Author's Notes

Human Trafficking is a blot on our society. To take anyone and force them to do things against their will is a terrible crime. However, it is my belief that to force a child to engage in sexual activity is unconscionable. This should not, must not, happen. Ever.

In 1990, I came across a story of a boy from St. Joseph, Minnesota, Jacob Wetterling, who at age eleven was abducted at gunpoint by a stranger wearing a mask in front of his little brother and his best friend. To this day, I have no idea why the tragedy of this story affected and stayed with me. It got to the point where I reached out to his parents, Jerry and Patty Wetterling, and offered my help. Honestly, I was only a high school counselor and didn't know what I could do, but I felt compelled to do something; anything.

I began to research the topic of child abduction, child sexual abuse, child safety, prevention, and education. I began speaking to parent groups, student groups, teachers, and faculty about the topic and how we can keep kids safe. It wasn't much, certainly not nearly enough, but I did what I could.

Jacob's story was the genesis of Taking Lives, which is the prequel of my trilogy, and each book of my trilogy, which includes; Stolen Lives, Shattered Lives, and Splintered Lives. These are works of fiction, yet based upon years of research, as well as the stories that kids and parents shared with me over the years. But it is a work of fiction, first and foremost. The statistics quoted in the stories are true, taken from the National Center for Missing and Sexually Exploited Children website. These dedicated individuals do such great work and go unnoticed by the general public. God Bless You! And while kids are abducted, some for a long time, kids do make it back home. We've read news reports about kids who do, and we rejoice. Sadly, some kids don't make it back home. Some kids are found dead.

Taking Lives and each book of the trilogy, Stolen Lives, Shattered Lives and Splintered Lives are meant to be stories of hope, a story of survival. Each of these books pays homage to law enforcement and other caring individuals who work to bring kids home safely.

I want to thank Jamie Graff, Earl Coffey, and Jim Ammons for their expertise in police, FBI, and SWAT procedure, James Dahlke for sharing his forensic science work with me, Jay Cooke, Dave Mirra and Bill Osborne for their IT expertise, and Sharon King for patience with all my medical questions. I also want to thank the folks at Sage and Sweetgrass, Robert Johnson, and various personnel at the

Navajo Museum for taking the time to answer my questions about Navajo culture, tradition and language.

I want to thank Theresa Storke and Winona Siegmund for their patience and their editing skills on each of the books. I want to thank Stacey Donaghy of Donaghy Literary Group for guiding my writing career, and of course, Natissha Hayden and the folks at True Visions Publications for giving me the opportunity to see my books in print.

Lastly, I can't tell you how supportive and encouraging my family has been. My wife, Kim, and my kids Wil, Hannah, and Emily have been so understanding and encouraging, never letting me give up and pack it in after each rejection. They stood by my side and supported me and whatever great or little success I might have as a writer. I am truly blessed for having been a husband to Kim and dad to my kids. I love you guys.

To you, the reader, thanks for taking a chance on an unknown writer, a guy who loves putting words on paper and seeing what might be made from them. I hope you enjoyed Taking Lives and I thank you for your willingness to continue the journey with me through the trilogy and beyond, and I hope I never disappoint you.

Happy and Thoughtful Reading,

Joe

Dedication

Stolen Lives is dedicated in love to my son, Wil Lewis, who at age 28, was taken from this earth much too soon. He is loved and deeply missed.

From Taking Lives

Prologue

2 years earlier

Brett walked home from school, but took his time so Bobby wouldn't be far behind him, in case his uncle was there waiting for him. He slowed his walk and searched the street. There were a couple of cars and a blue van, but not his uncle's car, and that was a relief.

He used the code for the garage, opened the back door, took off his shoes and dropped his backpack near the hallway that led to his room. As was his ritual, he got a glass from the cupboard, went to the refrigerator, used the ice dispenser to get a couple of ice cubes, and then filled his glass with water. Then he opened the refrigerator door, found an orange and went to the sink to peel it. He stuffed the rinds into the disposal, turned it on and ran water into the sink to wash them down. He took the orange and his glass of ice water back to the kitchen table and ate it. Bobby came into the kitchen.

"Hey."

"Hey."

Bobby dropped his bag near Brett's, went to the fridge and took out the orange juice. He went to the cupboard and took out a glass, filled it up, drank about half, and refilled it to the top. Then he sat down at the table with Brett.

Brett knew Bobby was going to ask him for the millionth time about him and Uncle Tony, so he went to the dishwasher, opened it, placed his glass on the top rack, and then picked up his backpack and walked down the hall to his bedroom.

He changed his clothes to shorts, a t-shirt, and basketball shoes. He stuck his head into Bobby's room and not seeing him there, walked back to the kitchen. Bobby hadn't moved.

"I'm going back to school to play some basketball."

Bobby nodded.

Brett studied his brother's face.

"What's wrong?"

Bobby shrugged, but didn't take his eyes off the glass he held. Brett sat down next to him.

"What's wrong?" He asked again.

"I have my piano recital tonight, and I've never played in front of anyone before."

"You don't have to worry. You're really good."

His little brother looked up at him, shocked.

"What, you don't think I listen to you?"

Bobby shook his head.

Brett smiled and said, "Sometimes, when you practice, mom and I come out to the kitchen and listen to you."

"You do?"

"We know you don't like anyone listening to you, but you're really good, Bobby."

Dumbfounded, Bobby didn't know what to say.

"You are. That song, Mandolin Rain, I like that one the best."

"You listen to me singing?"

"You have a good voice. Mom likes that Kip Moore song."

"Hey Pretty Girl?"

"Yeah, that one."

Bobby shrugged.

"It would sound better on guitar."

Brett punched him lightly on his arm.

"Bobby, you're really good."

"But tonight, I'll be playing in front of mom, dad, Grandma Dominico and a bunch of other people. And I have to play classical crap," he added with a "Blaahh," and his tongue sticking out.

Brett laughed. "And you'll do great."

Bobby smiled at him and shrugged.

"You wanna go play basketball with me?"

Bobby thought about it, almost said yes, but said, "Nah, I better practice."

"You sure? We can use one more guy."

"No, I better practice."

"Okay. You're really good, Bobby. Don't worry about it. I bet you'll be the best one there."

"Thanks."

With his hand on the doorknob, Brett stopped and stared at his brother. Bobby turned around.

"What?"

Brett wanted to tell him he loved him, something that he couldn't ever remember telling him. He wanted to tell him that he was sorry he didn't do more with him, that he was sorry they never talked or hung out. He wanted to apologize for not being a very good big brother. Mostly, he wanted to tell him that he was proud of him, and that from now on, he'd do better.

"What?" Bobby asked again.

"Nothin'. I'll see you later, okay?"

"Yeah. See you later."

Brett went back into the garage, found his bike, pulled it out of the garage and shut the garage door behind him. Then he jumped on the bike and peddled out of the driveway without looking back.

He took his time, peddling slowly.

No one was on the street, and there wasn't any traffic. He came to a stop sign and thought about blowing right through it, like he had done hundreds and thousands of times, and not knowing why, he slowed to a stop.

A blue van pulled up next to him, and the sliding door opened. Brett felt rough, strong hands pull him off the bike and clamp a damp smelly cloth over his mouth and nose. His bike fell to the pavement. He tried to fight back, but the cloth... the smell....

The sliding door closed, and the van pulled away from the stop sign. Brett tried to scream for help. He tried to fight back. He tried to push the hands away, but they were too strong. He tried to hold his breath, but it was too late. He felt himself getting drowsy, sleepy, and then there was darkness; nothing.

Brett was gone.

A half a block behind, Tony Dominico watched the brief struggle. He watched them pull Brett off the bike and into the van and watched the van pull away and drive down the street.

Dominico tried to summon up a feeling, any feeling, but nothing came to him. Nothing at all; it was all Brett's fault anyway, Brett's fault. Not his.

STOLEN LIVES

Where do the children go between the black night and the darkest day?
Where do the children go and who's that deadly piper who leads them away?
        Hooters, 1985 (*Rob Hyman and Eric M. Bazillian*)

Tuck you in, warm within, keep you free from sin, til the Sandman he comes.
Sleep with one eye open, gripping your pillow tight . . .
We're off to never, never land . . .
        Metallica, 1990 (*Kirk Hammett, James Hetfield and Lars Ulrich*)

Approximately Two Years Later . . .

CHAPTER ONE

The boy's muscles ached, and he longed to stretch out, but the handcuffs prevented him from doing so. His head hit the steel wall of the dirty van each time Frank drove over a rock or a rut or pothole in the dirt road. The boy's neck and shoulders had grown stiff from trying to cushion the blows. He shifted sideways so that his arms could take more of the pounding, but that was even more uncomfortable. He leaned as tightly against the wall as he could, pushing with his heels but slipped on a McDonald's bag, frowning at the mustard and pickle juice on his pants' leg.

The man wearing the baseball cap pulled low to his sunglasses merely glanced at the boy, but gave no hint of emotion. The boy had never seen him before, that is at least he didn't think he did. The way the man looked at him showing no emotion, no expression bothered him, but he wasn't going to give into that, so he ended up ignoring him just like the man wearing the baseball cap seemed to ignore the boy and the other two men in the van.

Ron, however, who sat in the passenger seat turned around and glared at him, his thick lips pulled back in a sneer. The boy looked away and stared at the tips of his worn-out shoes. His big toe poked out of one, and the sole flapped on the other. When the boy guessed that the big man wasn't watching him any longer, and when he felt that the man wearing the baseball cap wasn't watching, he turned back cautiously and strained to see out the windshield. Red fingers of rock poked the blue horizon. Bulky buttes formed walls on either side of the van like impatient onlookers at a passing funeral procession.

The boy guessed that they were still in Arizona. The last road sign he saw mentioned Tuba City, but that was before they had left asphalt and turned onto the dirt road.

"How much farther?" Ron asked the driver impatiently.

Frank turned onto a gravel road, crossed a cattle gate, and slowed to a stop as the boy watched a cloud of dust envelop the front of the van. Frank stared intently out the windows in all directions.

Satisfied, he nodded and said, "'bout as good a place as any."

The two men in the front got out of the van, and the boy braced himself. He had suspected, maybe deep down knew, what was going to happen. For the better part of a year, the boy had taken trips in the back of a van, sometimes handcuffed, sometimes drugged, as he was driven from one city to the next.

The man wearing the baseball cap and sunglasses sat in the van, staring at the boy, still showing no emotion and not interacting with either of the two men or with the boy. The boy looked at him expecting him to say or do something, but he didn't. He merely sat staring at him. Or at least, the boy thought he might be staring at him. With the sunglasses, he couldn't tell if his eyes were open or closed.

The side door slid open, and Ron yanked the boy's legs toward him. The boy tried to slow himself down, but the man was too strong. Before he knew it, both shoes were off and flung into the van. His socks followed shortly after that. Then Ron ripped off the boy's shirt and threw that into the van as well.

His eyes wild, the boy tried to kick, but the man was too big, too strong, and moved too quickly. With the boy's hands cuffed behind his back, he was defenseless. The man slapped the boy in the face, and then slapped him again.

"Not in the van!" Frank barked. "Just get his clothes off and bring him out here. We don't want a mess to clean up."

The man opened the boy's jeans and pulled them off along with his underwear, tossing them in the pile with the shoes, socks and what was left of the boy's shirt. Then he grabbed an ankle and yanked him out of the van with a thud. The boy hit his head on the door frame, but he didn't yell. No. He wouldn't give them the satisfaction.

"Get up!" the fat man said to him.

When the boy didn't move fast enough, the fat man kicked him.

The boy stumbled awkwardly to his feet and faced both men. Never more than then, facing those two men, knowing what was about to happen, did he miss his mother. He had never forgotten her face; how her green eyes danced when she smiled; how her nose turned up at the end—a ski slope he had teased her about. He remembered her gentle touch, her soothing voice, and the perfume she wore when she went out with dad. Never more in the whole year he was gone, did he miss her more than in that instant.

"Start walking," Frank said, exhaling smoke and tossing the last of a cigarette to the sand.

The boy walked slowly, the hot desert sand burning the soles of his feet. Now and then, Ron would give him a shove, and the boy would stumble, but not fall down.

The man wearing the baseball cap got out of the van but stood close to it. He didn't like the openness of the desert. He didn't like the sheep grazing up on the side of the hill. He tried to look that direction, but even with his sunglasses, he was staring into the sun and had to turn away. There was something about the place that gave the man an unsettled feeling. There was something he didn't like that was more than just the vast expanse of desert, so he stayed by himself and leaned against the side of the van near the passenger door and watched the two men and the boy.

"It's too fuckin' hot for this shit," the fat man grumbled quietly, so the man wearing the baseball cap didn't hear him. "We deserve more money."

Frank said nothing but wiped sweat off his face with the back of his hand and then felt for the gun in his belt.

"Okay, that's far enough," he said.

The boy turned around and faced both men and said, "You're going to kill me."

It was a statement, not a question, as if facing them and seeing the gun made it all more real. Final.

"Yeah."

"Just fuckin' do him, and let's go," Ron said.

Frank shrugged at the boy as if to say, *What am I supposed to do?*

A tear ran down the boy's face as he sobbed, "I wanna go home!"

"Yeah, sure," Ron said with a laugh.

"Why?"

Frank shrugged, waved the gun and said, "We don't need you anymore."

The boy looked down at the ground and then up at the men.

"I want to go home," the boy said again.

"Sorry, kid," Frank said, popping the cartridge and then palming it back into ready position. "Got orders."

"No one will find me," the boy said in panic.

Ron laughed and then spit. "That's the fuckin' point!"

The thought of being left alone in this place, this desert, with no one or nothing around him except for some sheep grazing in the distance and a hawk circling high up in the sky, made him feel desperate.

"Please?"

"Sorry kid," Frank said, walking behind him, putting a hand to the boy's shoulder, making him kneel down. "You won't feel a thing."

The boy shut his eyes, steeling himself against the blast of the gun. Frank stepped behind and away from the boy, aimed at the back of the boy's head and pulled the trigger twice. The boy fell forward, still handcuffed his face in the hot desert sand. Frank was right. The boy never felt a thing.

CHAPTER TWO

George Tokay sat among the pinion pine and Joshua trees on the side of the mountain after he had hidden his horse behind the ridge. He had heard the van even before it had appeared in the distance and had watched as it drove onto his grandfather's land, suspecting rustlers. Because the land where his family's sheep grazed was so remote, it happened often. Like his grandfather had taught him, George sat in the shadow, the sun to his back. That way, anyone looking for him would be looking almost directly into the sun.

Shadow.

Hiding in the shadow fit, because Shadow was the name given to him during his coming of age ceremony two years ago when he was twelve up on the mesa where he and his grandfather honored Father Sun. This was a ritual they had done together every day since, rain or shine. It began in the dark of early morning and ended as the sun peaked over the rim of the mountains. He wasn't singing now, though, and he wasn't with his grandfather. He was as alone as the boy.

George felt pity for him, disgust for the men, and curiosity as to why anyone would want to strip a boy naked, handcuff him and execute him. He chewed on his lower lip and then stopped himself. His grandfather had often, too often, reminded him that one of the *Dine'*—one of the Navajo people—didn't give away one's thoughts with expressions on one's face. Eyes shut, he held his breath, then let it out slowly and evenly, calming himself. Then he raised his binoculars, studying the scene again.

The fat man, with his back turned away from George and near the dead boy's feet, pissed a puddle that was quickly swallowed up by the hot sand. George watched as the fat man shook himself, then zipped up and faced the dead boy, muttering something to the tall, skinny man with the beard.

George studied the fat man's face; thick lips, broad, flat nose., dark brown hair, slicked with something other than sweat, parted sloppily on the right side of his head, big hands with thick, fat fingers, too far away to tell the color of the fat man's eyes. For sure, a *biligaana*, not interested in *hozro*.

George shifted over to the tall, skinny man with the scraggly black beard, bare in spots, thick in others. Not neat, but sloppy. Something about the beard—hiding something? Hair, brown. Hands, small. Fingers, narrow. George watched as the skinny man pulled out another cigarette—

Marlboro—and smoked, looking up into the hills, almost directly at George. With the cigarette clamped in his teeth, the skinny man pulled out his pecker and he too, pissed near the dead boy's body.

George decided that, like the fat man, he was a *biligaana*. Maybe Hispanic. Neither of them knew or worried about the dead boy's *chindi*, his spirit. They were both ignorant of the Way, of *hozro*, and his grandfather would be disgusted with them.

He flashed his binoculars back to the van and saw a third man, but because of the sunglasses and baseball cap, he couldn't get a good look at him. In fact, George couldn't tell if the man was particularly tall or short, slightly built or muscular, though his arms looked lean and tight. The hair under the baseball cap seemed long and dark, pulled back by the cap. George shook his head slightly in frustration, and then trained his binoculars back on the two men.

He watched both men discuss something while standing on either side of the dead boy, the fat man doing most of the listening. George shook his head, angry at how they defiled the boy, first pissing at the boy's feet, then talking over him like they would over a kitchen table. Finally, he watched them walk back where all three men got into the van.

George studied the van; Chevy, newer looking, black or navy blue, probably stolen. His cousin, Leonard, worked out of the Tribal Police station at Window Rock, and stolen cars with stolen plates were big crimes on the rez. So were murder, rape, rustling and everything else that went on in the world. His grandfather had lectured him that the *Dine'* were losing their way and becoming more like the *biligaana*.

George didn't move from his spot until the van had driven from sight, and just to be safe, George waited another twenty minutes before standing and stowing his binoculars in one of the saddlebags. He took out his canteen and drank warm water, wiping some across his face. Then he mounted Nochero, the big black stallion he had befriended two years previous, faced it down the hill and fingered the turquoise arrowhead around his neck.

A talisman to ward off evil.

And angry *chindi*.

Just to be safe, in case the talisman didn't work, he pulled the .22 from the scabbard.

George stopped about twenty-five yards away, what he thought was a safe distance. Nochero, impatient to get moving again, stomped its front hoof into the sand, flicked its tail at flies, snorting softly. George patted the stallion's neck and then dismounted. He pulled off his boots and pulled out a pair of moccasins from his saddlebags. He sat down, pulled his socks off and shook sand from them before stuffing them into his boots. Then, after slipping into his moccasins, George stood up and faced the dead boy.

The Navajo boy of fourteen, who stood facing the death scene, was afraid of the dead boy's *chindi*. But George reasoned that if he were to help find the dead boy's killers and bring them to justice, the *chindi* would be satisfied and leave his family's land. The worldly boy of fourteen, who wanted to join the tribal police like his cousin, was simply curious. He saw this as an opportunity to win respect and admiration from his family, and his grandfather, in particular. However, George was Navajo first and foremost.

So in a loud, calm voice, as confidently and as friendly as he could manage, said, "I have come to help find your killers. I want to help you. What was done to you wasn't right. I can only help if you allow me to come near. I bring you no harm."

He bent down, and as he walked toward the boy, picked up dried sticks and several stones no bigger than his fist.

"I'm coming now."

Taking care not to contaminate the crime scene, he stepped lightly, laying down the sticks and stones two yards away from the body, well away from where the two men had stood. He took the shirt off his back and tore it into narrow strips and stuffed all but one into his pockets. Then he picked up one stick and tied the strip of cloth in a knot like a kite tail and stuck the stick into the ground where the skinny man had stood, marking a footprint. He took another strip of cloth and stick, found the shell casings and marked them. Carefully, he moved to the other side of the boy, took another stick and strip of cloth and marked the fat man's footprint.

Then George knelt down and studied the body. A fly danced on the boy's shoulder, then onto the wound on his head. George waved his hand scaring the fly away temporarily, knowing that eventually, there would be nothing he could do. He touched the boy's shoulder gently, as if in apology, then got up and finished marking footprints, the skinny man's cigarette butts, and finally, the van's tire tracks.

As he went to mark the footprints made by the man wearing the baseball cap, something caught his eye, and he squatted down to study it closer. Between two tire prints, on the side of the van away from where George had sat watching the scene, he saw a dark spot on the sand. Careful not to touch or disturb it, he took one last stick and strip of cloth and marked it, thinking that it looked like blood, knowing that if it was, there might be more in or on the van.

At some point, the men must have hurt the boy before killing him.

At last, after marking every footprint and anything else of note, George knelt down at the boy's body and touched the boy's shoulder again.

"I will leave now, but I will be back with help. I will take care of you."

George walked away slowly, reverently, got on Nochero, took one last look at the dead boy and rode off to call his cousin.

CHAPTER THREE

Every now and then, Brett heard one or more of the boys weeping out of despair or loneliness. He could tell by the proximity or the voice who it was. He tried to shut his ears to it, but nothing he did could drown it out. Survive! Everything came down to survival, and Brett knew it, so did the other eleven boys.

He sat in the middle of the bed in a pair of stained beige-colored boxers with his chin resting on his knees, his arms wrapped around his legs. He had just had his fourth *date* of the day, and he knew he might have two or three more by dinner time and probably two or three more before he fell asleep that evening.

He never really slept though. Sleep was a rare commodity, and if it ever arrived, it was fitful and in snatches. It had been this way for the twenty-two months, two weeks and four days since he had been dragged off his bike and thrown into a van while on his way to meet some friends for a pick up basketball game at his middle school.

Brett had learned to close off all emotions after the third week or so in captivity. He was unreadable, and that was one way how he and the other boys survived. The only thing he couldn't control was the pure, unadulterated hate emanating from his large brown eyes. None of the guards or *dates* could read him. Only three other boys knew him well enough to guess at his feelings because they, like Brett and the rest of the boys felt the same things: disgust, anger and hate, along with the sense that somehow, some way, they needed to survive. So neither he nor the other eleven boys betrayed any feeling, any emotion, and they did what they needed to do to survive.

Though he hadn't been in them all, from what Brett could tell, all of the rooms were basically the same: concrete gray walls with chipped and faded green linoleum, windows that had been sealed shut with thick plywood and covered with steel bars. There was a cheap nightstand that had a box of tissues and a container of antiseptic hand wipes. A small garbage can sat on the floor near the bed. Each room had a beat up, stuffed chair that matched neither the bed nor nightstand. In Brett's room, the chair teetered back and forth because one leg was an inch or so shorter than the others. Its cushion had white stuffing leaking out of a tear in the back.

The boys were about the same age. All were locked in separate rooms that contained a lumpy double bed with faded sheets of a non-descript color that was either light green, faded yellow or tan. Perhaps the sheets and pillow cases had just been washed so many times the color had been faded to nothing distinguishable. The sheets and pillow cases were supposed to be washed every week, but that didn't happen. In fact, Brett couldn't remember the last time he had clean sheets. As a consequence, they smelled of cheap cologne, and of something deeper, darker. They had a greasy, slick feel to them. Yet, Brett tuned it all out. Used to it.

Brett's room, third on the left from the door and across from the glass control room, had been his from the time he had first arrived. All meals, if you could call items from the various fast food menus meals, were brought to him. He left his room only to shower and use the toilet. Brett tuned it all out, including the *date* he was with, no matter what the *date* did to him, Brett wasn't there.

Instead, Brett imagined himself on the track sprinting the 100 meter or the 200 meter, almost always winning because that was what had happened in almost all his races. He pictured himself on the basketball court playing with his traveling AAU team. Before he was kidnapped, he was the starting point guard, playing tough defense or setting up the offense. Before he was dragged off his bike, he played football for his middle school as a starter at halfback and free safety. So he'd imagine himself on the football field taking the pitch from his friend Austin Hemple and racing around the right side dodging a defensive end or linebacker, eluding a cornerback or safety on his way to the end zone.

In any case, Brett didn't operate in the present. He was absent, away, in another place and time, knowing that this was the only way he was able to survive. He had coached the other boys to do the same.

He had never imagined himself living this kind of life. He had never imagined that this sort of life had even existed. It certainly wasn't anything he had wanted to do-ever. So he and the other boys learned to channel all of their hate and all of their disgust onto the men and guards. It was the only way they were going to survive.

He and the boys couldn't say no, couldn't resist and couldn't even hesitate. To resist meant being taught a lesson in front of the other boys. They had to learn this lesson because their life depended on it: don't resist, don't say no, and don't hesitate.

He and the rest of the boys suspected they were in Chicago because every now and then, the guards would complain about the Bears, the Bulls, the White Sox or the Cubs.

Fuck the Bears.

From the time he was little, Brett had been told that he looked like a miniature Tom Brady. He had a compact, solid build neither short nor tall with the same intense eyes, but brown, and without the real Tom Brady's cleft chin. But being from Indianapolis, he was a rabid fan of the Colts, and Brett knew for certain that Peyton Manning was the best quarterback in the NFL. Tom Brady couldn't touch him. So in his mind, any comparison to Tom Brady, even if he did look like him, was an insult. And he really didn't give a shit about the Bears or Bulls.

Each boy was cute, bright, and each boy was a decent athlete. Brett excelled in track, football, and basketball, Tim, in basketball and baseball, Johnny, football and baseball, Patrick, basketball and soccer. The other boys were similar that way.

Even in captivity, there were leaders among the boys. Tim and Johnny led with kind words and gentleness, while Brett led with his actions. He had taken on the role of nurse, checking a boy for this pain or that malady. He was a listener who encouraged the boys to do sit-ups and pushups to keep themselves fit and as a way to fight boredom. But even with the sit-ups and pushups, the boys grew skinny.

Brett understood that boredom and loneliness were very real enemies. Long hours in solitary confinement with no one to talk to drove him crazy, so he did algebra problems in his head or tried to remember passages of books that he had read, but he'd reinvent the characters and the endings.

After almost two years in captivity, Brett had wondered if his parents and younger brother were still looking for him or if they had given up and forgotten him. Besides dying alone in captivity, this was his biggest fear, and he tried to shove those thoughts out of his mind as quickly as they would arrive. But arrive they would. Quietly, silently, like fog on a landscape: not there one minute, then suddenly filling the landscape like a thin white woolen blanket leaving Brett cold instead of comforted.

The boys had their own code used to communicate with each other that Brett and Tim had devised. A serious of clicks, gestures, even simple looks and slight nods were used to communicate. Their code included names the boys gave the men and guards.

Sometimes, the boys were given gifts. Brett *took* the gift, but never *accepted* the gift. To *accept* the gift was to somehow *accept* that what was happening to him was *okay*, was *alright*. But nothing about what had happened since his kidnapping was *okay* or *alright*. It was all very wrong and not okay at all.

So he took the candy from *Hershey*, giving a quarter piece to Tim, a quarter piece to Johnny and half of it to Patrick, one of the youngest of the boys and also one of the newest, only in captivity for six months. He took a cheeseburger from *Burger Man* but gave half to Johnny and half to Patrick. Though hunger gnawed at his insides, he had never taken anything for himself.

Recently, Brett and Tim had speculated in quiet whispers while in line for the morning shower that one of the boys was going to go away. It happened every month or so, usually when a boy had been sick for a while. Sometimes it happened when a boy got older. Johnny and Ryan had been sick for a while and neither of them had been having as many *dates* as the rest. Johnny had been held captive the longest, but Tim had been captive almost as long as Johnny. Because Johnny was his friend, Brett gave him whatever food or candy he could, encouraging him to drink a lot of water, to get better. They had to keep each other safe. They had to help each other survive.

It was all about survival until they could get help or escape. Brett didn't know how, but he knew that somehow, some way, they needed to survive until help arrived.

Whenever that might be.

CHAPTER FOUR

Pete Kelliher got a headache whenever he read in a car, and he had a sonofabitch grinding him smack-dab in the middle of his forehead. Of course, it could have been because of fatigue or the fact that he had only two cups of coffee instead of the six he would normally have by this time of day. He stuck a finger in the report, rubbed his eyes, readjusted his sunglasses and looked out at the lonely landscape of sand and sagebrush, butte and mesa. *How could anything or anybody live out here?* he wondered. *God! Did we screw the Indian!*

His mostly gray flat top screamed military, but he was miles from that. He grew up in the Vietnam era, and for his eighteenth birthday was gifted with the draft number of twenty-five and that year, they took anyone up through the two-hundreds. But thank God for allergies and asthma!

Pete had decided early on, however, that if drafted, he would go in as a Conscientious Objector because he'd rather carry a medical kit or a camera than a rifle, odd choice for a guy who spent the lion's share of his life in law enforcement. But he had actually only pulled his sidearm less than six or seven times by his count and never fired it, and he didn't plan on firing it in the near future either.

Pete was mostly serious, mostly quiet except to grumble about this or that, and off the job, kept to himself content to watch a Clint Eastwood or John Wayne movie in the dark of his living room in his three bedroom Colonial. A bowl of popcorn would be in his lap and a plastic twenty ounce bottle of Diet Coke on the side table. Of course, this would be after polishing off a small pepperoni and sausage pizza with extra cheese.

He was an average looking fifty-five year old, a bit over-weight and on the short side. He had barely managed to pass his yearly fitness exams, waiting until a month or so to begin the process of getting himself back into shape, and each year it took longer and the margin of passing became less.

He could put on an Armani suit with a Rolex on his left wrist and size nine Gucci shoes on his feet and still manage to look rumpled and disheveled. There was nothing rumpled or disheveled about Pete's mind, however. Many of the younger agents sought out his opinion or insight on a particularly tough case, and members of his own team deferred to him in meetings and strategy calls.

"Summer, what do you make of this kid?" he asked, rereading the report.

Summer Storm, his partner, slouched in the front seat with her head leaning against the passenger window. She received her first name because she was born in the backseat of a station wagon on a hot July night with hail, thunder and lightning rocking the car. Her parents thought first of Hailey, but settled on Summer, liking how it sounded together: Summer Storm. Pete saw her—and even treated her—as his daughter, and she grumbled about it, but Pete paid no attention.

They were an odd team: he sullen, rumpled and gray; she trim and proper, dressed like a model out of Vogue. Except for today, fighting jet lag, both looked rumpled. They were also very good at what they did.

Pete began as a beat cop in Baltimore and quietly rose through the ranks and ended up with a gold shield in the Homicide division. He had a knack for closing cases, and in Baltimore, there were plenty to close. The FBI recruited him, and he jumped at the opportunity. He was single, but married to his badge and gun, so changing jobs, especially for one with the FBI was a no brainer.

Summer was plucked out of law school at Louisville. She had a Pollyanna personality, definitely the glass half full type who laughed easily and had a great mind for details-names, dates, the little things that Pete seemed to slam over

in order to get to the end, the close. Neither had married.
Too busy with the job. No time. The team was family. The
partnership was marriage enough.

"Which kid?" she asked without raising her head or
opening her eyes.

"Um . . . the Tokay kid. The Indian boy."

"Pretty remarkable, huh?"

Kelliher nodded. In the three years since the
formation of the Crimes Against Children's Task Force—*The
Kiddie Corps,* as it was referred to inside the Bureau, they
had never had a break such as this, and this one came by way
of a fourteen year old boy, who had happened to be out
tending sheep when he witnessed the shooting, the perps, and
the vehicle used by them.

"Is the area secure?" he asked frowning at the report.

Summer glanced over at the driver, a young, tall,
gangly, dark-haired agent out of Albuquerque.

He shrugged and said, "We followed your orders."

"How far away are we?" she asked with a yawn.

"About an hour," the agent said, glancing at the
digital clock in the dash.

They had flown into Albuquerque from D.C.
spending five hours on a plane and another hour in the car

with more to go. Evidently, the FBI office in Albuquerque didn't believe in helicopters. Summer put her head back down and tried to get some sleep, knowing that once they arrived, sleep would be hard to get.

Kelliher reached into his breast pocket and grabbed his cellular phone, located the numbers from the crime report, punched in the numbers and spoke to a Window Rock Police Station dispatcher making sure the boy was still close by.

"He's there," the officer at the other end said.

"And I'd like two horses, one for the boy and one for me," Kelliher added.

The officer started to say something like, "No Problem," but Pete had already shut the cell phone off.

"What are you thinking?" Summer asked, turning towards the backseat to look at him.

Her short, natural blond hair looked as though it had been combed with an eggbeater. Her gray-green eyes had dark circles, and Pete wondered when she had last had a good meal.

"If this kid can ID these guys, we've caught a break. A big break."

"You still believe its child trafficking?" she asked knowing his answer before he said it, knowing it because they had discussed it over and over again.

"At least a dozen kids found murdered the same way . . . two shots to the back of the head from a .38, each kid missing at least a year, three missing more than two years. Each kid eleven or twelve at the time of the abduction. Yeah, it smells like it."

"Why not just three perverts picking up kids and getting rid of 'em?" the dark-haired driver asked.

Pete leaned forward between the two front seats and said, "Because other than the death scene, the boys were different. Three kids had brands . . . an upside down cross on the inside of the left ankle. The same three had scars on their backs as if they had been beaten with a whip."

He paused, sat back and looked out the window and then said more to himself than to the driver, "If there were only three guys picking up kids, all the kids would have the same." Perhaps feeling hope because the cased finally shifted to their favor for once, Pete slapped the report across his knee and said, "We don't know what else it could be."

Summer bit her lip, worried that he might be right. Actually, knew he was right. But three perverts snatching kids were hard to find. A bunch of assholes taking and using kids would be even harder to find, unless they got a big, big break. She wondered if this Indian boy might be the break they needed.

CHAPTER FIVE

The car pulled up in a cloud of reddish dust. The
three of them sat in the car until it had settled and until they
could actually see out the windows again. The problem was
that when it settled, it covered the windows in a fine sheen.

Three Tribal Policemen were gathered around a patrol
car. One officer sat on the hood with the other two leaning
against the front bumper. Two of the three chewed gum,
while the other spat brown tobacco juice over the side of the
car away from the crime scene.

Pete opened the door and whatever cool air there was
inside the car vanished in seconds. Air, the consistency of
oatmeal was hard to breathe. In fact the heat seemed to suck
all the air out of his lungs. *A freakin' furnace*, he thought.
Fuck dry heat!

He pulled his tie off and threw it along with his sport
coat in the backseat. He tucked the manila folder containing
the crime report under his arm, while he rolled up first one
sleeve and then the other.

Summer threw her suit jacket on the front seat and
surveyed the scene with her hands on her hips. The county
ME knelt down beside the body of the boy. An agent

snapped photos of foot prints and tire treads. Little yellow plastic tent tags with large black numbers sat alongside the stakes set up by the Indian boy. A couple of agents stood around not doing much of anything. In fact, they didn't even bother to try to look like they weren't doing anything.

Pete squatted down at the first stake and studied the tire tracks left by the van, marveling at how thorough the kid was. From a distance, the kid looked older than fourteen and not all that remarkable. A dirty white, beat up straw cowboy hat sat on his head. He had his arms folded over his chest, bare except for a leather vest and some sort of necklace around his neck. Medium height, maybe on the taller side, but Pete couldn't tell because he didn't know kids that well, at least, ones who were alive. The boy seemed skinny and lanky, yet showed the strength and agility of a basketball player. Skin the color of copper, darkened by the Arizona sun, with dark eyes and long black hair, neatly kept.

Pete scratched his head and motioned for the boy to come nearer. Still wearing his moccasins, the boy stepped lightly to Pete's side.

"Walk me through all this."

George nodded and pointed at the tire tracks.

"This is where they parked. You can tell by the depth of the track, compared to those over there."

Pete walked backward looking at the track, tilting his head at an angle to get a better look. George knelt down and pointed at the ground.

"I think this is blood. If it is, then they hurt him in the van," George said. "It could be that they pulled him from the van and his head hit an edge before hitting the ground."

Pete glanced at the boy and then frowned.

"When you look at the body, you'll see sand on his back. There's no other way that would have happened."

"You didn't see him fall?" Pete asked.

George shook his head, pointed and continued.

"Here is where the guy wearing the baseball cap stood."

Pete glanced at the report and said, "It says here that you didn't get a good look at him, but you described him as medium height with longish dark hair." He looked up at the boy and said, "How can you be sure?"

George shrugged, slipped his fingers into the back pockets of his jeans and answered, "I saw enough of him to be able to say that." George squinted at the man and added, "I judged his height by the van."

Pete nodded and fanned himself with the report.

They stared at each other and then George said, "These are the boy's footprints. The sand was hot and he was kind of hopping."

"And these?" Pete asked, indicating what looked like tennis shoe prints.

"The tall man with the beard."

"How can you tell?"

"Longer distance between steps and not as deep, compared to those," gesturing to the boot marks. "Those are deeper and closer together. Those belong to the fat man."

Pete nodded, smiling at George. The boy smiled shyly, knowing the older man had been testing him.

"The skinny man led, then came the boy, and then the fat man."

George walked lightly, but quickly up the road and pointed at the stake marking the cigarette butt.

"You said he smoked Marlboro. How did you know?"

"I thought I saw the red and white pack, but it wasn't until I saw this that I knew for sure."

"You touched it?" Pete asked.

"I used a blade of grass to roll it over," George answered.

Pete grunted.

"The fat man walks heal to toe . . . heavy. The skinny man walks on the front of his feet, like Cal Ripken."

"Like Cal Ripken?"

"Yes," George answered simply.

"Like Ripken," Pete said shaking his head.

Summer stood to one side, hands on her hips watching the photographer snap pictures. Pete motioned to her and she joined him and the boy.

"Any ID on the vic yet?" Pete asked.

Summer sighed, brushed some hair off her forehead and glanced back at the dead boy.

"We sent a photo to the Center and a preliminary ID came back."

The team worked closely with the Center for Missing and Exploited Children. The Center identified each of the boys they had found. Pete looked at her closely.

"There are so many of them," she said, glancing back at the boy and then turning away. "I wonder when it'll end."

"It'll end when we put these guys behind bars."

"Do you remember the Hart kid from Cincinnati?"

Pete frowned trying to remember specifics, but with so many missing kids, he didn't really know one from another. It wasn't that he didn't care, he just couldn't remember. Besides, Summer had always been better at that part of it.

"Paperboy, taken on a Sunday morning, they found his bike, the papers and one of his shoes."

Pete nodded, not really remembering, but letting Summer fill in the rest of the details.

"He was taken one month to the day before his thirteenth birthday and was missing eighteen months."

Summer sighed again, glanced back at the body and then at the three Indian officers about twenty yards or so away. The one sitting on the hood of the car was short and fat, barely fitting into his uniform, and it wasn't because of a bullet-proof vest. One was short and thin, leaning on the left side of the car. The third was the tallest of the three and had on the cleanest of the greenish-brown uniforms. Their uniforms sort of reminded her of Park Service uniforms.

"What's with them?" she asked.

"I dunno," Pete answered.

"Um..." George started, waiting for permission to speak.

Both adults turned towards him and waited.

"I think they're worried about the boy's *chindi.*"

"The boy's what?" Pete asked.

"The boy's spirit."

Pete squinted at the boy; Summer folded her arms impatiently.

George explained the Navajo belief.

"What do you mean *finished*?" Summer asked.

"The *chindi* will want justice, to know that the killer will be caught and that the body will be taken care of . . . *finished*."

"They believe in *ghosts*?" Pete asked skeptically.

George didn't answer but stared at him impassively, annoyed that he had failed to take the *Dine'* belief seriously.

"You knelt down right next to the body. Don't you believe in this . . . *chindi* thing?" Summer asked.

"I asked the *chindi's* permission, so I could help find the killers and bring the boy help."

Pete and Summer exchanged a glance, shrugged and then looked back at the deputies.

"I suppose if they don't feel comfortable, they can leave," Summer suggested.

"They won't," George said looking at his cousin Leonard - the short one standing on the left. "This is reservation land. They're responsible for it."

"This is a federal crime," Pete said. "They don't have jurisdiction."

"This is Navajo land," George said.

Summer and Pete shrugged at each other and then Pete walked over to the boy's body, looking closely at the wound. Small entries, fitting those of a .38 and similar to the wounds they found on the other boys. He glanced at the report he held in his hand.

Pete ran his finger through the report and asked, "George, where did they piss?"

"Over here," he said as he squatted near the foot of the dead boy. "Right here and over there."

"Did you guys get samples for testing?" Pete asked the gangly agent who had driven them to the crime scene.

The driver looked over at the other agents, and one nodded as he scribbled in a notebook.

"What about the blood sample back where the van was?"

"Just like you asked," the agent said impatiently.

Pete turned to the photographer.

"You get enough pictures?"

"I got everything you asked for. I got the body, the hands with cuffs, the wound, everything."

Pete gently turned over the body, almost reverently. Thankfully, the boy's eyes were closed, as was the boy's mouth. Sand covered his face.

"Take several more. I want close-ups of the face. Then send them to the Center, so we can confirm the boy's name."

"We already have a preliminary ID," one of the agents said.

"I want a firm ID," Pete said angrily.

George knelt down, placed his hand gently on the boy's chest and seemed to mumble something. He took a long look, then stood up and turned away to watch dust devils dance on the desert horizon. Pete and Summer noted the care and concern the Indian boy expressed in that gentle, simple gesture and took an immediate liking to him. Then Summer called over the Medical Examiner and asked him to give her a verbal report.

"Just what the kid said. Two shots, one exiting the left cheek indicating a back and right side angle, up from the vic's head. No exit on the other. Death within seconds if not instantaneously."

"Time of death?"

"I have no reason to doubt the kid's report," he stated rubbing his eyes.

"Summer, we need to make sure there are pictures of every footprint staked by George," Pete said, brushing sand off the dead boy's face.

Then he turned to the three other FBI agents and said, "And measure the distance between each of the footsteps as well as the boy's. I want a height and weight on them all."

One of them asked, "Why the kid's? The ME will do an autopsy."

"By guessing at the boy's weight and height, we can tell how accurate you are," Summer explained impatiently.

She was less than impressed with the Albuquerque office. She squatted down next to Pete and stared at the boy.

After a bit of silence she said, "I'm going to have casts made of the footprints and tire treads. They might come in handy somewhere down the road."

Pete got up and then lent a hand to Summer.

"George, let's take a horsy ride up to the spot you watched all of this from."

CHAPTER SIX

George politely offered the canteen to Pete before taking a drink himself. With a nod of thanks, Pete took a long drink and then gave it back to the boy who did the same. Pete rubbed his lower back, twisted and turned to work out the kinks. He hadn't been on a horse since he was a kid, and to be honest, he didn't like it much back then either.

"Do you have those binoculars?"

George pulled them from one of his saddlebags and handed them to the agent.

"Okay, now show me exactly where you were."

George led both horses away and tied them loosely to a Joshua tree and pointed to a rock just below the crest of the hill.

"See that rock, the one that looks like a chair? I sit there when I eat my lunch or take a break. I can sort of lean against the other rock, like a chair."

Pete smiled. The two rocks almost formed a chair, not quite at a slight recline. He sat down heavily, took out his walkie-talkie and binoculars and stared far below at the crime scene. He could see people move, but other than Summer, not well enough to make out who was who, much less what each brand of cigarette was used. Then he brought up the binoculars and suddenly, what was far away, became arm's length.

"Christ! How could they not see you?"

"The sun was in their eyes."

"Summer, come in," Pete said in the walkie-talkie.

"Here. How're you doing?"

"Sore as hell. Happy I'm not trying to have any children."

He actually saw her smiling, shielding her eyes to try to see him.

"I have to admit it's not often someone goes horseback riding in a white shirt, slacks and wingtips. You realize you're going to get a raft of shit from the rest of the team when I tell them," she said with a laugh.

"Yeah, yeah, yeah... very funny."

"What can you see, Pete?"

"Everything. I'm right on top of you."

"It'll hold up in court?"

"Right down to the last detail," Pete said smiling.

"Come on in, and we'll wrap it up."

"I'll be down soon. I have a couple of things I want to go over with George first." Then

Pete added with a smile, "And I want to build up my courage for the ride down."

*   *   *

George and Pete sat side by side thinking their own thoughts and chewing jerky that George had taken out of one of the saddlebags. George had gone over the whole thing again and then once more.

"Who do you think gave the orders?" Pete asked squinting down at the crime scene.

"I think the tall one was in charge."

"Why?"

George shrugged.

"A feeling... the way he acted. He was sort of cold, like he didn't care, like he didn't notice the fat man talking."

"What about the guy wearing the baseball cap and sunglasses?"

George squinted off in the distance, thinking.

"I'm not sure. He was sort of watching the whole thing. He didn't seem to be . . . involved," he said with a shrug.

"What was the fat man like?"

George stared at the scene, trying to picture the facial expressions of the men and the boy.

"Angry . . . impatient. Like an old bull being challenged by a young one."

"But you said he wasn't that old. In his thirties or forties, you said."

"He wasn't old. He acted like an old bull acts when he's challenged, that's all. Like that."

Pete thought about that for a bit, and then said, "You said the boy talked to them before the tall man shot him. What do you think he said?"

"I think he asked them not to kill him," George said quietly.

"Who do you think he asked?" Pete said curiously.

George thought about that for a moment. If he were the boy, standing in front of them, knowing he was about to die, which one would he ask? Pete watched him wrestle with this, knowing that he was going to make an incredible witness. And further down the road, make an incredible young man.

"I think . . . I think he knew he was going to die, so no matter what he said, it didn't matter who he talked to. Neither man cared. They were doing a job."

Pete couldn't comprehend the coldness, yet the reality of the statement. *Neither man cared. A job.* How is it possible that children couldn't be regarded as children? Just playthings, toys, to be gotten rid of when not needed anymore?

"May I ask you a question?" George asked, looking down at his moccasins.

"I think you deserve more than just one question," Pete said with a smile.

"Why did they kill him?"

Pete hung his head, his mind racing with statistics his own FBI accumulated in 1987; over one hundred-thousand *attempted* abductions each year, three hundred long-term abductions each year, one hundred-fifteen stranger abductions each year, forty-one percent still missing, twenty-seven percent found dead, thirty-two percent found alive. Pete slipped an arm around George's shoulders, squeezing him gently. George felt the man's pain coming off him in waves.

"I don't know, George."

They sat like that watching shadows grow before them, and when it was not quite dark, yet not quite light, they got up to start their trip back down the hill. George led the horses back to the trailhead, but before Pete mounted, George stopped him.

He took the turquoise and leather necklace from around his neck and said, "You might need this more than me."

Startled, admiring its beauty, he said, "What is it?"

"Protection. You might need it."

CHAPTER SEVEN

"How many ponies do we have in our Chicago stable?"

Frank *knew* the man knew, and Frank *knew* that the man *knew* Frank knew. Why this particular game was played was beyond him. Everything was on line, but the man liked a hardcopy backup. Frank looked through a three-ring binder listing the boys by name, complete with a picture and the boy's age.

Frank scanned a couple of pages, looked up and said, "It looks like twelve."

"How many are healthy?"

"According to Butch, all of them. The Vega kid has a cold or flu or something. Pretty much minor, but he's been out of work lately."

The short dark man ran a hand through freshly oiled hair, readjusted his robe and asked, "How long?"

"A week."

"I want him put down."

Frank didn't like all of the horse metaphors, but he had to admit it kept things simple. The word *Ponies* was a sort of shorthand or code that could be used in e-mail and phone calls, that sort of thing.

"It's minor . . . just the flu."

Besides, when Frank was in Chicago, Johnny was his favorite boy to mess with.

"We can't afford to have a sick pony. It's bad for business, and word will spread."

The short dark man glared at the skinny man, eyes narrowing, jaw set, and then he said, "If he doesn't improve by the end of the week, I want him put down."

Frank shrugged his shoulders. The dark man wondered if the gesture was one of insolence but decided it wasn't. Frank wasn't the type to be insolent. Ron was, but not Frank.

"What are the ages in the Chicago stable?"

Frank glanced through the book and then looked up.

"Three of the boys are fourteen, but they look young."

"How long have we had them?"

Studying the book, Frank said, "Two just over two years, and one just under two years. They still get quite a bit of business. One pulls down $1,800 a week and the other, the Pruitt kid, brings in $2,200 a week."

"Ah . . . yes, I remember him; strong, athletic."

"How many ponies do we have on the circuit?"

Frank flipped to the back of the binder and leafed through.

He looked up and said, "Four, all of them young, and all of them relatively fresh."

"How fresh?"

"Um . . . looks like the longest has been in rotation four months. The others are a couple of months old."

"Who is it . . . the one who has been in rotation the longest?"

"The kid from St. Louis . . . Montgomery."

The short dark man nodded with a smile, eyes glazed.

"We do have some beautiful ponies, don't we?"

Frank nodded.

"Our sources have good eyes, and you and Ron do a fine job picking them up. Beautiful boys."

The man reached for a cigar, took his time lighting it, offering one to Frank who declined.

"I should give you both a raise. How about an extra $500 a piece?"

"That would be fine," Frank said, though he didn't think it was fine at all.

He and Ron took all the risks. They were the ones who brought kids into the business and then disposed of them. And $500 was pocket change compared to what the man got.

The short dark man studied Frank and then said, "I know what you're thinking. You're thinking you deserve more."

Frank shrugged.

"Consider for moment the overhead. I have to make sure the ponies get fed, have a roof over their heads and clientele to pay for them. I set up the circuit, the stable in Chicago and the stable in Los Angeles. I pay for security and travel expenses. I pay for protection, and that doesn't come cheap. All of this takes money, and I have no doubt that the figures that appear in those ledgers are nowhere near what's actually brought in. I know that."

He rose from the padded leather chair, walked over to the window and gazed out across the pool to the rolling hills beyond.

"I'm certain of that, just as I know that both you and Ron take certain liberties with my ponies before you bring them to me, and that you pad your expenses for a little more pocket change."

The dark man turned around and stared at Frank with a sly, conspiratorial smile. Frank stared back, not willing to break eye contact first. He wanted to win this battle and show the dark man he wasn't afraid or worried.

The dark man turned back to the window, clasped his hands behind his back and said, "Knowing all of that, I think $500 is sufficient. Don't you?"

"I never said it wasn't," Frank said.

"No, but you thought otherwise, did you not?"

Frank said nothing.

The dark man let the silence drag on and then turned around, relit his cigar and said, "You and Ron take a trip to the Midwest . . . Wisconsin. Why don't you and Ron pick up another beautiful pony for me?"

"We can do that."

"We'll put him on the circuit, and put Montgomery in Chicago. Of course, we'll have to make some room for him there, but I'll let you and Ron make those arrangements."

Frank nodded and then got up to leave.

"And take Graham with you again. I want him to learn the ropes, because I'm thinking of expanding." Just before Frank got to the door, the dark man added, "And Frank, keep a leash on Ron. I don't trust him."

Frank nodded and left.

The dark man stared out the window. He watched Frank as he drove around the circular drive and down the mile long, tree-lined driveway. He continued watching long after Frank had disappeared, then stubbed out his cigar and sat down behind the desk. He took out his cell and punched in the numbers.

"Yes?"

"I have a job for you . . ."

CHAPTER EIGHT

Pete was restless, waiting for word—any word—on the three men who killed Tyler Hart in the desert and the other kids across the country. The descriptions of the men given by George Tokay and drawn up by a police artist were circulated to law enforcement agencies in California, Arizona, Nevada, New Mexico, Utah and Colorado. Nothing so far, but it was early.

The license plates drew a dead-end. The plates on the van had been stolen from a driveway in Scottsdale and had been substituted by ones stolen from a parking garage in Phoenix, which had been substituted by ones stolen from a parking lot in Flagstaff. Unfortunately, that was where the dead-end occurred, because the owner, Ralph Owens, knew his plates were stolen because none had been substituted for them. They were just taken.

In retrospect, it wasn't a *real* dead-end, because the trail led somewhat northeast, possibly from California. But who really knew? And, California was a big motherfucker of a state full of assholes. At least, that was Pete's opinion.

Summer had flown to Cincinnati, Ohio to speak with the parents of Tyler Hart. She could have had the Cincinnati office handle it, but because she took an active—perhaps, *too* active interest in the kids' lives, she felt obligated to deal with the endings, the deaths.

Pete worried about her involvement, cautioning her about crossing the line of objectivity, but she stated angrily, if not coldly, "They're kids, for God's sake! Parents deserve to hear it from me and not from a suit with a canned speech."

Pete felt equal parts of pity and admiration for her sense of duty, maybe a little guilt because he couldn't bring himself to face the parents.

"Chet, you have anything yet?" Pete asked.

Chet blinked at him, rubbed his eyes, shrugged and shook his head.

"What's taking so long?" Pete yelled in frustration, shoving his chair back into the wall behind him with a crash. "It shouldn't be this hard. We have faces, heights, weights and shoe sizes for chrissake. Even some sort of goddamn mole or scar on one guy's face, covered with a beard. We have one fat fuck, one baseball player-type, and one guy wearing a baseball cap and sunglasses. Isn't there some sort of data bank of known perverts we can get into?"

"I'm doing that, but it takes time," Chet answered through clenched teeth.

"We haven't *got* time, Chet, because these guys are already planning another kidnapping and maybe already stole a kid off some street. We've got to work faster, Chet."

"I'm working as fast as I can!"

Pete rubbed his hand over his flattop and sighed.

"I know, I know," Pete said sadly. "It's just so frustrating to be this close."

"We'll get 'em, Pete. I promise you that," Chet said as he turned back to his computer, stabbing at the keyboard.

Pete slapped the younger agent on the back, got up and left the bullpen head down and deep in thought and walked into another agent carrying a stack of papers, sending them to the floor in a jumbled mess.

"Jesus! Watch where you're going!" the agent yelled.

But Pete was already down the hallway and into his office.

"Jerk!"

$$*\qquad\qquad*\qquad\qquad*$$

Summer sat on a park bench watching a mother push her daughter on a swing. The girl laughed and giggled; the mother smiled and laughed along with her. The happy scene made Summer even sadder if that was possible. She had told

Richard and Tammy Hart that their boy, Tyler, had been found.

"How?" they asked. "Where?" they asked. "How do you know it was . . . is Tyler?" they asked.

Summer didn't want to tell them. She didn't want to give them all the sordid details, so she had given them an abridged version instead. But it all boiled down to the same thing: their son, Tyler Hart, had been found dead. His fifteen-month ordeal had ended. Another young boy dead; executed, alone.

Their ordeal, however, would never end. Not until their questions were answered.

Who took their boy as he had peddled papers on a city street? Why did they take him? Who would do such a thing?

Why? Who? Where?

Summer didn't have any answers. She never had any answers.

Maybe this time she would finally get answers once and for all. All she and Pete needed was a little luck, a break. Maybe the Indian kid would give them one.

Maybe.

As she watched the mother and daughter walk out of the park hand in hand, Summer pulled out her cell phone.

She had Thatch on speed dial and needed to talk to him. Thatcher Davis, tall, slender, stately and divorced, was her mentor and friend; always willing to listen, always willing to let her cry on his shoulder.

He had warned her that joining Kiddie Corps, as noble as it was, was not only a dead-end career move, but a hopeless one at that. He had warned her that rarely, if ever, would she find any child alive. He had quoted her the statistics: that of the abductions each year, most kids were killed in the first hour after being taken; if they lasted past that first hour, a girl more than likely found dead in the two weeks following the abduction; if a boy's body wasn't found in six months, it would most likely never be found.

And, he had warned her about working with Pete Kelliher, viewed by some of the heavy-hitters in D.C. as long past his prime and on the downward slide of his career. Summer had argued that she didn't want to be a suit; that she had wanted to do some good and make a difference. Something good. Anything. Even the *possibility* of good.

"Hi, it's me. I'm catching a plane for D.C. Do you have time for me this evening?"

"Always. Something happen?"

"I'll tell you about it tonight."

CHAPTER NINE

The Crimes Against Children Unit, or Kiddie Corps, was actually made up of two Special Agents in each fifty-six FBI Field Offices, serving as CAC Coordinators. These coordinators use all available FBI investigative, forensic, tactical, and informational and behavioral science resources to investigate crimes against children. They are charged with establishing and maintaining multi-agency, multi-disciplinary Resource Teams with participants from local, tribal, state and other federal agencies. Members of these teams include federal and state prosecutors and non-governmental organizations having roles related to child safety and welfare.

In short, a cluster fuck, at least in Pete's mind.

The only *real* team, the gang that ran the on-going cases on a *consistent* basis, consisted of the five individuals sitting uncomfortably around a metal table in what was called a *conference room,* but was actually only a little bigger than a janitor's closet on the third floor of the Hoover Building in D.C., housing the whole of the FBI.

The conference room was industrial gray, rather nondescript and certainly not as elaborate as those found on the upper floors. The large metal table taken from some other area in the building almost filled the entire room. The only nice feature the room had was the swivel chairs, which were padded and could rock back and forth. Yet, anyone sitting in them was crammed around the table with barely any room to maneuver behind them.

There weren't any windows. A whiteboard filled one wall. Pictures of dead boys were placed in columns on two of the remaining walls. Their names, birth dates, a map with the dates and locale of abduction and discovery, and other biographical data were listed underneath their pictures. On the last wall were pictures and criminal histories of the kids' murderers identified by a fourteen year old witness, George Tokay.

"Here's what we have," Summer said, handing out folders to the group. "Frank Ruiz, served five at Chino for pornography and child endangerment, ten more for sex with a minor, a boy. He was attacked with a knife in prison and has a scar on the right side of his face between his ear and his mouth. Ron Szymanski spent time in Chino for child endangerment and for pornography. Ruiz was paroled in May of '93. Szymanski in September of '94. As of now, their whereabouts are unknown."

"I'm assuming you checked with the LA office," said Logan Musgrave, the ranking agent in the room and technically in charge of the Kiddie Cops.

"Bogus addresses on both," Chet said with a sigh. "Ruiz worked for a meat packer as recently as five years ago. Szymanski last worked on the docks also five years ago. No known employment since."

"Anything on the guy in the baseball cap and sunglasses?" Logan asked.

"Nothing so far. We're looking at known associates with similar descriptions, but this guy's description is so vague . . ." Summer said.

Turning to Chet Walker, the computer guy, he said, "Did you look for any links they might have had with any of the boys or members of their families?"

"Nothing. The only thing I, we," nodding to Pete, "came up with were with the boys themselves and not much at that, just their closeness in age at each of their kidnappings and the closeness in their physical age at death."

Red-haired and freckled, Chet was the youngest member of the team. He had an aggressive, almost reckless personality and a bit of a nerd about him, a computer geek who could make something out of nothing when it came to computers. Rumor had it that Chet spent his free time hacking into anything, and everyone on the net and could do it with ease. More importantly, he could do it without detection. Or so it was said.

Pete believed it, and when he mentioned it to him, Chet merely shrugged and pretended not to care. That was confirmation enough.

"Just leave my boring, little world alone, will ya?" Pete had said with a laugh.

"Change your pin. Birthday's are way too easy," Chet had answered not even looking up from the computer screen.

That stopped Pete dead in his tracks.

And as if he was reading Pete's mind, Chet had added, "And stay away from your mother's maiden name."

"Their physical age at their death?" Douglas Rawson asked.

He was the beneficiary of Affirmative Action. But that being said, Pete and Summer thought he was a good guy with a good mind. A bit of a stuffed shirt, perhaps, dressing like a model from Ebony or GQ, but he was okay. And, he was on the climb, rapidly moving up the ladder in the agency.

"Our guess is that they executed these kids because they were either too sick or too old," Summer said.

"So . . . where do we go from here?" Musgrave asked.

Almost as one, they turned to Pete, who, though not the most senior agent in the room was the oldest. The warhorse, as Chet called him. He hadn't been listening to the conversation or reports that had been given, and actually sat half-facing the pictures of the boys on the whiteboard. When he noticed the silence, he turned around, startled that they were waiting for him to speak.

Logan asked again, "Where do we go from here?"

"You all know what I think because we've been through it ten different ways from sundown. I believe these kids were victims of human trafficking. These kids come from different parts of the country." He turned in his chair and gestured towards the white board with the pictures of the boys. "Monroe from Indiana. Nelson from Illinois. Watson from Ohio. Mullaney from California. Clarke from Arizona. Royce from Missouri. Babbitt from Minnesota. Collins from Wisconsin. Delroy from Nevada. Haynes from Michigan. Asher from Kentucky. And now, Tyler Hart from Cincinnati." Pete paused and stared at the pictures of the kids before continuing. "These kids were taken when they were between the ages of eleven and thirteen. Death occurred at least one year after their abduction, though three were killed two years after their abduction. Nelson, Clarke, and Haynes had some sort of brand on the inside of their left ankle. The same three had scaring on their backs. Best guess is whipped with a leather strap. None of these kids were found in the state where they were taken from."

"Despite what Chet said, he did come up with some links," Summer added. "The kids came from middle class or upper middle class, intact families. Most of the boys had at least one other sibling. All the kids were athletic. The type of sport doesn't really match, but their families and friends considered the boys athletes. They were bright kids, each on the honor roll and they were considered leaders. All were considered to be good kids. All were Caucasian."

Pete cleared his throat, and the group looked at him. He lowered his head and raised it, staring at Musgrave, then at the others.

"I've read these files over and over to the point where I can recite them word for word. This might sound a bit out there, but hear me out." He paused, stared at Summer and Chet, and then said, "I've been thinking these kids were targeted."

He had been thinking about this for quite a while and saying it out loud, solidified it in his mind. The group stared at him. Summer frowned at him, not in anger, but in thought.

Chet simply said, "Hmmm . . ." then chewed on the end of his pen.

"Look at these boys," Pete said turning from the group towards the pictures. "Look at them closely." He paused then asked, "What do you see?"

Chet got up from the chair and squeezed himself along the wall in order to get a closer look.

"Targeted?" Rawson asked.

"Look at the pictures and think about what Chet told us. Each boy was athletic . . . intelligent . . . on the honor roll . . . a leader . . ."

"Different hair color, but the boys are really cute, good-looking," Chet said.

"But targeted?" Musgrave asked.

It's just a gut feeling," Pete said with a shrug. "I have nothing to base it on, but there's some sort of connection these boys have . . . I just . . . can't . . . get a hold of it."

Chet turned from the board, frowning at Pete, not in disagreement, but more like he was trying to digest something distasteful. Pete recognized that look and knew Chet's mind was racing. Pete had called it 'high octane thinking'.

Exploring the theory further, Musgrave asked, "Chet, did you find any other . . . connection the boys might have had to one another or to the three perps?"

"We have nothing to connect them or their families with Ruiz or Szymanski."

"All of the deaths were similar," Rawson stated, surprising himself that he had spoken it aloud.

"Not similar," Pete said shaking his head. "The *same*. Each boy was nude, handcuffed behind their back, shot twice in the back of the head with a .38. They were found in remote areas. We figure all of the kids were kneeling when they were shot. Angle of entry would indicate that, and the Hart killing confirmed the theory."

"Did you look in the backgrounds of the individuals who found the boys?" Musgrave asked.

Chet nodded.

"Nothing there, especially with the last. That Indian kid . . ."

Chet looked at his notes.

"Tokay," Summer said, helping him out.

"Yeah, George Tokay. He's the same age or a year older than the boy he found." Chet shook his head. "Nothing."

"For the sake of argument, let's suppose you're right, Pete," Musgrave said after a long silence. "We can't *prove* its child trafficking, and we can't prove it *isn't*. We can't prove the kids were targeted. But the key to all of this is finding Ruiz and Szymanski. They're the key. We find them, we find the answers."

CHAPTER TEN

Two of the boys, Ben and Cory, weren't in the hallway. The rest of the boys, however, had filed out of their rooms as they were told to do, and they stood in front of their doors with hands at their sides in a sort of loose attention that wouldn't pass military inspection. This was a ritual that none of them wanted to witness or be a part of.

Brett caught Tim's eye and then Patrick's. He glanced at Johnny, sweaty and pale and leaning up against the wall just to keep standing. He coughed as quietly as he could into his hand. Tim moved as closely as he dared without the guards noticing and whispered something to Johnny who wiped sweat off his face and nodded slightly without drawing attention to himself or to Tim. He stood a bit wobbly but as straight as he could.

Brett looked back at Patrick, four doors down and too far away to speak to. He seemed on the verge of tears, and Brett silently hoped Patrick would keep it together until he went back into his room.

"Fuck me," Ian said in a very quiet whisper.

Brett, who stood one door away, shushed him without even looking at him. The door next to Ian's room opened and out came Ryan, led by the Fat Man and Skinny Beard, two of the guards the boys feared the most because when they showed up, one of the boys went away. As good as dead.

With the two guards was a young, tallish dark-haired man wearing a baseball cap, trim and fit and wearing sunglasses even though there wasn't any sun shining inside their little prison. The man took a long look at Ian and then at Brett, but barely glanced at the other boys. Brett and Ian exchanged a look, a silent question as to who he was. Ian shrugged slightly, while Brett shook his head. Neither of them had seen him before.

Ryan shuffled between the Fat Man and Skinny Beard with Mystery Man riding drag. Ryan was dressed in a gray t-shirt with a hole in one sleeve and another hole in the lower back, jeans that were about an inch and a half too short with holes in both knees, and in tennis shoes that had a hole big enough for his toe to stick out of the left, and with the sole on the right flapping when he walked. He actually didn't walk, though, because his legs were shackled forcing him to shuffle. His hands were cuffed in front of him.

He was a handsome boy with light brown hair and blue eyes. He was rather quiet, so none of the boys knew him particularly well, but he was one of them. Now, it seemed, he wouldn't be much longer. He never raised his eyes from the floor as he shuffled along. He reached the end of the hallway where the door led down, to where? The boys didn't know, but whoever walked through that door was never seen again.

Ryan turned back, managed to look at both Tim and Johnny before he was shoved by the Fat Man. Quietly, without a word or sound, the boys went back into their rooms and shut their doors behind them, which were locked by Butch, the ugly fat guard. Brett sat on his bed, his hands balled into fists, jaw set; more than angry and more than sad. More than frustrated that he couldn't call out, couldn't lash out. He wanted to hit someone or something.

Knowing that one way or another, some way or another, they had to escape before anyone else was taken away.

CHAPTER ELEVEN

Under the very best of circumstances, a five hour drive into the middle of nowhere is something he didn't want to do. A five hour drive into the middle of nowhere with Frank, Ron and a kid chained to the inner wall of the van being driven to his death was even worse. Yet, the Dark Man had given him an order, and because the Dark Man paid him a handsome salary, he was in the van. He passed his time by staring at the unchanging rural scenery and napping.

"Tell me again," Ron said, turning around from the passenger seat, squinting at him as he yawned tiredly. "Why did he send you with us?"

He shrugged and said, "Like I said before. He wants to expand to Miami. He wanted me to tag along, so I can learn how you do things."

The van made a left onto Highway 8 at Pembine, heading west and even the air-conditioning couldn't make the humid Wisconsin summer comfortable.

"But you did this before, right?" Ron persisted.

"Well, yeah, but other than that time in the desert, I never got rid of a kid. I help get 'em though. You know that, right?"

Ron faced the front, pursed his lips and shook his head ever so slightly.

"Nothin' to it, really," Frank said. "You take a kid, handcuff him, drive him to some spot no one will think of looking and pop him."

He looked at the boy in the back of the van. The boy seemed to stare at his shoes, but other than that, he couldn't tell what the kid was thinking.

"Why do you strip 'em?"

"First of all, you get rid of more evidence that way. The police have all that science fiction shit, so if the kid's wearin' nothin', birds and ants and shit's likely to get rid of him for you. See?"

Frank looked in the rearview mirror at him.

"Yeah, I guess." The young man glanced at the boy again. "The kid looks fine though. Why does the man want to get rid of him?"

"Who the fuck knows," Ron said, shaking his head. "Christ!"

Frank stared at his partner, then glanced at the man in the rearview mirror and shrugged. The young man in the back made a face and shrugged back.

After a bit of silence, Frank asked, "Who's the kid we're picking up?"

"A kid from Waukesha. We've been watching him. He plays baseball twice a week, soccer twice a week, hangs out at a quarry swimming with a bunch of other kids."

"Who's watching him?" Ron asked sullenly.

"Ace and me."

"Yeah . . . 'cept you're with us, right?" Ron said over his shoulder.

"Fuck! It wasn't my idea!" He leaned forward. "The man calls me and says, 'Get together with Frank and Ron. They'll teach you what they do.' So, here I am. It wasn't my idea!"

"Lighten up," Frank said, playfully slapping at Ron's arm.

"Keep your fuckin' hands to yourself! I don't like it."

"Think of it as a compliment. The man likes what we do, so we teach someone else how to do it."

"That's how I was lookin' at it," the young man offered.

They hadn't encountered more than a half dozen cars as they drove past Dunbar. They came to Jack Pine Road and turned right, drove about a quarter mile as the pavement changed from asphalt to dirt and from two lanes to one. Frank pulled off the road and cut the engine. The boy in the back looked up defiantly, but his lower lip trembled.

"Take the kid's clothes off, but watch his feet. They like to kick," Frank instructed.

The young man got up from the seat and moved cautiously towards the boy.

"Please, don't," the boy said quietly, a tear rolling down his cheek.

"Sorry, kid. Shit happens to everybody," the young man said as he yanked the shoes off the boy. "Today, it happens to you."

"*Please*!" the boy sobbed.

"What can I say?" the young man said, taking off the boy's jeans and boxers.

"Quit fuckin' around," Ron barked.

"Yeah, yeah, yeah," the young man answered, tearing the t-shirt off the boy.

"Now, take one hand and cuff him before you unchain the other hand," Frank said. "That's it. Now, easy does it. You don't want any mess in the van."

The young man helped the boy to his feet and moved him to the sliding door.

"Please, not here."

"This place is as good as any, Kid."

"I don't wanna die. Please," the boy sobbed.

"Nobody does, Kid, but like I said, 'Shit happens'."

The boy led the way into the woods, crying, pleading. Every now and then, Ron shoved him forward. Pine needles and small, pinkish and pointed pebbles pricked his feet. He limped and tried to move carefully, but Ron shoved him hard, making him fall, but he quickly got to his feet.

"Right here. Now!"

"Okay. Now what?" the young man asked, looking from Frank to Ron.

Frank reached into his waistband and pulled out a .38, checking the load as he did.

He pushed the boy's shoulder and said, "Kneel down, Kid. You won't feel a thing."

"Please . . . let me go? Please?"

"Sorry Kid, not today."

"You mind if I do him?" the young man asked, stepping forward. "I mean, I never did a kid."

"Fuck," Ron muttered.

"Sure, be my guest," Frank said, handing him the gun. "Stand over here and pop him from behind. Two shots."

"Two shots from behind," the young man repeated.

"Oh fuck, just do it!" Ron yelled.

"Okay," the man said, turning and pointing the gun at Frank. "Shit happens, right?" He pulled the trigger.

"God dammit! Oh fuck!" Ron yelled, backing up and stumbling.

The young man pointed the gun at him and pulled the trigger twice in rapid succession. He surveyed his work. Frank lay on his back, one shot to the face. Ron lay on his side, one shot to the face and one to the neck. Three shots. Each lethal.

"You dumb fucks . . . I've done my share of popping assholes like you," he said out loud to no one in particular.

The boy looked up at the man hopefully.

"Sorry, Kid. Your turn," the man said, stepping behind the boy. He pulled the trigger twice, watched the kid pitch forward face to the dirt and said, "Shit happens."

He spit on the ground and walked back to the van. He climbed into the driver's seat and took out his cell phone, dialed a number and waited.

"Yeah?"

"It's done. Give me half an hour."

"We'll be waiting."

He ended the call, started up the van and drove east on Highway 8, back to Pembine and then south on Highway 141 to Beecher and to a diner called *Mary's Place*. He climbed out of the van and locked it with the keys in the ignition and then went into the diner and joined two men in a corner booth and picked up a menu. No one said anything until a waitress stepped over to the table.

"What can I get you gentlemen today?" she said through a much-practiced smile.

*   *   *

First they heard the car door slam. Then they heard what sounded like crying and, though they couldn't make out the words, they knew somebody was angry. They were about to start up their ATVs when they heard the first shot. They froze. When the second and third shots rang out, they instinctively crouched down, searching for cover. Then, two more shots followed by silence and a car door slamming. Then silence and the car starting up and driving away.

Neither of them spoke.

They froze, just as if they were playing frozen tag or statues. They stared wide-eyed at each other, neither wanting to make the first move. Finally, the older of the two rose slowly, straining toward the sound of the gunshots and upon not hearing anything, motioned to his younger brother to stay put. The younger brother's silent and frantic protests went unnoticed.

The older boy moved slowly and ever so lightly through the woods, as if he were walking in a minefield, careful not to make any noise. After what he figured to be fifty or sixty yards, he stepped into the small clearing and saw the two dead men and the dead boy.

"Oh God! Jesus Christ!" he said, and threw up.

He ran, stumbled back to his brother.

"Call dad, quick!"

"What?" the younger boy asked.

"Oh God . . . they're dead . . . call dad . . . now!"

Recognizing puke on his brother's shirt and not understanding anything but the urgency in his brother's voice, he used a cell phone, and when his dad answered on the second ring, he yelled, "Dad, come quick! Something bad's happened!"

CHAPTER TWELVE

The Four Seasons in D.C. might look like just another upscale restaurant. It was here, however, that many deals on Capitol Hill were made. Mid-level aids would meet and broker deals over lunch, and then later that afternoon or evening, senators and congressmen would retool the deals into law.

On this late afternoon because of the summer recess on the Hill, few patrons were in the bar and fewer still ate early dinners. Towards the back of the room in a dimly lit booth with a table covered with a rich, dark red table cloth and a lit candle sat Summer in a navy jacket, cream-colored blouse and navy slacks. Thatcher Davis, having come from the office, wore a slightly wrinkled dark suit. Even wrinkled, Davis managed to look superior to everyone in the room, or anywhere else for that matter. He resembled a silver-haired college professor, and one would describe him as elegant.

"So, Barney Fife has you chasing a case of child trafficking," Davis said as he sipped his wine.

Summer ignored the bait and sipped her wine. It was difficult because he'd been at it since she had arrived.

"Do you have anything to go on? I mean, besides the kid's report from a mile or so away?"

"That boy is a credible witness. Everything he saw checked out, and based on his descriptions and the artist's sketches, we identified the perps."

"Let's hear it for the Indian boy," Davis said raising his glass in mock toast.

Summer tossed her dinner napkin on the table in disgust, frowning at him.

"Look, I'm sorry. I shouldn't have said that," he said trying to recover. "It's just that I see you wasting your talent with a dead-beat partner in a no-win department. You deserve better."

Summer looked away and watched a waiter deliver dinner to a near-by table. In some respects, she didn't know why she had decided to have dinner with Thatcher especially after the day she just had. He was condescending; cruelly so. He was also brilliant, wealthy and handsome in an aristocratic way, yet she never saw him as anything more than a friend, someone with whom to have dinner or a drink with. Someone she could talk to. She supposed she saw him as a kind of father figure. Not that he could ever come close to being anything like or as important to her as her father.

She loved her father and mother. They were hard-working ranchers, raising beef cattle on a little ranch near Crete, Nebraska. To add to their income, they grew wheat in three fields and leased out two others. Invariably, however, hail, wind, heavy rain or a combination of the three would ruin over half of their crop. While they weren't wealthy, they were happy, and that was more than many people in the world could say.

And, they were very proud of Summer for making it through the University of Nebraska and then law school at Louisville. Upon graduation, she went right to the academy where, being a pretty fair athlete and an even better student, she excelled. She could have gone into the Behavioral Science Department, which was her second choice, or the legal division, which she found utterly boring and consequently, was never considered. Instead, she opted for *cop work* as she called it. When the Kiddie Corps came calling, she jumped at it.

Kiddie Corps gave her an opportunity to not only be a cop, but to help families, and kids in particular. It made her parents even more proud of their little girl.

"I said I was sorry."

Snapped out of her reverie, she bristled.

"It isn't easy Thatch. I came here for support, and you mock me. I'm not having this conversation with you."

She wiped away a single tear and worked to compose herself.

"I said I was sorry." After a pause, he said, "But do you see what this assignment is doing to you? I don't like it. It's eating you up from the inside out."

"Drop it!" she said, causing others in the restaurant to turn in their direction.

"Have you considered my offer? I've held the position open for you for two years," he said softly, hopefully, gently taking hold of her hand.

"No, actually, I haven't, and I'm not going to."

She pulled her hand away. Thatcher didn't know what to say to that, so he sipped his wine without taking his eyes from her and then went back to his salad half-heartedly. The cell phone buzzed at Summer's belt.

She lifted it, looked at the caller ID, pushed the talk button and said, "Yes."

She listened, nodded and avoided eye contact with Davis. She hung up and gathered herself to leave.

"Officer Fife beckons?"

"We caught a break. I have to go."

"Good luck," Davis said, sipping his wine. "I hope something good finally comes out of this."

*   *   *

The bureau typically flew out of Ronald Reagan Washington National Airport in Washington D.C. Pete, grim-faced and sagging a bit more than usual, walked over to her as she got out of her car.

"Chet and Doug are coming with us. We're flying into Green Bay and taking a chopper north and west. We want to get there quickly."

Summer looked over at the plane, not seeing anyone other than the ground crew.

Frowning, she said, "Chet and *Douglas*?"

Pete shrugged, not understanding why Rawson was coming along either. He had never before accompanied them in the field. Together they walked towards the plane, but just before they got to the stairs, Pete took her elbow and stopped walking.

"When I got the call, I made a phone call to Albuquerque. I asked them to get the Tokay kid on a quick flight to Green Bay. He should arrive at about the same time we do."

Summer frowned at him. Flying a witness to the crime scene was irregular. Flying a fourteen-year-old witness to the crime scene was irresponsible.

"The way he worked the crime scene in Arizona, he might come in handy."

Summer still frowned at him, not comprehending, trying to find the logic. Surely, Wisconsin had a state crime lab that would process the scene. They were professionals. She didn't know how she, or he, would explain the presence of the boy to the rest of her team or to the local authorities. Still, she knew Pete worked on and followed hunches. This wasn't the strangest thing he had ever done. Not by a long shot.

She climbed the stairs without comment and joined Rawson and Walker, nodding at each in turn.

"What do we have?" She asked.

Chet handed her a manila folder and walked her through it.

"Two boys, brothers . . . Richard and Alan Zimmerman, were on ATVs. They stopped to take a leak. They heard voices and then gunshots. The older of the two, Richard, waits and goes to take a look. He finds a dead kid same as all the other dead kids; naked, handcuffed and shot in the back of the head twice."

Chet looked up at Summer, waiting for her to look at him.

"What?" she asked, looking first at Chet, then at Pete.

Chet glanced at Pete and then back at Summer.

"He also found two men who were shot. The men fit the description of our two perps."

He paused to let that sink in, but it didn't take long.

"Our two perps?"

Chet nodded and glanced back down at the paper on his lap. Summer looked over at Pete, who merely stared out the plane window.

"Our perps . . ." she said out loud as if saying it would help her digest it.

Now she understood why Pete wanted the Tokay kid in Wisconsin.

"What's the flying time?" She asked, taking control once again.

"About two hours." Rawson spoke for the first time. Then, as if he needed to justify his presence out in the field he said, "Logan thought Chet and I should go along. This case is getting complicated."

"Complicated . . . shit!" Pete said to the window. "Now we've got nothing!"

CHAPTER THIRTEEN

Ray Zimmerman raced to the boys after Alan had hung up. He found them hugging each other just off Highway 8 and Jack Pine Road. Rich walked his dad to the scene, and both came back pale and shaken. The younger boy was in tears, not understanding, not knowing what it was that Rich and his father had seen. Neither let Alan get near enough to find out.

This was how Officer Pat Blizel, the Marinette County Sheriff, found them. He followed Ray to the crime scene. A good officer who knew his limitations, Blizel took one look at the crime scene and realized he had a situation, a situation bigger than he could handle or wanted to handle. He radioed dispatch and told them to get a hold of the FBI office in Milwaukee. He was piped through and described in very brief detail what he had. The SAC in Milwaukee phoned D.C., who got in touch with Logan Musgrave, who got Pete and the team on a flight to Green Bay.

When the team landed in Green Bay, they hopped on a helicopter and flew to the scene. George hadn't arrived yet. The Wisconsin State Crime Lab, there are actually three of them; one in Milwaukee, one in Madison, and one in Wausau, was contacted. Because Wausau was the closest, they responded with a team of two: James Dahlke and Rosalind Wannager, who arrived about ten minutes after the team got there. State police and deputies from Marinette County had Highway 8 down to one lane a quarter mile either side of Jack Pine Road.

James Dahlke was a blond, pale, skinny young man with wire rim glasses, who looked as if he had just walked across the stage to receive his diploma- from high school. He didn't speak much, except to Roz. His partner was a plumpish redhead, who was normally quick to smile and laugh. She wasn't smiling or laughing on this afternoon.

Pete walked over to Dahlke and said, "You look barely old enough for this job."

James sighed, having heard these comments most of his college and graduate life. He was out of patience, and he wasn't about to take any crap from a suit.

"Actually, last month, I graduated from high school, got my B.S. from Carroll College in Chemistry and Forensic Science two weeks ago. Just yesterday, I received my M.S. in Forensic Science, with an emphasis in Entomology from Michigan State. I'm a bit accelerated."

Pete chewed on the inside of his cheek, shrugged and said, "Okay, Skippy. You and your partner do your thing. We have another person coming who worked a similar crime scene in Arizona. He's a civilian, but we think he might be able to help out."

"Okay *Boss Man*. We don't really need the help, but as long as this *civilian* is coming, he follows my orders, and we'll all get along just fine."

Summer had overheard the exchange and walked over and said, "Do we have a winner, or do we need to have both of you drop your drawers and take out a ruler?"

Pete laughed and said, "No, I think Skippy will do just fine."

"Whatever you say, *Boss Man*," Dahlke said over his shoulder, walking away to his truck.

About twenty minutes after the crime lab arrived, a helicopter carrying George Tokay landed on Highway 8, just inside the one-lane roadblock of the crime scene, but far enough so the copter rotors wouldn't blow away any of the crime scene evidence. George was met by a deputy, who escorted him to Pete. Pete shook George's hand, thanked him for coming and told him what they had found. He walked him over to Summer, Dahlke and Wannager.

"George, you remember Agent Storm," he said with a nod to Summer.

Summer shook George's hand. He smiled shyly and uncertainly.

"Skippy, this is George Tokay. We think the two perps are two of the three victims. At least, they fit the descriptions George gave us and the photos we matched from those descriptions."

James sighed at Pete, shook George's hand and introduced himself as James and his partner as Roz. He handed George two plastic booties and a pair of thin rubber gloves, the sort that surgeons wear, and asked that he put them on. George took off his cowboy hat, dropped his gym bag, dug out his moccasins, slipped out of his boots and put the moccasins on, followed by the plastic booties.

Dahlke handed him two large rubber bands and said, "Put these on your booties. That way, our footprints are distinguished from the others we'll encounter." He added in disgust, "A lot of pedestrians have already trampled the scene, so we have our work cut out for us."

George silently did as he was told, already feeling the heat and humidity that was vastly different from his native Arizona, and knowing it was only going to get hotter.

"We've worked a circular pattern around the scene, starting in the center where the vics are and moved out. Picked up some trace; a cigarette butt and some fiber," James said.

"We're about to work from the perimeter in," Roz said with a smile, wiping sweat from her face with her sleeve.

"Was the cigarette butt Marlboro?" George asked quietly.

Roz and James glanced at each other and then James spoke for both and said, "Yes. Why?"

"That's what I found at the other crime scene. The tall, skinny man smokes them."

James said to Roz, "We'll need to cross-check DNA on the tall guy with the cigarette."

George squatted down, glancing between the blacktop of Highway 8 and the gravel of Jack Pine Road. He bit his tongue, pretending to search the ground. He touched the turquoise and leather around his neck and silently asked forgiveness from the *chindi* for walking onto the scene of death. After he finished, he stood up.

"A lot of footprints."

"Wonderful, isn't it? Makes our job all the more fun," James said with disgust. "And time consuming."

"Did you check anyone's feet?" George asked.

"Nope, but we're about to."

James stuck a thumb and finger into his mouth and whistled loudly and sharply.

Walking somewhat sideways about four steps, he stopped and announced, "Anyone, and I mean *anyone*, who walked this far needs to report to my two partners right now. We need to check your shoes against the ones who messed up our crime scene."

Ray Zimmerman and his two boys came forward, as did Sheriff Blizel and stood in front of Roz and George.

When no more came forward, James said, "There are at least four or five more sets of prints here. Let's get moving. I'd like to finish before it gets dark."

Roz went to work studying the soles of the sheriff's boots and then started on the father of the two boys. Following her lead, George began inspecting the shoes of the two boys

Their father intervened and said, "Come here boys."

The boys hesitated and then moved over next to their father.

"We got a problem here?" Pete asked as he stepped up to George.

Ray Zimmerman didn't respond. Neither did Rich or Alan.

Pete slipped off his wingtip, handed it to George, and said, "Tell me what you see George."

Guessing Pete was making a point, George said, "Size ten, about 190, maybe 195. You mostly walk on your heals, but you roll the step, so you wear down the outside of the heal. Your left foot drags, because you're wearing a gun on your ankle. Probably small caliber like a .22 or .38."

"Thanks for the compliment, but I go 197," Pete said slipping back into his shoe. "How about the good sheriff?"

Sheriff Blizel began slipping off his boot, but George shook his head.

"Probably 210 or 215, about six two or three. Serious heal walker. No drag, so you don't carry a backup."

Blizel nodded and smiled at him. Anger getting the better of him, Pete stepped up nose to nose with Ray Zimmerman, glaring.

"This young man witnessed the execution of a boy his own age. He ID'd the perps and ran the crime scene slicker than anyone we have on the force." He let that sink in for a minute and said, "Thanks to this young man, we have our first break in this case."

Summer stepped over, handed her stylish, but dusty gray flat to George and said, "My, my, my . . . the testosterone is in the air today. I just might have to get that ruler out after all."

Chet Walker and Douglas Rawson walked over to George.

Walker stuck out a hand and said, "Hi, I'm Chet. I've heard a lot about you. Really nice work."

George smiled and shook his hand.

Rawson introduced himself, shook George's hand and gave him a wing tip, much like Pete's, but more expensive and polished. George checked it out and handed the shoe back to the tall black man.

James came over, smiling, but shaking his head slightly. He handed George and Roz thin wires with yellow numbered flags attached.

"Let's see what we have for prints. Let's get moving though," James said, urging them onward. "We've got a lot of work to do before it gets dark."

CHAPTER FOURTEEN

Although one year younger than his brother, William could have been George's twin. Their builds and temperament were about the same, though William tended to be a bit more lanky. George was more traditional than William, who didn't care for the old ways. He cared more for the white – *biligaana* world. His only concession to his Indian-ness was his longish black hair under a beat up cowboy hat.

In intense heat, the desert smells like nothing anyone could name, but it smells just the same. William was used to the smell of the desert, just as George was. And just like George, he was used to the smell of sheep and horse. His quick eyes picked out a jackrabbit perched under some sage, sniffing at the air, testing for danger. The sheep either didn't notice or didn't care about the diminutive interloper. They continued to graze or rest under the scorch of the sun.

Like his brother, William sat in the same spot in the shade of the pine at the top of the hill in the rocks shaped like a recliner as he watched for rustlers. Ever since the murder of the boy on their land, he and George were wary, nervous when they watched their sheep. Neither found they could relax like they once had. Ever since that day, the rifle lay across a lap and not in a scabbard on the roan William usually rode or the black stallion, Nochero, that George rode.

William was envious of his brother, who just that afternoon was picked up by a helicopter. George was nervous about the trip, but William wouldn't have been. He would have looked forward to it.

One day . . .

William took a drink of warm water from his canteen and swatted at a fly buzzing near his face. He combed his sweaty hair with his fingers and shoved his hat low on his brow. Just as his brother, he wore a pair of dusty blue jeans and a leather vest, but no shirt. In the desert, the boys knew enough about heat and dehydration to keep drinking liquid, yet he was hot. In other climates, sweat would pour out of you, but not in the desert. You could never tell, until sometimes too late, that you were over-heating. Beyond hot and wary and nervous, he was bored and uncomfortable.

His roan lifted his head and stamped a front leg. The sheep bellowed and moved further down the hill. William sat up slowly, looking towards the road. Nothing. No cloud of dust indicating a vehicle making its way towards the sheep. He gripped his rifle tightly, his index finger light on the trigger. He pushed his hat back on his head, and he stood to get a better look.

It was when he stood that he noticed the smell. A burnt smell. Something burning. He couldn't see anything off in the distance, yet the roan stamped and whinnied, the whites of his eyes showing. The sheep called to each other nervously. Gun shots caused William to jump. The shots startled both sheep and his horse.

He worked his way through the pine to look out over the other side of the rise, towards the ranch. He saw smoke and a lot of it. With one hand on his hat and other wrapped around the rifle, William squinted towards the ranch, trying to see what had happened. Then, remembering the binoculars, he started for the horse tied to a tree. That was when he heard it. He couldn't see it, but he could tell it was coming closer and was almost on top of him.

His first thought was that George might be back already. His second thought was that it couldn't possibly be George, because it had only been several hours since he had left. If it wasn't George, who was it, and why was it so close? He squinted up towards the sun.

Because of the glare, he couldn't see, even though the helicopter seemed to be right on top of him and getting closer. That was exactly what the men in the helicopter had wanted- for the boy to be blinded by the sun. While the boy stood transfixed, squinting upwards, trying to see what was happening, the helicopter hovered as its door slid open. A man aimed a high-powered rifle at the boy and carefully squeezed off two shots, nearly ripping William in half.

"Got him," one man said through his headset, still squinting through the sight.

"Make sure," his partner said.

The man with the rifle squeezed off two more shots into the lifeless body, making the body of the boy on the ground wiggle.

"That should do it."

The helicopter hovered a moment or two longer, then banked and flew off to the south, satisfied that the boy, along with the members of his family were dead.

All dead.

CHAPTER FIFTEEN

The heat and humidity of Wisconsin in late June was so much different than late June in the desert of the Four Corners Area. George found it oppressive, like being smothered in a warm, wet blanket. Breathing was difficult. Worse, swarms of little black flies, gnats, hovered around his face, his nose and his ears. Several times he found he had walked through a thick swarm of them.

He itched.

Rivers of sweat ran from under his arms and down his chest. His long black hair was wet and uncomfortable. He wished he had something to tie his hair up with. He wanted to take off his shirt, but he wasn't going to until James or Roz told him he could, and he wasn't about to ask. About taking off his shirt, George wanted to be proper and respectful and didn't know if, under the circumstances, he should do that. For the hundredth time, he ran his hand through his hair and wiped his face with his sleeve.

George sighed heavily. He was thirsty, and he wanted some water to drink. Yet, he would not ask for any. He would be patient. That was the Navajo way, the way of his people. Also, he didn't know if that would be the proper thing to do either.

George finished marking the last of the footprints, using the last of his flags James, or Skippy as Pete called him, had given him. He stood up and looked for James or his partner, and not seeing them, walked carefully to the death scene. He had recognized the two men at once and had confirmed that these were the two men he had seen murdering the boy in Arizona. James and Roz were squatting over the dead boy, talking quietly when he walked up to them.

Chet had downloaded a digital photo into the laptop, and sent it to The Center for Missing Children. It took them less than one-half an hour to ID the boy and faxed the data sheet along with a photo of a smiling dark-haired boy with brown eyes back to the north woods of Wisconsin. The boy turned out to be Ryan Wynn from St. Paul, Minnesota. He'd been missing for nineteen months, last seen playing a pickup basketball game on a school playground with some friends. Thirteen at the time. He never showed up for dinner that night, or for that matter, many other dinners.

Without looking up at George, James said, "How many sets did you come up with?"

"Agent Pete, Agent Summer, the sheriff, the father, the older boy, the other two FBI agents, the skinny man, the fat man, this boy, and one other. Not counting yours, your partner's or mine. Eleven total."

James smiled up at him.

"That's what we came up with. Nice job." He looked back down at the dead boy and said, "What do you see?"

George, the Navajo, didn't really want to get close to the boy, but George, the one-day policeman, squatted down next to Roz and squinted at the boy and studied him.

After a bit of silence, George said, "This is the way the boy looked in Arizona."

Patiently, James said, "We know that. What do you *see*?"

George looked at the boy closely, not saying anything. Not really sure what to say.

James said, "We assume the boy had sex with someone. With that assumption, we're going to use a Victim PERC or rape kit, and hopefully the boy will help us identify whoever did this."

George glanced at Dahlke, and then at Roz.

"We'll get some preliminary samples from the boy here and more detailed samples as we work with the coroner."

James stared at George, wondering what he was thinking. George was about the same age as the dead boy. This was George's second dead body in less than a week. The perps who executed the boy in Arizona lay dead not ten yards away. Both shot unceremoniously. Of course, James didn't give a shit about them, other than to catch the asshole who had shot them and the boy.

He had already assumed that neither of the dead men had shot the boy. There didn't appear to be any powder trace on their hands, though to make sure, they'd run the test for GSR. Also, there was no weapon at the scene. The third person, more than likely a male judging from the footprints, probably took the weapon, a .38, with him when he left the scene in what looked to be a van, judging by the type of tire tread and depth of the imprint in the gravel.

Dahlke had worked on a couple of dead bodies from boating accidents, a couple of hunting accidents and even a hiker or two. He had only worked a murder scene a dozen times or so and never anything this sick or gruesome.

Like most of America, he watched CSI and nodded with approval at their technique, lusted for their equipment, not to mention their budget, and laughed at how quickly loose ends were tied up. In the real world, at least James' world, fingerprints didn't pop up on a computer screen in seconds. In fact, with the current backlog and with any kind of luck, fingerprints didn't pop up for two or three weeks. With a "rush" on them, fingerprints still took five to seven days. DNA? Two to three weeks at the earliest, but usually longer. A "rush" might get you a week and a half, but that would be pushing it.

Roz was pretty new to the Wausau lab. Eventually, she would develop the thick shell most cops and coroners end up growing in order to deal with the ugliness of their work. She might even numb out with alcohol. He often wondered if she would last, and if so, for how long. Hell, he wondered if he would last. Dead kids in the north woods of Wisconsin, executed with their hands cuffed behind their backs wouldn't provide him with pleasant dreams in the dead of night. It certainly wouldn't be the stuff of telephone calls to his dear old dad and mom, Jeff and Rachel, living in Sturgeon Bay. *'Hey Dad, Mom. Guess what I saw today?'*

Hell, he knew he wouldn't talk to anyone about this. He only hoped he could forget what he saw and did on this hot summer afternoon near Goodman.

Not likely though.

*   *   *

Leonard Bucky ran his cruiser as fast as he dared, dodging potholes and ruts caused by rain runoff, fishtailing as he went. The smoke was easy to see against the Robin's egg blue sky and knowing the direction from which it had come, he was nervous. The closer he got, his nervousness changed to dread. A helicopter flew at him low on the horizon. This was unusual. Planes at a normal height, yes, but usually not helicopters, at least not on this part of the reservation.

It buzzed fast over his head. Leonard stopped and craned his neck out the window, trying to get a better look at it, but from his angle, he couldn't see any markings. It was white with red on it. Nothing else remarkable. Ignoring it for the time being, he stomped on the accelerator, kicked up gravel and dirt and shot ahead. He braked as he came up over the rise leading to the Tokay ranch and gasped at the destruction.

The blaze was nearly out. The small, wooden house, the barn and the out-buildings were gone, nothing more than charred ruins. He drove carefully into the yard and pulled to a stop. He yanked a handkerchief out of his back pocket and covered his mouth and nose and surveyed the damage. He saw the bodies.

He ran to the old man first. He was shot at what appeared to be close range by something powerful; rifle, maybe a large caliber handgun. A portion of his head was missing. He walked carefully over to the two women. George's grandmother and mother were shot where they had hugged each other. Near them were the bodies of George's youngest brother Robert and his younger sister Mary. They had died holding hands.

Missing was George, who had flown to Wisconsin earlier that day. Also missing was William. He skirted around the property with one hand holding the handkerchief and the other on the butt of his gun. Not seeing William anywhere, he got back into his car and drove through the opening of the fence and into the field and up towards the butte where he knew they tended their sheep.

As he drove, he thought about calling the Window Rock station to report what he knew thus far. The Tokay family had been murdered, and the small ranch leveled by fire. He wanted to know about the helicopter. He wanted them to do some checking on it and to ask for backup and the coroner. He decided to wait until he checked on his younger cousin, William.

Leonard saw the horse first. It was near the edge of the pine just on the ranch side of the crest of hill. As he drove nearer, it stamped its front hoof, flared its nostrils and raised his head. Getting out of his cruiser, Leonard saw the whites of its eyes. Clearly, the horse was scared or angry or both.

"It's ok, boy," Leonard whispered soothingly.

He unholstered his gun and hammered it back, not knowing what he might find in the stand of pine trees. Carefully, he stepped up to the horse and stroked its neck. He slapped the horse's behind, sending it towards the ranch and down the road from where he had just come.

He stepped lightly, watching for small sticks that might alarm anyone waiting on the other side. As he knelt behind a tree, he saw William on his back, rifle and binoculars dropped to the side. He had almost been cut in half. This was definitely the work of a high powered rifle; two, three shots, maybe four. Someone had wanted to be very, very sure.

It clicked, and he made the connection. Whoever it was had come looking for George. They must have stopped at the ranch first and then came for William, thinking he was George.

Whoever it was wanted George.

CHAPTER SIXTEEN

Pete's cell chirped.

He stepped away from the huddle of agents and said, "Kelliher."

He nodded two or three times and made eye contact with Summer who excused herself and moved next to Pete. He stabbed a finger on his phone to end the call and took Summer by the arm, so they could move further from the group.

"We've got problems."

"What?"

Pete glanced at the other agents, then at George who stood talking quietly with the two crime scene investigators and said, "Someone just burnt down the Tokay ranch and executed his family."

Summer went white.

"How . . . when?"

"That was Leonard, George's cousin . . . the Indian cop. He saw smoke and went to investigate. He also saw a helicopter leaving from that general direction. He found the ranch burned down and the family dead. He said it looked like large caliber weapons. George's younger brother, William, was tending the sheep. He's about the same size as

George, and whoever killed his family, must have thought they had murdered George."

"Oh God!"

Summer looked over at George, who noticed both Pete and Summer looking at him. She tried to smile and spoke quickly and quietly to Pete.

"Who knew about George?"

"Only our group," Pete said grimly. "Perhaps someone out of Albuquerque or the tribal police. That's it."

Pete let that sink in, and it didn't take long for Summer to catch the thought.

"We might have a leak."

Pete said nothing, only stared first at Summer, then looked over at Doug Rawson and then at Chet Walker. Neither noticed. He then stared at Summer.

"No way," Summer protested emphatically with a shake of her head.

"We don't know it's us, but we can't rule it out either. It could be as simple as the guy with the baseball cap and sunglasses . . . maybe tying up loose ends. George said the guy didn't seem to be involved . . . that was George's word, *involved.* Maybe he was the leader and decided to get rid of them."

Summer shook her head, not believing either possibility, but said, "Ok, so we don't rule it out. What's the plan?"

"What's the typical profile of a pedophile?" Pete asked.

"You know the answer," Summer said with impatience. "White male, twenty to fifty, single, doesn't get along well with his own peer group, tends to hang around kids of a specific age group and gender, no real friends."

"Right. Chet, Logan and I fit the profile. You and Doug don't."

"Forget it," Summer said, turning half away from him.

"Can't. You know we can't. We need to look at this objectively. You and Doug need to do some discreet digging. Discreet, but dig like hell. Once we're ruled out . . . or in, we can check out Albuquerque and the tribal police."

Summer turned back to Pete, crossed her arms and toed a small pebble without looking up at him.

"Do you have anyone in mind . . . I mean . . ."

"No. I don't think it's one of us, but again, we've got to dig, deep as hell if need be, discreetly, but we've got to dig. That's the only way," Pete said, running a hand through his grayish flattop and then wiping sweat from his face. "As

I said, it could be the guy wearing the baseball cap and sunglasses tying up loose ends."

"What about George. We've got to tell him, but I don't think we can send him back until we know more. It's too dangerous," Summer added.

"I'll tell him, and I'll find a safe place for him. Once I place him, I'll let you and only you know where he is, but it has to stay between the two of us."

Summer nodded.

"And," Pete paused and said, "I'm thinking on sending Skippy to Arizona to check the crime scene, but I think you should go too. I don't want to go too far out of the group, and I don't want this to get out too quickly."

"I'll go, but you just can't send Skip to Arizona, Pete. He's got to answer to somebody. Someone is going to want to know where he is."

"I'll work it out," Pete said walking away, knowing Summer was okay with it. He stopped and came back to her, "You take care of Doug but don't involve anyone else other than someone who can work a computer better than Chet."

"And who do you suppose *that* might be?" Summer said doubtfully.

Pete shrugged, believing Chet was the best. He turned on his phone, checked the recent calls and phoned George's cousin in Arizona.

"Leonard, this is Pete Kelliher. Who knows about this?"

"Just you. I need to radio in and get the coroner. Is George okay?"

"George is fine. Hold off on contacting anyone. I want a very, very tight lid on this. My partner is coming out along with a forensics guy by the name of Skip Dahlke. They'll arrive in roughly two hours. Can you trust one other individual who will give them an escort?"

"Yeah, I got a cousin. What about George?"

"I give you my word, George will be safe. After I tell him what happened, I'll have him call you, but don't give him a lot of detail. He's too young and doesn't need that right now. Okay?"

Leonard hesitated, but said, "Yeah, okay. But he'll be safe?"

"You have my word. My partner and Dahlke will catch a chopper out to Window Rock. Have your cousin meet them there."

"Got it."

"And Leonard, you've got to keep a tight lid on this."

*   *   *

While Pete spoke to Leonard, Summer spoke with Doug Rawson. The tall black man listened intently, squinting, a hand in his pocket, and every now and then he nodded at something she said. Luckily, Chet was busy with his laptop, so the conversation remained private between the two of them. Finally, Rawson nodded, turned away, pulled out his cell and made a call.

*   *   *

George listened silently, head down. Every now and then, he'd glance up at Pete, struggling to keep his composure. Pete admired him for that but knew that the struggle was intense.

"Everyone's dead?" George asked, lip trembling, eyes welling up.

"Yes. That's what Leonard said."

George dropped his head and folded his arms. Pete reached out and gripped his shoulders. George let him but didn't raise his head. He wiped his eyes but didn't look up.

"George, I need you to trust me, okay?" Pete said gently.

George nodded but didn't look up.

"I'm not going to let anything happen to you, but until we find some answers, I can't let you go back home."

"Someone will need to say prayers for my family," George said with a shaky voice.

"Can your cousin arrange that for you?"

George shrugged.

"I know you want to go back home and take care of your family, but I don't think it would be safe for you. Not yet, anyway."

George looked up at Pete, wiped his eyes and said, "It's because of me, isn't it."

Pete took George's face into his hands and turned it up so they were eye to eye.

"What happened was not your fault. You did the right thing. You helped solve a little boy's murder. That's a good thing. What happened to your family isn't your fault."

"But they killed my family because of me," George insisted.

Pete didn't say anything, but wiped away tears from George's eyes with his thumbs. George said nothing, but breathed deeply, took Pete's cell phone, turned and walked away. Pete let him go, knowing the boy needed some space, time and quiet. Instead, he walked over to the forensic team.

"Skip, can I speak with you a second?"

Dahlke recognized a difference in Pete's voice, had noticed him talking to George and had noticed George crying off by himself. He left Roz and walked over to Pete.

"Skip, I need a huge favor."

Pete told him about George's family being murdered, the family ranch being burnt to the ground and the need for him to fly to Arizona to cover the crime scene.

"You don't have anyone else?"

"No one I trust right now. I'm sure this is related to the murder George witnessed and the murder of this boy and these two assholes. I'm just not sure who or how."

James glanced over at George who had reappeared in the clearing, walking towards Roz.

"What's going to happen to him?"

"Nothing will happen to him. He's my responsibility now."

"What do I tell Roz? She's going to need to know," he shrugged and shook his head, "*Some*thing."

Pete chewed on his tongue and then puffed out his cheeks.

James said, "I'll give her directions and the protocols on this scene. I'm going to tell her I was asked to run another scene and that I'll be in touch with her. I won't tell her where or who. Fair enough?"

"Catch a ride with Chet, Summer and Doug in the helicopter. Summer will arrange for both of you to take a plane to Arizona and a chopper to take you to Window Rock, where someone will pick you up and take you to the ranch, or what's left of it. Call me when you arrive and after you check it out."

"You want me to use my gear, or do you have some for me?"

"I can get it, but it could take time. I'm not sure we have time."

James nodded and turned to walk away.

"Skip?"

"Yeah, *Boss Man*," he said with a smile.

Pete smiled and said, "I owe you."

James looked over at George and then back at Pete.

"No you don't."

CHAPTER SEVENTEEN

Pete phoned the Center for Missing and Exploited Children.

"There's a kid in Wisconsin I heard about who was a victim and held captive a couple, maybe three years ago. He works with families of missing kids or victims of sexual predators. Would you happen to know who he is and how to get a hold of him?"

The man on the other end paused before asking, "Can I ask why?"

Pete paused for effect and then said, "I'd rather not say."

It was the man's turn to pause and then he said, "His name is Randy Evans, and he lives in a suburb of Milwaukee. His father, Jeremy, is a high school counselor."

He gave Pete a phone number.

After thanking him, Pete signed off and punched in the number.

*   *   *

"What the hell were you thinking?"

The dark man smiled, smoked his cigar, blew smoke towards the ceiling and answered calmly, "Tying up loose ends."

"Do you realize that now they suspect they have a leak? They've begun an investigation into who that might be?"

After another puff on the cigar, the dark man said, "I pay you to keep things private. You'll just have to divert that investigation."

The man on the other end of the line said, "They aren't stupid . . . Kelliher isn't stupid and neither is Storm. It won't be that easy." He paused and asked, "Why? Why did you do this without first asking me?"

The dark man sighed and answered, "First of all, I don't have to ask you anything . . . not a thing. Secondly, they're Indians. No one in Arizona gives a shit about Indians, least of all me." He let that sink in and then said, "Besides, Graham was with them, and I need to protect him. You know why."

"Graham was the third man?"

"Yes. Now you understand?" the dark man asked.

The man on the other end swore and said, "It was still very stupid and dangerous. You could have just gotten rid of Frank and Ron. You didn't have to whack the kid and his family."

"I wasn't going to take that chance. That kid still might be able to identify Graham. You'll just have to divert the investigation."

Exasperated, the man asked, "You do realize that you're planning a pick up just hours from the deposit, don't you?"

"And?"

The caller on the other end was out of patience, tired of trying to explain the predicament the dark man put him in, so he said, "I think you're reckless."

The dark man smiled and said, "I'm a business man. I need to tie up loose ends and restock my stables."

"And I don't have to tell you what happens if you get caught."

"I pay you money to keep me from getting caught, now don't I? Not to mention an open invitation for certain privileges with my ponies."

A long pause.

"I just need you and your handlers to be careful."

"Of that you can be certain. I'll let you know when the pony is in our possession."

CHAPTER EIGHTEEN

Stephen Bailey, dressed in his tiger-stripped goalie shirt and his white Addidas gloves with finger spines, danced on his toes watching the play develop ahead of him. He had not been scored upon, but since the half, most of the play took place on his end of the field. A mid-fielder dribbled past a defender and down his right sideline.

Noticing his stopper down on one knee tying a shoe, he said, "Mike, watch the pass to the forward."

Mike Erickson straightened up and said, "Got it," and sprinted to intercept the pass.

He misplayed it, but it went off his foot out of bounds, giving his defense time to regroup. Stephen barked directions to his defense and moved to a defensive angle. The throw-in was headed by a defender and picked up by Stephen's forward, and the play moved to the other side of the field.

"Time?" Mike yelled to his sideline.

"Less than two," his coach yelled back.

"Nothin' past you, Mike!" Stephen yelled.

"Nope, nothin'."

The ball was stolen and launched to a quick forward on Stephen's left. The attacker dribbled nicely through the mid-field and past Stephen's left fullback. Mike slipped when he sprinted to defend it, and the attacker drilled it high to Stephen's backside. Somehow, Stephen laid out, knocking it out of the goal box. He scrambled to his feet ready for a second shot, but Mike had recovered and booted the ball to the far end of the field.

"Nice one, Mike!" Stephen yelled with a sigh of relief.

"Nothin' past me," Mike said with a laugh.

The two of them had been best friends since second grade, spending as much time at each other's house as their own. Stephen was a bit taller than Mike and was a strawberry blond, which he kept fairly short. Not only was he an excellent goalie, he was also a very good catcher on his baseball team, usually hitting third or fourth in the lineup. Mike, on the other hand, had dark hair, and he wore it a bit longer than Stephen. Soccer was his best game, though he played on the same baseball team as Stephen as a centerfielder. He was naturally quick, as well as fast, which made him ideal for each sport and the positions he played. Both boys also took tennis lessons, with Mike being the better of the two.

Three whistles, and the game ended in a 2-0 win. Cheers all around. Mike and Stephen, best friends, threw their arms around each other's shoulders and accepted knuckle bumps and low fives from their teammates, and as was their tradition, Mike and Stephen took off their shirts and waved them in the air. And as was the typical reaction to their tradition, their coach Barry Miller yelled at them to get their shirts back on. They did, but not before Mike did a nifty back flip and not before they squirted each other with their water bottles. Every win, the same routine, and so far, the routine occurred each game they had played.

The Spring City Revolution was fifteen and zero and ranked second in the boys U-13 age group in Wisconsin. They had high hopes for the Schwanz Cup Tournament in the Twin Cities in two weeks. After their team meeting, Stephen and Mike stripped off their socks and shin guards, slipped on their Addidas slides, picked up their gear and headed to the opposite sideline to catch up with their parents and finalize plans for the rest of the afternoon and evening. Typically, they alternated sleeping at each other's house after games, and it was Stephen's turn to spend the night at Mike's house.

"What time do you want me over?"

Mike glanced at his mom, who shrugged and said, "We're grilling out. Do you want to eat at our house?"

Stephen began to say yes, but his mom said, "If that's ok with you, Jennifer. Ted and I were going out tonight."

"No problem. What time would you like me to pick him up?"

"We can drop him off on our way."

Close by, a small, non-descript man listened in on the exchange with more than a little interest. He turned towards the parking lot and turned on his cell and placed a call.

"How soon?"

"We're about an hour away."

Ace told them the boys' plans and gave them the address. He glanced back to get another look at them. He got into his car, stolen from a Milwaukee parking garage, and waited until he noted which vehicles the boys got into. He checked the license plates he had written down in a small spiral notebook one more time to be certain.

One pony almost in the stable.

CHAPTER NINETEEN

Jeremy Evans lived in a modest, white, two-story with black shutters and a nice patio with a fire pit and barbeque in the backyard in a middle-class neighborhood on Waukesha's north side, not too far from Waukesha North High School where he was a counselor. His adopted son, Randy, lived with him as did Randy's biological brother, Bill.

Randy had come first. He had run away from an abusive home and was placed into foster care. Because Jeremy was on the foster list in hopes of eventually adopting a child, he ended up with Randy a little over two years ago. Billy, Randy's twin came along a little over a year later. It was a confusing mess.

The twins were born to a school-aged mom and were given up for adoption. Neither family had wanted a set of twins, so the agency agreed to separate them. Billy went to a couple in Milwaukee, while Randy went to a family in Marshfield in the north central part of the state.

Years later, a picture and story on adoption featuring Jeremy and Randy appeared in the Milwaukee Sentinel, and Billy read it and confronted his parents. While Randy had known he was adopted and knew about his twin brother,

Billy had not. It started a war in the Schroeder household and ended when Robert and Monica divorced. Monica moved out of the house to live on the east side of Milwaukee. Billy refused visitation weekends and eventually Monica gave up trying.

Robert died of a sudden heart attack a year or so ago and ever since the divorce, Billy wanted nothing to do with his mother. Living with his mother was not an option, and deep down, Monica knew that. Yet, she put up a fight, but when Billy threatened to run away every chance he got and threatened to move out as soon as he turned eighteen, she gave up and moved out of state never to be heard from again.

Billy moved in with Jeremy and Randy but kept his last name after he, too, was adopted by Jeremy. It was downright complicated for those who did not know the story. The boys were as close as two brothers could be ever since Randy's arrival. They were best friends. They shared the same friends and most of the same interests, except that Billy was more of an accomplished athlete while Randy was more cerebral and a writer and musician. Both were very bright, as well as perceptive and instinctive. They seemed to know what the other was thinking, and it seemed to Jeremy that a lot of communication between the two occurred with looks and gestures.

At first glance, they were identical, and anyone who was not a close friend could not tell the two apart. Both had soft brown hair and big brown eyes. They dressed the same, each wearing the other's clothes. They liked the same kinds of food, laughed the same, talked the same and used the same expressions. If you spent time around them, one would notice that Billy had a bit of a crooked smile, a glint in the eye that warned of mischief, wisecracks and practical jokes. Randy seemed a bit more serious; guarded. Yet, Billy who was eight minutes older would defer to Randy when plans or decisions had to be made. Randy was the leader and the quiet one, more reserved, and many times Jeremy had wondered if it was a result of the abuse he had endured or if it was just his personality to be so.

"That's how the twins ended up with me," Jeremy said with a shrug.

He and Pete sat in the kitchen at a blond-wood table with six matching chairs. A Diet Coke sat in front of both men. Every now and then one of the boys would cat-call or tease the other while they played Wii in the family room. The only voice that wasn't heard was George's, but that was understandable. He had just lost his family. His home was burnt to the ground. He had no idea where he was or who he was with or what was going to happen to him. So it was understandable if he was quiet. Pete didn't anticipate another boy in the house, but didn't think that it mattered.

"I can't give you a lot of the details. What I can tell you is that George witnessed a murder and saw the two perpetrators who committed it. The murder took place on the Navajo Indian Reservation in Arizona . . . on his land while he was tending his family's sheep. Someone murdered George's family and burned down their ranch. We suspect that the perps think they killed George because his little brother was shot multiple times, and he looked remarkably like George."

Jeremy glanced towards the next room and then back at Pete.

"No one knows George is here, and I need it kept that way . . . for his safety and yours."

"What do you mean by his safety and ours?"

"We believe that whoever killed that boy and those two men up north is still in the state. We believe he or they are tied to whoever killed George's family."

Jeremy glanced again towards the family room.

Pete knew what Jeremy was thinking so he said, "No one knows George is here, and I believe you and your family are safe. The problem is I don't know how long George will be here. Is that going to be a problem for you?"

Jeremy pushed his chair away from the table and leaned forward, elbows on his knees and looked intently at Pete. He was thirty-six years old, a single guy who had contemplated the priesthood for a long time before deciding that celibacy was a bit too much to deal with. Yet, he had never married and was far from promiscuous. Eligible, yes. A player, no.

As a former high school and college basketball coach and especially now as a high school counselor, he was used to problem-solving on the fly. He and Randy had traveled around the state and parts of the Midwest speaking to school assemblies, parent groups, and law enforcement agencies about the sexual exploitation of children and how to keep kids safe, especially in this day and age of the internet, social networks and cell phones. Law enforcement in four states brought the two of them in to work with kids who had been molested, as well as their parents. Jeremy knew the danger these men and groups posed.

"Let's suppose . . . what . . . if something happens to you during this investigation? What happens if somehow, some way . . . those people find out he's here? I don't care about me, but I have two sons to think about. And how do I explain George to the boys' friends or my family?"

Pete looked at him thoughtfully, fully appreciating the position he was placing him in, along with his family.

He shrugged and said, "He's a friend of the family or a friend of your sons, I guess. Try to keep it simple. The simpler, the better."

"And . . . if something happens to you or like I said if they find out he's here? Then what?'

Pete suspected the FBI had a leak. He knew there was the possibility that George's location might be found, but only if whoever killed George's family found out that it was George's brother who was shot on that hillside and not George. He explained this to Jeremy.

"Right now, they have no need to look for him and no idea *where* to look for him. I'm the only one who knows."

"Again, if something happens to you, then what?"

Pete ran his hands over his face.

"I have to let my partner know where he is. She and I will be the only two that know. Not even the rest of our team will know."

Jeremy looked down at his hands holding his Diet Coke.

Without looking up he said, "With your permission, I'd like to bring someone else into this . . . a friend who's a

detective on the police force. Jamie Graff. We're friends,
and I trust him. He knows my family."

Pete didn't want anyone else brought in, yet there was
logic in the idea. This detective could stay in the background
and keep a quiet watch. This could be good.

"I'll need to meet him."

Jeremy pulled out his cell and punched in Jamie's
number.

CHAPTER TWENTY

"Mom, it's only three blocks away, and it isn't real dark yet. We won't be gone that long," Mike pleaded.

"I don't think so. We have plenty of movies here you can watch."

Silence. That pleading look that killed her each and every time he wore it. Then, the fake puppy-dog look meant to bring about a laugh, which it always did.

"Take your cell with you and keep it on. You call me when you get there and when you start back home. You go nowhere else, and you stay together. You know the rules."

"Awesome! You're the best!"

"Remember what I said, Mike. Stephen, keep him in line," Jennifer said playfully.

Yet, there was this vague feeling of worry in the pit of her stomach. This wasn't the only time Mike had been allowed out at night in the dark, but something chewed at her. A mom's antenna maybe. Perhaps, nothing at all. Still, Mike was getting older, and he was with Stephen, a nice, calming influence on her son, who tended to be a bit more carefree.

"Be careful you two. And remember to call me!"

*   *   *

The team didn't have a firm snatch plan. They didn't have a firm snatch date other than by the end of the week. They couldn't afford to hang around more than two, maybe three days because of the stolen van and two stolen cars and even that was pushing it. They had decided to take the first available opportunity.

Down the block, Ace sat low in his car somewhat hidden by shrubs that ran in front of the house he sat in front of. Hedges were on the other side of the street also, but no one seemed to be home. He had pretended to alternately read a map and the newspaper and tried to blend in with the neighborhood. There weren't many people out and about. Most of the jogging occurred in the early morning. Every now and then someone walked a dog but pretty much ignored him or didn't pay him any attention.

That was what he had wanted.

He saw the two boys walk down the driveway and down the sidewalk away from him towards the van, which was on the other side of the street.

He punched speed dial and said, "Coming your way. Both of them."

"Got it," was all that was said on the other end. "Stay back and follow us when we have the package."

"One or both?'

"We'll see."

He watched the van start up and move down the street up ahead of the boys. It took a left, and Ace figured it would come back around the block and park at the corner where the boys would actually walk right to it. Rick drove while Shawn and Clay were the handlers. This was an experienced team, but not as experienced as Frank and Ron had been.

That was the A team while this was the B team. Ace didn't like working with this group, who tended to be a bit rough and who tended to take more liberties with the boys. But it was what he had since Frank and Ron had been disposed of.

Ace stayed a comfortable half-block behind the boys who were laughing and bumping into one another, taking their time without a care in the world. The way it should be, and the way Ace and the team needed it to be. The cell beeped.

"Yeah."

"At the corner."

Ace didn't respond, but clicked off and slowly drifted up the street, now past the Erickson house. A soft glow of light behind the sheer drapes. Quiet. Fifteen yards from the corner. The boys laughed at something. The van pulled into view at the corner. Shawn and Clay had crossed a yard behind the boys and quickly closed the distance.

Five yards, four. Each had a rag filled with chloroform in hand. Shawn came up behind the Erickson kid, Clay behind the Bailey kid. Arm around chest, rag covering the face, and the boys lifted off their feet and into the van. Door slammed shut as it pulled from the curb.

Total time: maybe a minute, probably less. Result: one new pony for the stable and one pony for the guards to use for a couple of days before he was disposed of.

Less than a block away, Jennifer Erickson finished with the dishes and sat down to read the newspaper, unaware that her son and his best friend were handcuffed to a wall in the van heading east on Blue Mound that would eventually take them to Interstate 895 south towards Chicago.

CHAPTER TWENTY-ONE

The flight back to D.C. was quiet, at least from Chet's point of view. He sat by himself towards the front of the coach deep into his laptop after taking a call on his cell. Doug Rawson had taken over a table in the back and worked his phone and scratched notes on a yellow legal pad.

On the flight to New Mexico, Summer had called Thatcher Davis to inform him of the possibility of a leak within her unit or just simply the guy wearing the baseball cap and sunglasses tying up loose ends, and to get a legal opinion and guidance, but demanding that he not share this information with anyone else. He had tried to question her first about Pete and the possibility that he played both sides of the street.

"What better way for him to maintain control on one hand and to keep tabs on you and your team, while taking care of his dark side on the other?"

Summer had dismissed that out of hand.

"Doug started on him before he and Chet left for D.C. and has just about ruled him out. No way it's Pete."

"Who's doing the background work?"

"Doug has a team of four; two on computers and two doing the files and phone work."

Thatcher had questions about Chet, the computer geek. Sort of a loaner, quiet and more into gadgets than people. The youngest member of the team, and therefore, not much in common with the other team members.

"Easy for him to cover his tracks and cover any trail that was left out in the open."

"I don't see it. Not him," Summer said shaking her head.

"Then you're telling me you have no leak, because you've covered everyone except for Logan, which I would personally rule out because he's a suit."

"Except for the fact that all information runs through him. He has access to everything and everyone."

This was Doug's theory actually. Summer tried it on for size, but it didn't fit.

When Summer told Davis that Pete was still in Wisconsin, but didn't know where, he asked, "Isn't that a bit irregular? Why the secrecy?"

Summer told him about George, the murder of his family in Arizona, and that fact that Pete had George flown to Wisconsin to help ID the perps and canvass the crime scene.

"Let me get this straight. You have a leak. One of the team members you suspect . . ."

"*Did* suspect. We don't anymore . . ."

"You *have* a leak, and one of the team members you *had* suspected flies in a fourteen year old kid to do forensic work, who is now in the hands of the same team member who you *had* suspected of being a leak, and *no one* knows where this kid or team member is. Do I have it about right?" There was a brief pause and then Davis said, "*Jesus*, Summer! What the hell are you thinking?"

Summer rubbed her forehead, nineteen different kinds of a headache grinding away behind her eyes.

"Or it's the guy wearing the baseball cap and sunglasses tying up loose ends. We can't rule it out, and it's looking more like that's the case."

"Oh come on, Summer!" Thatch yelled.

"You make it sound a lot worse than it is. As I said, we did suspect Pete, but we ruled him out."

"In what, an hour or two of digging? I'm thinking you have the world's best on this, or you've just not done a thorough job. It's sloppy and either you're slipping, or Barney Fife is rubbing off on you."

Summer caught Skip Dahlke's eye and the frown on his face.

"I've got to run. I'll be in touch."

"Keep me in the loop from now on if for no other reason than for you to have an outside, objective view." He softened and then said, "Sorry I was rough on you, but Summer, I'm worried. There's something really weird about this, and you have to take another, deeper look at Pete. Promise me you'll do that? Please?"

Summer sighed.

"I'll be in touch."

*   *   *

Pete got to the Holiday Inn Express on Blue Mound, about fifteen minutes from the Evan's house. He sat down on the uncomfortable chair at the cheap desk, pulled out his little notebook that he kept in his sport coat pocket, turned on the desk lamp and began writing. He had stopped at an Office Max a block from the hotel and purchased a pad of paper and two cheap Bic pens; one blue and one red. He began developing a timeline of what had occurred since he and Summer had flown out to Arizona, making a list of approximate times, dates, and the people who had access to the information. The times and dates he wrote in red, names and information in blue. The only thing he didn't have was a cork board to pin things on.

When he thought he had written down everything, he read it over and then read it over again. If there was a leak, he couldn't identify who it was or when it had occurred. Something didn't make sense. If it wasn't a team member, then it had to be someone close to the team, perhaps someone who was privy to the information or on the periphery of the investigation, or the guy in the baseball cap and sunglasses tying up loose ends. Which was it? He pulled out his cell and punched in Summer's number.

"You and Skip find anything yet?"

"Still looking. We landed almost three hours ago. It's a mess, and it looks like a massacre. It looks like the grandfather, women and children were marched out of the house. The women and children were huddled together, but the grandfather stood away from the group. Skip can't tell who was killed first. He thinks it was more bang-bang, not a lot of thought into it. I agree. The fires were an afterthought. Wood structures, dry country. They went fast. Large weapons, military-issue. They were meant to get the job done.

"George's brother could have been his twin, but a bit smaller, thinner. From a distance, they looked the same. We think the shots came from the helicopter. Same weapon.

Almost cut him in half. Really ugly, Pete. Meant to send a message."

"What are you going to do now?"

"Leonard and a deputy will wrap this up with one man from Albuquerque. Doug's already had him checked out, and he was told to keep this off the books for the time being. Skip is heading back to Wisconsin, and I'm taking a flight to D.C., should get there tomorrow morning." She paused and then said, "I thought you were going to call me when you had George placed. Where are you, and what have you been doing?"

Pete took the phone away from his ear, looked at it curiously, then replaced it and spoke slowly, annoyed and wondering why the quick change in her voice.

"I'm calling now. I needed to be certain George was safe. I think he is."

He told her about Jeremy, the twins, and Jeremy's friend, the detective.

"I think he's in good hands. I like the detective . . . he and Jeremy have been friends for years, so I think George is safe. But Summer, this information goes nowhere, only you and me, no one else on the team or outside the team until we figure this thing out."

"That's just it, Pete. Doug doesn't know where the leak is. He started digging before we boarded the plane in Green Bay and has been at it ever since; a team of four, good, young, aggressive. They've come up with no one. Nada. The only one left is Logan, but come on . . . you and I both know he's clean for chrissake . . ."

"He might have just scratched the surface, Summer. A couple of hours won't tell him much at all."

He told her about his timeline and his list of people who had access to the information, asking her to develop a similar timeline and a similar list.

"I've come to the same conclusion as Doug, but if that's the case, then it's out of Albuquerque, or . . ."

"Doug's already started to look at Albuquerque, but I'm not holding out a lot of hope. Something is right in front of us, and we're missing it. What is it?"

"If it's not a leak, it's the guy in the baseball cap and sunglasses. But someone might have something buried pretty deep that a couple of hours won't find. How soon can we clear Chet?"

"Doug's already ruled him out."

"Then bring him in the loop and have him do some magic with his computer. I'll catch a flight out of Milwaukee early and be in D.C. by ten. Meet me at the office and the three of us will put our heads together."

CHAPTER TWENTY-TWO

Mike woke first but didn't open his eyes right away. He tried to remember exactly what had happened, but only bits and pieces came back to him. His head hurt, and when he tried to move his arms, he found that he couldn't. He tugged, but that only hurt his wrists. He tried to shift his legs, but couldn't move them either.

Next to him, Stephen groaned. Mike opened his eyes and saw that Stephen was as naked as he was, and three men watched them. Stephen groaned again and woke up, and as Mike did, tried to move his arms and legs but couldn't.

"Where are we?" Mike asked.

None of the men answered.

"Who are you?" Mike asked. "Where are you taking us?"

Tears dribbled down Stephen's face as he said, "Please take us home."

A man with longish red hair looked at them and said, "You won't be going home. Not now, not ever."

*   *   *

The boys should have been there by now, and Michael should have called, Jennifer thought as she started out the back door, hoping they'd be sitting in the driveway or kicking a soccer ball back and forth. They weren't. She walked to the end of her driveway and down the sidewalk towards the mini-mart the boys had headed. No sign of them on either side of the street. She walked back into the house and grabbed her car keys.

"Honey, have the boys come back yet?" She asked, knowing they hadn't, or she would have known.

"No, they're probably horsing around. You know how those two get." Mark called up from the basement.

"I'll try calling again."

This was the second time she had called, and each time it rang and rang before going to voicemail. *Why won't he answer,* she thought.

"Mark, he's not answering his phone. I'm going to go look for them," she yelled, and not waiting for an answer, let the screen door slam behind her.

She backed out the silver mini-van or 'Soccer Mom Van' as the boys called it and drove slowly towards the mini-mart. While doing so, she tried calling Mike's phone again, but this time, a young girl's voice answered.

"Who's this?' Jennifer asked.

"Amber."

"Amber, where did you get this phone?"

"I found it on the sidewalk."

Reaching the end of the block, Jennifer saw a little blond girl, maybe eight or nine, talking on the phone facing a house on the corner. Jennifer stopped the van in the middle of the street and jogged over to the girl.

"Amber?"

"Yes, who are you?"

Frantic and not in the mood for twenty questions, Jennifer asked, "Where did you find that phone?"

"In the grass, there," she said, pointing to a spot near a hydrant.

Near the hydrant was a black Addidas sandal, the kind the boys wore. Without another word, Jennifer grabbed the phone and the sandal and ran to her car, pulling away with a screech of tires.

*   *   *

By the time Jennifer found the phone, each boy had been forced to take two pills each, one blue and one white, washing them down with beer. At first, Stephen spit them out but was slapped by the man with red hair. He picked the two pills off the floor and rammed them down Stephen's throat. Michael didn't know what the pills were but didn't want to get slapped around, so he swallowed them.

By the time the van reached the exit for Milwaukee International Airport, Jennifer had called 9-1-1 and was told that the police were on the way.

By the time the van reached the Illinois border, Mike had screamed himself hoarse as he was violated. Stephen didn't know if Michael had passed out or was dead. He made no sound. Stephen had watched helplessly, glad they weren't doing that to him, but guilty for feeling that way. That thought didn't last very long.

By the time they came to a stop outside a dirty red-bricked building, each boy had been forced to do things that no child should ever have been forced to do. And each boy wept silent tears as their dignity and innocence was stolen away and destroyed.

*   *   *

"Would there be any reason for the boys to run away?" the officer asked.

Frantic, Jennifer all but screamed at him. She shook the Addidas sandal and the phone in his face as she said, "No. They didn't run away. They were taken by someone."

Mark paced the living room like a wild animal, one hand on the top of his head, the other swinging wildly.

He stopped, turned on the officer and said, "If you don't call this in right now, I demand to speak to your supervisor! Now!"

Officer Bryce Fogelsang called dispatch and reported that two boys were missing under suspicious circumstances. He gave their names, ages, physical descriptions, and described the clothes they had been wearing. Mark and Jennifer gave him recent pictures of the two boys, taken from a bulletin board in Mike's room.

Ted and Sarah Bailey ran into the house, both yelling questions at the same time, Sarah crying and Ted angry, demanding to know how this had happened, even though Mark had tried as best as he could to explain to him with his phone call. Ted got into Jennifer's face, spit flying as he yelled, and when Mark stepped between them, Ted shoved him backwards into Jennifer. Deputy Fogelsang stepped between the two before the fists flew, threatening both men with an arrest if they didn't sit down and "shut the hell up!"

CHAPTER TWENTY-THREE

George, Randy, Billy and Jeremy were eating popcorn and watching *The Jackal* when the phone rang. Jeremy checked the caller ID and saw that it was Detective Jamie Graf, his friend, and the only other person to know about George.

"What's up?" Jeremy asked after swallowing a fistful of popcorn.

"Did you see it?" Jamie asked.

Jeremy sat up a bit straighter and asked, "See what?"

"Turn to any network station. Quickly. Now."

Jeremy left the room with the phone to his ear, entered the kitchen where there was a small TV mounted under the cupboard and turned it on.

"We repeat. An Amber Alert has just been issued for Waukesha and the surrounding counties and municipalities. Two boys aged twelve are missing under suspicious circumstances and are believed to be in danger. They are Stephen Bailey and Michael Erickson, missing since approximately 7:15 PM Central Standard Time from the 1700 block of Summit Avenue. Stephen Bailey is approximately 5'5" and weighs approximately 120 pounds. He has blond hair and blue eyes. He was wearing a light

blue Nike t-shirt, navy nylon sweat pants and black Addidas
sandals.

Michael Erickson is approximately 5'3" and weighs
approximately 115 pounds. He has light brown hair and
brown eyes. He was wearing a red t-shirt and khaki shorts
and Adidas athletic shoes. If you have seen these two boys or
have any information as to their whereabouts, you are asked
to contact the Waukesha Police Department at 262-524-3831
immediately."

He turned off the TV.

"I'm calling Pete Kelliher," Jeremy said urgently, but quietly so as not to arouse the suspicion of the boys in the family room.

"I'm coming right over. Make sure your doors and windows are locked. No one leaves the house, right?" Jamie cautioned.

"Got it." Then he added, "Jamie?"

"Yeah?"

"Please hurry."

"On my way. Ten minutes."

Jeremy ran his other hand over his face.

"Dad, everything okay?" Randy asked quietly.

The other two boys appeared in the doorway behind him.

"Jamie Graff is coming over. There's an Amber Alert for two twelve year old boys from Waukesha."

"The boy in Arizona and the boy north of here were about the same age," George said.

"Yes, that's why Officer Graff is coming over. I'm going to call Agent Kelliher and let him know."

Neither Randy nor Billy asked, but Jeremy read their eyes.

"We're okay." He turned to George and said, "George, no one knows you're here. Officer Graff will be here in ten minutes. To be safe, Billy, lock all the doors. Randy, make sure the windows are shut and locked. Then, let's stay in the family room together. Okay?"

*   *   *

Pete wasn't tired any longer, funny how adrenaline wakes you up. He weaved the rental in and out of traffic, slamming through red lights and intersections causing the blast of horns and the screech of tires, unheard curses and a minor fender bender; only one, not bad for doing 80 on city streets. Amazingly, he encountered no police cars though he's sure they were alerted to a crazy driver in a newer model blue Taurus.

As he drove, he gave Summer the update.

"How soon can you get back to Milwaukee?"

"I'll alert the team. Chet and I will lift off as soon as we can. Figure about two hours after we lift off."

"Are you going to alert the Milwaukee SAC?" Pete asked.

"No, not yet. We don't know *who* they are or *where* they are or *if* they're part of the ring we're working."

The silence on Pete's end said a lot.

"Pete, I'd rather keep this within the team for the present."

"You do realize that we might be bringing the leak to Wisconsin and ultimately to George, right?"

"Doug has been on this twenty-four seven. He's looked at bank accounts, text messages, phone records, fax transmittals . . . everything, you name it. It just isn't one of us. I don't know how that's possible, but it isn't one of us."

Pete slammed on the brakes, then punched it around a slow-moving Honda and almost took out a guy stepping out of his parked car, then took a left and quick right into relatively light traffic. *God Bless Suburban Neighborhoods!*

"Then it's the guy in the baseball cap. It simplifies things on one hand, but makes it all the harder on the other. We have no leads to speak of . . . none."

"Pete, you've notified the police on that end, right?"

"Well, not exactly the police . . . a detective."

"Good enough for me."

"Me too . . . for now."

Pete swerved to the curb in the cul de sac, took a quick look around, eyes missing nothing.

"Gotta go. I'm at the house. Looks quiet. Call when you're in the air."

CHAPTER TWENTY-FOUR

Jeremy Evans' home sat at the back of a cul de sac. The neighbor at the back of his home had a fenced in backyard because of their hyper Jack Russell Terrier named Gus, who yipped and yapped constantly. Jeremy and the twins had become oblivious to the barking.

The gray-blue two-story on the left was occupied by Mary Schuster and her son, Jerry. She never saw her former husband, and Jerry had long ago given up hope of one day receiving a visit from him. A monthly alimony and child support check, postmarked from three different cities in three sequential years was the only offering of fatherly love for his son.

Jerry was the same age as the twins, but attended St. William's Catholic School, the large private elementary and middle school three blocks down Summit Hill on Moreland Boulevard. Jeremy was one of the adult men who lent his presence to Jerry. It wasn't the same as having a real "dad", but it was better than having none at all.

On the other side of the Evans' home was a low one story ranch of dark wood owned by Jon and Bert Lane. Both retired, Jon was a former school psychologist, and Bert, short for Roberta, a former elementary teacher. Their only son,

Mike, had played shooting guard for Jeremy when he had
taught social studies and coached before becoming a
counselor. He had graduated the year Jeremy decided he had
done enough coaching, and had attended a smaller college in
a Chicago suburb playing some basketball. Currently, Mike
was in Chicago doing very well in the financial arena in spite
of tough economic times.

A head-high hedge of Arborvitae ran in an L shape
bordering the Schuster yard and the yippy terrier's yard set
up against their fence. Rose bushes and a garden of annuals
and perennials made up a border to the Lane's yard, set up
against a decorative fence that was more for show than for
function.

The three households shared an unspoken bond that
extended beyond the typical, neighborly "How are you?" or
"I think it's going to rain today" that more distant neighbors
tended to have towards each other. It wasn't uncommon to
have the three families share a grill in the back of one of the
yards at least one night a week or so during the summer.

Jon and Bert would not be classified as nosey
neighbors, but when Jamie Graff's unmarked squad car
appeared at the curb in front of Jeremy's house, they became
curious. There was very little traffic on this end of their

street, so when another vehicle they didn't recognize pulled up behind the patrol car, Jon and Bert became puzzled.

Jon watched the older guy with a buzz cut get out and stand at the edge of Jeremy's driveway looking in all directions with his right hand inside the breast of a sport coat. They knew something was up. The look had cop all over him, so Jon reached for the phone.

"Jeremy, it's Jon. Everything okay over there?"

Jeremy hesitated, wanting to say, *Hell no!* but instead said, "Yes. Jamie came over for a visit and brought a friend. That's all. Everything's fine."

"Okay, just wanted to be sure. You need anything, holler."

*   *   *

Garrett Forstadt saw the Amber Alert with the boys' pictures and recognized them immediately. The twelve year old had played soccer against them just three days before, getting trounced seven to zip. They went to Horning Middle School, while he went to Butler, the cross-town rival. He'd end up at North High School, while the two of them would attend South. They played basketball and baseball against each other too.

When he saw their pictures and heard the alert, it felt as though his veins suddenly filled with ice water, and a lead weight dropped heavily into his stomach. The small hairs on the back of his neck stood up straight, and he got goosebumps in spite of the warm summer night. He actually had to fight the feeling of having to throw up.

"Honey, do you know those boys?" Kim asked her son.

Garrett nodded.

"Garrett, what's wrong?"

Kim saw her son go visibly white before her eyes, with little beads of sweat appearing on his forehead and upper lip. Garrett didn't answer, couldn't answer. They were his age. They were in the same grade. He knew them. He also had a secret he had never shared with anyone. That wasn't true actually. Phil knew. Phil knew because he had a secret too.

The same secret.

"Honey, look at me," Kim said squatting down in front of her son. "What's wrong?"

"Nothing, Mom."

Garrett tried to stand up, but Kim put a hand on his shoulder. They stared into each other's eyes, but Garrett had to look away first because he was about to cry, and he didn't

want his mom to see that. If she did, he was afraid she might
see more than tears.

*   *   *

Pete, Jamie and Jeremy sat around the kitchen table
sipping ice tea and discussing the missing boys. Jamie had
called the reporting officer and had the copy of the report
read to him over the phone. He took small, scratchy notes
that were impossible for anyone to read but him. He was
reminded of that by anyone with whom he had worked and
who had tried to read anything he had written.

There wasn't much to go on. No witnesses. A time
interval that could have been minutes to an hour or more.
One Addidas sandal and a cell phone, both found on the grass
bordering the sidewalk, almost at the corner. It was decided
that *if* they were taken, they had been ambushed: grabbed,
lifted and tossed into a waiting car or van. Probably a van
since it was easier to get them into and out of quickly. Still,
nothing to go on. A dead end like many missing kids' cases.

The boys sat in the family room in front of a TV
supposedly watching one of the Jason Bourne movies on
HBO. Randy would glance up from the latest Jeffrey
Limbach thriller he was reading, while George sat on one of

the couches and dosed, only opening his eyes when there were explosions or tire squeals. He hadn't had much sleep since being whisked away in the helicopter and found that when he did close his eyes, his mom, his brothers and sister, and his grandfather would stand silently in front of him. Those images kept his eyes pretty much open.

Billy, who sprawled on the other end of the couch, would sneak a peek at George every now and then, wondering exactly what his story was. The twins weren't told much, other than George had seen a murder, visited a crime scene and that his family had died. It was just enough information to cause all sorts of ideas, theories and questions in an inquisitive kid's head. Mostly questions.

The phone rang, and since Billy was the nearest to it, he answered.

"Hello, the Evans and Schroeder residence."

There was a bit of silence, so Billy said again, "Hello?"

Randy looked up from his book, and George opened his eyes a little wider.

"Um . . . is Randy there?"

"Yeah, just a minute."

Billy shrugged at Randy as he handed the phone to him.

"This is Randy."

It was silent on the other end, so Randy just waited it out, already guessing what kind of phone call it was. He waved to get Billy's attention and then pointed at the kitchen.

Billy got up, leaned into the doorway and said, "I think Randy's got a phone call."

"It's okay to talk. I'm listening," Randy said patiently.

Jeremy had heard many phone conversations begin this way. He set a pad of paper and a pen in front of Randy and then pulled up a chair next to him. Jamie and Pete stood close by and watched. Very quietly, Jamie explained to Pete that these types of calls happened before: a kid seeking help or advice from Randy first, then Jeremy. The Amber Alert was a trigger. Pete merely shook his head in awe, wondering how a fourteen year old could do this.

He had heard about Randy through the pipeline. Summer had actually heard a presentation at a conference given by Randy and Jeremy a little over a year ago in the Twin Cities. They were invited by Patty Wetterling, whose son, Jacob, was abducted at gunpoint in front of his brother and best friend in St. Joseph, Minnesota in October, 1989. Despite hundreds of leads, Jacob was still missing. She and her husband Jerry, along with friends and the community, formed the Jacob Wetterling Foundation to bring awareness to the plight of missing and sexually exploited children. Jeremy was an unofficial member of the foundation, and on behalf of the foundation, gave presentations to parent groups, teachers, and community organizations, above and beyond his work as a school counselor. It was through these presentations, newspaper articles, and TV and radio interviews that he and Randy became known for what they do.

Randy heard a sniffle and knew where the conversation was headed. He nodded at Jeremy.

"You don't know me, but I go to Butler."

"That's where Billy and I go."

"You talked to my class at an assembly last September."

"I remember. What's your name?"

"Garrett. Garrett Forstadt."

Randy wrote the name on the pad along with *sixth grade at Butler,* followed by a question mark, signaling to Jeremy that he didn't know the boy. Jeremy held the pad up to Billy, who shook his head, letting him know that he didn't know who the boy was either.

"How can I help you, Garrett?"

Again, there was a sniffle and then an audible sigh.

"The two boys who are missing . . . I know them."

"How did you know them?"

Randy scribbled on the pad, *knows the two missing boys*. Jeremy showed the pad to Pete and Jeremy.

"I played soccer against them."

"Yes?"

"I think I know who took them."

*   *   *

Rachel Mader didn't like closing up her restaurant, but she was the owner, and the chief cook, and bottle washer. She did have pretty good help though. Still, closing up was closing up. On this day, closing up gave her the willies because of the mess on Jack Pine Road. That sort of thing didn't happen up here, and though the sheriff department didn't give anyone any information, everyone seemed to know anyway, or claimed they did because rumors were rampant, and a triple murder was ample fodder for stories and theories. Three dead bodies; one a kid. FBI flying around in helicopters. Deputies racing up and down Highway Eight and 141 like it was Daytona or something. She shivered more than once thinking about it.

Closing up Mary's Place, named after Mary Stinnett, who owned it before Harry Koel and before Chuck Rivers, and now Rachel, cut the costs. That was one reason, but the main reason was because she was able to keep an eye on the place. The teenagers she hired were a pretty seasonal bunch, home from college from late spring to late summer. A couple of the better high school kids helped during the summer and on weekends during the school year. When summer ended, she'd end up with the one or two high school kids and the rest would be made up with local help, which meant not much help at all. Who stuck around Northern Wisconsin if they had the brains and the opportunity to get the hell out? Well, she stuck around, and that was okay with her.

Rachel wiped off the last table, replaced the last dish on the shelf, checked the refrigerator and freezer thermostats and the back door to make sure it was locked, and then turned off the lights and locked the front door behind her. The parking lot was quiet and empty except for Brian Travers' beat up pickup, a dark van she didn't recognize and her two-year-old Explorer. Travers was probably tying one on at one of the bars. She could never figure out why the hell he didn't park his truck in the parking lot of the bar down the block. Maybe it was the walk up the highway to help clear his head when he decided he'd head home, or more likely, when Herman Strupp decided Brian had had enough.

The van bothered her. She hadn't recognized it, but had noticed it in the parking lot at one point during the afternoon, but not who the driver was. They did have a seasonal element that drifted up from Chicago, Milwaukee, and the Fox Valley, so maybe it belonged to one of the members of the summer migration. Still, with the triple murder and all, it gave her the willies. A part of her wanted to jump into her four by four and drive away, yet, there was a feeling and a hunch, and she was big on feelings and hunches. Ask anyone.

She slowly walked over and peeked into the driver's door and saw the keys in the ignition. She tried the handle and found it locked. She tried the passenger door, and it too was locked. Rachel walked around the van, memorized the plate- Wisconsin- and tried the other doors. They too were locked. She peeked into the passenger window as far back as she could and saw tennis shoes, a pair of jeans and a t-shirt. She backed away, stumbled, caught herself, then turned and ran to her Explorer, pulling out her cell as she climbed in.

*   *   *

Sheriff Pat Blizel hammered his patrol car down Highway 8 to Mary's Place, a trip that would normally take twenty minutes, but on this night took less than ten. He only hoped there were no deer or black bear crossing the road. He'd hate to think what would happen if Bambi or Smokey collided with his cruiser pushing ninety. He figured with the sirens and lights, he'd be pretty safe, and that any wildlife in the area would high tail it deeper into the woods that ran along both sides of the highway.

He took the intersection of Highways 8 and 141 at sixty and slammed hard into the diner's parking lot sending gravel and dirt flying everywhere. Mary started to get out of her Explorer, but Blizel motioned her to get back into it. She did and for good measure, locked it.

He pulled out his .45 and approached the van cautiously from the driver side, back to front, looking into the side mirrors and windows as he did: nothing and no one. A patrol car came screaming up 141 as he went back to his cruiser and called in the plate. Deputy Earl Coffey pulled to a stop on the other side of the van, opened up his door and crouched behind it with his .45 out, aiming at the passenger side door.

"It's locked and empty as far as I can tell," Blizel yelled. "What's the ETA on the tow truck?"

"Twenty to thirty minutes," Coffey yelled back.

"No time. Do you have a Slim Jim?"

Earl holstered, popped the trunk and pulled out a thin metal strip. He gave the van a wide berth as he came up to Pat's car.

"Want me to pop it open, or do you want to?"

Blizel spit into the dirt, wiped his mouth off with the back of his hand and said, "Cover me."

As Earl pulled out his piece and crouched behind Blizel's open door, aiming at the van, Pat holstered his .45 and pulled out surgical gloves. He moved to the driver's door and using the Slim Jim, popped open the door, causing the van alarm to go off. Pat pressed the panic button on the key fob on the key ring in the ignition and all was quiet again.

He pressed the unlock button and opened the side door on the driver's side. Nothing and no one, except for what looked like a boy's clothes. A pair of beat up athletic shoes, Levi's, a plain yellow t-shirt and soiled boxers. And trace amounts of what looked like blood. And handcuffs. One end open with the other attached to the interior wall of the van.

"Earl, call dispatch and tell them to get a hold of Wausau again. Tell them we might have a secondary crime scene."

Without a word, Earl called it in. Just as he finished, the report on the van's plates came back.

"Oh-one-eighty, this is dispatch. You copy?"

Pat walked over to his car and said, "Oh-one-eighty, over."

"The plates came back as stolen out of Milwaukee. Owner reported it two days ago. Over."

Pat glanced over at Earl and then said, "Contact Pete Kelliher right away and tell him what we have."

*   *   *

Garrett didn't know where to begin. He had started and stammered several times not sure what to say or how to say it, thinking he was being stupid, yet deep down knowing he wasn't.

"Garrett, why do you think you know who took the boys?"

There was a long silence before he spoke, again trying to find the words. This was his secret. A secret he had tried to forget, to deny it had ever happened. If he told someone, then it wouldn't be a secret any longer and even worse, he would be unable to deny it had happened.

"Because he did stuff to me . . . he does stuff to at least two of my friends."

"Would it be easier if you and I and my dad talked in person?"

"My parents don't know. I don't want them to know."

"Garrett, I know this is hard. It was hard for me too. You don't have to tell them by yourself. We can tell them together; you, me and my dad."

Silence, considering.

"I don't know . . . ok, I guess," he answered with a sniff and a sigh. "Ok."

His secret would now come out.

CHAPTER TWENTY-FIVE

When Randy and Jeremy first came to the door and introduced themselves, Keith and Kim Forstadt were puzzled. But the puzzlement grew to concern pretty quickly. Randy met with Garrett in his bedroom, while Jeremy met with his parents around the kitchen table. Garrett's older brother, Graham, was at a friend's house, as was his younger sister, Gwen. That made it easier to get his story without any distraction.

Jeremy faced dismay, denial, and anger, and it was nothing new to him. He had faced this eight times in the last two years, ever since Randy had come into his life, and ever since law enforcement agencies and various children's welfare agencies had heard about the two of them and their abilities to help with abused children and their families. He accepted the Forstadt's anger, their questions and their denial. Having been a counselor all these years had helped.

"What you have to understand is that what happened wasn't your son's fault. You have to understand that this man has practiced preying on kids. He grooms them . . ."

"He *what*?" Keith said, leaning forward, straining to understand. "He *grooms* them? What the hell does that mean?" his voice rising more than a little.

Kim placed her hand on his forearm, but he pulled his arm away.

"Has this man spent an inordinate amount of time with Garrett? Has he given him any gifts? Has he made some sort of promise to your son, given him extra attention or complements that might not ring true? Has he taken your son and others on a trip or had them sleep over?"

Jeremy watched realization wash over their faces, watched them look at each other as it sunk in, first with Kim and then with Keith.

"That's grooming," Jeremy said quietly. "These men are predators in every sense of the word. They prey on children and their innocence. They're not motivated by love or caring because they only want to control and dominate. Kids like Garrett don't have a chance."

"But how could Garrett let this man . . ." Keith asked.

"At first, Garrett probably saw this man as a mentor . . . a role model. He's flattered by the extra attention. He sees this guy as a friend. There is a *trust* that develops. Then, Garrett is led to believe that what he's about to do or has done is normal. He's shown pornography, pictures, or videos showing these acts as *normal*. Garrett is a kid. This is his role model, his coach, an adult. If *he* says it's ok, it *must* be ok.

"And then it happens, and he's afraid and ashamed. If he resists, or if the pedophile thinks Garrett might tell someone, Garrett is told he might get in trouble . . . that people won't believe him because he's a kid, and who would ever suspect a coach . . . someone who's successful, who's coached for five, ten, fifteen years? Who would believe him?"

"Jesus *Christ* . . ." Keith said quietly. "I never suspected," he said shaking his head.

"He's a nice guy . . ." Kim started to say, but let it drift.

"What?" Jeremy asked.

They exchanged a look between them, an unspoken message that married couples often give each other, and then Keith said, "He's a nice guy. He cares about kids . . ."

He and his wife exchanged another look.

"We just thought he's kind of . . . different . . . odd." Keith said.

"Some of the other parents felt the same way," Kim added. "But he was always good to the kids."

"Pedophiles are more comfortable with kids. They tend to not have many, if any, adult friendships or relationships. They tend to be single men between the ages of twenty and fifty, though there are cases where some have been younger or older and some who have been married. These predators gravitate to jobs that present them with opportunities to develop relationships with kids. They volunteer for opportunities that give them opportunities to be around kids."

Jeremy let that sink in and then said, "You saw the Amber Alert. The two boys are the same age as Garrett. We know it's a long-shot, but Garrett believes this man might have taken them."

"But really, what are the chances that Jim Rodemaker took those two boys?" Keith asked doubtfully.

"As I said, it's a long-shot. First, Garrett has to tell us his story, and that isn't going to be easy for him or for you. Garrett loves you, and like all kids, he wants you to be proud of him, to know that even though he made a mistake, you love him."

"My God! Of course we love him," Kim said, brushing away a tear.

"I know that, and you know that, and deep down, Garrett knows that," Jeremy answered. Then in a quiet voice, he said, "But he's scared and ashamed. His story will be hard for him to tell, and it will be horrifically hard for you to hear."

He looked at Kim and then at Keith and let that sink in. They looked at each other. Kim wiped away another tear, took a deep breath and nodded.

*   *   *

Pete drank black coffee, while Jamie nursed a coke. Billy had a strawberry shake and George a chocolate one. There were only two other customers in Hardee's, teenagers who might have been on a first date. They shared fries, and in general, were pretty sappy. Jamie wanted to gag.

Pete's phone chirped, and he answered by simply saying, "Yeah."

It was Summer.

"We've just landed. Chet's done some digging on this guy; no records, single, never married, pays his taxes on time, nothing out of line, and has two older sisters and a younger brother. The sisters are married. One lives near Madison in Monona Grove, and the other lives near Green Bay in Suamico. The brother lives in Brown Deer, which is just north of Milwaukee. His father is deceased; died three years ago. His mother is in a nursing home in Milwaukee. Rodemaker manages a pizza place. He's just sort of ordinary."

"Yeah . . . ordinary."

He glanced at the two boys. Billy pretended to drink his shake, while George lowered his eyes and then turned his head and stared out the window.

"Jamie has him under surveillance."

"Where are you?"

"We're waiting to talk to the boy. We're expecting a call any minute. Once we get some details, we'll move on the guy. We have a judge waiting to sign the warrant."

"We should be there in forty-five minutes or less."

"I'll keep you posted."

*   *   *

Jeremy had heard Patty Wetterling speak about missing and sexually exploited children a half-dozen times, and while there were many things she had said that stuck with him, there was one statement that had resonated with him more than any other: *All it takes is one brave kid to put a pedophile away.* Sitting in the Forstadt family room listening to Garrett tell his story, Jeremy couldn't help but apply that statement to the boy. He struggled in front of his mother and especially in front of his father. His posture expressed shame, regret, and profound sadness. Yet, the more he talked, the more relieved he became. It was apparent to Jeremy what a heavy burden this secret had been.

Garrett was nervous, but Randy's pep talk in the bedroom had helped. Randy sat on one side of him while his mother sat on the other side. His father stood off to the side near the fireplace. Pete stood next to him, while Jamie stood behind Jeremy, who sat in a chair facing the couch. Billy and George were outside, sitting on the front porch.

It took forty minutes for Garrett to tell his story. He spoke in a voice just above a whisper, and he buried his chin into his chest. When he did look up, he'd glance furtively at his father and not at his mother at all.

Jeremy would ask a question or two for clarification or to get him started. When Garrett would seem stuck, he would prompt him with an open-ended sentence. Other than that, Garrett described what took place, where it took place, and how it took place.

It was painful for him to talk about and painful to listen to. Jeremy watched Randy as much as he did Garrett, because each time a story like this was told, Randy relived the night he was abused, molested and raped. Jeremy knew that he'd have to pick up the pieces once they got home and for a couple of days after. But this was different somehow.

There was something going on in Randy's mind as he listened to Garrett.

"Garrett, there's probably a lot you want to tell us. There's probably a lot you need to tell us just to get this off your chest. I know it isn't easy," Jeremy said looking intently at the boy. "I want you to know how incredibly brave you are. I know this isn't easy, not for you or for your parents."

Garrett nodded and took a deep breath. A tear ran down his face. Kim saw that and took his hand in both of hers.

"It's okay, Garrett. It wasn't your fault, no matter what you think," she said.

Garrett lowered his head and wiped tears from his face. Randy reached over and grabbed a couple of Kleenex's from a box on the end table and handed them to him.

"He said that he wanted me to be the captain of the team, but that he needed to trust me, and that I needed to trust him. I told him he could. He said that he needed to get to know me better, and that he had to be absolutely certain that he could trust me running the team on the field." Garrett shrugged and said, "I told him he could."

Garrett wiped his eyes with the Kleenex, and then blew his nose. Without asking, Randy took them from him and handed him fresh ones.

"He put his arm around me, and he kissed my head. He held me and then . . . then . . ."

And that was how it went. For forty minutes, Garrett told them about the night with his coach. Kim put her arm around the boy, but Garrett seemed to sink further into the couch.

"I didn't like it, but I was afraid to tell him not to. I wanted to be captain, and if I told him to stop, he wouldn't trust me, and I wouldn't be captain."

His chin lay on his chest and he was quiet for a bit before Randy said, "Go ahead, Garrett."

"He said that he knew what might help, and he went over to the TV and turned on a video."

He looked squarely at Jeremy, then at Jamie and said, "It was sick."

"What was the video?" Jamie asked.

"I don't know the name, but it was Coach and Phil doing stuff to each other."

"Phil Kuehl?" Keith asked incredulously.

Garrett nodded.

"Phil is a teammate of Garrett's. He and Garrett were friends, and they used to hang out but not lately," Keith said.

His eyes widened as he realized what he had said, and now he understood why they hadn't been hanging out.

"If we go to Coach Rodemaker's house, will we know where the video is?" Jamie asked.

"He has all kinds of videos on a shelf next to the TV. The ones of . . . you know . . . they're in a cupboard behind the TV."

"There are others besides the one of him and Phil?" Jamie asked.

Garrett nodded and said, "Lots of them."

"Did you recognize any of the boys in the videos?" Jamie asked.

"Some. Danny Pickett. Brett Connolly. There were other boys I didn't recognize."

"These videos, were they filmed in his house?" Pete asked.

"Some . . . the ones with Danny, Brett and Phil. But the ones with the boys I didn't know were filmed someplace else. I don't know where."

"Garrett, think for a minute. You saw the videos. Do you think the boys knew they were being video-taped?" Jamie asked.

He screwed up his face in thought and then shook his head.

"I don't think so."

"Why?" Pete asked.

"They were doin' stuff that was gross. It was embarrassing, and if they knew they were making a video, they wouldn't have done that stuff."

"Were there any pictures of kids?" Pete asked.

Garrett hung his head and then nodded. Jamie and Pete exchanged a look, as did Randy and Jeremy. Keith and Kim knew something had happened, but weren't sure what it was.

Changing the subject, Jamie asked, "About how many of these videos do you think he has?"

Garrett shrugged, puffed out his cheeks and said, "A bunch."

"Garrett," Jeremy said, "I know this is really difficult, but you're going to need to be specific about what he did because the police are going to arrest him. That way, he won't be able to do this to any other boys."

Garrett's face turned blank, empty. *A thousand yard stare* were the words Jeremy used to describe the look to parent groups and to law enforcement agencies. Once you see it, you know it and won't ever forget it.

He told his story, and once he began, he didn't stop. He didn't look at his mother or his father, but studied his hands clenched and tight in his lap. As he spoke, there was a certain determination, perhaps resignation, but also relief.

"Did anything else happen?" Jamie asked.

"We watched a couple of videos, the ones like with Phil and Danny and Bret, but with other boys I didn't recognize."

Garrett looked down at his hands and was quiet for a while.

"Coach said it was okay. We were friends and beginning to trust each other and that I was on my way to being the captain.

"That night, he made me sleep in his bed. I told him I could sleep on the couch, but he looked all sad. I knew that if I didn't, he wouldn't trust me. So I did."

"That's enough. No more," Keith said.

"You're right," Jeremy said. "Garrett, look at me." and then he repeated, "Look at me."

When he was sure Garrett was looking at him and ready to listen, he said, "You're the bravest person in this room. What you did tonight will save many other kids from having to go through what you went through. No child, no young man should ever have to go through what you went through. Ever." He let that sink in and said, "You're incredibly brave, and I'm very, very proud of you."

"I know you don't feel like it right now, but you'll get over this, just like I did," Randy said. "You *will* get over this. You're parents will help . . . and I'll help."

Garrett wiped away more tears and buried his chin on his chest.

"I feel dirty," he said through sobs.

"No!" Randy barked. "Never feel like that. If you do, then that asshole's won, and you can't let him win."

Garrett looked at him.

"You can feel sad and maybe feel ashamed for a little while. You told us your story and because of that, you're going to send that son of a bitch away for a long time. That's something to be proud of."

Jeremy had not heard Randy speak like this in a long time. He stared at Randy who was breathing hard, staring intently at Garrett. Finally, Garrett nodded at Randy, and Randy gave him a hug.

"Garrett, your dad and I love you very much no matter what you think. We always will."

"That's right, Kiddo. You're my son, and I love you," Keith said.

"I'm sorry," Garrett said looking up at him.

"Hey, weren't you listening?" Keith said as he strode across the room to kneel in front of his son. "No matter what, I love you."

Garrett nodded as he let his dad and mom hug him.

"I never did get to be captain."

"I know," Keith said. "It's okay, Kiddo. It's okay."

Pete and Jamie huddled for a private conversation and then broke apart and pulled out their cell phones, and during his conversation on the phone, Jamie motioned to Jeremy to join him.

"We're getting the warrant signed," he said to Jeremy half-covering his phone, and then to both whoever was on the other end and to Jeremy, he said, "We'll meet you there. No, we won't move until we get the warrant. Yeah, Boss."

"Ready to roll?" Jamie said to Pete.

"Yup. They're about ten minutes out and will meet up at the house."

CHAPTER TWENTY-SIX

The ride was silent except for the noise of tires on asphalt. The radio wasn't on and none of the boys spoke. Randy sat in the back staring out the window at nothing in particular. Jeremy spent as much time watching him through the rearview mirror as he did on the road ahead of him. Every now and then, Billy, who sat shotgun, would turn to look at him, but Randy didn't or wouldn't make eye contact. For all Jeremy or Billy knew, Randy didn't even know Billy had turned in his seat to look at him. He was in his own world thinking God knew what, Jeremy couldn't fathom.

George sat next to Randy in silence. Jeremy figured that part of his silence, perhaps a great deal of his silence, was the profound sadness if not shock of losing his entire family. He hadn't even had time to grieve. Jeremy was concerned about George, but Randy was his son. He had never seen Randy react like he had before this evening at the Forstadt house. Something had triggered it, and he wasn't sure what it was. And given Randy's disposition, his stubbornness, it would be a while before Randy would talk about it with him.

But he also knew that Randy was an incessant journal writer, and it wouldn't be long before Randy's journal would appear open on Jeremy's bed or somewhere else he'd be sure to find it. Jeremy would read it and then the two of them would talk.

He was equally certain that Randy and Billy would talk much sooner than he and Randy would. Though they had only been living together for just under three years after being raised separately for the better part of eleven years, there was both a spoken and unspoken bond between the twins that seemed eerie at times and downright spooky at others. One would begin a sentence that the other would finish. There were times when they would look at each other, somehow communicating silently with each other. Other times, when one was sick, the other knew it and took on the same symptoms. They were never far apart from each other. Billy would read while Randy wrote, or Randy would listen to music, while Billy watched TV. One might be in a different room, but they would have to check in on each other if only to verify they were nearby.

Jeremy had phoned ahead to let Jon and Bert know they were coming. He walked the boys into the house, briefly told Jon and Bert what had taken place and asked that they be watchful of both Randy and George. Jon shook Jeremy's hand, then gave him a hug and said he and Bert would take good care of them until he returned. As he left, he turned to look at the three boys sitting silently on the couch; Randy, looking out the window; Billy, studying his hands; George, staring at the floor.

*   *   *

Jeremy sat in the back seat, while Jamie drove with Pete riding shotgun. They didn't say much to each other as they were into their own thoughts. Jeremy was worried about Randy, feeling guilty because he wasn't helping George through his grief, and guilty because he wasn't worried about Billy. *What the hell kind of counselor and father was he?*

Pete's phone went off.

Not recognizing the number, he said, "Kelliher."

"Pat Blizel, Marinette County Sheriff. You were up here earlier today investigating a triple homicide."

Earlier today? Pete thought. *Impossible! That was days ago, wasn't it?*

"What have you got?" was all he said.

"I think we found the van involved in the homicide. Ran the plates. It was stolen from a parking garage in downtown Milwaukee. We've contacted the Wausau Crime Lab and Roz is on the way."

"Let me give Skip Dahlke a call. He was in Arizona running a crime scene for me, and I think he might be in your area. Button it up until he gets there. Nothing gets touched. No one moves a thing."

"Got it. I'll wait to hear from you," he said punching off.

Pete checked his phone log and found James Dahlke's number and dialed it.

"Yeah," James said through a yawn, sounding more than tired.

"Skip, where are you right now?"

"On my way to Pembine. Why?"

"Is that where the triple homicide took place?"

"Yeah. Got a call from Roz. She's meeting me there, but I should be there first."

"Thanks. I owe you. Try to get fingerprints and DNA if possible. Keep me posted, Skip, okay?'

"Yup. Call you later."

*   *   *

There were several neighborhoods on County Road F that led one after the other to the fringe of Waukesha County and eventually to the city of New Berlin. Small, single-story ranches on quarter- to half-acre lots, gave way to two-story homes on half- to three-quarter acre lots. Then there were large homes with expansive lawns and long driveways. These houses sat on five- and six-acre lots. Finally further out on F was horse property with all the trimmings on fifteen-plus-acre lots.

Rodemaker lived in one of the first neighborhoods, a fairly large, but older ranch in the kind of neighborhood where you'd find bicycles on the lawn, kids shooting hoops, and adults jogging or walking the dog. There was an attached two-car garage on the right side of the house, with a dark, Toyota Four-Runner in the driveway. That meant the two year-old Mazda was in the garage. A large hedge-row of Barrel Arborvitae ringed the backyard, but in front of the chain-link fence making the backyard a square and fairly secure and very private. A cement and red brick patio with a grill, hot tub, picnic table and chairs, and a hammock, sat in front of a sliding glass door. According to the officer on surveillance, the hot tub was in use, and the slider was open. A screen door separated the patio from the family room. This would make entry through the back fairly easy.

There was at least one youngster in the house with Rodemaker, and according to the officer, the boy didn't seem to be there against his will. The officer could hear conversation between the two, and though he couldn't make out the words, it seemed friendly. There was laughter and a familiarity between Rodemaker and the boy.

*   *   *

A total of four detectives from the Waukesha Police Department including Jamie, two Sheriff Deputies from the Waukesha County Sheriff Department, a uniformed patrolman from the Waukesha Police Department, the Captain of the Waukesha Police Department Detective Unit, who was Jamie's boss, and members of the FBI Crimes Against Children Unit including Pete, Chet and Summer huddled around the hood of the car. Jamie would be the lead detective. Jeremy stood behind them listening but not contributing to the discussion. The only reason he was there was because there was at least one child in the home, possibly more, but from the surveillance, that was doubtful. He was there to work as a counselor.

Captain Jack O'Brian, the scene supervisor, held the warrant for the search of the Rodemaker home. The search included anything and everything in the home, from videos and DVDs and any equipment for recording and playback, to any paper documents, to cell phones and their records, PDAs and anything else that seemed pertinent. If there was a computer, it too could be taken, and a second warrant gave them permission for a forensic computer search. Detective George Chan, who everyone called Charlie, held the video camera and would record all of it.

It was a Knock Knock Search, which meant that the doorbell would be rung and then entry by ramming the door open. The house would be breached from the front, while two detectives and a sheriff's deputy would secure the backyard in case anyone tried to run. They decided on a Knock Knock Search rather than a Dynamic Entry with SWAT because it was determined that Rodemaker wasn't a known violent offender. He had no record. The child or children didn't appear to be in any danger, and a Dynamic Entry might place the child or children in danger unwittingly. Therefore, they would announce and enter.

Seven would enter from the front and none from the back because they didn't want to create a crossfire situation. Jamie had laughed at and told Jeremy that the stuff everyone watched on TV shows was crap and only for glitz. Detectives Reilly and Gates would find the child or children and protect them. Guns would be drawn and held in first positive safety, which meant that fingers would be on the barrel, not on the trigger, not only because Rodemaker wasn't known to be violent, but also because a child or children were on the premises. FBI would serve as backup and enter with the group from the front. Jeremy would remain in a car and would be summoned only when the house had been completely cleared, and it was safe to do so.

Everyone had a radio with earpiece, and each did a final check to make sure they were on and working. The groups split up, one working its way around the back, while the other waited down the street until everyone was ready.

"Captain . . . we're in position."

"We're moving now. On my go, only. Do you copy?"

"Copy."

CHAPTER TWENTY-SEVEN

A patrol officer rang the doorbell and announced, "Waukesha Police Department, we have a warrant," and another officer blew the door open.

First through the door, Detective Gary Fitzpatrick took off down the hallway after seeing Rodemaker jump up from the couch and run. Fitz threw a shoulder into him, sending him headlong on shag carpet. His head made a dull thud as it hit the wall at the end of the hallway, near a bathroom. Fitz smiled to himself, satisfied, then planted his knee firmly in the small of Rodemaker's bare back as he simultaneously read him his rights and handcuffed him.

Jamie knelt at the couch hovering slightly over a shocked and crying boy, placing a hand on the boy's shoulder to comfort him, but listening as his detectives yelled "Clear" one after another as various rooms were entered with guns drawn. It seemed like a long time, but in truth, it took only fifteen seconds before the main floor was determined safe. The basement was searched next and in the same way. The entire process took only twenty-six seconds from the entry to the final "clear".

Jamie led the boy to a back bedroom where he was given his clothes and told to dress. Jamie radioed for Jeremy who came into the house in a jog. He hesitated in the entry way, stepping lightly, cautiously, into the foyer, and then followed Pete's direction to the back of the house, peering into rooms as he went. By the time he found the room with Jamie and Detective Gates, the boy was dressed except for his bare feet. He sat on the bed and hung his head, still crying.

Jamie said, "Son, what's your name?"

The boy didn't look at him, but said, "Scott . . . Scott Carrigan."

"Scott, I want you to talk with my friend Jeremy and with Detective Gates. They're going to ask you some questions, and I want you to be as honest with them as you can. Then, we're going to take you to Waukesha Memorial Hospital, so you can be checked by a doctor. Okay?"

Scott nodded, but asked, "Am I in trouble?"

"Don't you fuckin' say anything! You hear me? Don't say a fuckin' thing!" Rodemaker yelled from the hallway, just outside the room.

"Shut the fuck up you fuckin' pervert," Fitzpatrick snarled, grinding his knee deeper into Rodemaker's back making Rodemaker groan.

"No Scott, you're not in trouble," Jeremy said. "We're just going to talk for a bit before you go to the hospital. But I want you to believe me when I say you are not in any trouble."

The last part he said, taking hold of the boy's hands.

"You have no right to be in my house. Get the fuck out! I'll fuckin' sue you! I want my lawyer."

"You're gonna need one!" Fitz said into his ear.

While the boy was at the hospital, his parents would be notified in person by Jamie, Pete and Jeremy, which according to Jamie, "will fuckin' suck so bad!"

Jamie nodded at Jeremy as he left the room to direct the search, leaving Jeremy to interview the scared boy with Gates taking notes.

"Fitz, take that scumbag into his bedroom to get some pants on and then into the other room so Jeremy and Gates can have some privacy with the boy."

Fitzpatrick yanked Rodemaker up off the floor and pushed him into the master bedroom and threw a pair of black, nylon sweatpants at him, telling him to get dressed. When he did so, struggling because his hands were cuffed behind his back, Fitz pushed him a couple of times back to the front of the house and then pushed him one last time onto the couch.

George 'Charlie' Chan and Summer moved through the house looking for everything and anything that could be used against him. Given the information Garrett had provided, they found the DVD collection in the cupboard behind the TV. Thanks to Rodemaker, they were nicely categorized with the name of each boy, the date, and in some cases, the location. Two of the DVDs were listed as taken in Chicago with a boy named Tim and the other with a boy named Johnny listed on the case. One DVD was listed as taken in Los Angeles with a boy named Colin.

"Get the fuck away from my DVDs," Rodemaker yelled. You have no right!"

Summer turned to Chan and said, "You get that?"

He nodded and said, "Yup. Crystal clear."

"This your stereo system and computer?" Summer asked nonchalantly.

"Damn right," Rodemaker snarled. "Get the fuck away from it."

"Camera and cell phone too?"

"This is my house. I own it and everything in it. Get the fuck out of here. I know my rights!"

"Shut up, Pervert," Fitz muttered.

"Dusting for prints will be easy," Summer said with a smile. She turned to Rodemaker and said, "Thank you."

Rodemaker didn't answer. Just glared at her.

Nothing was touched without it being filmed and numbered. Videos were placed in paper bags, so there wasn't any chance of moisture damaging them. The outside of each bag was marked with the numbers on each of the videos. Other items were placed in clear evidence bags but marked with its contents.

Pete had a fleeting idea to contact Skip Dahlke, but knew Dahlke was already knee deep in the investigation of the van in Pembine, about five or six hours to the north. Besides, Waukesha had its own forensics team and would use the crime lab out of Milwaukee to analyze and process any DNA found in the house, on the boy's clothes and the PERK kits. Still, Pete kind of liked the innocent 'geekiness' of Dahlke; bright, very bright actually, with a quirkiness that was endearing.

Chet hadn't moved to work on the computer at all, instead focusing on Rodemaker's home theater and stereo system. Pete had told him that the videos Garrett saw of several boys were taken in Rodemaker's house. That meant that there had to be a camera system connected so he could film himself with the boys he brought here. That also meant that the cameras were connected to a recorder somewhere in the house. It wasn't visible, or at least, not that Chet had seen so far.

Loud enough so Rodemaker could hear, he said, "Pete, pretend you were a pervert like Rodemaker, and you wanted make home movies reliving your conquests. You would place the cameras in places where the kids wouldn't see them, yet film everything you could." He paused and looked at Pete. "Where would you hide them?"

"Garrett said he started in the hot tub."

Both men walked to the patio, turned on the lights and searched the perimeter of the house for any visible cameras. They didn't find anything that remotely looked like a camera.

Pete walked over to the hot tub, put his back to it, and faced the house. He was staring at the sliding patio door. To the left and right were patio lights. Ordinary looking. Nothing on the roof looking downward. To the left of the sliding door was a window behind the kitchen sink. In front of the window sat a small box planter with a mix of yellow marigolds and purple and white petunias.

"Chet, check the lights on either side of the slider."

Chet first inspected them and then carefully unscrewed the top, carefully exposing the light bulb.

"Well hello," Chet said. "Look what I found?"

"Summer, can you and Detective Chan come out on the patio?"

Summer led Chan out to the patio with Chan still taping. Chet pointed to the small, but high-powered camera.

"This is wireless, and I'm willing to bet it's motion sensitive."

He inspected the other light fixture in the same manner but didn't find any other camera.

"Garrett said after the hot tub, they went to the couch. There's got to be a camera stashed opposite the couch because that's where Rodemaker molested him again."

The group went into the family room and stood in front of the couch. They faced a forty inch, high definition, flat screen Samsung TV with a Panasonic Home Theater System. On the left was the now empty cabinet that had contained the DVD collection. On the other side were two bookcases. The one closest to the TV contained more DVDs, but of the commercial variety, and heavy on action-adventure. The other bookcase contained books (John Sanford, James Patterson, and Michael Connolly mostly) and various knickknacks with a few scented candles. The room was lit by a ceiling fan with a light kit, as well as recessed lights above the TV. Table lamps sat on end tables on either side of the couch.

Pete said, "Fan is a little high, but a possibility. I'm guessing somewhere on or around the TV system."

Captain O'Brien and Detective Reilly joined the others in the room as they searched for hidden cameras. One of the officers found a stepladder in the garage, brought it in, and Reilly climbed up and searched the ceiling fan and light kit.

Eventually three cameras were found. Reilly found one in the ceiling fan, while Chet found one in one of the speakers in the home theater system, and Summer found a camera in one of the table lamps. As they went through the house, they also found a camera in the guest bathroom air vent. They found another in the master bedroom ceiling fan and one in the light on the nightstand. They found an additional camera in the guest bedroom ceiling fan. Eight cameras found in all. Yet, they had not found the recording device the cameras fed.

They moved back to the family room to examine the wall facing the couch. Walls were tapped to determine if there were any hollowed out pockets or false walls.

Nothing.

"The DVDs of the kids were in this cabinet," Summer said pointing to the cabinet on the left.

She wrapped it with her knuckles trying to find a hollow spot. She pushed it once, then twice, and it swung open a couple of inches. She opened it the entire way and found a recorder, still on, still recording.

"Detective Chan, can you please film this?"

As he did so, Pete's cell buzzed.

CHAPTER TWENTY-EIGHT

"Kelliher."

"This is Deputy Leonard Buckey," he sounded agitated, out of breath. "George's cousin."

Pete sighed, impatient.

"Yes, Leonard, I remember."

"I did some digging on the helicopter, the one I saw leaving George's home."

Pete was suddenly interested.

"They're dead. The pilot and two passengers . . . probably the shooter and the spotter."

"Wait . . . wait!"

Pete moved towards the kitchen, turning his back to the group in the family room.

"Start at the beginning."

Leonard searched for the helicopter he saw leaving the ranch. He figured it was probably hired in one of the bigger towns or cities within a hundred mile radius or so of the Tokay homestead. He found a small charter company owned by Hugh Janovic out of Gallup, New Mexico. In addition to one small aircraft of the site-seeing variety, he owned two helicopters, one red on white and the other blue on white, neither having a company logo.

He was found shot at close range, two shots to his face. Two other men were found shot presumably as they stepped off the helicopter with one, Mathew Dooley, still holding a Springfield MIA semi-automatic .308 caliber with a 4 by 14 scope. Leonard figured the other guy, Daryl Fisher, was the spotter.

They were found by the wife of Janovic. He had not come home for dinner and had not answered the seven phone calls placed to him by her throughout the day. The ME figured they had been dead for approximately twelve hours, putting the time at approximately 1:00 PM MST, within an hour or so of the killing of the Tokay family.

"Is George safe?" Leonard asked at the end of his recital.

Thinking of the implications, he missed Leonard's question.

"*Kelliher*, is George safe?" Leonard yelled into the phone.

"Yes, yes . . . he's fine. I'll have him call you in a couple of hours. We're in the middle of something here. I promise you he's safe."

"What the hell did he get himself into?" Leonard said more to himself than to Pete.

"Shit, Leonard, I'm not sure."

*   *   *

Pete, Summer and Chet huddled in the kitchen with the door closed so he could tell them about Leonard's phone call.

"The rifle matches the caliber of bullets Dahlke and I found at the Tokay ranch. Who is tying up loose ends, and why is he . . . they . . . one step ahead of us? I don't get it!" Summer ran her hand through her hair and stared up at the ceiling.

Pete pulled out his notes and showed them to both Summer and Chet.

"In all my spare time," he said with a wry chuckle, "I created this. I don't think I talked to anyone out of the circle. I've looked at my cell call log, both incoming and outgoing, and unless my cell was traced, there is no one outside of the team, except for the folks at the Missing Children Center, Jeremy Evans, Skip Dahlke, and Jamie Graff, the detective in there, George's cousin, and the sheriff up north. Did either of you create one like I suggested?"

Chet shook his head, as did Summer, who took the notes from him. She scanned them, then turned her back from them and leaned against the counter. She spun around, looked up at them, eyes distant, then turned back to the sink and threw up.

"What?" Pete said.

"Get Doug on the phone. Now!"

Pete punched Doug's number into his cell and pushed the button so it was on speaker.

"Pete, who is with you?" Rawson asked.

"Summer and Chet."

"How secure is this conversation?" Musgrave asked.

"Logan?"

Odd that the two of them happened to be together at the same time, especially this late into the evening.

"How secure is this conversation," Musgrave asked again, this time more forcefully.

"How secure does it need to be?" Pete asked, looking from Summer to Chet.

There was a long pause before Doug said, "I think we've found our mole."

"Who?" Pete asked.

"It was me, wasn't it?" Summer asked.

"Bullshit," Pete laughed, but looked at Summer and noticed she was ashen.

*   *   *

Before the end of the conversation, it was agreed that Doug would run surveillance on the suspect; four teams of two, twenty-four hour coverage. This would include phone taps, surreptitiously looking into computer files and monitoring cell traffic where and when possible. Logan would be control, with all parties reporting directly to him. No one outside of the team other than those already in was to be involved from here on. In fact, any information to anyone outside of the team had to be approved of in advance by Musgrave. Pete phoned Dahlke and asked him for a preliminary report on the van found in Pembine.

"We have a lot of prints. Some match Ruiz and Szymanski and the boy . . . Ryan Wynn. We found blood on the floor of the van, along with clothes that the boy might have worn. There is trace DNA in the boy's boxers. Roz is going to type it against both men and the boy. If it doesn't match, then it might be the DNA of the third man . . . the man who killed all three in the woods."

"Skip, I need you to be careful."

He gave him Logan's cell number, as well as Chet's and Summer's cell.

"In case you need anything local, contact Detective Jamie Graff with the Waukesha Police Department. Don't contact anyone else. Fax the reports directly to Musgrave in D.C."

"What's going on, Pete? How bad is this?"

Pete paused and then said very quietly, "Skip, if something happens to me, you need to get George back to Arizona."

He gave him Jeremy's number and the number of George's cousin, Leonard.

*   *   *

Informing Greg and Marcia Carrigan had really royally sucked, just like Jamie had thought it would. How could it otherwise? It was impossible to tell parents gently that their son had been molested. No, just like Jamie thought, it fuckin' sucked.

There was anger, threats to kill Rodemaker, which were modified later to just beating the shit out of him, feelings silently shared by Pete, Jeremy and Jamie. Finally the only emotion left was the profound sadness they felt because they believed they had let their son down.

Jeremy explained that Scott would need their love and support now more than ever. He told them that Scott wasn't the only boy that had been molested by Rodemaker, though he couldn't give them names when they had asked. The whole process took less than thirty minutes and then Jeremy went with them to the hospital, while Pete and Jamie left for the station to formally interview Rodemaker.

*   *   *

Rodemaker waived his right to an attorney after Jamie and Pete explained that his only chance at any sort of deal would be to cooperate. A deal, however, would be up to the US Attorney.

The FBI, particularly the members of Summer's and Pete's unit were formally in charge due to the fact that two of the boys in Rodemaker's video collection, Tim Pruett and Johnny Vega had been missing for more than a year. They had been identified by a worker bee at the Center, who was told that potentially, there was a lead on them but that he needed to keep this quiet until it was thoroughly investigated.

Pruett was from West Bend, Wisconsin, while Vega was from El Paso, Texas. That meant that kids had been transported across state lines. This was among other charges yet to be filed, inter-state trafficking and kidnapping. The only bright side to all of this was the fact that the date showing Rodemaker with them in Chicago a month or so ago meant that they both could still be alive. This absolutely validated Pete's theory that the human trafficking ring existed. There was no longer any doubt.

Even though the FBI was officially in charge, it was Summer's and Pete's idea to let Jamie take the lead. Musgrave gave them the green light to let it play out, so Pete sat in on the interview.

Jamie Graff was a six foot, two hundred pound guy with dark hair and sometimes with, sometimes without a mustache. This was a time he had the mustache. He was described by his boss, Captain Jack O'Brien, as a thorough investigator, probably the best detective on the force and the best interrogator. He had a soft voice and was naturally reserved and thoughtful. He usually took on the role of the nice guy, the friend who wanted to help the suspect out. Almost always, it worked.

While, Jamie and Pete worked on Rodemaker, Summer and Chet worked on Rodemaker's cell phone and his computer, the subject of the second warrant.

They discovered a gold mine.

CHAPTER TWENTY-NINE

Jeremy found the kids barely awake at Jon and Bert's house when he rang the doorbell. They looked sleepy and greeted him with yawns as they got up from the couch in the Lantz family room and trooped out of the house to the Evan's house next door, still yawning and heads drooping.

In very brief detail, he explained to the boys what had transpired. He didn't give any names, since some of the boys attended Butler Middle School just as Randy and Billy did. The names of the kids and many of the details were confidential and way beyond what was appropriate to share despite what Randy had heard and had been through himself.

George shuffled off to the spare bedroom after going to the bathroom to wash up and brush his teeth with the toothbrush and toothpaste Pete had bought for him. He changed into clean boxers and gym shorts, which were among the clothes Pete had purchased at a discount chain store. Even though George typically wore either cowboy boots or moccasins, Pete reasoned that every kid should own a new pair of Addidas, so he asked George his shoe size and bought him a pair. No sooner than his head hit the pillow did he fall asleep.

Jeremy stuck his head in the room hoping to have a quiet word with him but noticed the heavy rhythmic breathing of a very sound, and tired, sleeper. So instead, he tiptoed over to the bed, stroked his cheek, then left, closing the door to a slit. He felt guilty because he had not said much to George and certainly had done nothing to comfort the boy. He'd make amends in the morning.

He knocked on Randy's and Billy's room and walked in. It was a small room, cozy, just a bit larger than the spare room. There were three windows. Two were in the corners over each boy's bed and a third was positioned in the middle of the room sort of like a line of demarcation defining which side of the room was whose.

However, there really didn't need to be an artificial separation between the two halves because the boys shared everything. Yet, it was easy to figure out which side of the room belonged to which boy. Billy had posters of sports figures like Milwaukee Brewer Ryan Braun and Green Bay Packer Aaron Rogers. There was a book shelf that was filled with various baseball and basketball trophies, along with several biographies and autobiographies of sports figures. A basketball sat on the light blue carpeted floor next to a baseball stuffed in a baseball glove against his dresser.

Randy had posters of Carrie Underwood, Taylor Swift and Tim McGraw. On his book shelf were paperbacks by Stephen King, a hardcover volume of *The Complete Mysteries of Sherlock Holmes* and an older hardcover collection of Nathaniel Hawthorne short stories and full-length stories. There were CDs and an IPod with a docking station hooked up to speakers. A Yamaha acoustic guitar sat in a stand in the corner next to his dresser.

Jeremy was surprised that the boys were still awake, though each was in their own bed on their respective sides of the room. Each had their head propped up on an elbow.

They looked at one another and then Billy said, "We think George should live with us."

Jeremy sat down on Randy's bed, which was nearest the door, not saying anything.

"He doesn't have any family," Billy continued. "We have room, and we like him."

Jeremy looked over at Randy and then back at Billy who said, "I think we should at least ask him."

"He has a cousin, but I'm not sure who else he has left," Jeremy said. "Have you talked with him about it?"

The boys looked at each other and then Randy said, "We thought we should talk to you first."

"We really don't know anything about George," Jeremy said gently. "We only met him a couple of hours ago."

"Can you at least think about it?" Billy said.

"You both feel this way?" Jeremy asked, knowing that both of them did, or Billy wouldn't have brought it up.

"Yup," Billy answered for both of them.

"I'll think about it. Promise," Jeremy said. "Now, both of you need to get some sleep. He got up and kissed Billy's forehead and said, "Goodnight." He moved over to Randy, ran his hand through his hair and said, "You okay?"

Randy nodded.

"What happened tonight at the Forstadt house?" Jeremy asked.

"It was the pictures," Randy answered. "He took pictures and sent them in e-mail and over the internet. It made me angry."

"And reminded you of what Mitch and Ernie did to you," Jeremy said.

"Yeah. The thing is, I don't know, and Garrett won't know . . . ever know, who has them or who has seen them . . ." Randy's voice trailed.

Jeremy kissed the top of his head, then took his face into his hands and said, "Talk in the morning?"

Randy nodded again.

"Okay," Jeremy said, caressing his cheek. He bent down to kiss his forehead again, but Randy held him in a hug, whispering, "I love you."

"Love you too, Randy," his voice catching. "You too, Billy. I love you guys a lot."

"Love you too," Billy said.

Jeremy took a long look at the boys, who had rolled onto their sides facing each other, then turned off the light and shut the door to a crack. Then he went to the family room and phoned Jamie to let him know what Randy had told him about the pictures.

*   *   *

"Here's what we have Mr. Rodemaker," Jamie said rifling through pages of notes and glossy 8 x 10s. "We have you on multiple rape charges, sodomy, and molestation, indecent liberties with a minor, contributing to the delinquency of a minor, and possession of pornography, distributing pornography, and possibly, accessory to kidnapping along with accessory to murder."

"I never kidnapped or murdered anyone!" he shouted. "I think I want a lawyer."

"That's certainly your right," Jamie said with a nod. "The FBI wants to fry your nuts over a stoked fire, but we've been talking. I've been given some latitude in the charges that might be filed. It all depends upon how much you cooperate . . . or not, as the case may be."

Pete leaned over Rodemaker getting into his face.

"I'm not into deals, but I have my orders. In the next room, I have a computer expert who is giving your computer, your cell phone and anything else electronic a proctoscopic, so here's how it works," he paused for effect. "The faster you talk and the more you cooperate, we deal with you. The minute you lie, deny or mislead us, this interview is over, and we *will* build a fire and fry your nuts. You understand?"

Rodemaker nodded so vigorously, his head was in danger of unhinging and falling off his neck.

"I already told you I'd cooperate."

Jamie shoved a piece of paper and pen across the desk, explaining that the paper Rodemaker was about to sign waived his right to an attorney, that he voluntarily cooperated with the investigation and that he acknowledged that the interview would be both videotaped and recorded. Rodemaker barely glanced at the forms before he signed and initialed them. He couldn't do it fast enough.

*   *   *

This was the kind of stuff Chet lived for. When he sat down at a computer, nothing and no one else existed. He could begin a project, and hours, even days, could pass before he realized it. Diet Coke and Snickers kept him going long into the night or early morning. Of course, he didn't have all night to dive into and make sense of Rodemaker's computer and cell phone because the lives of two missing kids might possibly depend upon what he found.

Rodemaker had given Chet a user name and password he said he used on the computer, and Chet had written it down on a pad of paper but set it off to the side.

He set up Rodemaker's computer and turned it on and then he opened up his own laptop and turned it on. He opened up a black case, which contained a number of disks. He selected one and inserted it into Rodemaker's disk drive.

"What are you doing?" Summer asked.

"I'm using a system CD to boot up Slimeball's computer to access the file system on the hard drive," Chet answered not even looking at her.

"Why don't you just use the user name and password he gave you?"

Chet turned to her with a puzzled expression and said, "Why do you think he'd be honest with us? The goodness of his heart? The sudden desire to repent and come clean?"

"We have him six different ways from Sunday on about a dozen different charges. He's trying to lessen the impact," Summer answered.

"Yeah, right. Or . . . he could be trying to erase contents on his hard drive. By using a specific user name or password, he could have set up his computer to erase everything automatically."

"Huh," Summer said, sitting back to watch Chet work.

Chet booted up Rodemaker's computer using his "special" system CD and made an exact image of the hard drive to an external USB drive, so it could be used as forensic evidence. Then, he opened the original hard drive in the computer and went right to the Documents and Settings folder to look at the various user names on personal folders within.

He looked up the user name Rodemaker gave him and discovered that it was indeed rigged to automatically run a disk erase utility to clean off the hard drive.

"Told you . . . he rigged it! He must have all sorts of crap on here he didn't want us to see."

"So he's not cooperating." Summer didn't pose that as a question.

"In a word, no way."

"That's two words," Summer said.

"But you get my point," Chet said. "He's trying to cover his tracks."

Chet looked at the other user folders and found one called, '*pizza_guy*'. He then looked into the settings folder for the Firefox history and cache but didn't find any user folders.

"Huh," he said with a nod.

"What?" Summer asked.

"He's trying to cover his tracks."

"You said that already."

He didn't answer, but went to the BookMarks.html and found various links anyone might have: CNN, CBS Sports, ESPN. Then he found a link to a site called, '*Desert Ranch Ponies*' and became curious because it didn't fit an otherwise ordinary pattern.

"We went through his financials, and there was nothing in there about a ranch, farm or livestock, right?"

Summer opened a folder, ran a finger down pages notes and pages of bank records and then answered, "No, nothing. Why?"

"Not sure . . . I'll tell you in a minute."

Chet switched to his work computer and went to the Desert Ranch Ponies web site. Nothing special, except that the page was a beautiful picture of three ponies set against a red-orange sunset, with red hills and Joshua Trees in the background. He then switched back to Rodemaker's computer and combed through the pizza_guy user settings looking for any additional traps, but found none. Then, he rebooted the computer using his Ophcrack Live CD.

"What are you doing now?" Summer asked with a yawn.

"I'm running a password cracking utility to find out what Rodemaker's password is for his user name." Before she had a chance to ask, Chet said, "His preferred user name is '*pizza_guy*'."

It was just a matter of minutes before he found Rodemaker's password, which was '*love2loveboys*'.

"Sick sonofabitch!" Chet said through clenched teeth.

Next, he logged in as *pizza_guy* with the *love2loveboys* password and looked at Rodemaker's email, finding acknowledgements to email sent to a list serve. The list would have to be checked out in case these were addresses of perverts collecting and sending Kiddie porn as

Chet suspected they would be. He printed out the list and asked Summer to fax it to Musgrave.

"How do you know they're pervs?" Summer asked.

"Hunch," Chet grunted.

He went to sent mail and opened up the email sent to the list serve and clicked on the first attachment. Chet and Summer found themselves staring at a frontal nude picture of an unsmiling Scott Carrigan, the boy they had found with Rodemaker earlier that evening. He clicked on the second and then a third attachment and found similar pictures, all pornographic.

"Sharing his own personal memories with a few of his closest pervert friends. Can I shoot the sonofabitch now?" Chet asked Summer through clenched teeth.

He clicked off the picture, turned to Summer and said, "I know I've not been doing this as long as you and Pete, but I don't understand these sons of bitches. How can they do this to kids?"

Summer shook her head. She had given up trying to answer that one a long, long time ago.

In a little over twenty minutes, Chet had unearthed hundreds of pictures of nude boys in various poses in a folder simply titled '*Boys*'. Some of the pictures showed boys handcuffed to what looked like the inside of a van. Others were pornographic.

He uploaded all of the photos to the Center for Missing Children and then to Logan Musgrave in D.C. for cataloging. It wouldn't take long to match the kids in the photos with the names of missing kids, unless the kids were local victims. Both Chet and Summer figured there would be many of those, given the number of videos taken in the search of Rodemaker's home.

Chet knew from FBI statistics that by the time a pedophile is tried and convicted, he or she- mostly a he- would have, on average approximately 200 victims. That figure still staggered Chet's imagination. At least with this pervert behind bars, kids would be safer. And, the names on the list serve might lead the team to members of the sex ring and perhaps, missing kids.

One could hope.

"Hmm," Chet mumbled.

"Ok, now what?"

"Why would Desert Ranch Ponies be a site with only one page?"

"How many pages should it be?'

Chet didn't answer, but glared at the screen, willing it to give him an answer. He grabbed another Snickers, took a bite, but stopped chewing. He glanced at Summer and went to his keyboard.

In the web address bar, he typed */boys* after the IP address of '*www.desertranchponies.com*' and waited, staring at the screen.

A directory listing of files showed up on the monitor. He looked them over and then clicked on a file that said, '*StartHere.html*' and then a graphic site opened up with three nude, unsmiling boys. Two of the boys were blond, one had light-brown hair, and each appeared to be about twelve years old.

The screen dissolved again like an animation in a PowerPoint, and the three boys appeared on the screen again, this time however, performing sex acts. The screen dissolved again . . . and again . . . and again. What looked like the final screen had menu options scripted over the boys who were caught in a close-up of the brown-haired boy.

The first menu said, '*Chicago*'. A second said, '*Los Angeles*'. A third said, '*Coming To Your Area*'. A fourth said, '*Share Your Pictures and Stories*'.

At first, Chet and Summer stared at each other. But there was a sudden charge of adrenaline that had nothing to do with the three Diet Cokes and four Snickers consumed by each of them in the last two hours.

Summer phoned Musgrave, gave him the IP address to *Desert Ranch Ponies*, and asked him to do some quiet digging. It was time to have heart to heart with Rodemaker.

CHAPTER THIRTY

Stephen sat on an unmade double bed in a simple room that had an ugly chair covered in green fabric that had more worn spots than actual fabric, and a cheap table someone might have purchased at a discount chain store, except this one had assorted nicks and chips. A cheap fake wood lamp sat on the table along with a box of wipes and box of Puffs. The shade on the lamp was dusty and dirty with some sort of stain on it. Stephen thought the color was tan, but because of the dust and dirt, he couldn't tell for sure. The sheets on the bed and the pillowcase smelled and were of an indeterminate color. Perhaps tan, maybe some pastel, but who knew. Stephen didn't.

The room had cheap, peeling, flowered wallpaper and a window that was sealed from the inside with plywood and steel bars. The floor was dirty green linoleum that was chipped and faded. There was a threadbare rug at the side of the bed. He had been taken directly to this room and locked in upon his arrival.

He only had a glimpse of the building he was brought to because it was dark and late at night. The van drove into a dark alley alongside a dirty red brick building on one side and an even dirtier gray brick building on the other. He could tell the colors because of the street lights on each corner. The buildings looked to be about three stories high. A roll-up metal garage door opened up and swallowed the van and when it entered, the door rolled back down.

He was alone, very alone, and had never been this frightened before in his life. He was particularly alarmed that his eyes refused to focus. He'd move his head to the right, and it felt like his eyes dragged slowly behind. He had to blink several times before his eyes caught up with his head. There was a general dizziness. He had a major headache and a stuffy nose.

Stephen didn't like any of this; none of it. He wanted clothes to cover himself up with, something, anything to wear. Mostly, he wanted to go home, but he knew that might not be possible, might not *ever* be possible, but each time that thought came up, he pushed it away because it was too terrible to think about. The possibility of never seeing his family or friends again terrified him.

Every now and then he had heard muffled screams and knew they had come from Mike, or at least he *thought* they had come from Mike. The last time Stephen had seen him, he was being dragged down to the far end of the hallway, still in handcuffs. Mike was still bleeding from his nose and mouth because the men used him, punched him, and slapped him when he tried to fight them off in the van. They had beaten him up pretty badly.

As time went on, Stephen had wondered if Mike was still alive, but after hearing his muffled screams, Stephen knew he was. He had tried covering his ears to keep out the screams, but it didn't work. Whether the screams were real or just in his head, he wasn't sure. He thought they were real. And at least if he believed they were real, Mike was alive, and Stephen wasn't alone. That was his only happy thought.

He heard the door unlock once again.

Stephen recognized the fat, sweaty man with long, greasy, black hair as one of the men who had used him over and over again. This time however, he led two boys into the room and then left, shutting and locking the door behind him. Stephen had not seen the boys before. In fact, up until they walked in, he had thought that he and Mike were the only boys in the building.

The two boys were dressed as he was: wearing nothing. At first, the two boys stared at him warily, but then the taller of the two, a lanky blond boy came over and sat down next to him, while the other one, a brown-haired boy a bit taller than Stephen stood in front of them at an odd angle.

"I'm Tim," the blond whispered. "This is Brett. We don't have much time, so you have to listen, okay?"

Stephen tried to nod, but it felt awkward because his eyes couldn't focus, and nodding made him feel nauseous.

"The room has a camera. All the rooms have a camera. We think the rooms are bugged too . . . you know . . . so they can hear what we say, but we're not sure. Brett is kind of blocking the camera, so we have to talk fast."

"We're supposed to make a movie . . . you know, do stuff with each other . . ." Brett said. "We don't like it any more than you do, but while we do this, you have to listen. You have to remember what we tell you. Okay?"

Stephen remembered what had happened the last time he nodded, so he whispered, "Yes," instead.

"It's important to listen and remember what I tell you, okay?" Tim said.

Stephen began to cry. He was so scared, and he couldn't believe what was happening to him.

"Shhh," Tim whispered, putting his arm around him. "That doesn't help," but he let him cry nonetheless, holding him close.

"We have to get moving, so . . . you ready?" Brett said.

Stephen wiped away his tears and in a tiny voice said, "Yeah."

"Nod or shake your head when I ask you a question," Tim whispered. "We think we're in Chicago . . ."

There were eleven boys. With Stephen and Mike, there were now thirteen. Stephen was the boy they had really wanted, while Mike was going to be used for a couple of days by the guards and then disposed of, probably in front of them to make sure the boys knew who was in charge. They meant to send a message: none of the boys would never, ever leave.

There were times when one of them was taken away in handcuffs never to be seen again. That had happened several times in the almost two years Tim and Brett had been there and as recently as that morning. With Stephen now among them, someone was surely going to go away again.

At some point in the morning, Stephen would be visited by the *Dark Man*. Tim had whispered this like it was a real name, and someone to be feared. The boys thought the Dark Man was the boss or owner because the guards treated him like he was a king or something. Behind his back however, they made fun of him or flipped him off.

The Dark Man always came the morning after a new boy arrived.

Stephen would find out on his own that the Dark Man liked to cause pain. Warning him ahead of time would only make it worse. The only man that liked to cause pain more than the Dark Man was the *Cop*. The boys thought he was a cop because one of them saw an identification tag and a nightstick, though it was only a glimpse, and there had been no time to read it. So the boys referred to him as the *Cop*.

There were at least three guards on duty at any one time. Butch, the fat, greasy man was the guy in charge, unless the Dark Man was present. The guards rotated every three or four days. Shawn, the red-haired man and Clay, the guy with the buzz cut were not guards. Those two guys along with a dude named Ace and another creep named Rick were only around long enough to bring boys to or from the building.

Usually it was two other guys, *really bad* guys, who brought boys to and from the building. A couple of the boys had overheard the guards talking that Frank and Ron weren't going to be coming around anymore, but the boys didn't know what that meant.

Each morning, the boys were fed fast food breakfast items along with two pills. One pill was either blue or yellow, and the boys thought this was Viagra or something. Stephen was told that he needed to take it because it would help him. It would give him a headache and stuffy nose, but in time, maybe he'd get used to it. Stephen was told only to pretend to take the other pill. The boys didn't know what it was, but they were convinced that it did nothing but fuck up your head, so when the guard wasn't looking, Stephen was told to spit it out and hide it somewhere but then pretend like he was high.

Sometimes a man might make him do lines of coke, smoke a joint, or drink beer or whiskey, and Stephen would have no choice but to comply. He wouldn't like it, but maybe he'd get used to that too. The guards were forbidden to use the boys like the other men who visited them. The boys were off limits. Stephen paused and looked up at him with a puzzled look on his face, but didn't say anything.

"I said they aren't *supposed* to do anything with us. I didn't say they *wouldn't*," Tim said seeing the question on Stephen's face as he looked up from what he was doing to Tim.

They were all pigs and assholes, not to be trusted. The boys only had one another. The boys were called 'ponies', and they hated that name. Each new boy, or 'pony', in this case Stephen, was responsible to memorize the names and faces of the other boys in case he outlived them all. That way, their families would know about them. It was a system

Tim had made up. For as long as Tim had been there, Stephen was the tenth new boy. Each morning, the boys would be lined up one behind the other to take a shower.

"In the morning, we'll make sure we line up in alphabetical order . . . or try to. I'll stand behind you and whisper names. Each of the guys will make an excuse to turn around, so you can see them. It's important," Tim said urgently, but in a whisper. "You've got to memorize our names and faces. Okay?"

Stephen nodded.

They were to obey without question, and if any boy refused, he'd be severely punished. Punishment, Tim explained, was to be dragged to the end of the hallway, handcuffed to chains that hung from the ceiling and whipped in front of the other boys, so that all of them could watch. The message was simple: obey or else.

If one of the boys tried to escape, that boy would be dragged down the hallway, handcuffed to the chains, whipped, and then branded with an upside down cross on his ankle. Stephen was warned not to try to escape, but he didn't need the warning. He would obey because he didn't want to get whipped or branded.

Brett looked up from between Stephen's legs and said, "You can't give up. Never, no matter how bad it gets or how long you stay here. You can't give up, because the rest of us depend on you." Brett stared intently at Stephen and said, "You got that?"

Stephen nodded slightly.

"And remember this . . . this is *really* important, you can't ever, *ever* like this shit. No matter how long you stay here. You can pretend . . . you can act, but you *can't* like it." Brett paused and then asked, "You understand?"

Stephen stopped what he was doing and said quickly, "No fucking way!"

"Good," Brett answered. "Last thing . . . don't trust *any* of 'em. *No* one. Just us, especially me and Tim. Maybe Johnny, but we think he might be the next one to go away. He's sick and not getting any better."

The boys finished, and a short time later, the door was unlocked and the two boys were led away. And, Stephen was alone.

*   *   *

Chet and Summer knew they had something big, really big. Chet got up from the table and walked in rapid laps around the room with both hands on the back of his head. His eyes weren't focused on anything in particular.

Summer watched him while talking on her phone to Musgrave.

"It's bigger than we thought, Logan."

Musgrave was silent on the other end of the phone and then said, "We've matched pictures of the twelve dead boys on our board with pictures from Rodemaker's computer. We're assuming the pictures were sent from the Desert Ranch Ponies website. We're getting information on all the addresses on Rodemaker's list serve. We were able to quietly obtain warrants to find out the names and locations of all of the men from the various dot coms and dot nets.

"We need Chet to find out who set up this website. We find who's behind the website, we shut down this ring."

"Chet's working on that now, but he thinks a warrant might slow us down. He's worried about those two boys."

"Put Chet on."

Summer caught Chet making his third trip around the table, placed a hand on his arm to stop him and then handed him the phone.

"Walker," was all he said.

"How can I help you find who set this website up?" Logan asked.

Chet didn't answer him directly, but instead seemed to think out loud.

"We know the picture of the original website . . . the one with the ponies and the Joshua Tree was taken in the southwestern part of the US. We also know there is no Desert Ranch listed anywhere in the Four Corners area of the United States. It doesn't exist. But I believe, given the area, we're looking at a remote location, probably a real, legitimate ranch of some sort."

"There has to be money behind this. The site is slick, and the setup is even slicker. This isn't an average Joe. It has outreach to Chicago and Los Angeles and a traveling component that moves kids around the country."

"I was thinking the same thing. I guess Pete was right."

Chet kept going as if Logan hadn't said anything.

"In order for this to be as big as it is-"

"-We know." Logan interrupted, not wanting either of them to vocalize the obvious.

"I want your permission to reach out to someone who can help. Someone I trust," Chet said.

"Do I know this person?" Logan asked.

"No you don't. He's not FBI. Hell, I'm not sure what he is other than he is the best computer guy I know. He could be CIA or NSA. He might not be anything at all. I'm not sure, Logan, but I trust him, and I need his help."

Logan knew this request didn't come lightly. Chet was one of the best computer guys in the FBI. Still, there was a risk. Logan knew that if he asked, Chet wasn't going to give him his name. There was already one leak, and he had come to the same conclusion Summer and Chet came to: a ring this big had serious protection. The question was, was this guy Chet was about to reach out to part of that protection, especially if this guy worked for some government agency?

"How much do you need to share with this guy?" Logan asked.

"Not sure, really. I'll play it by ear. I'll start shallow, nothing in depth. Only so much that he can get the job done and not tip off anyone that we're on to this. We need to find those boys. If there are two, there might be twenty," Chet reasoned.

There was silence on the line, but Chet knew Logan was going to give him the go ahead.

"Chet, I'm going to trust you, but I want to be in the loop each step of the way."

"Got it."

"I don't have to tell you how sensitive this is. If any of this leaks . . . *any* of it . . . we'll lose everything, including those boys."

CHAPTER THIRTY-ONE

It had been a while since Chet had dialed the number, and he worried that it might have changed and that the guy had dropped off the grid. He needn't have worried.

"Yeah."

"I need help. It's urgent. Two boys depend on it," Chet said.

"What do you need?"

*   *   *

Summer listened to the conversation, not understanding more than a sentence or two. As far as she was concerned, it was Geek-Speak.

"There were alerts sent to our pervert's IPhone. Someone at the top or near the top sent them to this fuckhead and others like him. I don't believe they're coming from a computer, but an IPhone like our pervert's."

"So, give me the MAC and the cell provider, and I'll set my computer at five minute intervals searching for the dynamic DNS . . ." the voice on the other end of the line said.

After Chet had hung up, Summer said, "Can you explain in very simple English what you and this guy are doing?"

Chet chewed on the inside of his cheek and tried to explain in Non-Geek what was happening.

"Each IPhone has its own unique MAC, which stands for media access control. Each service has a unique set of IP addresses. IP stands for Internet Protocol and in many cases are written as part of the TCP/IP. That stands for Transmission Control Protocol/Internet Protocol. A DNS enables people to type in a name like CNN or NBC instead of an IP address. Usually, the IP address is a static number that does not change. There are dynamic DNS servers where you register a server's name, and they keep track of what the IP address changes to.

"The network firewall, router or server an individual has will send updates to the dynamic DNS server to let the dynamic DNS server know it's been changed. A dynamic DNS allows you to type in a server name that goes to a server that has a changing Internet address.

An interesting twist has occurred with the development of the IPhone. Someone's IPhone could actually be the web server."

Summer was very bright. Top Ten in the Law School at Louisville indicated just how smart she was. Yet, she stared at Chet as if he were talking a foreign language or something.

Chet sighed, but continued on.

"So, there's an ordinary web page on any site, just like Desert Ranch Ponies. You click on a picture or a word, and it links to the IPhone. The IPhone web server uses dynamic DNS so the link works whenever the guy turns on the app on the IPhone. Whenever this guy feels it isn't safe, he just turns off the app and/or the IPhone.

My guy, and he is the God of Geeks, is going to do two things. First, he's going to try to find the owner of the IPhone by backtracking off Rodemaker's phone. The second thing he's going to do is locate where this guy is in real time."

"Jesus, Chet. I have absolutely no idea what the hell you just told me."

Chet shrugged.

"Best non-geek explanation I can give."

"Okay, so what are we going to do?"

Chet smiled and sat down at his computer.

"We're going to find who might be the owner of Desert Ranch Ponies."

*   *   *

"You said you'd cooperate with us," Pete said as he came back into the room with Jamie. "And I told you what I was going to do if you didn't."

Rodemaker didn't say anything but looked from Pete to Jamie.

"You haven't been all that honest with us, so I think we're going to add Obstruction to the list of charges, along with accessory to kidnapping and accessory to murder. We have established that absolutely." Without taking his eyes off Rodemaker, he said to Jamie, "We're no longer dealing with this piece of shit!"

Rodemaker started to get up from the chair, but Pete pushed him back down and said, "Don't you move a fuckin' inch!"

"We warned you," Jamie said gathering up his files, pictures and papers. "We had a deal, and you blew it."

"I *was* honest with you," Rodemaker cried. "I *told* you *everything*!"

"The hell you did you perverted motherfucker!" Pete said through clenched teeth. "Not by a long shot!"

Pete opened a file filled with pictures and began showing them to Rodemaker; one by one without commentary. Pete held up a picture of two boys handcuffed to the interior wall of a panel van, showing it first to Jamie, then to Rodemaker.

"The boy on the left is Stephen Bailey. The boy on the right is Mike Erickson. These boys were abducted earlier this evening from Waukesha. And within a couple of hours, you have their picture on your cell phone. With all the *honesty* and *cooperation* you've given us, it's amazing how we found this website on your laptop."

Pete placed a color photo of Desert Ranch Ponies website in front of him and then the pictures of the three boys from the same website as they appeared in order on the computer screen.

"You didn't think my guy would find this?" Pete asked. "You didn't think he'd find the auto erase program on your laptop if he were to type in that bogus username and password? You didn't think he'd find the hundreds of pictures on your hard drive in a folder titled, '*boys*'? You thought you were going to fool us and get away with it, you stupid mother fucking pervert?"

Rodemaker hung his head, buried his face in both hands and began to cry.

"I warned you my computer guy is the best. I warned you what he was going to do to your computer and cell phone. I warned you, didn't I?" he asked rhetorically.

"Sorry, Rodemaker," Jamie said quietly. "I wanted to deal with you, but you blew it. The deal is off, and I can't help you."

Sobbing, head still in his hands, Rodemaker said, "Please, you don't understand. They told me they'd kill me if I ever said anything. We were all told that."

He looked at Jamie, then at Pete.

"They will *kill* me."

"I don't give a fuck, Rodemaker. Sincerely, I couldn't give a shit. Hell, if you don't tell me now who *they* are, I'll kill you my*self*."

"You don't understand," Rodemaker cried. "They got cops and FBI. They're gonna fuckin' *kill me*!"

Jamie and Pete exchanged a quick glance that Rodemaker didn't catch because he had his head buried in his hands.

"Look," Jamie said patiently like he was explaining it to a four year old. "You have one shot left. You tell us what we need to know, and we'll deal. We'll even protect you. If you don't, we'll advertise you to the guys behind this whole thing. We'll get out of the way and let them have you."

Rodemaker dropped his head back into his hands and sobbed, then looked up and nodded.

"I'll help you, but you gotta protect me. You gotta protect me."

*   *   *

Chet's fingers flew over the keyboard. He stopped only long enough to swallow some Diet Coke, to check his notes, or simply to frown at the screen.

"Okay . . . from the picture of the website, the ranch is in the southwest, right?" Without waiting for an answer, Chet said, "And we also know there is no Desert Ranch anywhere, right?"

Summer frowned at him and said, "What are you getting at?"

"A pedophile is generally a male between the ages of twenty and fifty-five, right?" Chet asked.

"Generally single . . . never married," Summer added.

"So, we look in the southwest for any ranches owned by a single male between the ages of twenty and fifty-five and see what we get," Chet said as his fingers typed away.

"Do I want to know how you're going to get that information?"

"Most of it will be legal . . . you know, public record."

"You said most of it," Summer said.

"Yeah most of it, so you don't really want to know," Chet said without looking at her.

CHAPTER THIRTY-TWO

Chet rubbed his eyes. He'd been at this for six hours, and it was after midnight. Despite the Snickers and Diet Cokes and adrenalin, he was crashing. Summer was pretty far gone too. To keep awake, Summer would alternate between looking over Chet's shoulder and watching Pete and Jamie tag team Rodemaker, who suddenly couldn't shut himself up. Anything and everything about Desert Ranch Ponies and the website, the prostitution, the entire human trafficking details utilizing boys, the Chicago and Los Angeles operations and the traveling component all came out. Summer had watched through the glass, fascinated at the extent and sophistication of the operation, yet sickened beyond belief that so many men seemed to be involved. Not to mention the obvious money, power and protection this organization had.

"Summer, I think I have something," Chet called.

Yawning and stretching with both arms over her head, she walked back into the little office where she and Chet had holed up.

"I've checked this over four times, making sure the parameters are correct. We have sixteen ranches owned by single men. There's several in southern Colorado, but these guys are either divorced or widowed, so I guess they're candidates, but long shots. There's several in both Arizona and New Mexico but with the same results. The guys are either divorced or widowed. But there are two in Arizona, and both are prospects because they're both single. Neither are married . . . neither are divorced, and neither are widowers."

Summer looked over his shoulder at the results on the screen.

"Where are the two ranches?"

"One is near Chandler, a burb of Phoenix. The other is closer to the Four Corners area. Near the Navajo Reservation."

"Logic would tell us to go with the one near the reservation, but that almost seems too easy," Summer said. "Something about it doesn't feel right. So, how do we know for sure?"

"We wait until my guy calls," Chet said, folding his arms on his chest. "If we dig anymore than we've done so far, we might tip the pervert off or maybe the protection. We can't afford that because we'll never find those two boys or the rest of the missing kids."

"Then let's hope your guy calls soon. The longer those boys are missing . . ."

"I know, Summer, I know."

*   *

*

It took almost forty-five minutes for Rodemaker to spill his guts. He rolled on two or three other local men who shared his perversion, though he didn't see his desires as perversion.

"You have to understand . . . I loved those boys," Rodemaker pleaded.

Jamie almost flew over the table at him. Pete had to *decide* whether or not to let him, but in reality, only took a second or two before he restrained him.

"Don't you even fucking think we'll understand you, you mother fucking son of a bitch!" Jamie yelled, shrugging off Pete's hold on him.

He reached for the folder of pictures and pulled out the one of the two kidnapped boys, handcuffed to the interior wall of the van.

"Explain to me you fucking pervert, how this is love?" Jamie held that up for Rodemaker to examine. "Explain to me just how this love of yours allows kids to be taken from their families and raped by fucking sons of bitches like you."

Jamie reached for one of the photographs of Ryan Wynn taken earlier that day in Pembine and held it up to Rodemaker so closely that Rodemaker had to pull his head away in order to focus on it.

"Look closely, Asshole. This boy was found with two bullet holes in the back of his head. Explain to me, Shithead, how this is love."

Rodemaker turned his head away and began to cry again.

"That's right . . . you can't. You can't because you don't know what the fuck love is, Mother Fucker. You have no fucking clue, so don't you *dare* try to explain all of this shit as love, *Mother Fucker*! I'm not buying it and neither is anyone else."

Jamie gathered up the photos, and without looking at Pete, went to the door, opened it and looked back at Rodemaker and said, "You fucking piece of shit!"

It was then Pete noticed the tears in Jamie's eyes.

*   *

*

Morgan Billias was a mild-mannered, easy-going, middle-aged guy with a wife, two daughters and a son. He had an easy laugh, a ready wise crack, and could find humor in most anything. He didn't work for the CIA or the NSA or any of the other alphabet groupings that belonged to the government. Chet never asked Morgan what he did or where he lived or whether or not he was married and had two or six children. And Morgan never told him.

They met at a computer expo a couple of years back in San Francisco, got to talking about computers, had a couple of beers together and basically, hit it off. They kept in contact off and on over the months, with Chet reaching out to him whenever a "puzzle" needed to be solved. Nothing great or grandiose, just puzzles.

The puzzle of the IPhone being a server was much bigger than anything Chet had reached out to him for, and it was the only time Chet had actually sought permission for.

The phone beeped, and Chet answered it with his customary, "Walker."

"You're right about it being a mobile phone."

Chet smiled and nodded at the news.

"I kept asking myself why the IP address was AT&T one minute, then Panera Bread the next, only to be Starbucks the next."

"Has to be an IPhone," Chet said. "You did an nslookup?"

"Yeah . . . and he's mobile," Morgan answered.

"So, do you have a name?" Chet asked hopefully, but knowing the answer.

"Yup. I called a guy at AT&T, and he looked up the MAC . . . Gary Sears, but both of us know it's fake."

"How much . . ."

"-nothing. He knows not to ask, and I didn't volunteer anything," Morgan answered.

Chet didn't realize it, but he was holding his breath waiting for Morgan's answer because he had remembered Logan Musgrave's caution about leaks. He sighed audibly.

"Which Panera Bread and which Starbucks?" Chet asked, grabbing a piece of paper, jotting down notes.

"Panera Bread in Chandler, Arizona and then Starbucks at the airport in Phoenix."

"So, we could contact the IT guy at either and see if we can get him on tape," Chet said more to himself then to Morgan.

"And then you'd have to compare the two tapes against the times the MAC was in use to determine who the guy is," Morgan answered.

"We'll have to get the tapes," Chet said.

"Um . . . check your computer. There will be an e-mail from me with two video files attached with my notes. I think you'll find the guy in them."

Chet was stunned. He opened his mouth to speak, but never said a word.

"Morgan, I owe you big on this, but how . . ."

"Don't ask because you don't want to know, right? And, you don't owe me anything," Morgan continued. "I hate perverts. If I had my way, they'd all get gang-raped by six hundred pound gorillas so their assholes would end up looking like Mammoth Cave."

*   *   *

Jamie leaned against the window staring out at the Waukesha night. It was misty and quiet. Traffic was light after midnight. Bars and restaurants were closed. No one was on the street. A lone street sweeper drove down the street weaving in and around parked cars cleaning up sand, dirt, McDonald's wrappers and other debris from the city streets. He had composed himself and was back in control.

He met Jeremy Evans the first day of new teacher orientation at Waukesha North High School six years ago. Jeremy was a social studies teacher and head boys' basketball coach back then, while Jamie was the newly appointed school liaison officer. They were two of the J's as they were called. The third J was Jeff Limbach, a new English teacher. The three of them developed a fast and lasting friendship that survived Jeff's divorce, Jeremy's transition to counseling and eventually Jamie's move out of the school system to the rank of detective. Barbeques at the pool at Jeff's house, golf at one of the local courses, movie nights, all of it continued. Jeremy was Godfather to Jeff's son, Danny, who lived half of the time in Omaha with his mother after the divorce. Jeff was Godfather to Randy and acted like one to Billy. The three J's shared an unspoken loyalty, a bond that few friends ever shared.

Pete cleared his throat to let him know he was in the room and then asked, "You okay?"

"Yeah."

Jamie pushed off the wall and walked over to the table and opened up the file with all the pictures. He flipped through them until he came to the two he wanted, the ones he noticed earlier that evening and pushed them across to Pete.

The first picture was of a crying brown-haired boy whose face was contorted in obvious pain. The second was of the same boy, obviously embarrassed and scared, posing nude for the camera. Jamie watched Pete's face, looking for any sign of recognition.

When he didn't see it, Jamie said, "Look closely at the boy."

Pete held the picture closer, frowning in concentration. He shook his head and looked back at Jamie and shrugged.

"You met him earlier this evening. He's two years younger in the photos."

Pete looked at the photos again, recognition dawning over him.

"Sweet Jesus!"

"Yeah," Jamie answered.

CHAPTER THIRTY-THREE

Jamie pulled out a chair and sat down, half facing the window. Pete sat down on the other side of the table and waited.

"He was about eleven or twelve. The man in the picture is Ernie Caturano. He's serving a forty year stretch in Waupun State Prison. His partner, Mitch Lyons, is serving forty years in Omro.

"Randy had run away from his home in Marshfield the night before and hitched all the way to Milwaukee where they picked him up at a Burger King."

"What made him run away?"

"Randy had known he was a twin and adopted. Identical. His adoptive father hated him for some reason God only knows and beat the shit out of him every chance he could. His adoptive mother did nothing to prevent it. Randy finally ran away, thinking that if he found his twin, he could live with him."

Pete gave him a dubious look.

Jamie shrugged and said, "What can I say . . . he's a kid."

Pete sat silently and looked at the two photos again and then turned them upside-down.

"Caturano and Lyons spotted him alone and vulnerable, bought him dinner and offered to help him find his twin. They took him to Lyon's apartment and raped him, sodomized him, whipped him, and burned the inside of his leg with a cigarette. He escaped after Lyons and Caturano passed out from pot, pills or alcohol . . . who knows. A couple of good Samaritans protected him and called us.

"Jeremy was looking to adopt and was on the list as a possible foster home as a way of moving up on the adoptive parent list. Randy was placed with him after a week and a half stay in a hospital. It was rocky at first. Randy didn't trust Jeremy. He wanted to, but the years of abuse by the adoptive father made trusting too difficult. But Jeremy worked his ass off to prove to Randy that he'd hang in there with him, and well," Jamie shrugged. ". . . you see how they are together."

"Why wasn't Randy sent back to his adoptive family?"

"Because of the abuse Randy suffered and because the father refused to take him back. His mother didn't put up much of a fight."

"Fuck!" Pete said shaking his head.

"At the trial, Randy refused a video-taped deposition. He wanted to face Caturano and Lyons in person."

Pete looked up, puzzled and in disbelief. "Really?"

"Yeah, I know . . . a twelve year old kid. What you don't know is how really remarkable he was that day . . ."

Randy stood in the witness box, raised his hand and swore to tell the truth, the whole truth and nothing but the truth. He told his story almost entirely without prompting by the prosecuting attorney. He never blinked, and he never wavered. He stared directly at those two assholes, facing them down.

The defense attorney, a small, skinny, balding man complimented Randy on his bravery and then asked the first of three questions- the only three he would ask Randy that day.

"You ran away from home. You hitch-hiked from Marshfield to Waukesha. And these two gentlemen offered to help you find your twin brother. Is that correct?"

"Yes, Sir, except they aren't gentlemen."

Stenzel chuckled at the joke while the rest of the courtroom laughed out loud, causing the judge to use his gavel. However, the judge had trouble hiding the grin.

Stenzel went on to say, "They bought you a meal. They took you to Mr. Lyon's apartment. You took a shower. Mr. Lyons washed your clothes. Is that correct?"

"Yes, Sir."

"Now, Randy . . ." Stenzel dramatically turned to face the jury. ". . . there is a difference between consensual sex and rape. Do you know the difference?"

"Objection. The witness is a minor and too young to consent to having sex with an adult."

"Objection sustained. Counselor, you know better than to ask a question like that," Judge Henry Catlett said.

"I'm sorry, Your Honor. Let me rephrase the question. Randy . . ."

"I'd like to answer that question, Your Honor." Randy stared back at the man without blinking. "But I want to make sure I understand it."

"Fine," Stenzel said with a smug smile, standing in the center of the courtroom with his hands behind his back.

"By consensual sex, do you mean those two guys . . . the defendants . . . shoving objects up my rectum so that I ended up with more than twelve stitches?"

The defense attorney opened his mouth to speak, but he only looked at the judge, then back at Randy.

"*By consensual sex, do you mean those two gentlemen taking photographs of me posing naked, making a movie of them raping me and then sending it over the internet to whomever they wanted and then forcing me to give them oral sex?*"

"*Your honor, I object . . .*"

"*Counselor, you asked the question,*" *Judge Henry Catlett said. He turned and smiled at Randy and said, "I believe he has the right to try and understand your question, so objection overruled.*"

Randy smiled back at the judge and then continued.

"*By consensual sex, do you mean forcing me to drink shots of whiskey and smoke pot? By consensual sex, do you mean that fat guy whipping me with a belt buckle so hard and so many times that I have scars on my back? By consensual sex, do you mean that every time I said 'no' to them, they'd slap me? And finally, by consensual sex, do you mean that skinny guy biting me so that I still have a scar, or the skinny one burning me with a cigarette on the inside of my leg? Is that what you mean by consensual sex?*"

Randy sat silently watching the attorney's mouth open and close without any words coming from it.

"*Because if that's what you mean, then I do understand the difference between consensual sex and rape.*

And what those two guys did to me was rape. I didn't want to have any kind of sex with them that night or at any time since then, and I sure don't want to have sex with them now, or for that matter, have sex with any man."

The courtroom was silent. No one spoke and it seemed that no one breathed.

Stenzel stood in the middle of the courtroom, hands hanging at his sides, sweaty and pale, knowing he had lost his case and that it was too late to change pleas or ask for a deal.

"Counselor, do you have any more questions for the witness?" Judge Catlett asked.

"No, Your Honor."

"Son, you may step down," the judge said with a smile and a nod of his head.

"Your Honor, I would like to say one more thing if that's okay," Randy said.

"Yes, Son?"

"I want to make sure everyone knows I'm not gay. And I want everyone to understand that what they did to me shouldn't be done to anyone. Sex shouldn't be forced on anyone, and those two . . . the defendants . . . forced me to have sex with them."

Randy stood up briefly but sat back down, staring first at the defendants, then at Stenzel.

"If you think I consented to what they did to me, than you're as sick as they are."

Then Randy stood and left the witness stand without waiting for the judge to dismiss him.

Jamie couldn't help smiling at the memory.

"I'll never forget that day as long as I live. I swear to God it happened just the way I told it. You can ask any cop in Waukesha, or I can give you Judge Catlett's number and you can ask him yourself."

Pete smiled and nodded.

"You know, I saw those pictures of Randy taken from Rodemaker's computer, and I freaked," Jamie said. He made a fist, then relaxed and looked at Pete. "Randy's a remarkable kid. If Jeremy wouldn't have adopted him, Kelly and I would have. I'd be proud if my son grew up to be the kind of boy Randy is.

*   *   *

Pete, Summer, Chet, Jamie and Jamie's boss, Captain Jack O'Brien, sat around a metal table in one of the department's conference rooms. Everyone was pretty wasted because it had been a long day. Rodemaker had been photographed, printed, booked and then taken to lockup. He had asked to be placed in solitary confinement, and he was accommodated for his own safety because of the crimes he had committed.

Jamie, Pete and Summer tag-teamed the update for Musgrave and Rawson who were present via conference call. It was agreed beforehand to keep the IPhone, Desert Ranch Ponies and the fake name off the record and out of the report for the time being.

"We've gotten all we possibly can from Rodemaker and from the website. He's gotten updates routinely, including pictures and the latest picture was of the two boys kidnapped in Waukesha," Chet said while rubbing his eyes.

"We need to move quickly but carefully to rescue those two boys as well as any other kids who might be there," Summer said.

"Do you have a plan?" Logan asked.

The group around the table looked at one another, but it was Pete who spoke up.

"It'll take a couple of days, but we're setting up a small team for Chicago; four or five max. We'll do recon ahead of time, but because of the potential number of kids and the fact that we have no idea of the fire power inside the building, we think we'll need recon for at least two, maybe three days."

"Three *days*?" Musgrave barked. "Pete, who knows what will happen to those boys if we wait that long. And, we still have the leak, and if it gets out we're this close to shutting them down, we'll never see those kids again."

"And if we rush this, Logan, we potentially lose those two boys and every other kid," Summer answered. "Can you live with that? I can't!"

Jamie chimed in, "And, I'm not all that certain we know enough in the first place. Rodemaker lied to us too many times tonight. It could all be bullshit."

There was silence on the other end of the line, and the team in the room could only hear snatches of conversation between Musgrave and Rawson.

"We got a federal warrant for tomorrow, but we'll have it reissued given the circumstances," Logan mentioned. "I just don't like the possibility of this leak getting out in the open."

"We've been through these six different ways," O'Brien said, looking from Pete to Summer to Jamie, "and there really is no other way."

"None of us like the wait, but there's no getting around it," Pete said.

"Do you have your team picked?" Doug asked.

"Jamie, two guys from the local PD and me," Pete said.

"Doug will be there sometime tomorrow. In the meantime, keep me in the loop, and that means, every move by anyone associated with this case."

"Do you need anything more from us?" Doug asked. "Anything we can help with?"

"A couple of prayers might help," Summer said lightly.

"You've got that," Doug said. "I'll see you at some point tomorrow. I'll call ahead."

"Pete, one last thing," Logan said. "How's the Indian boy . . . George? Is he okay?"

"He's fine, Logan. He's with a good man and his family . . . in good hands."

"Good. Glad to hear it," Logan said. "Okay, keep me in the loop."

O'Brien punched off the phone and room was silent. For good measure, Pete lifted the receiver off the cradle and listened for a dial tone. The phone was off. They sat and stared at each other for a moment and then Pete's cell signaled an incoming text. Pete opened up the phone, read the text and motioned for Chet to follow him. In the other room, Pete showed him the text, and Chet wrote it down on a pad and then went to his computer. As he began to type, Chet's cell went off.

"Walker."

"Your favorite pervert is on the move."

"Chicago, right?"

"Yup," Morgan answered.

"Okay, got a second number for you. Ready?"

"Yup. I get off on chasing perverts, even late at night when it's past my bedtime."

"Thought you might," Chet said. "And since when do you have a bedtime?"

"Hey, Smart Ass, I have a nine to five job too, you know."

"Yeah, sure," Chet laughed.

"I'll let you know what I get when I get it," and Morgan clicked off.

Pete and Chet walked back into the conference room and sat down at the table.

"Think he bought it?" O'Brien asked.

"We have eyes on him and the other guy," Pete said. "Only time will tell."

CHAPTER THIRTY-FOUR

"We'll need to move quickly to make sure we're there before they move the kids," Chet said.

"But not so quickly that we're careless," Summer cautioned.

"When was the last time we heard from Fitz, Kaupert, or Reilly?" O'Brien asked.

"They've been checking in at fifteen minute intervals," Jamie answered. "All is quiet except for a steady stream of perverts entering and leaving the two buildings and the motel. They've taken pictures of each scumbag, so we can match them to the serve list. They've also given us quite a bit of detail on the entrances and exits and the set up in general."

Given the fact that there were few options because of leaks, Jamie, Pete and Summer decided to go with local law enforcement hand-selected by Jamie and O'Brien. There were a few outsiders brought in for help. A road-weary, Skip Dahlke was flown in from Green Bay along with Marinette County Sheriff Deputy, Earl Coffey. Dahlke would serve as the videographer and would handle forensics in Chicago. Coffey was a gun and would be a part of the Kansas City team. He was former military and Appleton SWAT, who had

moved to northern Wisconsin because of a love of hunting
and fishing, walks in the woods and the peace and quiet that
only the forest can give. He was proficient with virtually any
weapon and had a solid, spotless record in both military and
law enforcement.

O'Brien and Jamie picked members of the team that
had raided Rodemaker's home earlier that evening, including
Gary Fitzpatrick, George 'Charlie' Chan, and Paul Gates, all
from Waukesha PD, and from the Waukesha County Sheriff
Department, Deputies Patrick O'Connor, Tom Albrecht,
Ronnie Desotel and Paul Eiselmann.

Each member of the team had been vetted by Chet.
Each team member knew what was expected of them and
knew that they would have no backup from any local law
enforcement. They were on their own.

Summer had worked up a statement of notification
that would be sent to each enforcement locality once the
three teams made their move. This was coordinated by Pete
at the upper-most level of the FBI. Regular channels
couldn't be used for obvious reasons.

The members of the three teams had been briefed by
Jamie and Pete and had been given their assignments and
deputized as federal agents. Once the teams landed in their
respective city, they'd be updated by the detective on site.

Before they left, O'Brien addressed the group with his hands on his hips. He reminded Pete and Summer of Mr. Clean, like in the commercials. He was completely bald, a chiseled and solid, two hundred ten pounds on a five foot-eleven inch frame. He didn't speak right away but held them at attention with his eyes. Even Pete, Summer and Chet paid attention.

"I like happy endings," was how he began. "I want nothing less for this mission . . . each mission. I expect everyone, including the kids, back home in one piece." He surveyed each person on the team. "Do I make myself clear?"

Almost in unison, each man facing him said, "Yes, Sir!" including Chet and Skip.

Pete nodded and Summer said, "Yup!"

Detective Gary Fitzpatrick, a big red-head who had a passion for weight-lifting and guns, had driven to Chicago the minute Chet and Summer had an address. He'd been undercover for almost two hours as a street person, panhandling for spare change under a street light on the corner of the alley across from the target building. He'd call to the perverts asking for change, and when they turned around to see who had called or when they exited the building, he'd take their picture with a mini camera that had a three gig memory stick.

With his cell, he took pictures of the front of the building, the alley, the front door and a service entrance that had a steel roll-down door, much like the bay of a car service center. He had limped along the wall of the building adjacent to the target building, using the gray brick wall as a support as he scouted the back of the building. He urinated against the wall but also took a picture of an entrance that seemed to have been seldom, if ever used, judging by the amount of debris and overgrown weeds.

He ambled back to the front of the alley, resisting the urge to charge in and save those kids. The urge wasn't easy to suppress, but he did anyway knowing that by going in solo, he'd do more harm than good.

There were security cameras above each entrance that would somehow have to be avoided before entering, and then neutralized as soon as possible when a team member gained access. Rodemaker said he saw at least three guards on duty at any one time, but there could be any number of men watching over the kids, more or less than the three he had seen on his visit. If there were guards, there would be guns. If there were guns, there would be a battle. And if there was a battle, kids might get in the way and get hurt or worse, killed. They'd have to work it out so that didn't happen.

Detective Gavin Reilly, who considered himself a cowboy even though he lived in a city, flew to Los Angeles at just about the same time Fitz left for Chicago and mirrored what Fitz had done in Chicago. Like Fitz, Reilly had posed as a homeless man and worked the corner across from a three story building in the warehouse district of west Los Angeles, near Long Beach. The building had a similar look to the one in Chicago but seemed to serve more perverts judging by the foot traffic. It had a dirty, gray color, and like the Chicago building, had three entrances, two of which were used, and one that was a vehicle entrance.

In Kansas City, Kansas, Nathan Kaupert, a Detective with the Waukesha County Sheriff Department who was known for stale donuts, stale coffee and stale jokes followed the same game plan as Reilly and Fitzpatrick had. This was trickier, however, because the site was a low rent, run down motel adjacent to a truck stop. Kaupert dressed in a red flannel shirt and jeans and baseball cap. He wore boots and shoved a pair of gloves into his back pocket, playing the part of a trucker.

According to the Desert Ranch Ponies website, four boys would be "available for your every pleasure" for the next five days. Judging by the foot traffic of men going to and from the motel, Kaupert guessed that there was one boy in each of four rooms. There were no back doors, only a front door on each unit that opened to a side of the hotel, perpendicular to a courtyard. There were no security cameras. The four rooms were visible from the motel office but were otherwise blocked from site by the rest of the motel. Kaupert reported to Jamie that a team of five would be needed: one officer for two rooms each, with the other three covering the guards.

Kaupert spotted three of them.

Chet's cell chirped.

"Walker."

"Sears is at a Sheraton in downtown Chicago. I know this because he was called by one of the numbers you had asked me to watch."

"You're positive," Chet said more as a statement than a question.

"Yup. More importantly, you've got a problem," Morgan said.

"Pete, Jamie . . . you better listen," Chet said. "I'm going to put you on speaker."

"I don't think you should. Make sure you're secure."

Puzzled, Chet motioned to Summer, Pete and Jamie to follow him into the conference room.

"Okay, we're secure," Chet said putting the cell on speaker.

"Who's we?" Morgan asked.

The three of them looked at each other, then back to the cell.

"This is FBI Agent Storm," Summer said. "With me is my partner, Pete Kelliher, Detective Jamie Graff of the Waukesha Police Department, and Chet Walker, who you already know. What's going on?"

"Chet gave me three numbers to monitor. The first, Gary Sears, who we think is running the kiddie porn website from his IPhone is now in downtown Chicago staying at a Sheraton. He received a phone call from the second number you gave me to monitor. The call was made approximately ten minutes ago, but if you like, I can give you the exact time and the duration of the phone call."

Summer frowned at the cell, then at Chet. She shrugged to say, 'Okay, what's the big deal?'

"You said we had a problem," Chet said.

"A call was made by Sears to the third number you wanted me to monitor, belonging to another FBI agent, who I believe you already know. This guy is also in Chicago, at the same Sheraton.

"The problem is that this FBI agent contacted still another mobile number," Morgan said. "This call was made approximately two minutes after the first call ended."

"And?" Pete said, beginning to get annoyed.

"And . . . the guy who received the call is in Waukesha, Wisconsin. That's where you are, correct?"

"Who received the call?" Jamie said, bending down over the cell.

"Working on that . . . should have a name for you in about fifteen minutes or so."

"Can you pinpoint where the call was received?" Summer said.

"I followed the cell towers. The receiver is headed west from the downtown area. The next tower that picked up was a Verizon tower on Sunset, but the call continued north. I'm figuring the guy is in a car moving at approximately twenty-five miles an hour, a city speed limit. The call switched to a Verizon tower just east of Highway 57, which is when the call ended. It lasted approximately nine minutes."

"You said you were looking for a third man . . . from the Arizona shooting wearing a baseball cap and sunglasses," Jamie said. "Any chance this could be the guy?"

Pete, Summer and Chet looked at Jamie. Then, Summer turned back to Pete showing the alarm in her expression. A slow realization spread across Pete's face.

She said, "Pete, what is the possibility the guy who shot those two assholes in Pembine is still in Wisconsin?"

"Possible. Why?"

Jamie answered for her. "Because someone had George's family killed, and this same someone had intended to kill George. George is still in Wisconsin . . . Waukesha to be exact. And according to Chet's contact, he might be headed to find George."

Pete and Jamie left the conference room on the run, with Jamie pulling out his cell.

CHAPTER THIRTY-FIVE

A light breeze blew through the slightly open window in George's room. He had been sleeping with just a sheet because Jeremy liked to have windows open at night, opting to keep the air conditioner set at the mid-70's before it turned on. He was used to the dry heat of Arizona, but was having trouble adjusting to the humidity of Wisconsin.

He woke up from a troubling dream . . . perhaps. Perhaps, because the Navajo believed in the spirit world and the spirit world was interwoven in dreams. George had to consider the possibility that his grandfather had visited him. George didn't think he actually spoke to him, however. His grandfather was present, but George couldn't decide whether his grandfather had beckoned him or had warned him. Beckoned him to where? Warned him about what?

He lay on his back, arms under his head, staring at the ceiling fan that didn't produce much of anything by way of cool air. He hadn't noticed until just then that he had been crying. George was profoundly sad. He had loved his mother and grandmother, his brothers and sister. But who he had really missed was his grandfather. His grandfather was his greatest teacher, his greatest influence, his greatest mentor. His grandfather was his best friend.

He began to weep again. Where would he go? Where would he live? He had no answers, no ideas. He was scared. And lonely.

He got up out of bed, took his knife and crept down the hall soundlessly, past Jeremy's room, past the twins' room, down the stairs to the kitchen and the back door. He opened it and shut it quietly behind him, and sat down on the cement porch step facing the backyard. The night felt good. The mist was light and cool.

He sat head down, staring at the knife his grandfather had given him. The blade was shiny and sharp. The shaft was eight inches long, and the handle was an extra four inches and made of elk bone bound to the shaft with leather. It had balance and heft and fit his hand much like it was naturally made for it. His grandfather had wanted to give it to George during his coming of age ceremony on top of a plateau facing a sunrise with only his grandfather and George present, but instead had given to George a couple of weeks early.

His grandfather had practiced with him each day in the morning just before sun up. To a casual observer, the routine looked much like karate or some other form of eastern combat. It was defensive in nature, using slashes, slices and cuts rather than thrusts and stabs. Though he was predominantly right handed, George was proficient with either hand. He was quick and lethal, dancing lightly on the balls of his feet, breathing evenly through his nose. His grandfather encouraged him and taught him to think calmly and clearly because his life and the lives of others would depend on it; could depend on it.

He had learned at an early age how to observe, to watch the land around him, to study the people nearby. He had listened to his grandfather and had learned how to study sign, to listen to changes in sounds around him, to smell scents that changed. His grandfather had taught him that all of life, and ultimately death, was connected. He learned that he needed to be respectful towards life, reverent.

His grandfather was a singer, which in the Navajo religion was similar to a priest or minister. George was learning the traditional songs and prayers of the Navajo, which he and his grandfather performed after the lessons with the knife as the sun rose in the east over their land each and every morning; each and every morning for the past two years.

He had grown up speaking English, Spanish, and Navajo, which is a very difficult and now almost extinct language that only his mother, his grandfather and grandmother spoke in his family. His brother, William wasn't interested, and his younger brother and sister were too young to understand the importance of this tradition, the Navajo language. His cousin Leonard knew only a few words or phrases.

George stared at his knife and came back to his dream. His grandfather was in front of him, a worried look on his face. Was he beckoning him to something, or was he trying to keep him away from something? George couldn't decide. He was deep into his thoughts, but was not startled to find Jeremy sitting down on the step next to him. Though Jeremy had moved quietly, George had heard him.

He put his arm around George's bare shoulders, and George moved closer to Jeremy, allowing himself to be held. He liked Jeremy, found him to be sensitive and caring. There was goodness about him. His grandfather had taught him to look for those qualities in others and then to surround himself with the people who had possessed these qualities. He liked both Randy and Billy and thought that in another time, in another place, they would be good friends. George didn't know many biligaana, but George understood that his grandfather would have liked this little family. He flashed back to a discussion with his grandfather years ago about biligaana with hearts of the Dine.

"George, I can't imagine what you're going through," Jeremy said softly, almost in a whisper. "I'm so sorry."

A rabbit hopped out of the hedge line on the left side of the yard, separating the Evan's house from the Schuster house, a family he had not yet met. George lowered his head, weeping again. Jeremy hugged him closer and kissed the top of his head.

George was as tall as the twins, maybe a bit shorter, and lankier. He wasn't as solidly built, but that wasn't to say he wasn't strongly built. Jeremy had coached for years and knew an athlete by a certain look, a certain walk. George had both.

"The boys and I have been talking, and we'd like you to consider living with us."

Jeremy stopped at that. The boy had just lost his family, and they knew nothing of one another. Yet, Jeremy had a gut feeling about George, much as he had about Randy when he had first met him. In so many ways, he had the twin's sensitivity, Randy's seriousness, and Billy's athleticism. Again, it was only a hunch, but Jeremy rarely missed on people.

Yet, they had only known each other for less than a day, and George had to be reeling from the loss of everything in his life, including all of those who had meant so much to him. He couldn't imagine the loss this boy experienced. Even in his grief, his sadness, George caught a scent of cologne, different from the deodorant he or Jeremy used. It was faint, but present. At first he thought it was the lilacs at the corner of the house, but it wasn't. He had recognized it as being similar to the cologne or aftershave various male tourists wore when they visited or drove through the reservation.

Jeremy noticed that George had said nothing and was just staring off into backyard. Perhaps he should have waited until morning to have had this talk. *Real* morning and not the *middle of the night* morning.

"I hope you consider the offer. We'd love to have you." Jeremy said sincerely.

It didn't even seem like George had heard a word.

"Mr. Jeremy, I'm tired," George said with a yawn and stretching. "Let's go back inside and go to bed."

They stood on the porch facing each other, and Jeremy held George's face gently and said, "It might not seem like it right now, George, but things have a way of working out. You'll be okay."

George embraced him and then without another word, George opened the door and waited for Jeremy to enter. He did, and before George followed, he took one last look at the backyard and then shut the door behind him, taking care to lock the dead bolt and the chain.

Jeremy turned to say something, but George put a hand on Jeremy's chest and said very calmly, "Mr. Evans, there's someone in the backyard."

*   *   *

"He's not answering!" Pete said through clenched teeth. "How much longer?"

Jamie stared straight ahead driving as fast as he dared. They had decided not to use police frequency for fear of it being monitored, and they didn't want to call the house land line because it might alarm the intruder, especially at this late hour, so they reluctantly decided to use cell phones.

"About fifteen minutes."

"I hope that's not fifteen minutes too late," Pete said as he tried calling Jeremy again.

*   *   *

"Are you sure?" Jeremy asked. "I didn't see anyone," he added, though he also had to admit to himself that he wasn't really looking for anyone either.

"Yes, Sir . . . positive. He was in those trees or bushes on the left side . . . towards the back of the yard. He was trying to be quiet, but he made noise."

"Not a cat or dog or something?"

"No, Sir."

Jeremy moved towards the window, but George held him back.

"Don't. I don't think it would be a good idea for him to know that we know about him. I think you should call Agent Pete or Detective Jamie and then wake up Randy and Billy. Tell them not to make any noise though."

"My cell is in the bedroom. I'll make the call, but I want you to head down to the basement."

Jeremy went to the door and held it open for him. George nodded and started to walk that direction. As Jeremy headed down the hallway to the stairs, George took hold of the door and shut it just as quickly. Instead of going down to the basement, he headed to the living room and out the front door. George couldn't explain it, but it seemed that his grandfather walked with him, actually leading him. That calmed him some, though his heart thudded in his chest.

"Shadow, be calm. Think clearly. Move quickly, but silently."

"Yes, Grandfather."

"He cannot see you until it's time to strike."

"Yes, Grandfather."

George never said a word out loud, but the conversation was clear, just as the vision of his grandfather was clear. He was never so happy to see him.

"Slow down. Control your breathing. Concentrate. Focus."

George did as he was told. He stayed in the shrubs and bushes at the front of the Evans' house, but he felt very exposed, and the mulch stuck to and poked his bare feet. Still, if his grandfather was leading him, this must be where he needed to be.

At the corner of the house, George stopped; stooped low and peeked around the corner looking for the man. He didn't see the man right away but saw his grandfather holding his arm out, telling George to stay where he was. George nodded that he understood. His grandfather turned and smiled at him.

"Now, Shadow. Slowly, very quietly. Control your breathing. Focus."

George nodded and then crept forward and peeked around the side of the house. There, fifteen yards in front of him, stood a man in black, looking into one of the family room windows. George looked up and saw that the window was just below the window to the room he had been sleeping in.

The man stood about six-one, was slender, and when he moved his right hand from the window screen, a glint of light shown on the gun he held.

*   *   *

"Dad, where's George?"

Randy and Billy had sprinted down the stairs in the dark expecting to find George waiting for them.

"George, where are you?" Jeremy called softly.

"George . . . George," Billy called.

"Dad, he's not here!" Randy whispered urgently. "Where is he?"

Stunned, Jeremy had an idea where he was but didn't like that thought, at all. He turned on his cell and called Pete back to report that they were in the basement, but George wasn't with them.

*   *   *

"Almost there," Jamie said. "Five minutes."

"That was Jeremy," Pete said.

Jamie glanced over at Pete because of the tone of voice he had used.

"George is missing."

"Jesus *Fuck*!" Jamie said. "Call O'Brien and tell him what's happening. We'll need backup."

"Just get us there, God Dammit!"

*   *   *

George crept low, knife out in front of him. He was silent. He felt nothing, no emotion. His breathing slow, rhythmic. Focused.

George stared at the man's right hand, because that was the hand that held the gun. He'd have to attack the man before the man attacked him.

Five yards. Four.

The man, perhaps sensing someone was close, began a slow turn to his right, just as George thought he might. George, under control, closed the distance quickly, much like how a wrestler might approach an opponent.

George had an advantage the man didn't recognize: the man underestimated George because he was a boy.

As the man turned to face George, his right hand came up. George slashed with his sharp, heavy knife and connected. At first, the man didn't realize what had happened or who or what had hit him. It felt is if someone had batted his hand, but then it began to sting, then ache, then throb. The pain was on him suddenly. The gun was on the ground, along with three and a half of the man's fingers. What was left of the hand pulsed blood.

"What the . . ." the man said.

He stared at George, then down at his hand, then back at George.

"You little Mother Fucker!" the man snarled.

He took a step towards George and swung at him with his left hand. George stepped deftly to the right, under the man's swinging arm and sliced his inner thigh, high up towards the groin. He danced back to his left and sliced the man's other inner thigh, again up high. The man stopped, felt the pain and understood the danger, then blindly, stepped forward once again, swinging wildly with both arms.

George danced first left, then right, and in two quick moves, sliced the man's right armpit. George knew that the groin was one of the more delicate and vulnerable spots for any opponent, especially men, but the armpit controlled the arm.

The man stopped in his tracks, then staggered backwards, reaching for the side of the house with his left hand to brace himself.

"What the fuck did you do?" the man asked.

George knew the man was in shock, and his thinking would get less clear as time went on, coinciding with the loss of blood.

"You're bleeding to death," George said softly, not gloating, but just stating a fact, much like one might comment on the weather.

The man looked down at his hand, then at his groin, which was now throbbing with pain and slick with blood. His right arm hung uselessly at his side. He noticed the gun and his fingers on the ground.

"Don't," George warned.

The man smiled, staggered forward, and bent to reach for the gun with is left hand. George stepped forward and swung, slicing through skin and bone as if nothing was there. And in fact, nothing was there as more fingers fell to the ground next to the gun, and like the other hand, what was left pulsed blood.

The man stared first at his left hand, then at his right and then at George. He seemed to want to say something, perhaps to scream, but nothing issued forth. The man staggered backwards, fell against the house and slid to the ground among the mini-rose bushes that had been planted there. George stared at the man, lowering the knife to his side. He heard a car break to a stop out in front of the house, and then heard the heavy footfalls of men running.

"George, are you okay?" Jamie asked.

"Yes, Sir," George said, then pointing at the side of the house with his knife, he said, "He's dying."

CHAPTER THIRTY-SIX

As Jamie and Pete ran up to George, Jeremy came racing out the back door calling George's name. No one had time to answer before he rounded the corner and spied him with the two men.

"George, are you alright?"

"Yes, Sir."

Jeremy gripped his shoulders and gave him the once over, noticing the bloody knife. He dropped his hands off the boy and took a step back.

"What the . . ?"

Neither Jamie nor Pete said anything, but both turned towards the man slumped over in the rose bushes.

"He's gone," Pete said.

"George, what happened?" Jamie asked.

He explained about not sleeping well, getting up and sitting on the back steps. While Jeremy talked with him, he noticed the man hiding in the hedge row at the left side of the yard.

"Jesus, George," Jeremy said, taking hold of his shoulders again. "You scared me to death. Are you sure you're all right?"

"Yes, Sir . . . I'm okay," George said, hanging his head. "I'm sorry."

Pete approached the boy and said, "Start at the beginning, George. What happened?"

George stared at the ground as he told the story, minus the vision of and conversation with his grandfather.

"Where did you learn to use a knife like that?" Pete asked.

"My grandfather taught me." George showed them the knife and said, "He gave me this when I turned twelve. We practiced every morning." Lowering his head again, he added, "I'm sorry."

Jamie called O'Brien and told them what had happened. O'Brien had actually started over to the Evan's house with Summer, and said they'd be there in less than ten minutes. Pete told Jamie to send for Skip Dahlke to run the forensics.

"We'll need the ME," Jamie said to his boss.

"Let us get there before we decide exactly what to do," O'Brien answered.

*   *   *

George sat at the kitchen table, hands in his lap and his head down. Randy and Billy tried talking to him but had given up because George didn't answer. So, Randy and George sat in silence, while Billy watched through the kitchen window that was over the sink. O'Brien, Jamie, Pete, Jeremy and Summer had huddled together in the backyard. O'Brien and Summer did most of the talking from what Billy had seen.

When the adults started for the backdoor, Billy quickly sat down across from Randy and said, "They're coming."

The group entered the kitchen through the back door, and Jeremy asked the twins to go to their bedroom while they spoke with George. Randy gripped George's shoulder as they got up from the table. George looked up briefly at Jeremy, eyes brimming, and then back down at the table.

"George," O'Brien began, "What you did was incredibly dangerous."

George nodded just once.

"It was also incredibly brave."

George didn't agree or disagree, but wiped his eyes with the backs of his hands before replacing them in his lap. The men looked at each other and then at Summer.

"George, can you tell us one more time what happened and don't leave anything out, okay?"

This time, George told them about his dream, then sitting on the porch, seeing the rabbit hop from the hedges, smelling the cologne, and then finally, seeing the man hiding in the hedges. He told them about the vision and the conversation with his grandfather. He never looked at them. He never lifted his eyes off the table. He didn't move but once or twice to wipe tears from his eyes.

"That man came here because of me. I could not let him hurt Mr. Jeremy or the twins. I think my grandfather understood that. I think that is why he came to me. I did not mean to kill him, though."

"George, no one . . . and I mean *no one*, thinks you killed that man on purpose," Summer said.

"I had to make sure he would not use the gun," George sobbed. "He was reaching for it with his left hand, and I warned him. I said, 'Don't.' He knew what I meant, but he had a kind of sick smile," George sobbed again. "I could not let him get the gun," he repeated to Summer, and then to Jeremy. "I could not let him hurt you or the twins."

"George, look at me," Summer said reaching for his hands. "Look at me," she said again softly.

George looked at her but kept glancing at Jeremy, who remained unreadable, arms folded across his chest.

"What you did was self-defense. You defended and protected Jeremy, Randy, Billy and yourself. If you wouldn't have, he most certainly would have killed you and everyone in this house." She paused to let that sink in and then repeated, "Self-defense."

George dropped his eyes back to the table and wiped them with the back of his hands before he did so.

"What you did was very, very dangerous," Summer said. "But like Captain O'Brien said, it was also incredibly brave." She paused, took his chin in her hand, so he was looking at her. "Just please, don't ever, *ever* do that again. Okay?"

George nodded, but stole a glance at Jeremy before looking back at the table.

*   *   *

With all the noise, cars, ambulance and people milling around the Evan's house, Jon Lane had phoned to ask if everyone was okay. Jeremy had assured him that all was fine and that he'd explain in the morning. A story had been concocted by Jamie, Pete and O'Brien that someone was thought to have been in the backyard, but it was a false alarm. Still, given the circumstances of the evening, it had to be checked out thoroughly. Fortunately, none of the police nor the ambulance used sirens or their light bars. And luckily, Mary Schuster and her son had been out of town, while the rest of the street had simply slept through all of it.

Before transporting the body back to the basement of Waukesha Memorial Hospital, the ME and Skip Dahlke had photographed, printed and catalogued the fingers of the man, hoping to use them to identify him. It was gruesome picking up fingers from the ground swimming in a pool of blood. The ME would put together the meat puzzle, matching the fingers to the placement of the hand back at the coroner's office.

The man was carrying an Arizona driver license with the name Graham Porter, but Summer thought it might be a fake. She had taken a picture of the license with her cell and sent it to Chet, and then waited for him to do some digging on it.

Skip Dahlke worked the scene, asking George to walk through it with him. Still in bare feet, George pointed to the side of the house where the man stood, then at the ground where the fingers had been, where the gun was, and where the blood still appeared like thick, chocolate syrup on the ground.

He and George walked through the backyard backtracking, looking for any signs of where the man might have walked. Finally they walked slowly through the hedges shining the little flashlight James held. When all the evidence had been collected and there wasn't much left other than the scene of the knife fight, the gun and the blood, Skip said good night and drove back to the station, and George went into the house.

A light was on over the kitchen sink, and the rest of the house was dark. George tiptoed up the stairs to the hallway bathroom and cleaned himself up and then went to his bedroom and crawled into bed. He lay on his stomach with his arms under his pillow and wept, feeling more alone now than ever. The way Jeremy had backed away from him, had looked at him, had barely spoken to him seemed to tell him that Jeremy didn't want anything to do with him. Jamie had taken the knife his grandfather had given him, because it was evidence, and George hoped he'd get it back, but was afraid to ask.

Jeremy said he was welcome to live with them and while he hadn't even had time to think about it, he knew there was no way they'd want him to live with them now. Not someone who had murdered some guy, self-defense or not. A man was dead because of him. Yes, he did it to protect himself, Jeremy and the twins, but a man was dead.

He felt guilty and ashamed. He had been taught from little on to respect life. Yet, his grandfather had woken him up and had led him out to fight the man. Clearly, his grandfather had wanted him to protect himself and the others. It was confusing, but the confusion didn't help remove the shame or the guilt.

He heard the door open and knew Jeremy had waited up for him. He didn't know what Jeremy would say, but George was afraid, sad and lonely. It did no good to pretend to sleep, because he was crying quite heavily. Jeremy sat down on the side of the bed and gently rubbed George's bare back and shoulders. George didn't move nor speak and seemed to cry harder.

Jeremy didn't speak for quite a while, but when he did, he said, "George, I want to thank you."

George said nothing.

"Like they said, what you did was dangerous, but it was also very courageous. You saved our lives as well as your own."

Still, George said nothing.

"I was so frightened that something had happened to you or that someone had taken you. You were entrusted to my care, and I was afraid I had failed you. I was angrier with myself than with you, angry that you had confronted that man instead of me."

He was silent again. He stroked George's soft, long black hair, moving it away from his face, pushing it behind his ear.

"George, I don't know how I can ever repay you. You saved Randy's and Billy's life, as well as yours and mine. I can't ever repay you for that."

George snuffled and wiped his eyes with the sheet.

"George, can you look at me?"

George rolled over onto his back and blinked back tears, trying to hold eye contact with Jeremy.

"I meant what I said earlier tonight. We'd like you to live with us." Gently, Jeremy wiped tears away from George's eyes with his thumbs. "Please consider it, okay?'

George nodded, and Jeremy bent down to kiss his forehead.

"The boys and I would like that very much."

George nodded again, tears welling up in his eyes. Jeremy kissed his forehead again, got up from the bed and left the room, leaving the door slightly ajar.

CHAPTER THIRTY-SEVEN

About the same time Jeremy and George had fallen asleep; two charter planes took off from Mitchell International Airport. One plane carrying Patrick O'Connor, Paul Eiselmann and George "Charlie" Chan flew to Los Angeles where it would land in Long Beach. The three officers would then hook up with Gavin Reilly who was already there doing recon on the building holding twelve boys as prisoners.

O'Connor could be described as non-descript. He wore his brown hair longish, had a narrow, hawk-like look about him, was of medium height, thin build and was made for undercover drug work, which is what he did for the Waukesha County Sheriff Department. His best friend since high school was a red-haired, freckle-faced guy named Paul Eiselmann, who was a head shorter than O'Connor and built like a fire hydrant. His looks made it impossible for him to work undercover. So instead, he was muscle on the gang task force and usually took point on SWAT work. "Charlie" Chan, of course worked technology, usually a camera, but was good and dependable to have on your side during a fire fight.

The other charter carried Earl Coffey, Tom Albrecht, Ronnie Desotel, and Paul Gates to Kansas City, Kansas, where they would hook up with Nathan Kaupert at the sleazy hotel where four of the boys were held as sex slaves. Coffey kept his words as short as his dark hair, wore a perpetual smirk on his face and had a laugh ready. When he put on a SWAT jacket, he was all business ready to kick ass. Tom Albrecht and Ronnie Desotel were as good of friends as O'Connor and Eiselmann were. Like O'Connor and Eiselmann, Albrecht and Desotel were Waukesha County Sheriff Deputies. Albrecht was a stud athlete in high school, started smoking sometime afterwards, and usually had one hanging out of his mouth unless he was working SWAT. Then, he'd tuck a plug of chew in between his lower lip and his teeth. Desotel, dark, short with a quick wit and a very smart mouth, constantly rode Albrecht to quit. So far, Albrecht hadn't listened.

As the two planes took off from Mitchell Field, two vehicles drove in a caravan to Chicago, about an hour and a half south and east of Waukesha. One vehicle, a dark panel van driven by Jamie Graff, carried Pete and Skip Dahlke. They would hook up with Gary Fitzpatrick, undercover as a homeless man outside the building where thirteen boys were held captive and forced into prostitution. The other vehicle, a non-descript, four door driven by Jack O'Brien, carried Summer and Chet. They were headed to a Sheraton in downtown Chicago.

Chet had pleaded to go with Pete and Jamie, but Summer had held firm, knowing he would be needed at the Sheraton. Like 'Big Brother', Morgan Billias was on stand-by from some undetermined location monitoring cell phones and locations of several of the players. Sulking in the backseat, Chet had dosed off.

Each of the teams would have wire microphones that would fit unobtrusively on the inside of a shirt collar. They would also have matching wireless ear pieces in order to hear one another. One member of each team would have a small, but powerful camera that would fit onto a shirt button. These cameras would give eyes to the backup entry team who would let them know what was taking place inside. They would wait on the outside for a predetermined signal from the team member who entered the site before they entered to free the kids, and then arrest whoever was on the inside stupid enough to put up a fight.

Each team was armed with a federal warrant signed by a judge in Milwaukee. Summer had made a phone call to a number in D.C. while standing in the living room of Judge Robert Packwood at 2:34 AM CST. She then handed the phone to Packwood standing impatiently in his pajamas and bathrobe, who listened to the voice on the other end and without another word, signed the four warrants allowing No Knock searches and Force As Necessary with dynamic entries even though minors were present. The thought was that a Knock Search might put the kids and the officers in more danger. The signed warrants also allowed the officers to seize any and all electronics, including thumb drives, cell phones, floppy disks, CDs and DVDs, as well as any papers or documents that might be found on the premises. Summer also obtained arrest warrants for three individuals, two of which she knew by face and name. She looked forward to reading them their rights.

The teams were heavily armed. Besides .350 Magnum side arm they would also have at their disposal Springfield M1A semi-automatic .308 caliber rifles using 168 grain bullets. Ironically, this weapon was identical to the weapon used to kill George's family. Fitz, in Chicago, preferred a pump action shotgun, and he always carried it on SWAT detail, as did Earl Coffey, who was on the plane to Kansas City.

The fact that Graham Porter had driven to Waukesha under orders to kill George and perhaps Jeremy and the twins, forced the four teams into action sooner than they had planned. And purposely, they did not tell Musgrave or Rawson they were moving forward that soon.

On a hunch and on advice from Chet, Summer used Porter's IPhone to send a reply to a text message Porter had received that gave him Jeremy's home address. She had taken it with her when she left the Evan's home and after the body had been removed from the premises.

Her message simply said, "Job completed."

Moments later, Summer received a message back that said, "Meet us in Chicago in the morning."

Summer smiled as she read the reply out loud to O'Brien and Chet. She was looking forward to meeting them in Chicago and couldn't wait to see the expressions on their faces as she walked in on them.

Morgan Billias phoned Chet to confirm that the message was received and then sent by one of the phones he was monitoring and that the location of this phone was the Sheraton in downtown Chicago. Summer, O'Brien and Chet thought the sending of the message and the reply bought the four teams time, as well as an element of surprise. Everyone was exhausted. There had been very little sleep and only a quick bite to eat from a brown sack that held more grease than food. At least, it was warm and filled the stomach . . . sort of.

The three assault teams had planned their penetrations and tactics based upon the recon provided by eyes and ears on the ground, as well as information given to them by Rodemaker. No one deemed Rodemaker's intel very reliable because of the pattern of lies and deception earlier that evening. Even the carrot of a 'deal' in 'exchange for cooperation' didn't make anyone believe Rodemaker. Still, any information was better than no information.

*   *   *

Fitzpatrick ambled two blocks to a dark alley, took off his green army jacket and his scruffy gray wig, walked back to the street and climbed into his tan Ford Taurus and drove five blocks to a small all-night diner. He studied his rearview and side mirrors as he did so. In the parking lot, he sat quietly watching for passing cars or anyone following him and when satisfied that there was no one or nothing out of the ordinary, got out of his car locking it behind him and went in.

He took a few steps in and waited until his eyes adjusted, then spied Jamie and Pete and a young skinny kid with short blond hair, a pointy nose and Harry Potter-like wire rims. He slid into the booth next to Jamie.

"Hey Fitz," Jamie said as he shook his hand. "You remember Pete?"

Fitz said, "Nice seeing you again," and shook his hand.

"This is Skip Dahlke," Pete said. "He's going to run forensics for us, videotape if need be, and be an extra gun. You and he will take the alley entrance, the one with the garage door, while I enter from the front after Jamie gives the all clear."

"I've not seen anyone leave that didn't go in. I sent the pictures to Chet with my phone, but it's almost dead. I'm charging it."

"How many guards do you think?" Jamie asked.

Fitz shook his head, taking a sip of the hot, black coffee Jamie had ordered for him.

"No way to tell. Could be three . . . could be five . . . could be fifteen. No way to know until we're inside."

They stared at each other and drank their coffee in silence.

*   *   *

Similar conversations took place in Kansas City and in Long Beach, with similar answers. It turned out that

Kansas City might be the easiest to take. There were only four rooms, one for each of the boys, and two others on either end of the four that served as bookends for the guards. One had two men in it, while the other had one. The office manager would have to be taken, since he had to know what was taking place in his motel. In Long Beach, the situation was very similar to Chicago. There was no way to know how many guards were on the inside.

It was decided that one person from each team would have to pose as a paying customer. In Chicago, it would be Jamie. In Long Beach, it would be Pat O'Connor. In Kansas City, it would be Tom Albrecht, minus his chew. That would be a first.

The three teams readied themselves a block away from their targets. They were silent and grim-faced, but determined. They knew the stakes were high, and they knew that the odds were stacked against them. It wouldn't be easy, but somehow, some way, they had to save those kids.

CHAPTER THIRTY-EIGHT

Summer, Chet and O'Brien arrived at the Sheraton at 4:37 AM, CST. O'Brien and Chet stayed in the background while Summer went to the front desk. She asked the young female desk clerk named Bethany for the night manager.

A tall, skinny man in his early thirties wearing a green blazer with a white button-down shirt and green tie came to the front desk and asked, "How can I help you?"

Summer displayed colored pictures of three men, printed earlier that morning at the Waukesha Police station.

"Can you tell me if these three men are here at the hotel?"

"I'm sorry . . . I can't give out that kind of information because we have to respect the privacy of . . ."

Summer took her FBI credentials out of her pocket and said, "*Now*, can you tell me if these three men are here at the hotel?"

The manager mumbled and then took hold of the three pictures, played a bit with his computer console and nodded, "Yes, well, two of them, I do believe, they've arrived. They checked in separately." He separated one of the photos and tapped it with his index finger. "Not this man. Would you like me to ring them?"

"No. I don't want them to know I asked about them."
Then Summer asked, "Do I make myself clear?"

"Yes, Ma'am, very clear."

"Good. Because if one or all of them find out I've asked about them, you'll be arrested for obstruction, and the hotel will suffer needless embarrassment. Do I make myself clear?"

"Absolutely, Ma'am."

Summer and Chet went into the restaurant to get some coffee and to wait. O'Brien grabbed a free USA Today and sat in a comfortable chair in the lobby facing the bank of elevators. Chet set Summer up with a small, rather innocuous looking tube that resembled a pen that was in reality, a very powerful microphone. Hooked wirelessly to his computer, he could record virtually any conversation that took place in the restaurant. No one but Summer, Chet and one waiter were in the restaurant at that hour, however it would fill up quickly with patrons for the breakfast buffet.

The waiter asked what he and Summer would like, and Summer ordered coffee for both of them and one to go for O'Brien. The waiter nodded and disappeared through a doorway in the back.

Chet called Morgan to let them know they had arrived and that he'd be hacking into the hotel security cameras to monitor several areas at once using split screen.

"I'll be waiting," he said with a yawn.

"Thanks. I owe you."

"I already told you, I want these perverts as bad as you do, so you don't owe me anything."

He clicked off and Chet nodded at Summer.

"We're set."

*   *   *

Jamie pushed the buzzer just as Rodemaker told him to. Fitz, in the guise of a homeless wino, who had watched pervert after pervert push that same buzzer earlier that night and early morning confirmed that this was the procedure.

"Yeah?" was the response from the other end.

"Um . . . I have money and would like to spend it," Jamie said, not sure what else to say.

Silence. It seemed like a long time, and Jamie thought about giving up and walking away and rejoin the others to come up with a different plan.

"It's fucking early," the voice said.

"I wanted . . . you know . . . before I went to work."

"Third floor. Meet you there."

Jamie resisted the urge to give a thumbs up to the others because he knew about the camera above the door, as well as the camera in the alley. Fitz had begun ambling down the alley, listing and leaning against the far wall just as he had done all morning. He even called out to Jamie asking for money as he had done with all of the other perverts entering and exiting the building. Jamie, playing along, obligingly flipped him off without turning around.

Pete waited impatiently around the corner for Jamie to let him know all was clear. Dahlke had circled the back of the building keeping his distance from Fitz until Fitz let him know when to come forward.

"Guys, stay sharp," Pete said. "Jamie's in."

"Born ready," Fitz said, pumping a shell into the chamber beneath the green army jacket.

"Almost there," Dahlke said breathlessly.

This wasn't what he had in mind after graduating in Forensic Science. In fact, he had never fired a weapon in his life, unless you count suction-cup darts from a toy pistol or bullets from a Nerf gun. And now he was armed with an assault rifle with several extra clips of ammo and a .45mm Magnum. To say he was nervous was an understatement. Yet, he felt that he needed to be there. He knew the importance of being there. He just didn't want to let anyone down, or worse, get himself or anyone else hurt or killed.

Perhaps reading his mind, Pete said, "Take it easy, Skip. You'll be fine. Just listen to what's going on, watch everyone and everything around you, and do what Fitz tells you to do."

"Yeah," was all the response Pete received.

Jamie took the stairs silently, smoothly but not too swiftly. He lingered at the door to the second floor, tempted to take a peek, but resisted the urge, spotting the camera on the landing heading up to the third floor. He moved up the steps, took a deep breath and stood outside the door on the landing.

*   *   *

Chet had moved to the outer lobby after receiving the two coffees. He and O'Brien sat at different ends away from each other. Chet was known by at least two of them, so he had to blend into the woodwork and remain as close to invisible as possible. No one knew O'Brien, so he could hide in plain sight.

Chet had screens open to him on his laptop, which allowed him to monitor the action in the hotel. He'd have to rely on cell calls to get updates from the three locations and relay info to and from them.

Morgan had his ears tuned to what was being said on the three IPhones. Currently, the IPhones were silent. But if Morgan didn't know what was happening in the three different cities, he could at least imagine, and perhaps it was the imagination that had him sitting on the edge of his seat waiting for updates from Chet on what was taking place.

Both Summer and O'Brien were wired for picture and sound. It was Chet's job to monitor and record. Hoping that the three targets would meet and eat before heading to the building in Chicago, Summer sent a text to one of the IPhones letting the person on the other end know that *he* was in Chicago and would wait for him in the hotel restaurant. There wasn't a response yet, but when the phone was turned on, it would let the person know a message was waiting to be opened.

Every now and then, Summer would ask O'Brien if he had seen anything. He held the newspaper and pretended to read it, but couldn't tell you anything about any of the articles other than a headline or two.

Cop work was often sitting, waiting and writing reports. The glamorous stuff you see on TV was fiction. Seldom, if ever, were cops pulling triggers or dodging bullets. So, the three of them waited impatiently, worrying about the three teams trying to free the kids.

*   *   *

Tommy Albrecht went to the motel office, pushed it open, looked over his shoulder, and then shut the door quietly behind him. There were cobwebs in the corner near the window and dead flies lying on the window sill. Dusty tan curtains hung limply from a bent curtain rod. A window air conditioner ran but didn't produce much cool air. A small, skinny, sweaty man in a button down dirty blue shirt, open to reveal a wife-beater t-shirt stood behind the counter.

"Um . . ." Albrecht said.

"You need a room?" the skinny man said with a smirk.

"Well . . . yeah . . . I guess," he answered uncertainly.

"How about the *special*?"

Albrecht didn't answer right away because he wasn't sure exactly what to say.

So after a bit, he simply said, "Um . . . yeah."

The small man just looked at him, not moving, not saying anything.

So Albrecht asked, "Can I have a choice?"

"Just a minute," the man answered with a sly grin.

He reached down and using a key, opened a drawer and took out a thin notebook. He opened it to reveal pictures of four boys, each nude.

"Look through this and you can pick out the one you want. Each kid is available at the moment."

"How much?"

"Depends on how long you want one. The prices are at the bottom of each picture, and there's a price sheet on the back page."

Albrecht browsed through the notebook, sickened at the pictures he saw. In none of the pictures was the boy smiling. Each boy looked scared, maybe angry.

"I think I'll take Cory Rowell for an hour," Albrecht said, sickened at the thought.

"Good choice," the manager said with a smile. "That's $300."

Albrecht counted out three one hundred dollar bills, and as he did so, the manager went to a corner and selected a key from the many that hung there.

While the man was busy getting the key, Albrecht said, "Got it?"

Evidently, the manager didn't hear Albrecht's question, because he said, "Here's the key. You have one hour from now. It'll be $75 for every five minutes you're late, so you want to make sure you get back here on time."

Desotel came into the lobby and shut the door behind him. Seeing Desotel, the manager quickly closed the notebook and dropped it into the drawer behind the counter in the event Desotel wasn't looking for the *special*.

"Can I help you?" the manager asked Desotel.

"Not really, you fuck. You're under arrest."

The manager backed away from the counter, but Desotel hopped over it with ease and threw the man into the wall knocking him down. While he Mirandized him, he pulled plastic ties from the pocket of his light-weight jacket and used them like handcuffs, binding the man's hands behind his back and then used them on his feet. The man complained they were too tight, so Desotel obliged him by taping his mouth shut, dragged him to a back room by the back of the dirty blue shirt and shut the door, and gave him the warning that if there was any noise, he'd make up an excuse to shoot him. The man knew he wasn't kidding. Desotel knew he wasn't kidding either.

The key Albrecht held had a red oblong tag that gave the name of the motel and the room number, which was 110. That meant the room was the second last in the group of four, which put it in the middle of the rooms, two away from the room holding the guards. Desotel handed him the keys for each of the other rooms holding the boys, as well as the keys for the rooms holding the guards. Albrecht walked out of the office, while Ronnie Desotel took the manager's place behind the counter, posing as the manager.

As Albrecht neared the group of four rooms, he said quietly into his shirt collar, "So far, so good. No perverts but me. I have the keys. Meet me half-way, and I'll give them to you. Wait until I enter and shut the door. Earl, take the first room, and Paul, take the sixth, but wait until Nathan and I secure the kids. Nathan, take the second and third rooms. I'll secure the fourth and fifth."

As he put the key into the door lock, Albrecht added, "Good luck guys. Everybody goes home safe."

*   *   *

Jamie stood just inside the third floor doorway in a kind of outer lobby with nothing in it except a computer on a wooden table. He presumed the voice on the other end of the call box belonged to the fat man with long, greasy black hair and a three or four day old beard leaning against the door. He wore a dark green t-shirt that seemed two sizes too small, revealing a fat roll falling over the belt of his jeans. Six pounds of sausage in a two pound casing, Jamie thought. The man's body odor assaulted Jamie about as much as the pictures on the computer console.

Jamie viewed the pictures of eleven boys, but none of whom were of Stephen Bailey or Mike Erickson, the boys taken the evening before. Disheartened, Jamie started over again.

"What type you lookin' for?" the fat man asked.

"Um . . . I don't know," Jamie answered.

"Blond, black- or brown-haired?"

"Brown, I guess."

The fat man tapped the computer screen and pictures of all the blond- and black-haired boys disappeared, showing only five boys, each with brown hair.

The fat man pointed to one of the boys and said, "Try this one. Athletic. Aggressive."

Jamie almost gagged at the man's breath. He looked at the photo and saw a tough, strong boy, eyes shouting hatred and defiance. His name was Brett.

"Yeah . . . Him."

The fat man nodded.

"Be $500 for an hour."

Jamie counted out five one hundred dollar bills and handed them to the fat man, who recounted them again and then stuffed them into his back pocket. He pulled out a set of keys and opened up the door for them.

He led them into a darkened hallway with chipped and dirty industrial green linoleum. On the right side was a small room with glass windows. From the little Jamie saw as they walked past, it held what looked like video equipment, about a dozen, dozen and a half small surveillance television screens, and a phone.

On the left side were metal doors, one after the other like you might find in a prison hallway, but without the bars. Just past the glass-windowed room were more rooms just like the ones on the opposite side of the hallway. Each of the doors opened inward.

The fat man stopped at the third door down on the left side, inserted his key and opened it. Jamie took one last look at either end of the hallway. No one was there. No sounds were heard. He bent down quickly and pulled out a gun clipped to his ankle and shoved it into the man's neck just behind his ear.

"Inside and get on the floor. Don't make any noise, or I'll blow your fuckin' head off. Move . . . now!"

CHAPTER THIRTY-NINE

Tommy Albrecht and Nathan Kaupert timed it so that they had entered their respective target room each at the same time. The first problem they encountered was that each boy had one arm handcuffed to an old fashioned metal bed frame.

"Earl . . . Paul, do either of you have a handcuff key?" Albrecht asked in a whisper.

"Ahh, fuck!" Desotel said. "You shittin' me?"

"I don't," Coffey whispered.

"Neither do I," Gates said quietly.

Albrecht went over to the bed and looked at Cory Rowell, half-hiding under a filthy sheet.

"I'm with the FBI. We're going to get you outta here, but I'm gonna need your help." He paused and then whispered, "Okay?"

Rowell nodded once.

"How much slack do these have?"

Albrecht gently lifted the boy's arm and followed the chain to the bed frame. Not much room to maneuver.

"Can you get down on the floor?"

Rowell got out of bed and went to the side of the bed and was able to lie down awkwardly with his arm up against the bed frame. Albrecht got him a pillow and a blanket to wrap around him, and as he did so, told Kaupert what to do with his boy, Sean Jarvis, next door.

"Cory, stay wrapped up and on the floor. One of us will be back to get you. I promise."

Rowell, who hadn't said anything, nodded.

Albrecht met Kaupert outside the next rooms and signaled to Earl Coffey and Paul Gates to watch the guard's doors. Then on a three count, Albrecht and Kaupert opened the next two rooms; the ones right next to the rooms where the guards were.

*   *   *

"How many guards?" Jamie asked quietly.

The fat man said nothing, so Jamie squatted down in front of the man and loosened the duct tape covering his mouth.

"I asked a question, and I want an answer."

The fat man spit at Jamie who answered by slamming his gun into the side of his head and wiping his face off with his sleeve. Then he replaced the duct tape.

"Seven," the boy said from the bed.

"Seven?" Jamie was shocked.

He and Pete had figured three or four. The boy didn't answer or move. Jamie grimaced and then spoke into his collar.

"Pete, we have at least seven guards, probably all with weapons."

"Christ! Nothing's easy," Pete answered. "Fitz . . . Skip, you copy?"

He received almost simultaneous answers to the affirmative.

"Jamie, we need to get in there and secure the kids," Pete said.

"Working on it."

Jamie turned to the brown-haired boy sitting on the bed.

"You're Brett, right?'

"Who's askin'?"

"I'm Jamie Graff, a policeman working with the FBI."

"There's a cop two doors down fucking Tim. Is he workin' with the FBI too?"

Jamie opened his mouth to answer, but shut it without saying anything. The boy glared at Jamie daring him to say something.

"Look, you don't have to trust me, but I want to get all of you home today, so I'm going to need your help."

The boy continued glaring at Jamie. It was a silent standoff, Jamie hoping for the boy's help, and the boy, not sure if he could trust Jamie.

"I'm Brett . . . McGovern," the boy finally said. He pointed at the fat man groaning on the floor and said, "That fat piece of shit is Butch. Right now, he's the only one awake. What time is it?"

Jamie looked at his watch and said, "About twenty to six."

"We have about thirty . . . maybe forty-five minutes tops, and the others will wake up. The cop should be finished with Tim about the same time. We better hurry."

Naked, he jumped off the bed, and stepped over to the fat man so that he knelt in front of him.

"Hey, Fuckhead," he whispered. He grabbed the fat man by his ears, lifted his head up as far as the fat man's neck would allow and slammed his face into the floor twice in rapid succession. "That should keep you quiet . . . Fuckhead!"

He stood and smiled at Jamie.

"Um, do you have anything you can wear?"

He shook his head.

"None of us do. They don't want us to wear anything at night. We don't get clean boxers until after we shower each morning. Problem is, we're not in 'em all that much."

Jamie was disgusted, angry and sickened at the way the boys were treated, but frankly, he hadn't known what to expect. It was more than horrible and more than a crime. It was beyond anything he had ever worked on or would ever want to work on.

Ever.

Nothing, absolutely nothing could take this memory away. He longed to hold his wife, Kelly, and to hold his son, Garrett. Once he had them in his arms, he vowed to himself right then and there he'd never let go.

"You okay?" Brett asked.

Jamie wiped his eyes and said, "We have to get my men into the building, and we have to get the rest of the kids safe."

"Come on," the boy said he went to the doorway.

He looked both ways and then sprinted quietly to the room with the windows. Jamie caught up with him, and together, searched for the control to the door on the street.

Not finding any, Jamie said, "Go back to your room and wait. I'll go down and open the door."

"No," Brett said. "You stay here and protect the guys. I'll open the door, but you'll have to open it for us because they lock it from the inside."

"Move quickly and silently," Jamie said, not liking the plan at all. "You've got to be careful."

Brett nodded, stuck his head out the doorway, looked both ways and then ran silently to the door, opening it and then shutting it quietly without making any noise.

"Pete, get to the door. Now!"

*   *   *

Albrecht and Kaupert went into their respective rooms and did the same thing with the second set of boys as they had done with the first set. Albrecht helped Greg Montgomery to the floor just as he had with Corey Rowell next door. Kaupert helped Mike Faustino in the last room. The four officers huddled quietly outside of Rowell's room.

"We don't use the key because it'll tip them off," Albrecht said.

"We'll have to smash the door on the first try, or we're toast," Coffey said.

Albrecht was a bit smaller than Coffey who was broad, strong and compact. Kaupert was bigger than Gates, who was tall and slender. It would be Coffey on one door and Kaupert on the other. Albrecht teamed with Earl Coffey, while Kaupert teamed with Paul Gates.

"On my count," Albrecht said.

They moved to their respective doors with Albrecht and Gates standing just off to the side, crouched, on first positive safety: gun safety off, with trigger finger on the side of the barrel. Albrecht nodded, *one . . . two . . .* and both men broke through their doors at the same time, splintering the doors as if they were made of plywood. Albrecht and Gates were on the guards before they had a chance to move out of bed. Handguns were in reach on the nightstands, but neither had a chance.

"FBI! On the floor, Asshole!" Gates said.

Albrecht echoed it in his room.

Both guards were on the floor, hands bound behind their back, feet bound together, duct tape over their mouth.

"Nathan, any problem with your two guards?"

There wasn't a response right away, but then Gates said, "Only one guard here. We thought you had two in your room."

Coffey and Albrecht looked at each other and then Albrecht said, "Guys, we're missing a guard."

*   *   *

The door opened, and Pete came in, followed by Skip Dahlke who had race-walked back up the alley, so he could enter the front door. Fitz, still in the guise of a street person, took his position in the alley opposite the metal garage door. Brett put his finger to his lips to keep them quiet and motioned to the two men to follow him. Pete reached out and gently held the boy's shoulder.

"What's your name?"

"Brett."

He started back up the stairs, and the two men followed closely behind.

At the second floor landing, Brett stopped and put his finger to his mouth again, then whispered to Pete and Skip, "We think the guards sleep on this floor. We don't have much time. They'll be awake soon."

He ran up the next flight and Brett motioned to Pete and said, "Tell the detective we're here."

Pete spoke into his collar, "Jamie, we're here. Open up."

The door cracked open, and the three of them slipped through.

"There's a cop with one of the boys," Jamie said. "Brett said there are at least seven guards."

The three men looked at Brett and Pete asked, "You sure he's a cop?"

"Positive," Brett said.

Pete wanted to know how he knew, but he didn't have to ask because deep down, he knew the answer.

"What room is he in?" Pete asked.

Brett pointed to the fifth door on the left.

"You have a key?" Pete asked Jamie.

"Yeah . . . a master, I think."

"I'll go in and tell him Butch is giving him me on the house," Brett suggested.

"No," Pete said gently. "Let us handle him."

"The guy's a pig. He'll want me."

Pete, Jamie and Skip looked at each other, then back at Brett.

Jamie took hold of Brett's shoulder and said, "Brett, listen . . ."

"I'll be ok. I've done it before with this asshole."

"Jesus!" Pete said.

"*I* don't like it, *Asshole!*" Brett said through clenched teeth.

Pete shook his head.

"That's not what I meant," he said quietly.

"Whatever," Brett said. "Gimme the key," he said holding out his hand to Jamie. "You be ready to move when I get in."

Jamie didn't like the decision but gave the key to Brett and followed him to the door, as did Pete. Skip stood behind Pete on the other side of the door. Jamie took Brett's shoulder and bent low to whisper into his ear.

"What side is the bed on?"

Brett poked his thumb to the right.

"When you get in, move to the right as close as you can to the wall. I'll come in on your left. My gun will be out and pointed with the safety off." He paused and asked, "You know what that means?"

Brett nodded and said, "You better tell these two guys to watch the hall doors. It's getting late."

Pete nodded and motioned Skip to move back to the front entrance. Pete moved to the other end.

"Skip, stay against the wall and stay low."

Brett waited until Pete and Jamie were in position, then he looked back at Jamie and nodded. He inserted the key and heard a voice on the other side.

"Hey . . . what the . . . it's not time yet."

Brett pushed open the door, entered and said, "Butch thought you might want me."

Jamie heard the man say, "Oh, you! Okay!"

Brett moved to the foot of the bed, close to the wall, and just like that, Jamie rushed into the room and shoved his gun into the man's neck.

"Get off the kid . . . now!"

The man didn't move.

"I said, NOW!"

Jamie grabbed the man by the hair, pushing his gun further into the man's face. The man climbed off, hunched low and moved to the floor.

"You know the drill . . . hands behind your head and lace your fingers." Then he said, "Pete, need your help."

Pete came on a run, gun out and ready.

"Keep your gun on him," Jamie said.

When the man turned to look at Pete, Jamie slammed the butt of his gun into the side of the man's head.

"Keep your eyes straight ahead, Fucker!"

Quickly, just as he had done with the fat man, he cuffed the cop's hands and feet and duct taped his mouth shut while he Mirandized him.

Pete went through the cop's clothes, taking the wallet out of the man's pants and opened it to find the driver's license. He shoved the gun into his belt at the small of his back and kicked the tazer, handcuffs, and nightstick to the side away from the man.

"Robert Manville . . . Cop," Pete said with disgust.

Tim hadn't moved off his stomach, but watched the two men suspiciously.

"Timmy, you're bleeding," Brett said.

He took a handful of moist wipes and began cleaning Tim off.

"That hurts!"

"Sorry, I'll go softer," Brett apologized.

Brett finished wiping Tim off, threw the wipes into the waste basket and then stepped over to the man on the floor and said, "You like the nightstick, don't you, Fuck Head?"

The cop glared at him but made no sound.

"I'm going to come back, and we'll see how much you like it."

He stood, looked at Pete and said, "We have to get the rest of the guys safe before the guards wake up."

"How do you want to do this?" Jamie asked Pete.

"Skip gets the kids; you and I watch the doors."

"I'll get the guys because they don't know you. You two watch the doors. That other guy looks scared," Brett said.

"We're all nervous, Kid," Jamie said. "Foolish not to be."

"Do either of you have clothes or something to put on?" Pete asked.

Brett glared at him. "Well gees . . . I guess we forgot to put on our fuckin' tuxedos!" Tears spilled out of his eyes. "You think I like runnin' around like this? What do you think I've been doing for the last two years . . . Fuck Head!" The boy angrily wiped tears out of his eyes. "You think we *like* this?"

"Kid, I'm sorry. I just . . ." Pete apologized.

"Shut the fuck up, Asshole, and do your job. We wanna go home."

"Brett, they're trying to help," Tim said softly, wiping some tears from his own eyes.

Ignoring the two officers, Brett asked, "Timmy, can you walk?"

Tim pushed himself off the bed and stiffly moved first one leg, then the other off the bed and stood, leaning with his hands on the nightstand. Brett stepped over and took one of Tim's arms and laid it across his shoulder, holding around the waist to help him walk.

"Bring the key and follow me," Brett said to the two officers. "But first, lock this asshole in. Make sure Butch is locked up too," he said already moving out of the room and down the hall with Tim leaning on him.

"Put me in Ian's room," Tim said. "Get all the other guys except Johnny and the new kid, Stephen. Get them last."

"You mean the other new kid, Mike."

"No. You'll need Stephen to get Mike. Mike won't know you, but he'll recognize Stephen. That way, he'll go with you."

*   *   *

"Ronnie, we're missing a guard," Albrecht said.

"I heard. You want me there or here?"

"There, but be ready."

Moving low, away from the door, Albrecht moved to the window and peered out. He tried looking as far left and right as he could.

"Paul, stay low and get to the window. What do you see?"

Just as Albrecht had done, Gates moved to the window, moved the curtain, and that's when a gun barked, and the window shattered.

*   *   *

Pete stood guard at the back door, while Jamie watched the front. Skip Dahlke went into the control room and videotaped everything he could. He found recording equipment and DVDs – dozens of them. He catalogued them, gave each of them a number and placed them into paper bags and then stored them in the black duffle bag he had brought along.

After he did all he could in the control room, he went back into Tim's room and began collecting DNA traces from the filthy sheets and the soiled wipes from the garbage can, cataloguing them as he had done with the DVDs in the control room.

Brett ran from room to room waking the other boys and escorting them to Ian's room where they would stay until they left the building. Some sat on the bed, while others sat leaning against the wall. They were confused and scared, but hopeful. The only two boys left were Johnny Vega and Mike Erickson. Brett went to Johnny's room and woke him up gently.

"Johnny, we're going home. You need to get up and come with me, but we have to be quiet, and you have to come now."

Johnny raised himself up, tried to smile and began to cough. He was pale, sweaty and very weak. In fact, he looked worse than he had in the past few days. Unless they got him out today, Brett didn't know if he'd make it.

"Johnny, we have to move . . . now! The guards will be up soon," Brett said.

Johnny pushed himself up off the bed, and with Brett's help, moved slowly down the hall to Ian's room. When they reached the room, Brett lowered him to a position next to Tim, who took him into his arms and held him. Johnny laid his head on Tim's shoulder, and together, they wept. Brett took a look at him and Tim and at the other boys who stared back at him. A few were crying. All were scared.

"Guys, we're going home." But even as he said it, he didn't know if he believed it. "Stephen, I need your help. Let's get Mike."

Stephen got up, and the two boys ran on tiptoes down to the end of the hallway. Pete saw them coming and met them before they got there.

"Is Mike in the last room," he turned and pointed, "There?"

Brett nodded suspiciously. "Why?"

"Because I don't think he's alone."

*   *   *

"Paul's down . . . Paul's down," Nathan yelled. "Head shot!"

"Fuck!" Albrecht swore. "Ronnie, the shot came from one o'clock from my position. Circle from behind, from opposite the courtyard."

"On my way," Desotel said breathlessly.

Albrecht pulled out his cell and dialed up Chet in Chicago.

"Get the cavalry moving . . . now! Paul Gates was shot. Head wound. Don't know his status."

He didn't wait for an answer but closed the cell and went back to the window. A shot broke glass and splintered the back wall behind him. The walls were thin, the doors cheap, and for all he knew, the bullet was still traveling.

"Ronnie, what's your twenty?" Albrecht asked.

No answer, which meant that Desotel was close to the target, looking for the shooter. To help him out, Albrecht tossed the curtain near the window without getting up. Just like that, a shot rang out throwing the curtain up in the air and piercing the back wall.

"Drop it!" Albrecht heard Desotel shout.

Two shots rang out in rapid succession.

"Shit . . . I'm hit . . . I think I got him, but I'm hit," Ronnie said.

"How bad?" Albrecht asked.

"I spun him, and he's down . . . can't see him . . . I'm down."

"Ronnie, how bad?" Kaupert asked.

"Bleeding . . . hurts like a whore!"

Coffey moved to the window opposite Albrecht and peered out. No shots were fired.

"Gotta take a chance, Tom," Earl said. "Man down."

Albrecht knew he was right, especially not knowing how badly Ronnie was shot. Somehow, he . . . they had to get out of the room and to Desotel without getting shot. That is, if Ronnie didn't finish him off.

"Nathan, can you get out of your room and go left away from the shooter?"

"Yeah . . . can do," Kaupert said, more determined than scared.

"I'm going to go right," Albrecht said. "Earl, lay down cover fire if you need to. Any movement, fire!"

Albrecht breathed slowly in, then slowly out
gathering his thoughts, getting ready.

"Nathan, on my count . . . one . . . two . . . now!"

As Coffey leveled his semi-automatic rifle out of
what was left of the window, Nathan and Albrecht sprinted
from their rooms. Nothing or no one moved.

*   *   *

"Stephen, go back to the room and shut the door.
Don't say anything to the guys," Brett said.

"You're going with him," Pete said.

"Listen to me. We don't have time. The other guards
will be here soon," Brett said, watching Stephen's bare butt
disappear down the hall.

Pete began to swear at the boy, but Brett interrupted
him.

"Listen, just listen," Brett said urgently, but quietly.
"Mike wasn't the one they wanted. It was Stephen. Guards
aren't allowed to use us. We're just for the men. So
sometimes, they get a kid like Mike and use him for a couple
of days."

He stopped and pointed to the bloody wall where empty chains and handcuffs hung from the ceiling, and the small grill that was filled with cold ashes and a branding iron.

"After they're done with the kid, they whip the shit out of him, sometimes brand him, and then if he's still alive, they kill him. This is done in front of us to teach us a lesson."

Pete put his hand up to his face, rubbed his jaw, and then looked back at Brett.

"We need to do this my way, and we need to do it quick before the rest of the guards come, or no one will leave here alive," Brett said.

Pete looked at Jamie at the far end of the hallway. His expression was unreadable. He looked at Skip Dahlke and got the same expression, which was nothing at all.

"Keep the gun in your back. Unbutton your shirt about halfway down and pull out one side. Unzip your pants," Brett said yanking out Pete's shirt. "You have to make it look like you and I just . . . you know."

"Fuck no!"

Brett didn't listen to him. Instead, he picked up Pete's hand and put it on top of his head, closing it into a fist.

"Grab a handful of my hair. When we get into the room, throw me on the bed. That way, I'm out of the way, and I can protect Mike. You tell the shithead in there that you wanted to get rough with me, but Butch wouldn't let you. You tell him that Butch said you can do anything you want with Mike. You tell the guard that if he wants, he can have me. When he makes his move, you have the gun."

Pete dropped his hand to his side and shook his head slowly, first looking at Brett and then at Jamie.

"This isn't going to work," Pete said.

Brett grabbed his hand again, placed it on his head, crying now.

"Please, we don't have time! Trust me!"

"Jesus Christ Almighty!" Pete said.

"He hasn't been here in a long time. He's packed up and moved away. We have you, me, Jamie and that other guy. That's it."

Pete clenched his teeth and grabbed a fistful of hair.

"You forgot your zipper. Pull it down. You have to act. It's our only chance. Honest!"

Pete took one last look at Jamie, shook his head and lowered his zipper. Then, playing the part of pervert, he yanked Brett down the hall towards the room and instead of using the key, knocked on the door.

"Give me a minute," a voice said from the other side.

Pete heard the door unlocking and it opened. The first thing he saw was a .45 pointed at him.

"Hey, hey, hey . . . lower it, Man. Butch said I could have some time with that kid in there. You know . . . kind of rough. He said I can't be rough with this kid."

He shook Brett by the hair, lifting him off his feet. Brett reached up and slapped at Pete's hand. The door opened wider and the man stepped to the side to let them enter.

"Kid, you know better than to hit a client," the skinny man with long red hair said, lowering his gun.

Pete threw Brett onto the bed, and the man with red hair turned to watch him land, almost but not quite on top of Mike. Brett scrambled to a position covering the other boy, cradling his head in his arms. As the man turned to watch the two boys, Pete grabbed the wrist and arm of the younger man and slammed his hand on the door frame once . . . twice . . . three times and the gun dropped to the floor. As Pete twisted the man's arm behind his back, his right foot kicked the gun out into the hallway, while his left foot and leg kicked the man's left leg out to the side, sending the man to the floor with Pete on top of him.

Pete saw movement behind him and felt a hand reaching for his gun, but he couldn't go after the gun or the hand because to do so, would be to lose his advantage over the younger man. He heard the gun cock. It was loud. Far louder than it should have been. Perhaps he only imagined how loud it was.

"Stop moving or I'll shoot."

Pete and the younger man stopped wrestling, though Pete still had a good, solid hold on him. He turned and saw Brett holding the gun in a classic shooter's crouch: both hands on the gun, legs spread at shoulder width.

"Cuff him," Brett said.

The man with long red hair smirked and said, "Like, you're gonna shoot me."

Then he laughed.

"I'm holding a .45 Beretta. It carries eight rounds in a cartridge in the handle. Let's pretend it's loaded with hollow points. If I cluster three shots center mass, they'll enter your scrawny ass about the size of a quarter and come out the other side the size of a baseball. You don't have a chance."

He paused to let that sink in.

"Or, I could aim one glancing shot just in front of your left temple and take out your frontal lobe. That way, you might live, but you'll be a veg. You'll piss in a tube and shit in a bag, and you'll eat Gerber Baby Food the rest of your life. But, hey, you won't care because you'll be a veg."

He paused again.

"You wanna try me, Fuck Head? I've been hoping for a chance like this for two years. So go ahead and try me!" Brett said.

The man's smirk disappeared from his face, and Pete used the plastic ties on his hands and feet and duct taped the man's face. But instead of using one short strip across the man's mouth, Pete wound it three times around the man's head.

He stood up huffing and puffing and put both hands behind his head breathing deeply. Then he bent at the waist, breathing some more. Brett gently depressed the hammer, slipped it into safety, and held it out to Pete for him to take.

"You guys have it under control?" Jamie asked from the doorway.

He stood in a shooter's crouch, the same crouch Brett had been in. The only difference is that Brett had relaxed, while Jamie still had the gun trained on the red-haired man on the floor.

"This fuck head's name is Shawn. He was one of the guys who brought in Stephen and Mike."

Pete stood up-right, buttoned his shirt and tucked it in, then zipped up. It was only then he took the gun from Brett. He and Jamie exchanged a look that anyone could have read as, '*WHAT THE FUCK!*'

"Mike, I'm Brett. These guys are cops. We're all going home today."

CHAPTER FORTY

Mike Erickson crawled as far into the corner as he could have, trying desperately to get away from Brett and the two men. His left eye was swollen shut and was dark blue-black, the color of a Midwestern thunder cloud. There was blood around his nose, and he had a badly swollen lip, cracked with dried blood around it. Pete thought he saw at least two teeth missing, but because the boy wasn't smiling, Pete wasn't sure.

"Could one of you go get Stephen . . . fast? We don't have much time," Brett said to Pete and Jamie while not taking his eyes from Mike.

He reached towards the boy with both hands slowly, palms up, speaking softly and slowly.

"Mike, we have to get out outta here. Jamie went to get Stephen. You're not going to be hurt again . . . ever again. I promise."

Stephen came into the room on a run but stopped as soon as he saw Mike. His mouth opened and closed, opened and closed.

"Oh Mike . . . I'm sorry . . . Mike . . ." in a whisper that was barely audible.

"Mike, Stephen's here," Brett said, motioning to Stephen to come closer without taking his eyes off Mike. "Can you walk?"

Mike watched Stephen step forward cautiously, hanging back a bit, and then looked back at Brett. He shook his head.

"I'm going to take a couple of wipes and clean you up a little, okay?" He repeated, "That okay?"

Reaching very slowly for the wipes on the nightstand, he took a handful, showed them to Mike, then gently, oh so gently, touched them to Mike's face, dabbing at the dried blood around his nose and mouth.

He did the best he could, which wasn't much at all, and said, "Mike, can you roll over a little? I want to get your legs, okay?"

Mike stared at Brett, then at Stephen who stood a little behind Brett crying silently, then back at Brett. He reached for the wipes in Brett's hand, and Brett gave them to him. He knelt and wiped himself off.

"Do you want me to help?" Brett said.

A tear fell from Mike's eye, the one that wasn't swollen, and then more tears fell. He nodded and turned around. Brett took a couple more wipes and helped Mike clean himself off. To Pete and Jamie, it seemed like a lifetime, but in reality, took only five or ten minutes.

"Okay, Mike . . . Stephen and I are going to help you walk to the end of the hallway where the other guys are. We're going home today, okay?"

Mike nodded and tried to get out of bed. Brett was right there, putting Mike's arm around his shoulder, while Stephen came up on the other side. With both of his arms around their shoulders, and both Brett and Stephen holding him around the waist, they walked as quickly as they could to the end of the hallway.

They opened the door to the room where the other boys were gathered, and the three of them entered awkwardly trying to fit themselves in the doorway.

"Give him to me," Tim said, holding out his arms. "You're Mike?"

Mike didn't answer, nor did he acknowledge that anyone had spoken to him. The two boys lowered Mike into Tim's arms, just as Johnny was lowered into his arms earlier. Johnny had moved, so that Tim could hold Mike in his lap, cradling Mike's head on his chest. Stephen sat down on the other side of Mike. He hadn't stopped crying.

"It's okay, Stephen," Tim said. "We're all going home today."

*   *   *

Albrecht and Kaupert circled around the back unit where they thought Desotel had run, moving slowly, cautiously.

"Nathan . . . anything?"

"Not yet."

"Earl . . . anything?"

"No movement," he said from his position in the motel.

"Ronnie, you okay?" Albrecht asked hopefully.

"Fuckin' hurts," came the answer. "Shit!"

If he was swearing, it was a good sign. Albrecht moved a bit quicker and saw a pair of legs. They weren't moving.

"Throw your gun and raise your hands!" he commanded.

There wasn't any movement.

"Nathan, anything?"

"I see Ronnie. Leg wound. Looks like it's in and out."

"It's fucking on fire!" Ronnie answered.

"I said, 'Throw your gun out and raise your hands!'" Albrecht repeated.

He aimed and put a shot into the near foot that was visible. Other than jumping from the gunshot, it didn't move. Tom stood cautiously and moved towards the body on the ground, gun at the ready out in front of him. He rounded a stone bench and found the man lying on his back spread-eagle, gun still in his right hand. Albrecht kicked the gun away and felt for a pulse at the man's carotid artery. It wasn't really necessary to check since Ronnie put a hole into the man's chest at the location of his heart. Nothing. He was gone.

"Nathan, we're clear. Get to Ronnie," Albrecht yelled. "Earl, take care of the kids. One of the guards must have a cuff key. Find it and put the kids in one room and cover them."

Kaupert reached Desotel, took off his belt and used it as a tourniquet over the wound in spite of Ronnie's colorful objections. In the distance, there were sirens. The cavalry was on the way.

*   *   *

"Where did you learn about guns?" Pete asked.

"My fuckin' uncle's a cop," Brett said. "He used to take me shooting with him."

"*Fucking* uncle?" Jamie asked.

"Yeah . . . *fucking* uncle," Brett answered defiantly.

Pure hate boiled up and out of the boy.

"He's the reason I'm here."

Pete and Jamie stared at him, then at each other.

"Explain," Jamie said.

About two weeks after he was taken, his uncle visited him and used him the same way as the Dark Man had.

"I thought he had come to take me away," Brett said quietly. "But he came to use me just like all the other men who came in my room. He said that he had wanted me for a long time."

Brett wiped tears from his eyes.

"One time, when he had taken me shooting, he kissed me. I thought it was weird, but I figured, 'Okay, no big deal.' Then he stood behind me as I took aim, and he was like coaching me, telling me to concentrate on the Campbell's Soup can on the rock by the river. He had his hands around my waist. Then he . . . he . . . I told him not to. He kept . . . he did . . . I didn't know what to do. When he was done, I threw the gun down and ran. I ran and ran.

"I never told anyone. I was afraid. After Ron and Frank took me, about a week or two later, he came. He told me it was all my fault. That if I just let him do stuff with me, I'd still be home."

Jamie had his hands over his eyes. Pete stared at the boy not comprehending the brutality and coldness of it.

"The other boys . . ." Pete said. "Did someone . . ."

Brett nodded.

"Yeah, all of us. We're here because somebody wanted us here."

"What's your fucking uncle's name?" Pete asked.

"Detective Anthony Dominico," Brett answered. "He's in Indianapolis."

Pete's hunch was correct. Each of the boys was targeted by someone and then they were snatched and abducted. He walked over to Skip, explained the situation and what he wanted and told him to send it to Chet as soon as he was finished. He told Skip to tell Chet to get it out to the rest of the teams. Dahlke pulled out his cell and went into the room with the boys.

One by one, each boy gave the name of the man responsible for his being there. The only two that didn't know who was responsible were Stephen and Mike.

"They wouldn't know yet," Tim explained.

What he didn't say was that they might never know.

*   *   *

Pete shook his head in exasperation, nervous and perhaps fearful for the first time in his life. He had three partners to worry about, plus thirteen kids locked in a room. It was beginning to take on the appearance of a runaway train, and he felt like he was trying to stop it by hanging onto the caboose and dragging his feet. Pete knew that the only thing that would accomplish would be a pair of broken legs, or maybe death; his and others.

He dialed up Chet and said, "Send the cavalry now. We're running out of time, and we're undermanned. The kids are secure . . . for now. There are more bad guys than good guys, and they have more guns than we do. Hurry!" Pete said.

"Will do."

Pete rang off and found Brett in the hallway outside the room with the cop.

"Hey, Brett," he said quietly. "Can we talk?"

He never got the chance. Fitz got his attention.

"Um, guys . . . we have company."

The hairs on the back of Jamie's neck stood at attention. He went to the door, put his ear to it, turned back to Pete and shook his head.

"A rusted out Camaro, red on white, Illinois tags 479GCE is rolling up the alley. Door going up. Two men."

"Fitz, any way you can get in after them without being seen or getting shot?"

"Yes on the first . . . I'll try real, real hard on the second."

"Skip, did you get the kid info to Chet?"

"Done."

"You gave him the names of the kids and where they were from-"

"-everything!"

"Good. I want you in the room down the end of the hall with me. You do as I say, when I tell you. Keep your head, stay calm. Jamie, take the front door."

Brett entered Ian's room and whispered to Tim what was happening, as much as he had heard anyway. Listening to one conversation, he had to guess at the rest. Tim nodded solemnly and gripped Brett's forearm. Their eyes sent each other a message. The bond between the two of them and Johnny was incredibly strong.

"Brett, stay with us," Patrick pleaded. "Please!"

Brett hugged Patrick, kissed his forehead, and said, "You have to trust me, okay?"

"Brett, please!"

"I'll be okay. I promise."

He took one last look at the boys and locked them in.

He looked both ways to make sure none of the cops were watching. Earlier, after he had left Mike's room and after he had deposited him in other room with the boys, he had taken the .45 lying in the hallway, the one taken from the red-haired man, and hid it. Slowly, he backed into the room next to where the rest of the boys were. Quickly, quietly, he built himself a barricade to hide behind, yet be able to see down the hall in either direction.

Breathing easily and calmly, he waited.

CHAPTER FORTY-ONE

When Tommy Albrecht moved his team forward in KC, and when Jamie put his gun to the fat man's head in Chicago, it was only 3:30 AM PCT in Los Angeles.

The building in Los Angeles that Gavin Reilly had monitored was dissimilar to the building in Chicago in that it was newer. It was in a lousy part of Long Beach near the water front just off the industrial corridor. Its colors were a dirty gray on the outside with a very plain tan or beige color scheme on the inside. It was similar in that men had to be buzzed in from the outside, walk up three stories to a computer kiosk of sorts, where the *customer* would then browse through a series of pictures to select the boy he wanted, just as Graff had done.

Once inside the third floor, the set up was the same, though O'Connor didn't know it. A long hallway with doors on either side opened to what O'Connor thought to be bedrooms. A similar control room like the one in Chicago was on the right near the third floor landing.

There were some customers in the building, and two of the three guards were sound asleep when Pat O'Connor pulled his gun out and forced the sleepy guard, a short, squat balding man, to the floor in Colin Chapple's room.

Colin sat up in bed and watched in fascination, not quite believing it was happening. Rather, he thought the whole thing was staged as some sort of sex game before he was raped by the man with the gun.

After O'Connor had Jack Andrews on the floor in similar plastic ties that Desotel had used in Kansas City and like Graff had used in Chicago, and after he had duct taped Andrews' mouth shut, he pulled off his jacket revealing a navy t-shirt. He pulled a Velcro patch off his left breast that revealed an FBI logo and removed a similar Velcro patch off his back shoulders that revealed FBI in even bigger, brighter yellow letters.

"Kid, I need your help," O'Conner said. "I'm a Sheriff Deputy working with the FBI. My team is outside waiting for me, and I have to get them inside and secure the guards and get all you boys home safely. Will you help me?"

Very leery, nervous, and still not quite believing what was happening, yet ever so slightly hopeful, Colin nodded but didn't move from his bed.

"Do you know how the front door works to let people in?"

Colin nodded again, but didn't move.

"Well . . ." O'Connor started. "Kid, we have to move. Right now, I'm assuming the other guards are asleep. I don't know how many other men are in the building, but I think our spotter said two, maybe three. So, will you help me or not?"

Colin got up off the bed, walked over to the guard bound up and lying on the floor, and slammed his foot down on the back of his head driving his face into the floor. Then he went to the doorway, looked both ways, and ran to the control room with O'Connor following and pushed the buzzer, allowing Charlie Chan and Paul Eiselmann into the building. Then he and O'Connor went to the door that opened to the third floor hallway and let the two men in to join O'Connor.

"How did you know where the buzzer was?" O'Connor asked him.

Embarrassed, Colin turned red and said, "Jack brought me in there a couple of times for, you know. I watched him buzz guys in."

Chan went to work filming and collecting evidence as Dahlke had done in Chicago, downloading the contents of the computer kiosk and the various electronic gadgets in the control room to Chet at the Sheraton. He checked in with Chet letting him know what he had found, so he could pass it on to Dahlke in Chicago so they could trade their intel. Eiselmann and O'Connor huddled.

"We think the other two guards are still sleeping. You could start on one end, while I start on the other. We get the guards squared away and free the kids."

"What about any assholes who might be with the kids?"

O'Connor thought about it for a minute and then said, "You and I get the assholes first, then the guards. Start on that side of the hallway at that end," pointing to the end farthest from the control room, "and I'll start on this end."

"Can't," the boy said.

"Why?" Eiselmann asked.

"Only one key."

O'Connor sighed and revised the plan once again. He would enter the room with Eiselmann standing guard just outside the door and ready to help if O'Connor needed it.

"We let the kids stay in their rooms?" Eiselmann asked.

"Um . . ." Colin said.

"What?" O'Connor asked.

"I'll get the kids and move them to one or two rooms. That way, we're together and ready."

"Ready for what?" Eiselmann asked.

Puzzled, Colin looked first at Eiselmann, then at O'Connor and said, "To go home."

Paul Eiselmann nodded and smiled at the boy and said, "Right you are, Kid. Everyone goes home."

The three of them set to work quietly and efficiently. Inserting the key; opening the door. If there was just a boy, Colin would wake him gently, whispering into the boy's ear and then move him to a room towards the end. If a *customer* was with the boy, then O'Connor would bind and gag him with plastic ties and duct tape, while Colin took the boy to the end of the hallway.

In less than twenty minutes, the boys were in two rooms, and four men were bound up and gagged and locked in the rooms they were found in. With Chan watching the third floor and with the master key taken from Jack Andrews in hand, O'Connor and Eiselmann went down the back stairs to the second floor to take care of the guards.

*   *   *

Fitz rapidly went through various scenarios and possibilities and finally settled on a bull rush. As the Camaro slowed to enter the garage, Fitz got up from his sitting position and stripped off his scraggily wig and green military coat and left them in the middle of the alley revealing the FBI T-shirt he had worn underneath it. He ran across to the garage door at an angle so as not to be seen by either man. He waited by the entrance and as the door started down, sneaked himself around the corner behind a white van that sat in the right side parking slot.

The garage was dark, dirty and dusty with oil stains on the cement floor. It was also bigger than he had originally thought, taking up what seemed to be most of the first floor of the building. A couple of cheap frame and drywall unused offices faced each other. The glass in the windows was either broken or removed, and neither had doors. There were stairs on either end of the garage that Fitz assumed went up to the second and third floors. The outside door that he knew to be unused stood closed and padlocked behind a pile of old tires, oil drums and other accumulated debris. Two other vehicles, a '98 dark blue Grand Prix, and a '94 silver Chevy Lumina were also in the garage. Fitz loved cars, especially fast ones, but these were nothing to admire, and he didn't have the time to admire anything at the moment. Basically, he recognized these as pieces of shit he wouldn't be caught dead in.

He slid along the back of the van and waited until the door rolled down completely and until he heard the car doors open and the two men shuffle out of the vehicle. One man laughed at something the other man had said.

Fitz allowed his eyes to adjust to the darkness and then he stepped out and yelled, "FBI, hands where I can see 'em."

Neither man moved except to turn around at the sound of his voice.

"I said-" he never got to finish.

A tall, skinny guy who was on the passenger side reached for his gun but was blown backwards by the shotgun blast to his chest. As Fitz jacked another shell into the chamber, the driver pulled out his gun and fired two shots. Fitz ducked, but not soon enough. He was hit in the shoulder and was spun around and down behind the passenger side of the car. Lying down where he could see the other man's legs and feet, Fitz fired.

The shotgun sent a blast of pellets in a cluster the size of a softball shattering the man's lower shin, and in the process, blowing his foot off leaving only a bloody stump. The man landed in a thud screaming, but another shotgun blast to the side of the man's head ended his screams as quickly as they had started.

Fitz's ears were ringing. Sound was muffled like he was under water and had cotton packed in both ears. If anyone had come to his or to the two asshole's rescue, he'd never know it. His left arm was useless, which was sort of okay since he was right handed. Yet, he was bleeding badly.

He picked himself up off the floor, moved first to the passenger, felt for a pulse, and not finding any, picked up the man's gun and shoved it into his belt. He moved to the other man but didn't even bother with the pulse because most of the man's head had disintegrated into a gooey mass of bone, blood and brain matter. He picked up that man's gun, too.

Both Jamie and Pete had heard the gunfire and knew that if they could hear it on the third floor, there was little doubt the guards on the second floor could also. If they weren't awake before, they would be now.

"Fitz, what's happening?" Jamie asked.

"Two down, but I'm hit. Shoulder," he shouted in answer.

"How bad?"

"Trouble hearing you . . . my ears are all fucked up," Fitz yelled. "My left arm is bad. Bleeding."

"*Fuck!*" Pete muttered more to himself than to Jamie.

"Pete, I gotta go . . ."

"Be careful. Those guards . . ."

"Yeah, I know," but Jamie was already moving through the door leading down to the rest of the building.

"Skip, I need you in the front. No one, and I mean no one, comes through that door. If he, she or it doesn't identify themselves as FBI, you shoot first and ask questions later. You understand?"

Dahlke licked his lips and nodded solemnly.

Pete placed a hand on his shoulder and said, "You'll be fine. You breath nice and easy, short, shallow breaths. Aim waist high."

Dahlke nodded again then ran back up the hallway to the front door. He stood ten feet from the door and looked around, feeling exposed. Brett came out of the bedroom carrying a chair and set it on its side where Skip stood.

"Get down and use this to steady your rifle. It isn't much protection, but it might help you aim."

He ran back into his bedroom and pulled the pillow off the bed and brought it back to Dahlke.

"Don't know if this will help or not. Up to you."

He ran back to the room once more, picked up the .45 and ran down the hallway where Pete stood half in, half out of the bedroom where the red-haired man lay bound and gagged on the floor.

"What the fuck are you doing out here? Give me that gun!"

"No. I'm keeping it for protection," Brett answered calmly, coolly.

"You're a kid. They see you with a gun, you become a target," Pete yelled through clenched teeth.

"I'm a target one way or the other. At least I'll be a target with a gun," Brett answered.

"Fuck!" Pete said pounding the wall.

"Those guards are awake, and they'll either be coming this way or going down to where Jamie went. He's going to need help."

"Don't tell me my job, Kid!"

"Just sayin' . . . this door is locked, and anyone coming through it has to unlock it. I'll shoot first, just like that guy," Brett said, jerking his head in the direction of Dahlke. "But, that other cop is going to have a shit storm coming down on him, so you better get moving."

Pete started to say something with his finger pointing at Brett, but thought better of it. Quickly, he ran through the options and came to realize there weren't any. Two guns on the backside of the building were good, and the fact that the door locked behind him was even better. The kid could handle a gun, but still, Campbell's soup cans were a hell of a lot different than men with guns. But the door was locked, and both Jamie and he would be armed.

He frowned at the boy, turned and said to Dahlke, "Skip, I'm going to help Graff. You have the front door. *I'll* have the back door," he said as much to Skip as he did for the benefit of the boy with the gun, "but I'll be on the first or second floor. Got it?"

"Yup, just go!"

Seething, Pete shook his head once and cautiously opened the door, listening for any sound or footfalls. He looked back at Brett, then moved onto the third floor landing and shut the door quietly behind him.

*   *   *

In their years together in SWAT, O'Connor and Eiselmann had developed a silent hand-signal system they had modified into a kind of shorthand, bred by their close friendship. They entered the second floor assault style, one behind the other, with Eiselmann leading low to the right, and O'Connor entering high to the left. Pat kept his hand on the door, so he could shut it softly behind them.

No one other than Pat O'Connor and Paul Eiselmann were in the hallway. Listening for any sounds out of the ordinary, Pat signaled Paul to move ahead and to the left side, while he would trail slightly to the right.

The first room they came to was an empty and darkened kitchen. The only lights were the digital time on the microwave and on the oven. They moved onward and came to the first door. O'Connor signaled to Eiselmann to try the doorknob on a count of three. Eiselmann did, and the knob turned easily. He pushed it open, and the two of them entered the darkened room swiftly and silently. The bed was made, no one was present and there weren't any signs that the room had been used. Both looked at each other and almost simultaneously sighed in relief.

They moved down the hallway, and the next two rooms were the same as the first: dark, empty and unused. Knowing that at least two guards were still asleep, they had four doors left to check. They gripped their guns tighter, took a deep breath and Eiselmann reached out cautiously, and slowly turned the doorknob.

It was locked.

He showed the key to O'Connor, who nodded. Eiselmann inserted it as softly as he could, and the door unlocked with a soft, yet audible click. He opened the door quietly to the sound of slow, heavy breathing. O'Connor nodded at Eiselmann and turned facing the hallway in a crouch.

Eiselmann moved to the side of the bed, clamping one hand down on the mouth of the man sleeping, waking him up, while shoving his gun into his cheek just below his left eye.

He bent low and whispered, "You make one sound, and I'll blow your fucking head off. You understand?"

Now wide awake, the man nodded cautiously so as not to have the gun go off accidently. Keeping the gun in his face, Eiselmann took his hand off the man's mouth and used it to grab the man's hair, yanking him up and out of the bed, forcing him to the floor. Paul bent low and in a whisper, ordered the man to put both of his hands behind his back, which he did. Then using twist ties, bound the man's hands and feet, and duct taped his mouth shut. It took Paul less than five minutes. He locked the room behind him and joined O'Connor in the hallway.

Three doors left and behind them, one or more sleeping guards. Hopefully, sleeping guards.

*   *   *

"Fitz, I'm on the landing just above the first floor . . . I'm coming to you. Do you copy?"

"Yeah. All clear down here. Better watch your ass though," he answered hoarsely.

Jamie backed up against the landing wall and looked up towards the second floor. He was exposed if anyone should come down. He needed to move and move quickly.

"I'm coming now, Fitz."

He came down the landing with his gun out, head on a swivel looking both below and above him. The air smelled of gunpowder, oil, dirt and dust. There weren't any lights and the little that filtered in from under the garage door was negligible.

"Fitz, where are you?"

"Your twelve o'clock, twenty yards on the other side of the Camaro. I saw a light switch to your left on the wall as you come off the last step."

He found three lights and flicked on the first, which turned on two lights on the far wall over the van and the Camaro. He didn't turn on any others, thinking that he could find Fitz and use the darkness in the rest of the garage to their advantage.

Jamie covered the ground quickly, yet cautiously. He rounded the front end of the Lumina, then the Grand Prix and saw one of the guards lying on his back in a syrupy pool of thickening blood. He had to step over the other man to find

Fitz, sitting down against the side of the van, listing to one side.

"How you doin' Buddy?" Jamie said as he knelt down to check Fitz's shoulder.

"Just ducky! Gonna play a couple rounds of golf when we get back," he answered through a cough.

He had lost a lot of blood, and he had to get help in a hurry.

"Pete or Skip, call Chet and find out the ETA on the posse."

Pete heard him in the earpiece as did Dahlke but didn't answer because of his closeness to the second floor door. Dahlke responded by saying he'd place a call right away. Distracted, Pete didn't hear the door open. Not just one, but two guards came through the door, and one placed a gun to the back of Pete's head, cocking it, while the other one took Pete's gun from him. Pete raised his hands, and one of the men shoved his face into wall, kicked his legs apart and frisked him, but found nothing.

"Let's go back upstairs and see what's happening," a man whispered into his ear. "But first, how many guns up there?"

"Fuck you, Pervert," Pete spat.

The man with the gun wrapped it hard on the back of Pete's head while the other one punched him twice in the lower back in the area of his kidneys.

"No matter, you'll go through the door first. You're gonna be our Kryptonite, Mother Fucker. You'll get the first bullet while we take out whoever's left."

Hoping that the two guards didn't know about him being wired, and hoping that Dahlke would listen and understand what was about to happen, he said, "As long as you two guys get shot, I don't care if they take me out. They can pull the trigger on you two and keep on shooting until the well is dry for all I care."

One of the guards grabbed Pete roughly by the back of his jacket and shoved him up the stairs.

"Just get your ass up there and don't try to be a hero, or I'll be the one to cap your ass. Got it Mother Fucker?"

"You two are so brave . . . you fuck eleven and twelve year olds. You two guys are so tough. I'm real worried."

Pete kept up a running commentary of bullshit, repeating "two guys" often enough that Dahlke was bound to understand, wouldn't he? But would he tell the kid with the gun he was going to walk in on? How would he react?

CHAPTER FORTY-TWO

O'Connor and Eiselmann stood in the hallway knowing that behind one of three doors, a guard lay in bed sleeping.

Hopefully.

And then there was always the possibility that there was more than one guard sleeping behind those doors. Eiselmann moved to the next door and softly tried the knob. Locked. As he did before, he inserted the key quietly and then stood off to the side and pushed the door open.

Two shots from what sounded like a .38 blasted from the darkness of the room and harmlessly into the hallway, hitting neither Eiselmann nor O'Connor. Pat signaled that he'd watch the hallway to see if there were any other guards in either of the two rooms across the hallway, while Paul would deal with the shooter in the room.

While O'Connor moved away from the open door and crouched low facing the two unopened doors, Eiselmann concentrated on the man with the gun in the dark bedroom. How to flush the guy out?

"Look, there are more of us than you have bullets, so why don't you just . . ."

Two shots in rapid succession rang out and into the door and wall across the hallway just like the first two shots, far away from either officer.

"We have all night, Asshole. In about five minutes, this building will be crawling with FBI so . . ."

One more shot rang out.

"How stupid are you?" Eiselmann asked.

There was silence.

"It doesn't have to end like this, Dumb Shit. Really, it doesn't."

It wasn't textbook negotiation, but at this point, Eiselmann didn't care. He just wanted it done. This was met with silence. It stretched on and on. No one came out of either door. There was no sound in the building other than slight movement from inside the open bedroom door and distant sirens that came gradually louder and closer.

"Buddy, the posse is almost here. We don't have much time. We can end this with flash bang grenades and a full out fire fight, but . . ."

A single shot rang out, followed by a thud from inside the room, along with metallic clatter as if a gun had fallen to the floor. O'Connor and Eiselmann looked at each other and knew it was over, other than to check the other two rooms.

Eiselmann snaked his arm around the doorway and found the light switch and flipped on the lights. No shots. No sound. O'Connor chanced a glance into the room from the low right side of the doorway and saw the man lying in his underwear on the floor. Blood pooled around the man's head in a crimson satanic halo.

He shook his head at Eiselmann and motioned that the man was prone, down on the floor, and chopped his hand in a way to convey it is over, done. Eiselmann took a quick look into the room, then took his time and entered the room slowly, cautiously.

It was over in Los Angeles.

*   *   *

Jamie and Fitz heard Pete's chatter. Two of the three guards had him on the stairs and were headed to the third floor. Some way, somehow, he had to help protect those kids and Pete.

"Skip, did you copy that?"

"Yeah . . . so, what do you want me to do?"

Jamie looked at Fitz who seemed to be sweating as much as he was bleeding. He was in a bad way. With his good hand, Fitz waved Jamie off as if to say, 'Go help Pete'.

"What did Chet say about the cavalry?" Jamie asked.

"Fifteen, maybe twenty minutes."

A hell of a lot can happen in fifteen or twenty minutes.

"Skip, you can't let that door open. One of them might have a key, and they're going to use Pete as a shield. You *cannot* fire until he's clear. Do you understand?"

"Yeah, I get that. I'll hold them off until you or somebody gets here," he said solemnly.

"Fitz, I'm going to follow up the stairs, so I can help Pete. You gonna be all right down here?"

Fitz nodded and waved him off again. No, Jamie thought, Fitz is not going to be all right unless somebody gets here quickly.

He got up from between the van and the Camaro and moved in a quick walk towards the stairs when the first of two shots rang out slamming into the back concrete wall, just missing him. He was able to duck back between the garage door and the broken down office.

They had to have come from the other side of the garage towards the front of the building, meaning: sleeping guard number three was wide awake and shooting. That also still left the possibility of two other guards roaming the building. Jamie got onto his belly and waited for any sound that might give the guard away.

"Skip and Pete, Fitz and I are pinned down. I'll get to you as soon as I can. Guys, be careful."

*   *   *

Skip and Brett had come up with a plan. Or actually, Brett came up with the plan, and Skip reluctantly agreed because it sounded half-way plausible, but a whole lot dangerous. Skip stayed in a room where he could see both ends of the hallway, yet closer to the back end where he knew Pete would come through the door. Brett stayed half in, half out of the room where the red-haired man was. His right hand carried the .45 with the safety off, finger slightly on the trigger, not visible from the back door. Brett was to move out of the way, so Skip could get a good shot at the two guards.

Brett heard the key slide in the lock and saw the knob begin to turn. He had time to shut his eyes, breathe deeply and let it out slowly. Pete came in with his hands in the air and stopped short, eyes wide in horror as he saw the boy. Luckily, he was shoved forward, which gave Brett and Skip the room they needed.

"Kid, what are you doin' out here?" the guard asked.

Brett knew him as Ace.

"Butch told me to fetch one of you as soon as you showed up."

As the two guards lowered their guns, Brett stepped fully into the hallway, pulled his gun up with both hands and took out Ace with two shots to the chest. It took only a second before the other guard registered that the kid had a gun, which didn't make sense to him, but for that guard, it was a second too long. As he swung his gun up, Brett shot him first in the stomach, then in the chest. The guard got off one shot spinning Brett around, knocking him to the floor.

Before Pete could react, Skip put three shots into the guard and a fourth in the wall high and to the right.

"Jesus Fucking *Christ*!" Pete yelled as he ran to the boy and knelt down. "Brett . . . Brett, you okay?"

No answer but moans and groans. Blood everywhere. Brett held his shoulder, blood oozing out of the wound and between his fingers. He rolled slowly around on the floor, finally stopping, and curled up in a fetal position.

"Skip, I need help . . . now!"

Dahlke came on a run, dropping his rifle on the floor, kneeling down beside the boy.

"I need something for bandages. Quickly! Water, if possible."

"Is he going to be all right?" Pete asked desperately.

"How the hell do I know?" Skip shouted. "I work on dead people!"

Brett looked up at both men, but his eyes didn't register or focus. He tried to smile, but the pain was too intense. He began to shiver. Skip ran to the bedroom and grabbed the blanket and pillow off the bed and wrapped the boy in it, laying his head on the pillow. Pete had run off to find anything that could be used as bandages.

"Kid, hang in there. This doesn't look that bad," Skip lied. "But you have to fight, okay?"

He didn't know if Brett had heard or had understood him as there was no reaction from him. Brett had shut his eyes and had become pasty-white. Skip recognized that at the least, he was going into shock. Hopefully, he wasn't dying.

Pete pulled out his cell and dialed up Chet.

"We need two ambulances, maybe three . . . *NOW*!" he yelled running back to Skip with an armful of sheets. "We need the cavalry *NOW*, goddammit!"

He didn't wait for Chet's reply but clicked off the phone and shoved it back into his pocket. Skip had already taken off his shirt and was tearing it in strips.

"Can't use sheets, Pete. Too risky given what was done on them," Skip said calmly. "Go help Jamie. I got this."

As Pete was leaving, he added, "We need to wrap this up in a hurry," nodding at the boy.

"Pete, if you're coming, use the front stairs. That way, we'll have the asshole between us. Just don't get caught in my crossfire. And remember, there might be more than one guard down here."

Jamie had often made fun of shows where cops storm buildings from more than one entrance. It never really happened that way in real life because of the possibility of shots being fired at each other. It was always better to seal one exit and enter through a different one. That way, there wouldn't be the possibility of anyone getting shot with friendly fire.

Pete took one last look at Brett who seemed so small wrapped in the blanket. Skip packed the wound with strips of his shirt trying to stem the flow of blood. Brett, the little boy who had acted so tough, but was so gentle helping the other boys. The little boy who had been through so much.

No way can he die when he and the other kids were so close to going home. No way.

Pete picked up the rifle Skip had used and took off down the hallway on a run, checking his ammunition. He burst through the door and onto the third floor landing, stopped at the second door, opened it up cautiously, shut it quietly behind him and then ran down the stairs as cautiously, quickly and as quietly as he could to the first floor.

"Jamie, I'm at the door. Give a couple of bursts to keep the asshole down. I'll come through low and to the right. I'd prefer not to get shot."

"I'll see what I can do. On my count."

Jamie let loose a burst of gun fire, five or six shots and said, "One . . . two . . ." and he let out another burst of fire. "Three!"

Pete stayed as low as he could and opened the door quietly, looking around to see as much as he could, as he dared. He found himself on a landing, six steps from the garage floor. He shut the door quietly behind him.

In the distance, sirens.

"Hey, Asshole!" Jamie yelled. "You don't have much time. Hear those sirens? They're coming our way."

A shot rang out below and to Pete's left. In the semi-darkness, the muzzle flash was bright. The problem was that it was too bright, and it left an imprint on Pete's eyes. He shut them briefly and then opened them up, and while still present, the imprint was dimmer.

He saw movement in the general vicinity of where the gunfire had come from. He looked around for something, anything, to throw and had to settle for twenty-three cents he had in his front pocket. He threw the coins against the wall opposite him.

The guard stood up and fired three shots in rapid succession and that was all Pete needed. He opened fire in a general spray pattern, saw the man get lifted up off his feet and over a barrel.

"Pete, you okay?"

He didn't answer right away, but instead fired another spray in that direction.

"Pete?"

"I think he's down. No movement."

"Stay where you are. I'll come up the far wall. Where do you think he is exactly?"

"From your position, one o'clock, ten yards from my position on the landing."

"Got it."

Jamie moved in a crouch up the far wall, and Pete saw him coming. He'd stop every so often behind a barrel or a pile of one thing or another, until he was maybe fifteen yards from the position of the guard.

"There's been no movement," Pete said.

"On the wall by the last step are light switches. Turn them on, and I'll cover you."

Pete took the last six steps very quietly, slowly, then flicked on all three lights and suddenly, the entire garage was filled with light.

Sprawled over a barrel on his back spread-eagle, a man lay still and unmoving. Both Jamie and Pete approached him warily, guns at the ready. He was almost cut in two. In fact, the only thing keeping him together was his torn shirt which was dripping with blood and various internal organs. The sirens drew ever nearer and that was when Pete's phone chirped.

"This is FBI Agent Vincent Cochrane of the Chicago Field Office. We have two ambulances on stand-by with EMTs, with a third ambulance handy in case we need it. We also caught two armed men as they ran out the front of the building. We have the perimeter secured, and we're waiting for your go ahead."

CHAPTER FORTY-THREE

Once the duct tape came off Luke Clyborne's mouth, he couldn't talk fast enough. The same could be said for the two remaining guards at the motel in Kansas City. They had hoped that by cooperating with the FBI, their role in the prostitution of the boys at the motel might be minimized. Together, they provided contacts, e-mail addresses, account numbers, and turned over money, photos, and DVDs. The manager was so sleazy that he probably would have pointed a finger at his own mother had she been involved. Fortunately, she wasn't involved because she had been dead for two years after crawling into a bottle of gin seven years previous.

Albrecht, Coffey and Kaupert had given statements to the KC FBI, which were accepted verbatim. Because it was a shooting, their weapons were taken and would be held until the review was completed. Old and well-worn territory for these three vets. Paramedics had taken Ronnie Desotel to the hospital despite his protests because he had wanted to be there with the rest of his team.

As the gurney carrying the black body bag containing Detective Paul Gates was pushed out of the motel room, Albrecht, Coffey and Kaupert stopped talking and turned and watched in silence.

"A wife and a young son," Albrecht said softly.

No one responded.

*   *   *

Pat O'Connor and Paul Eiselmann sat next to each other on the floor in the third floor hallway drinking Coke. Both of them had wanted something much stronger but had accepted the Coke gratefully from one of the cops sent by his boss to a convenient store. The harder stuff would be waiting for them later.

O'Connor had his eyes shut, but he was alert to every sound and foot fall. FBI from the LA office scurried around collecting any evidence Charlie Chan might have missed, which meant they hadn't and wouldn't find anything.

Chan lugged a heavy, dark green, canvas duffle wherever he went, never leaving it outside of his reach. Thick red evidence tape sealed the bag, and he wasn't about to lose chain of custody until it was delivered to the federal attorney.

Gavin Reilly sat down next to Eiselmann. O'Connor and Eiselmann knew he was pissed about not being part of the siege team inside the building, but they also knew that the building had to be covered on the outside as a precaution.

Deep down, Reilly did too. Eiselmann reached out and slapped his leg playfully.

"You okay?"

Reilly grunted something Eiselmann didn't understand, but he didn't care. He was exhausted as was everyone else, and more importantly, the kids were safe, and everyone was heading home, except one pervert who chose to blow his brains out.

Good riddance, Fuck Head! No one will miss your sorry ass, and the world will be that much safer for kids! he thought to himself.

As if reading his mind, O'Connor turned to his two teammates, smiled and said, "Not a bad night's work, huh? All the kids go home. No bullets. No blood. Everyone safe."

He took a sip of Coke, leaned his head back against the wall, shut his eyes and repeated, "Not a bad night's work."

*   *   *

Pete and Jamie had huddled briefly just outside the control room after letting the FBI team, led by Vince Cochrane, into the building. Jamie decided he didn't do

'Feeb-speak' very well, so with a pat on the back and a smirk, Jamie walked down the hallway to get out of the way and to help Skip Dahlke with Brett.

"Smart ass!" Pete called after him.

Jamie didn't turn around or even break stride, but waved a hand as he kept on walking.

Agents ran around everywhere. Four paramedics jogged through the door pushing a gurney and lugging bags of equipment. Pete stood in the center of the hallway and pointed towards the other end. He grabbed the fourth man by the arm as he was about to pass.

"You treat that kid as if he were the president. He's the real hero here. He saved our asses, and if it weren't for him, we'd be dead and those kids wouldn't be going home." He paused and added, "Understand?"

"Yessir."

One of the agents came up to Pete and said, "What's with the guy with his dick fried and a nightstick sticking out of his ass?"

Pete stared at the guy, not having any idea what the guy was talking about. He chose to say nothing because he didn't have anything to say. The agent motioned to Pete to follow him.

He stopped outside the room where they had found the man raping Tim. Pete entered and saw the cop, Robert Manville, on the floor in obvious discomfort, if not agony, with the electrodes to a tazer clamped on his penis, which was now the color of a grilled hotdog and the handle of his nightstick sticking out of his ass.

Pete almost laughed, bit his tongue and said, "I have no fucking clue."

Jamie came over to see what was happening, stuck his head in the door, and laughed. "What, a copcycle?"

Pete did laugh and said, "No fucking clue."

Vince Cochrane came over, took a look, shut the door behind them and with a smirk said, "I think we need to talk."

The four of them huddled and decided that no one knew what had happened, though Pete had a pretty good idea as did Jamie, but neither of them had volunteered anything.

Instead, Cochrane grabbed a wipe from the box on the nightstand, wiped down the handle of the nightstick, none too gently, but didn't remove it. Then he went to the tazer gun and wiped that down, too. After a minute or two, he radioed down and called up another set of paramedics to transport Manville to the hospital.

When they arrived he said to them, "Not sure what happened, and I pretty much don't care. He was found with one of the boys. When he's admitted to the hospital, I want him as far away from that boy as possible. Do you understand?"

A burley, barrel-chested black man with a mustache asked, "A cop?"

"A pervert cop," Jamie answered.

"Found him with one of those boys?" he asked.

"I had to shove my gun in his face and yank him off the boy by the hair."

"The hair on his head, I hope," the medic asked.

Pete, Jamie and Cochrane laughed.

The medic looked at the cop on the floor and said, "I guess he got what he deserved, huh?"

"That's what we're thinking, but we don't know how it happened," Cochrane said.

"Huh. Interesting." The black man dropped his equipment on the floor next to the man and said, "Huh."

Pete left the room and from a distance watched three medics and Skip Dahlke lift Brett onto the gurney, wrap him in a blanket and then secure him with straps. An IV was started as was oxygen. He looked so small, vulnerable. His eyes were shut, and his expression was a grimace.

"Is that Brett?"

Pete turned around and saw Tim and Patrick standing next to him.

"Yeah, but it's not as bad as it looks."

The boys continued to watch in silence.

"He was hit in the shoulder, but I think he'll be okay."

At least Pete hoped he would be. They moved forward to speak to their friend. Pete took a gentle hold of Tim's arm to prevent him, but Tim shook it off and limped to the side of the gurney, followed by Patrick.

The medics stepped back and watched while Tim smoothed Brett's hair and wiped some tears off Brett's cheeks. He wasn't conscious, but Tim bent down, whispered something and then kissed his forehead. He backed away and the medics wheeled him down the hall.

Jamie ruffled Tim's hair and asked both boys, "You guys okay?"

Neither of them answered but watched the medics and Brett in silence. With Patrick helping Tim, both boys turned and went back to the room to be with the rest of the boys.

Jamie walked over to Skip and said, "You should go with him."

Skip looked up and down the hallway at the agents scurrying around, knowing it had been combed over by him thoroughly and that whatever they'd find wouldn't amount to anything. He had his black duffle bag containing the evidence and videotape he had gathered earlier.

"He shouldn't be by himself," Skip said softly watching the gurney pause before going through the doorway, "but what about the sick boy . . . Johnny? Mike and Tim are in bad shape too. What about Fitz?"

"We'll take care of the boys, and Fitz already left. You go with Brett and stay with him, okay?"

Skip handed the duffle bag to Jamie and turned to leave, but Jamie called after him, "You did really well today."

Skip stopped briefly, and he looked like he had wanted to say something, but he didn't. He dropped his chin to his chest, and he walked quickly to catch up with Brett. Stephen stuck his head out of a doorway and motioned for Jamie to come to over. Jamie did, and Stephen introduced a blond boy.

"This is Ian."

Jamie smiled and nodded at him.

"Um . . . can you find us . . . all of us . . . clothes? We don't want to leave like this," Ian said indicating his nakedness.

Jamie had actually gotten used to it by now, watching Brett run around all morning.

"Oh, yeah . . . you bet."

He looked around for Pete, but he was talking to Cochrane. He grabbed an agent who had happened to walk past them.

"I have thirteen kids who need clothes. Shorts, shirts, maybe flip-flops. Can you rustle something up?"

The agent glanced into the room and saw the boys huddled together, staring back at him.

"Yeah . . . probably." He checked his watch and said, "Problem is, it's too early for anything to be open."

Two more teams of paramedics came through the door, pushing three gurneys.

A short, skinny, bald medic with a mustache walked up to the agent and Jamie and said, "A guy . . . Skip something, said three gurneys were needed to transport three kids . . . um, Mike, Tim and Johnny."

Jamie had an idea.

"How many hospital gowns can you get your hands on?"

The short guy looked into the room and said, "How many you need?"

"Thirteen, with slippers. These kids aren't leaving the building without something on."

The small guy nodded, keyed his lapel mike and said, "Two-eleven to base. I need thirteen hospital gowns and slippers now, like yesterday. Do you copy?"

There was pause on the line, and the medic was about to repeat his request, perhaps a bit more forcefully judging by his expression when a voice on the other end said, "Copy. A cruiser will transport now. Expect delivery in ten, fifteen minutes. Copy?"

"Two-eleven . . . thanks!"

The two bad guys were stuffed into body bags rather rudely and were dropped onto gurneys roughly and taken down the hallway. The cop with the nightstick still stuck in his ass was placed on his side onto a gurney and rolled down the hallway. The boys saw him and began to clap and cheer. Jamie and the agent turned to them and smiled. Butch and the red-haired guy were led away in handcuffs, and the boys cheered even louder. Pete and Agent Cochrane walked down the hallway and joined Jamie, the other agent and the teams of medics.

Pete stuck his head into the room and said, "What's all the noise about? Maybe it's time to get out of this place?"

The boys cheered and clapped and hugged one another. Jamie placed two fingers into his mouth and whistled, and the other agents stopped what they were doing and began to clap, whistle and cheer along with them.

The medics went in and found Johnny, Mike and Tim and prepared them for transport. Blood pressure, temps and heart rates were taken. Johnny was given oxygen and an IV of something. Tim told the medics to take care of Mike and Johnny first. The medic assured him that they would all be taken care of.

He climbed off his gurney and limped over to Johnny, bent down and whispered something to him, and then went over to Mike and did the same. Mike reached out and took hold of Tim's arm.

"It's okay, Mike. You're going to ride with Johnny. You won't be alone."

Mike held Tim's arm, and Tim patted his hand, and then kissed his forehead just as he did to Brett. "You'll be okay, Mike. You're going home."

Mike let go, but continued to look at Tim, who smiled and waved as he was pushed down the hallway.

Pete helped him get back onto the gurney and helped him lie down and asked, "You okay, Kid?"

"I'm worried about Brett," Tim said.

Pete and Jamie looked at one another, then at Tim.

"He's going to be okay," Pete said.

Tears leaked from Tim's eyes.

"Do you want someone to ride with you?"

He didn't answer. He stared at the ceiling, then shut his eyes and cried. Just as he was out of the room and in the hallway, he motioned to Pete, who moved quickly to his side. Pete took hold of the gurney to keep it from moving.

"Patrick is really close to Brett. If he rides with me, he'll get to him quicker. That okay?"

"Absolutely. I'll get him for you," Pete said.

But before Pete left, Tim said, "And you have to tell the other guys about Brett . . . that he saved us. They need to know."

Pete nodded and promised Tim that he would. It wouldn't be easy, but he would.

CHAPTER FORTY-FOUR

Just before dawn in Waukesha, Wisconsin, in the backyard of the Evans' house, George stood facing the east in nothing but his boxers and gym shorts. Bert Lane watched from her kitchen window fascinated with what he was doing. She could hear him chanting, and she watched his gentle hand and arm motions. His eyes were closed in concentration, and she assumed he was praying. What she wasn't sure was if he was praying for his family who had been murdered or if this was a morning ritual. She was curious enough to ask him but not until he was finished. She didn't want to interrupt or intrude in any way because there was certainly a reverence in George she had not seen in the many who went to her own church. At times, she herself included.

She tended to her bacon, turning it over, making sure it wasn't going to end up like Joan of Ark. She had cornbread in the oven, which she knew Jon and Jeremy liked with honey, and the twins liked with butter and warm syrup. Every so often during the week, the twins would appear at her backdoor sniffing the air in an act of what she had referred to as 'breakfast shopping' to see if her breakfast was better than the one offered by Jeremy. Usually they ended up sitting down at the Lane table and packing it away. She was amazed at how much they could eat. Much like her son Mike had done at their age.

She didn't think George would come over on his own, so she had decided that when he was finished with his morning prayers, she'd invite him over. Hopefully, she would have an opportunity to call to him before he disappeared back into the Evans' house. And maybe later that morning, she'd get him to help her plant some flowers she had wanted to plant next to the hedge row separating the Lane yard from the Evans yard.

The sun came up, and George was silent for a short time, eyes open with an expression she couldn't read. Then, he began chanting again with gestures a bit more animated but not any more loudly than he had done when the sun was still down.   At last he finished, wiped sweat from his face and then sat down on the back step; the same step he sat on just a few hours before.

He stared off into the yard. The shadows grew smaller inch by inch, foot by foot and Bert wasn't sure if he was watching it or just thinking. Thinking, she decided. She went to the back door, stuck her head out and softly called to him.

"George, come on over for breakfast."

At first he didn't acknowledge her call. Then he raised his head and turned around at the Evans' door, and then got up and walked over.

"Ma'am?" George asked shyly.

"I have cornbread and bacon for breakfast and a lot of it, so you have to help eat it. The twins and Jeremy will be over later, I'm sure, so come on in," she said opening the door wider.

"I don't have my sandals or shoes, and I'm not wearing a shirt," George said, turning a darker shade of red.

"I guess we'll have to make an exception." She added with a wink, "Chances are, Billy'll be over dressed the same way."

George came in and stood awkwardly in the entry way, not sure where he should sit or if he should even be there. He remembered how worried Jeremy was the night before, and he didn't want to worry him again. He also didn't want Jeremy to become angry with him. He noticed there were six places set at the table, enough for the twins, George, Jeremy, Jon and Bert, as if she had somehow expected everyone to show up. This was something his grandmother would do.

He smiled to himself, but remembering the image of his grandmother made him sad, and his smile quickly faded away as quickly as it had appeared.

"Have a seat anywhere. Jon usually sits there," she said gesturing to the seat at the end of the table nearest the hallway. He'll be here in a minute."

"Maybe I should let Mr. Jeremy know where I am," George said shyly.

"A bit early for Jeremy. We'll call him in a little bit. Come on, sit and eat."

George sat down and waited. Bert took a bright red hot pad, went to the oven and brought out the cornbread and placed it on a trivet in the center of the table. She took a knife from a wood block and cut it into good-sized portions. There was a pitcher of water, a pitcher of juice and a plastic gallon of milk already on the table. There was butter in a dish along with a plastic squeeze bottle in the shape of a bear filled with honey.

His stomach rumbled. He hadn't realized how hungry he was.

"Well, you're up early," Jon said as he came into the kitchen.

He put a thick arm around George's neck and rested a cheek on the top of George's head in a hug.

"Good morning, George."

"Good morning, Gran- . . ." he caught himself, hunted for something to say and settled for, "Sir."

He felt himself turning crimson, even with his naturally copper-colored skin.

"I'll take that as a wonderful complement, George, because I know how much your grandfather meant to you. Thank you very much."

Embarrassed, George smiled at Jon, then at Bert, and waited with his hands in his lap until Jon sat down to eat.

"Pour yourself something to drink, George. No need to be shy around us," Bert said.

Bert was loading bacon onto a plate between layers of paper towel to soak up some of the grease, and Jon was at the counter pouring himself a cup of coffee.

"What?' Bert asked.

"In my family, we wait until our elders . . . my mother, grandfather and grandmother begin to eat before we do."

"Oh," Bert said. "Don't wait for me or everything will get cold. Jon, sit your butt down and start eating. George is hungry."

George had to smile at the two of them as they made faces at each other, then Jon turned to George and said, "She's rude this morning, don't you think?"

Bert snapped him in the butt with a dishtowel, and George laughed as Jon danced away after a 'yelp'.

He sat down and said, "Do you and your family say 'grace'?"

George looked confused, not sure what he meant.

"George already said his prayers this morning," Bert said placing the plate piled with bacon on the table. "That's what you were doing, right?"

"Yes," George said simply, offering no further explanation.

"I watched, and I thought it was beautiful," Bert said. "Do you do that each morning?"

"Yes."

"I noticed you faced the east."

George nodded.

"Toward the rising sun."

She nodded.

"With all the trees, it must be different for you here than in Arizona," Jon said.

George knew they were curious, and he didn't mind. So he explained that each morning ever since he was little, he and his grandfather would ride on horseback up the nearest mesa that overlooked a valley with a winding creek that seldom had water in it. They would face the east and pray to father sun, honoring him.

His grandfather was a singer, which to the Navaho was similar to a priest or minister to the *biligaana*; someone who wasn't Navaho, except among his *'Azee'tsoh dine'e,* which translated to The Big Medicine People Clan, and their neighbors, his grandfather had the reputation of being more similar to an archbishop or cardinal in the Roman Catholic religion. He knew this because many of his people converted to this faith, something neither he nor his family had done. But his grandfather was that important. Slowly, George learned the songs and had hoped to one day become a singer like his grandfather.

Bert exchanged a look with Jon as George reached for a piece of cornbread and then the bottle of honey. He squeezed a good amount on it, loaded up his fork and took a bite.

"How long will it take you to be a singer?" Jon asked.

George thought about that and didn't answer right away. Trouble was, George didn't know, especially now. He knew of other singers in his clan, but none well enough for him to ask to teach him. Maybe this was as far as he was going to get, and maybe he'd never become a singer like his grandfather.

"I don't know."

As he reached for bacon, Bert asked, "George, is there going to be a funeral for your family?"

George turned red, and explained that the Navajo didn't have funerals. In fact, they seldom if ever talked about the dead, family members or not. There was too much superstition, especially among the elders. Because the elders didn't talk about the deceased, the young didn't either.

"But," Bert said, "if they were important to you as they must be, it seems only fitting there should be some sort of memorial."

George looked at her, smiled and said, "I was thinking about that, but I don't know how I'll do it. Someone needs to say prayers for them."

He shrugged and ate some bacon.

"Have you thought about where you will live now?" Jon asked.

"I have a cousin . . . Leonard. He's in the Tribal Police. He's not married, and he lives by himself in a trailer near a creek."

He didn't say that with any enthusiasm. In fact, it was more resignation than enthusiasm.

"Do you think he could help organize your memorial?"

George shook his head.

"He's superstitious."

"Hmmn . . . maybe Bert and I can go to Arizona with you. We'll help," Jon said. "It would be a nice vacation for us. We'll ask Jeremy and the twins to come along. You can show us where you used to live and sort of be a tour guide . . . if you want to, that is."

Tears filled his eyes. These people were so kind. They didn't even know him, but were willing to help him anyway. He was very grateful, and a big lump rose in his throat. He could hardly talk and couldn't swallow. He took a drink of ice water. Thankfully, there was a rap at the backdoor and Randy walked in.

"There you are," he said punching George in the arm. "Dad was wondering where you were and figured you'd be over here."

He sat down next to George without waiting to be invited and loaded up his plate with cornbread and bacon.

"We better eat before Billy comes over or there won't be any left," Randy said with a laugh.

George smiled at Randy, then at Bert and Jon, nodding a silent thank you to them.

Billy came running to the door, fumbled with the handle and said, "You guys started without me?"

And just as Bert had suggested, Billy was dressed just as George was: bare feet and no shirt.

"How far behind is Jeremy?" Bert asked.

"Right here," he said walking through the door. "Mornin' guys!"

He and Billy sat opposite George and Randy, and finally Bert sat down, and the six of them ate breakfast with talk of Billy's baseball, flowers to be planted, and the humid weather. More than anything else, there was laughter. A lot of laughter.

CHAPTER FORTY-FIVE

"He's awake, and the website is up. I'm on him. No sign of the other two yet, but I'll keep you posted."

"Thanks, Morgan."

"Watch yourself, Chet."

He clicked off without giving Chet a chance to respond, and Chet went back to monitoring the computer with his back to the front door and out of sight from the elevators. Summer was seated next to the wall in a booth in the corner of the restaurant not clearly visible from the doorway. Captain Jack O'Brien of the Waukesha Police Department, not in uniform, still pretending to read the newspaper, was in the lobby with Chet, but at a distance from him. He sat near the door in a comfortable dark, red leather high-backed chair facing the elevators.

"Mike check," O'Brien said softly for the fourth time.

"Loud and clear," Chet responded. "Summer, you okay?"

"Yeah," she said tiredly. "Anxious to get this over with."

The hotel was coming to life. Two members of the hotel cleaning crew had already come through, one with a dust cloth and the other with a vacuum cleaner. The hotel smelled of wood and some rather pleasant cleaning spray or polish that O'Brien couldn't name. An instrumental version of an Air Supply song played softly in the background. A TV on mute was tuned to CNN. They had hoped to contain the media, so the fact that there was no story on the siege that took place in Chicago, Kansas City or Los Angeles was welcomed, especially in the Sheraton in downtown Chicago.

A couple of early birds were lined up at the counter ready to check out instead of using the rapid checkout by phoning the front desk and leaving the keys on the desk inside of the room. An older couple dressed in summer leisure clothes walked out of the lobby going for an early stroll or perhaps breakfast somewhere other than the hotel. A very tired looking mom carrying a steaming hot coffee from room service and a Chicago Tribune followed after a boy that looked to be about nine and a girl about seven, both dressed in swimsuits and sandals obviously headed to the pool. O'Brien didn't think they'd be lucky to have the pool open at this time in the morning, but it didn't hurt to try. Two middle-aged men in suits, one carrying a briefcase came in from the street chatting and walked into the restaurant.

O'Brien looked at his watch and saw that it was two minutes faster than the lobby wall clock, which annoyed him.

Depending upon which one you looked at, it was either 7:02 AM or 7:04 AM, both Central Standard Time.

Any time now.

The Los Angeles and Kansas City sites were all wrapped up, as was the Chicago site. The kids were safely at hospitals getting checked out, but more importantly, were under guard. No one was going to hurt those kids ever again. O'Brien was concerned about the boy who had been shot because Chet had told him that when the boy got to the hospital, he went immediately to surgery. No word on him yet.

He was pissed and saddened that Paul Gates had lost his life, and that Ronnie Desotel and Fitz had been wounded. Fitz also went into surgery as soon as he entered the hospital, but he was a tough guy. It'd take more than one bullet to keep him down for long. But still, Gates, Fitz and Desotel were his guys, and that kid was, well, a kid. Shouldn't have happened.

He had to control his anger and not let it get the best of him because he had to watch Chet's and Summer's back.

Chet rechecked his connection to the hotel's security cameras. By using split screen, he could monitor the two floors where the targets were located, the restaurant and the outside camera, which covered the front door, so he could monitor traffic in and out of the hotel. He spotted one target leaving his room on the fourth floor, walking to the elevators while checking his IPhone.

"About to have company, Jack," Chet said to O'Brien. "Watch the elevators."

Chet's cell vibrated.

"Number two is awake, cell on. He phoned number three, and he's close to your position. Be careful." Morgan said.

He was anxious, not sure how this was going to play out and wishing he could do more to help.

"Got it, Morgan. We're ready."

Chet sat a little lower in his chair because at any moment, he expected someone to enter the lobby. He and Summer had already guessed who it would be.

"Game time, folks. Target just stepped out of the elevators," O'Brien said.

"Summer, Target One is headed your way in one . . . two . . . now."

"Gary Sears, aka Victor Bosch . . . the Dark Man," Summer said quietly.

A man and woman entered the restaurant just a step or two behind Sears/Bosch and took a booth kiddy-corner from him. The restaurant now held four people besides

Summer, including the two men in suits who came in just before the Dark Man and sat in a booth near the door.

A different waiter from the one who was in the restaurant when she and Chet first entered it was on duty and stepped over to Summer offering her a refill on her coffee and very quietly without making eye contact said, "I'm Kevin Thigpen from the Chicago office. The man and woman in the booth are with me. Agent Vince Cochrane sent us, and Pete Kelliher said to say hello. We're here to assist and support."

He left as soon as he finished.

"You guys catch that?" Summer asked.

"Copy. Always nice to have back-up," O'Brien said quietly.

"Jack, on your six. Our second guest will be entering the hotel in one . . . two . . . now," Chet said. "Dapper as usual." Then Chet added, "Smug son of a bitch."

O'Brien tensed as the impeccably dressed man walked passed him, but he didn't even pay Jack any attention as he walked directly into the restaurant. The well-dressed man walked to the table where Bosch/Sears was seated, and they shook hands, though Bosch/Sears didn't get up to do so.

"Jack, watch the elevators," Chet advised. "On one . . . two . . . oops, a stop on two. Wait a bit . . . wait . . . okay, on one . . . two . . . now. Everyone present and accounted for."

The third man entered the restaurant and sat with the other two men at a table towards the back of the room, out of direct line of sight of Summer who also sat in the back but in a booth and not near them. The waiter/agent went to them and took drink orders; coffee all the way around, along with ice water with lemon for the Dark Man and one guy. The well-dressed man ordered tomato juice.

The Dark Man reached into his inside breast pocket and took out two thick envelopes and handed one to each man and said, "I appreciate all you've done. Once I close down the operations, we'll have to lay low before we begin again. I'm thinking of an extended stay in Amsterdam or Lichtenstein. I believe I can make some profitable contacts there and . . . *enjoy* myself while doing so, if you know what I mean," he said with a humorless chuckle.

"You'll have to shut them down today, though. They said they'd move on them in two, maybe three days," the well-dressed man said. "All evidence, and I mean *all* evidence will have to disappear. That means the kids and the guards."

"You can't stall them another day?" the other man asked the well-dressed man.

"Not without arousing suspicion. Storm isn't stupid and neither is Kelliher."

"No, we can't take the risk," the Dark Man agreed. "I'm going to visit the Chicago stable and spend some time with my new pony . . . a good, long time with him." He took a sip of water and then said, "His name is Stephen, and he came in last night. You want to see some pictures?"

The well-dressed man waived him off, but the other man asked to see them. Bosch/Sears handed him his IPhone.

The older man took his time looking at the pictures, and then said, "I have some time before I have to get back to Washington. I think I'll go with you. There are two boys . . . Tim and Brett." He took a sip of coffee and said, "I like those two boys."

"Have you heard from Graham yet?" the well-dressed man asked.

"No," the Dark Man answered looking around the restaurant. "He said he'd meet us here."

"Did your nephew tell you how it went in Waukesha?"

The Dark Man answered, "All he said was, 'Job done.'"

The conversation came in loud and clear. The powerful microphones and hotel security cameras recorded everything. Summer thought to herself, *that was who was tying up loose ends*. Graham Porter, the Dark Man's nephew.

She asked her partners, "We have enough?"

O'Brien answered, "Chet, you get all of that on tape?"

"Every word. Summer, we need their cells, especially Bosch's before he can erase anything. Text him from Porter's phone telling him you went to the restroom, and that you're walking to the restaurant now. That'll keep him busy. I'll tell you when to move. Jack, you might want to move into position now, but don't enter the restaurant until I give the go ahead."

"Texting now," Summer said. "Jack, Chet will tell you where the phone is, you get it before Bosch can do anything with it. Break his fingers if you have to."

"My pleasure. Might break 'em even if I don't have to," O'Brien answered.

"Text sent," Summer said.

Chet watched, and Summer and O'Brien waited impatiently. Time moved ever so slowly. The waiter arrived at their table and took orders. The men ordered off the menu rather than the having the breakfast buffet, during which, the Dark Man checked his IPhone.

"Okay, he checked the text." Chet announced.

"Let's move. Now!" Summer said.

The waiter stood with his back to Summer as she approached the table. As O'Brien came into the restaurant, she moved across the room in such a way as to appear to head to the doorway. The waiter blocked the one man's view of her, and the well-dressed man had his back to her. This was all good because she was on them and at the table before anyone realized it, taking the three men seated at the table by surprise.

"Hands on the back of your head, Gentlemen," she announced. "FBI, and I have warrants for your arrest."

The waiter/agent reached for his .9M Glock under his apron and held it on the three men, as the man and woman from the booth came to assist behind each man. As Bosch reached for his phone, O'Brien grabbed the man's hand squeezing tightly, and there was no real struggle as he took the phone and pocketed it.

The two businessmen in the booth towards the front watched in fascination. When the guns appeared, they left the restaurant on a run.

"Summer, I . . ." the well-dressed man started.

"Save it, Doug. Whatever you're about to say is bullshit."

Deftly, she took his left hand and cuffed it, pulling it behind his back. As she reached for his right hand, he started to come out of his chair, but she rapped the back of his head with the butt of her gun hard enough to stun him, but not to render him unconscious. She thought about pistol-whipping him, but didn't.

"Sit your ass back down and stay there until I tell you to move," Summer said.

Thatcher Davis hung his head briefly and then raised his ashen face towards her.

"I'm sorry," was all he said.

"You're a piece of shit, Thatcher," Summer spit. "You were a friend! I trusted you!"

Bosch took a sip of ice water and then said, "I want a lawyer."

"You'll need one. Kidnapping, child endangerment, pornography, sex with a minor, sodomy, just to name a few of the charges. Oh, and I forgot . . . murder."

"We'll see," he said smugly. "We'll see."

"Yup, and I can't wait," Summer said as he was cuffed by the waiter/agent. "And by the way, the kids in Chicago, Kansas City and Los Angeles are all safe."

She turned to Doug Rawson and smiled wryly.

She turned back to Bosch and said, "Oh, and I almost forgot. Your nephew . . . Graham Porter . . . isn't in the restroom, and he's not in Chicago. He's dead, killed by the fourteen year old Indian boy you sent him to kill."

She waved Porter's cell at him.

"In about a half an hour, arrest warrants will be served on every participant in this ring. So yes, you'll need a very good lawyer, but probably not one of the seven you have in your network. They'll need one, too."

As she stepped around the table towards Thatcher Davis, he snatched up a serrated knife. The lady agent moved to intercept him, but it was too late. Davis jammed it into his juggler and blood sprayed and pulsed out of his neck. His eyes found Summer, who looked impassively at him, then turned away.

The male agent moved to pull out the knife, but O'Brien held the man's arm preventing him from doing so. The puzzled agent looked at him.

"Safer to let him bleed to death."

The two agents took a step or two backward.

The expression on Bosch's face was that of smug contempt.

He turned to Summer and said, "What do you think you'll prove by arresting me? Hmmn?"

Summer didn't have any intention of responding.

"Don't you realize that there are other men out there with similar appetites, similar tastes? Put me away, and someone else will step forward. Put him away, and another will step forward. You think you ended this? You didn't. There will always be other men to take my place and other ponies to fulfill their needs. Whether those beautiful boys know it or not, they like what we do with them. We fulfill their need as much as they fulfill ours. It's reciprocity, that's all."

"No, you sick son of a bitch. It's sickness . . . it's filth. And those boys? They hated it, and at your trial, they'll step forward and tell you so. That's a promise you sick bastard. I'll see to it!"

"Summer, I was undercover. I was playing a role," Rawson pleaded.

"Save it," O'Brien said. "Your bank records, your cell records, and your travel arrangements tell us differently."

"Summer . . ."

He never finished. Summer punched him on the nose sending him crashing to the floor.

CHAPTER FORTY-SIX

Hospitals have a certain smell; not quite clean, not quite dirty, something in between and not altogether pleasant. Sort of like one's grandmother's house, minus the freshly baked bread or aerosol air freshener. Of course the hospital was bright, sunny and clean. It just didn't smell that way. A sour smell, perhaps, Skip couldn't decide. It was different from the lab where he worked, even different from the lab where he performed his autopsies. Different.

He never liked hospitals. Not that he ever spent time in one, not even one night. He had never known anyone close to him who had spent time in a hospital. And, it was interesting that he chose Forensic Science as a career considering how he felt about hospitals.

Skip sat in the waiting area for word on how Brett and the other boys were doing after surgery. The little dark-haired boy, Patrick, sat with his head against him, mouth slightly open and sound asleep. Skip had one arm around the boy protectively. Every now and then, Skip would brush his lips against the boy's brown hair, kiss him and give his shoulder a squeeze. Patrick never noticed. He was sound asleep.

The doctor felt that the Erickson boy would be pretty routine, thinking that five or six stitches might do it. The fact that it was inside his anus and rectum necessitated him being placed under sedation. Of course, you never knew what they might find once they enter, but the preliminary physical and evaluation resulted in a "minor" diagnosis. It would be the after-surgery that would require care. He also had a shiner, and his face was beaten up badly, but there weren't any broken bones. He had, however, lost two teeth and at least one other was loose.

Tim Pruitt's surgery was similar to Mike Erickson's, but because he was penetrated with an object, then raped, the attending physician thought it might be more than minor. Just how much, he wasn't sure until he took a closer look.

Fitz and Brett were different stories. Both had shoulder wounds, but the bullet in Fitz rattled around a bit, nicking his lung and in general, "created a bit of havoc" to quote the surgeon. In Brett's case, because he was so small, malnourished and dehydrated, the bullet did even more damage. It didn't touch the lung, but it nicked several large veins, just missed an artery, damaged muscle and other tissue and eventually exited out his armpit and entered his upper arm, nicking his triceps. His surgery would take more time and the rehab even longer.

Johnny Vega was in intensive care being treated for dehydration, complicated by pneumonia, or vice versa. The doctors weren't sure. He was on oxygen and an IV drip, and he wasn't allowed visitors yet. Skip had looked through the window at him, and Johnny tried to smile, but it came out more as a grimace. He did manage to flash a weak thumbs up, which Skip reciprocated. Then, Johnny shut his eyes and seemed to fall asleep.

Pete and Jamie entered the waiting area and found Skip sitting in a chair, one arm resting on his knee, the other around a sleeping Patrick, head hung low and cell phone in his hand. It had been almost two hours since they had seen him, and the only thing they had heard was that Fitz, Brett, the Erickson boy, and Tim were in surgery, and that Johnny Vega was being treated for pneumonia. They wanted an update.

Their butts dragging, Jamie dropped into a seat next to Skip, while Pete sat across from them. Jamie shut his eyes and rested his head on the back of the chair, legs stretched across the cramped sitting area. Pete wiped his eyes with his hands, ran his hand over his face and yawned.

"I'm too old for this shit," he said softly.

Jamie answered, "I'm too young for this shit."

He clapped Skip on the leg and asked, "So, what have you heard?"

Skip gave them as much information as he had, then paused and added, "And, I'm out of a job."

Jamie glanced sideways at him, then straightened up and said, "What?"

"Wisconsin's closing the Wausau office due to budget cuts, and everything will now be handled out of Milwaukee or Madison."

"Can't you get on with one of them?" Pete asked.

He shrugged. "Roz called and said all of us received one month's notice and that we were encouraged to apply to Milwaukee or Madison, but there weren't any openings at the moment."

Jamie and Pete exchanged a glance, Pete's face screwed up in thought.

"Let me make a phone call," he said, lifting himself up from his chair.

He knew he was tired but didn't realize just how much until he had sat down.

"Things'll work out," Jamie said as he smacked Skip on his arm.

Skip didn't respond.

*   *   *

Pete, Summer, Chet, Jamie, Skip and O'Brien sat around a table in the hospital drinking coffee or Coke, picking at pastry and talking about what they had accomplished that morning. The adrenaline rush had long since vanished. It had been a long, sleepless night. Brett was still in surgery and had been for the past hour, and the attending physician was instructed to call Skip when he was out, but he hadn't yet.

Fitz was out of surgery but in post-op and wouldn't be allowed to have visitors until later that morning. Tim and Mike were about to be moved from post-op and would share a room together at Tim's request. Everything went well with them, though both would be uncomfortable until the stitches dissolved.

Johnny was comfortable and though the doctors hadn't said it, they were worried.

Cochrane and several of his agents from the Chicago office, along with Pete and Jamie interviewed each of the boys. Their reports would be compared to the reports obtained from Kansas City and Los Angeles. One story was as depressing and as disgusting as the next. The common theme was perversion at the hands of sick men. Worse, there was the constant theme of isolation.

Another constant was the lack of food and water. The boys were given a bathroom break every hour or so, and were given water periodically, but inconsistently during the day.

The agents found the stash of pills on the second floor of the building in Chicago, and it was determined that one pill was Viagra or a similar drug. The other pill was either a depressant or a stimulant. The idea was to keep the boys submissive, as well as dependent.   The type varied, and there were at least three different kinds that were found, including Adderall, Ritalin, and Amytal. Because the boys had learned to fake taking the pill and just pretend, among all the other things that were wrong with them, addiction wouldn't be one of them. Each boy had snorted cocaine, smoked marijuana, and drank alcohol, but not with any regularity that would cause addiction. Each Saturday, the boys were to cut their nails because they had to look their best for each 'date'. Haircuts were perhaps once a month, which was why each boy's hair was long.

"It's a wonder the boys survived this long," Jamie said.

The others at the table didn't say anything, but their anger was a thick blanket wrapped around them.

All three networks and CNN now carried the story, though a general, sanitized version was put forth. The FBI had pleasant looking PR people prepare and then read statements from all three sites. They also mentioned that 147 arrest warrants were issued across the country, including several prominent local, state and national politicians, judges, lawyers, sports figures, music and movie industry folks, teachers, coaches, priests, ministers- virtually every walk of life. The only common factor, and not surprising at all, was that all were male. The charges ranged from receiving or possessing pornography, sending pornography, to the much more serious rape, sodomy, and in several cases, murder.

Most of the parents of the boys had been notified and were either on the way or making plans to get to their sons as soon as they could. Those who hadn't been contacted would receive phone calls until they were. The Pruitts lived in West Bend, Wisconsin and were already in route, as were the Baileys and Ericksons, parents of Stephen Bailey and Mike Erickson, the boys taken the night before from Waukesha, Wisconsin. Jamie had also contacted Jeremy Evans to see if he and Randy could come and speak to the parents and perhaps the boys. Jeremy had agreed, as did Randy, and had at least an hour lead on the parents.

Summer spotted Cochrane picking up a cup of coffee and made room for him at the table.

"We finished the interviews." After a sip, he added, "Pretty fucking grim."

"At least they're alive," she answered.

"I wonder how damaged the kids are . . . I can't imagine," Chet said.

"How can they *not* be damaged?" Jamie said. "Starved, locked in a fucking room, some of them over a year . . . and God knows what else. Jesus *Christ* . . ." he trailed off.

"This Jeremy Evans . . . can he help them?" Cochrane asked.

"Hell, I don't know. He's good, and the kids deserve a shot, but hell, who knows?" Pete said.

"The Erickson kid hasn't said a word since we found him," Skip added. "Not even a grunt."

There was silence then. Sips of coffee or Coke. The pastry no longer tasty, pushed away from whoever had it sitting in front of them, losing their appetite, thinking about the demons the kids will be wrestling with for a long, long time.

"Can I ask . . ." Cochrane started, "there are rumors that there was a leak."

Summer nodded. "Chet and Pete found it."

"Nah, you and Chet," Pete said.

"How?" Cochrane asked.

"Someone was a step or two ahead of us, and we couldn't figure out how," Pete said.

"When did you suspect?" Cochrane asked.

"We were in Pembine, Wisconsin at the scene of a triple homicide. We got word that George Tokay's family was murdered, and their home burnt," Pete said. "It was just luck George was with us at the time."

"We had two possible theories," Summer explained. "One was that the third man that had been seen in Arizona was tying up loose ends. We wanted to believe that one, but it didn't seem likely because he wouldn't have gone after George or his family the way he did."

Cochrane looked puzzled and pulled out his notebook searching for George Tokay's name.

Pete helped him out and said, "He's a fourteen year old Navajo boy. Two of the victims in Pembine were ID'd by George in Arizona. We flew him to Wisconsin to positively ID the two men as the assholes he saw executing a kid . . ."

". . . Tyler Hart from Cincinnati," Summer corrected.

". . . executing Tyler Hart," Pete said. "We made a decision to have Doug Rawson investigate each of us to see where the leak might be."

"Why him?" Cochrane asked.

"Because he's black. He didn't fit the typical profile of a serial rapist of white boys. We thought he wouldn't be involved . . . guess we were wrong."

"He allegedly investigated and didn't come up with anything on any of us," Chet said. "That was odd. It *had* to be one of us."

"Then, Summer remembered having a conversation with Thatcher Davis and passed that on to Logan Musgrave, our boss, and Doug. Doug said he'd put Davis under twenty-four hour surveillance," Pete said.

"But Davis was on the lawyer side of the FBI. He didn't have regular access to our work and wasn't a part of our meetings," Chet said. "So, that still left one of us, or either Doug Rawson or Logan Musgrave."

"So Chet had a buddy of his do some digging on the two of them and had him monitor their cell phones," Pete said.

"You monitored your boss' cell phone?" Cochrane asked, eyebrows raised.

"I got the okay from Tom Dandridge," Pete answered.

"*Dan*dridge?" Cochrane asked.

"You never mentioned that you reached out to Dandridge?" Summer said, a little annoyed that Pete had kept that from her.

"My guardian angel. He and I go back years, and he's a friend. I needed a consult," Pete explained with a shrug. "Besides, kids were dying, two kids were just kidnapped, and a family was murdered. The gloves were off," Pete said with another shrug.

"You never told me that," Summer said. "Why?"

Pete shrugged. "I wanted your butt covered in case I screwed up. I didn't want it to touch you."

She glared at him and then continued.

"In Waukesha, Chet's buddy intercepted a phone call from Rawson to Graham Porter giving him the location of George Tokay with a kill order. At the same time, Chet finds accounts for both Rawson and Davis with quite a bit of money in them."

"Almost a half-million apiece," Chet said. "I found it easily. Rawson should have found it just as easily, but he claimed he couldn't find anything on Davis. He's not dumb enough to wave his account at us and say, 'Here I am.'"

"Chet matched deposits from what might have been withdrawals from Victor Bosch's account," Summer said.

"Still, it wasn't until the two of them showed up at the Sheraton that we were one hundred percent sure."

"But what I don't understand and can't figure out is why Bosch would risk letting us know there was a leak by going after George and his family," Chet said.

"I can only guess," Summer said shrugging her shoulders. "Arrogance . . . the feeling that he can and will get away with it . . . that he was untouchable . . . and the fact that Porter was his nephew who shared the same perversions, and he needed to protect him from being identified by George. That's all I can figure," Summer said knowing that they'd never know for sure.

"Why Rawson? Why did he get involved?" Cochrane asked.

"Greed . . . old fashion money," Summer answered. "We don't think he ever took advantage of the boys . . . at least there's no record or video of him in Chicago or Long Beach."

"Chet looked into the agents in Albuquerque and Phoenix and found someone in each office with almost as much money as Davis and Rawson. We think the pilot was clean and was coerced into taking the helicopter up. We suspect the agent out of Albuquerque of executing the helicopter pilot and the two guys who murdered George

Tokay's family," Pete said. "You know, tying up loose ends. We'll never know who pulled the trigger for sure."

"Why did you suspect someone in Albuquerque or Phoenix?" O'Brien asked.

"George's cousin, Leonard, is a deputy with the Navajo Tribal Police, and he had discovered the helicopter service was out of New Mexico. We knew Bosch's ranch was outside of Phoenix in Chandler. We figured he had to have protection or at least eyes in both places," Pete answered.

"We also uncovered protection from local PD in Chicago, Long Beach and Los Angeles," Chet said. "This whole thing was well organized with a lot of money that helped with the organization."

"And the rest . . . well, you know the rest," Summer said.

"Nice investigative work," Cochrane said.

Pete and Summer exchanged a smile, and Pete winked at Chet. He smiled for the first time in a long time.

CHAPTER FORTY-SEVEN

Jamie and O'Brien left to check on Fitz, Skip left to check on Brett, and Cochrane left for his office. Pete had asked that Summer and Chet stay behind, so he could speak to them. They sat around the same table where they had been sitting, Pete on one side, with Summer and Chet facing him.

"Guys, I've handed in my resignation. I'm too old for this."

"Come on, Pete," Summer said. "You're tired, that's all."

"No," he said shaking his head. "A boy hangs onto a gun and gets shot when I should have shoved his butt back with the other boys. Two assholes catch me off-guard, and I'm running up and down stairs out of breath and wondering what the fuck is happening. I can't do this any longer."

"Oh bull!" Chet said.

"I've already sent a message to Dandridge."

Deputy Director Thomas Dandridge was in charge of the wing that Logan Musgrave and others on that side reported to. His kingdom, as he liked to call it, ranged from computer crime, to auto theft, to crimes against children, including the Rapid Response Team that were the actual first responders in abduction cases. He and Pete had entered the

FBI at the same time and had become friends and stayed friends, even though Dandridge had moved quickly and quietly up through the ranks, while Pete stayed with cop work. Pete had quietly kept him in the loop ever since he had received the phone call from George's cousin while investigating the murder scene in Pembine.

"Pete, we just closed a ring that ran across half the country, and we saved a bunch of kids. Probably more when you consider this ring could've kept going on and on for who knows how long. It was your hunch . . . your gut that closed it. Ask Dandridge to sit on it for a week or two, and then see what happens," Summer pleaded.

Pete looked down at the empty and chipped mug that held the last drops of coffee he drank earlier. He held onto it with both hands, and he didn't respond, so the three of them sat there in silence, not sure what to say.

*   *   *

The nurse didn't want to let them in at all, but the doctor overruled her, allowing them in the boy's room for a moment to just have a quick word.

Brett's eyes blinked open, but he lay still, first staring at the ceiling, then out the window, and then the wall at the foot of his bed. He stared at his left arm that had an IV in it, and it seemed that he noticed that his left shoulder ached under the heavy bandage. He turned his head slowly to his right and spotted both Skip and Pete and he smiled weakly.

"I'm not sure who you are, Kid," Pete said. "I'm used to having you run around naked and calling me names."

He mouthed something, and Pete bent low so he could hear him.

"Lift the sheet and take a peek, Fuck Head," Brett said quietly with a smile.

"That's the Brett we know," Pete said to Skip with a laugh. "Had us fooled, didn't he?"

Brett reached out his right hand, and Pete took it and held it, and then Brett shut his eyes still smiling.

After a short time, he opened them, focused on Skip and said softly, "Sorry for not sticking with the plan."

"It worked out okay," Skip said.

"I could've gotten everybody killed." Tears filled his eyes.

"Kid, you saved everyone's life. *Everyone's* life," Pete said. "Don't forget that."

Brett looked at Skip and said, "Sorry."

"Nothing to be sorry for, Kid. You're one of the bravest guys I know," Skip said. And then with a laugh added, "Probably one of the most stubborn too."

Brett smiled, turned his head and fell asleep. Skip's cell vibrated and he got up, looked at the number but didn't recognize it, so he stepped into the hall to take it. Nurses moved up and down the hall. The overhead intercom asked for this doctor to call that number. Orderlies pushed patients in wheelchairs or on gurneys this direction or that direction. Lots of hustle and bustle, all purposeful and orderly.

The phone vibrated again and he opened it up and said, "James Dahlke."

"Please hold for Deputy Director Dandridge," a women's voice said.

He had heard about him just that morning but was puzzled as to what this was about. Probably Pete called this guy in order to have him running off again to look at a crime scene. He guessed that would be okay, since he didn't have much to do at the moment. After a pause, he heard someone pick up and then a man cleared his voice.

"Skip Dahlke?"

"Yes, this is James Dahlke."

"My name is Tom Dandridge. I'm a Deputy Director with the FBI, and I'd like you to work for us. You've come highly recommended, and I've seen some of the results of your work."

Skip guessed who it was that had contacted him. He glanced through the window into Brett's room. Brett was asleep, and Pete sat in the chair with his head in his hands. He looked like he was dozing.

"Oh and I also want you to give a message to Kelliher for me," Dandridge continued. "Tell him to take his resignation and shove it up his ass. Tell him I'm not accepting it. Got that?"

"Um . . . yes, Sir."

*   *   *

While Randy made the rounds talking to each of the boys, mostly listening, sometimes sharing tears, Jeremy met with the Pruitts, the Baileys and the Ericksons. Understandably, the parents didn't want to meet with him but instead wanted to be with their sons. Yet, they listened respectfully, asked questions, and sought advice.

He repeated what he had shared with the Forstadts the night before, after their son had phoned Randy and told him that a pizza owner, Jim Rodemaker, might have had Stephen

Bailey and Mike Erickson. That conversation seemed so long ago, days ago and not just a few hours ago.

They sat around a dark oak or mahogany table in soft leather chairs in a comfortable conference room used by the hospital for telling loved ones about imminent death or required surgery or surgical complications. Fortunately, there would be none of that at this meeting.

"Your boys will be anxious to see you, but at the same time, nervous and ashamed."

"Nervous?" Jennifer Erickson asked, not in anger, but in confusion. "We're their parents."

"Yes," he said nodding, "But nervous and ashamed because of what these boys had to endure, go through . . . do. These boys had to survive any way they could. They obeyed. To *not* obey meant severe beatings or even death. Stephen and Mike didn't witness this, but the others did."

He paused and started again.

"All kids want to please their parents . . . make them proud. Your sons want no less. Because of what they were forced to do, they might feel you'll be disappointed in them . . . they might feel they let you down."

"But we aren't disappointed in them. They're our kids." Mark Erickson said.

"Exactly" Jeremy said. "But remember, it isn't what *you're* feeling, it's what the *boys* are feeling. They're confused. They're tired. They're angry."

Jeremy paused and said, "They had a good-sized chunk of their lives stolen from them, and they won't get it back. Ever. The best they can do . . . with *your* help, with *your* love and with *your* support is to go on from here."

The parents looked at one another not quite sure what to make of Jeremy or what exactly had happened to their kids. They were also pretty sure they didn't want to know what had happened to their kids.

Sitting around the table with Jeremy were Detective Jamie Graff, Captain Jack O'Brien, and Agent Summer Storm. Sitting off to the side were the two surgeons who had worked on Tim and Mike. They listened intently, nodding every so often to a point Jeremy made or a question that was posed to him, but otherwise just listened.

"We were told Tim had surgery," Thad Pruitt said. "Why?"

The two surgeons looked at each other, deciding who would answer the question. Finally, Blaine Flasch cleared his throat, took his glasses off and sort of played with them, debating what words to use. Finally, he shook his head and ran his hand through his hair, giving up on any polite, sanitized way to say what needed to be said.

"Both Tim and Mike had similar injuries to their anus and rectum. They're going to be fine in the long run, but in the short term, there will be discomfort and some pain. They'll have to wash carefully, take Sitz baths, apply antiseptic ointment, but they're going to be fine."

The parents stared at him, not comprehending what he was saying, and then slowly the meaning of his words seeped in, showing first on their faces. Two of the mothers covered their mouths. Tears spilled out of each of the mothers' eyes. The fathers grew pale, and Thad Pruitt clenched his fist.

"Our sons were raped." Ted Bailey didn't ask the question.

He merely voiced what had registered in each of the parents' minds.

"They were . . ." he didn't, couldn't finish.

"Oh my God," Sarah Bailey said, clutching Jennifer Erickson's hand. "Oh my God," she repeated.

Thad Pruitt put his arm around his wife's shoulders, their heads together in a silent hug.

"Tim'll be fine," he said softly.

"This is what you meant when you said it would be difficult for the boys to tell us what they went through, isn't it?" Mark Erickson asked.

"Yes," Jeremy said nodding. "At the very least, these boys have been forced to do things that we don't want to imagine children doing. In some cases, the boys were tortured and what they experienced no one . . . not me, not you . . . no one can imagine."

Jeremy paused then said, "They might not *ever* tell you exactly what happened or what they went through, but what they *do* tell you will be painful for them to share and painful for you to hear."

"What about . . ." Ted Bailey searched for the words, and then finally said, "AIDS?"

The other adults turned and looked at Doctor Flasch who shrugged and said softly, "The boys will have to be tested every six months for at least a year or two, maybe longer."

The statement was met with silence. It was a thick and living thing, enough to choke, enough to suffocate. Each adult wrestled with their thoughts, their feelings. They tried to rationalize and deny. They were angry. But mostly, they were helpless. There was nothing they could do to make it go away, to make it disappear, and they certainly couldn't have a do over, either for themselves or more importantly, for their sons.

Jeremy had seen this same reaction in each of the adults he had spoken to in the years he'd been on call for law enforcement agencies. Hell, he still felt this way at times when he looked at his son, Randy.

"What now?" Laura Pruitt asked. "What do the boys need now? How can we help them?"

Jeremy smiled sadly.

"They need each other. The boys suffered together. They cried together. They watched other boys get taken away, never to be seen again. They need you."

The parents nodded and wiped away tears; took Kleenex and wiped their eyes, their noses. Somehow, someway, they garnered up their courage. Jeremy saw it building, if ever so slowly, weakly, but it was there. A resolve.

"Wouldn't it be better if they didn't talk about it? You know, just move on?" Laura Pruitt asked.

Jeremy shook his head and said, "No. That would just bottle things up. If you discourage them from talking about it, that might confirm to the boys that you are disappointed in them and that what they did, even though they didn't have any choice in the matter, was wrong."

"Can the boys talk to you?" Sarah Bailey asked.

"I'm willing to work with them, but they might need someone with more experience. But yes. We'll make sure the boys have my number as well as my son's number. My son, Randy has been through this too, though not as long or as extensively as your boys."

The adults stared at one another in silence. Mark Erickson puffed out his cheeks and slipped an arm around his wife, Jennifer. Thad and Laura Pruitt rested their heads on each other. Sarah and Ted Bailey said nothing. They had been feeling guilty because they had blamed Mark and Jennifer because the boys had been taken from their house. Though they had apologized and though that apology had been accepted, the guilt was still there and would be for a long time.

Trying to lighten the mood in the room, Jeremy said, "Don't forget . . . these boys survived. They lived. They have incredible courage . . . and hope . . . and resilience." He paused and then said again, "They survived. Honestly, you can be very proud of them."

*   *   *

Tim had climbed up and sat on the end of Brett's bed. He wasn't supposed to be there, but Skip had snuck him in and guarded the door so the friends could talk.

"Tim, I'm scared."

"Why?"

"I don't want to be alone," Brett said tears running down his cheeks.

Tim stared at his friend, not understanding what he was trying to say.

"My parents won't be here until tomorrow, maybe the day after. You're leaving along with some of the other guys tomorrow. The doctor said I'll be in the hospital for another day or two. I don't want to be by myself," Brett said. "And then what? What happens next?"

Tim got up from the foot of the bed and lay down next to his friend, carefully slipping his arm around his shoulders. Brett laid his head on Tim's shoulder.

"You and Johnny are my best friends, and Patrick's like my little brother," Brett said absent-mindedly wiping his tears off on Tim's robe. "Are we ever going to see each other again?"

"God, I hope so," Tim said. "I don't know if I would have made it without you, Brett."

Brett looked up at his friend, shook his head and said, "You were the strong one, Tim. Everyone looked up to you."

"I don't feel very strong, and I didn't feel like a leader," Tim said, wiping tears from his face with his free hand. "Besides, you were always the toughest."

"Tim, promise me we'll stay in touch," Brett pleaded. "Promise? Really promise?"

Tim turned and kissed the top of Brett's head and said, "We'll always be friends, Brett. I promise."

They lay there side by side, Brett's head resting on Tim's shoulder, Tim with his arm around Brett's shoulder.

Brett reached over and took hold of Tim's hand and said, "I'm so scared, Tim. I don't know why, but I'm scared. Even when I shot those two assholes, I wasn't afraid." He paused, looked up at his friend and asked, "What does that mean?"

"Dunno, Brett." Tim kissed the top of his head again.

"The doctor told me that I probably won't be able to play football for at least a year. Maybe not ever again," Brett said.

Tim nodded and clenched a fist.

"I used to play basketball . . . my favorite sport. I played baseball and could hit it a ton . . . pitch." He paused, shook his head and clenched his fist again. "I haven't played in over two years. I don't even know if I can play anymore."

"We're kind of fucked up, huh?" Brett said with a humorless laugh.

Tim held him tighter.

There was a knock on the door and Ian stuck his head in.

"Can we come in?"

Without waiting for an answer, the door opened, and the boys from Chicago filed in one by one, crowding around Brett's bed. Randy entered last and stood against the door.

"Hi guys," Brett said, straightening up and wiping the tears off his face. "Mike, sit down here," pointing to a spot on his bed. "You need to get off your feet."

Stephen and Ian helped Mike up on Brett's bed. It was painful to sit, so like Tim, he sort of leaned back, resting on his elbow and his hip. Patrick ended up next to Brett sitting half on, half off the bed. Brett took a hold of his hand and gave it a squeeze before letting go. They were treated as if they were brothers, and both of them still felt and would still feel as if they were.

"You have a hell of a shiner," Brett said to Mike.

Mike nodded and smiled, pointing at his missing teeth.

"Shit, they really fucked you up!"

The boys laughed, including Mike.

Patrick said for all of them, "We wanted to thank you."

Brett looked at Patrick, then Tim, and then at each of the boys, who smiled back at him and nodded. Ian spoke for the group.

"Skip told us that if it weren't for you, we might not be here."

"'Course you had to go and get yourself shot all hero-like," Tim said bumping his head into Brett's.

The boys laughed and then talked all at once about the phone calls to their parents, when they would arrive and get to go home. Randy watched them, mostly watching Tim and Brett. Tim's eyes locked on Randy's and he nodded.

"Randy, some of us were talking . . ." Tim said.

Everyone settled down and looked at Randy, who blushed and remained glued to the door. He felt like an intruder because while he went through much of what they did, he was only held captive for one night before he had escaped and was rescued.

"Some of us are worried about being alone."

Tim felt Brett elbow him slightly, not unnoticed by Randy.

"You have each other. You have e-mail, cell phones, landlines, and Facebook," Randy said as he sat down on the arm of a chair that a smaller boy, Ben sat in. "You can always visit with each other. And more than anything, you have one thing in common that no one can take away."

"Yeah . . . Butch gave all of us showers . . . and hand-jobs," Ian said. "Every so often, a blow job."

The boys laughed, including Randy.

"And about a thousand meals from McDonald's and Taco Smell," Patrick said.

The boys laughed some more.

"A fucking million meals!" Charlie said.

"We didn't watch TV for a year!" Zach said. "Cory and I turned it on, flipped through some channels, and turned it back off. I guess we didn't miss much."

The boys laughed some more and then Tim said, "What? What do we have in common?"

The boys turned back to Randy who said, "You had the courage to survive. You didn't give up. You guys are tougher than anyone I know."

"You too," Brett said.

Randy shook his head.

"Not like you guys."

"Tell them about George, the Indian dude," Ian said.

Randy told them about George and how he had witnessed the murder of the boy and how, because he had come forward, had lost his family and home.

"Where's he now?" Patrick asked.

"For now he's staying with me, my dad and my brother. We've invited him to stay with us, but we don't know if he will."

"It was because of him that we were saved, wasn't it?" Ian said.

"Well, yeah," Randy nodded. "He started it all, but there's another boy, Garrett, that turned in his coach. That's who led Jamie and Pete to you."

"We should thank this Garrett guy too," Tim said.

The boys agreed, but didn't know how that might be accomplished.

Stephen waited until the boys were quiet once again and then said, "Um . . . what do we tell our parents?"

"As little or as much as you want. It's up to you," Randy said.

Randy paused, looked at his hands as if he were ashamed.

"At first, I didn't tell my dad anything because I was embarrassed. I didn't really know him," Randy said.

He explained about his running away, about getting picked up by Mitch and Ernie, about escaping and being in foster care and then getting adopted by Jeremy.

"I was ashamed." He looked at each of the boys and said, "I know it's hard and just like you, I didn't want to talk about it. My dad didn't push me, but over time, I told him everything."

"Everything?" Cory asked.

"Yeah, everything," Randy said nodding.

He looked around the room at each of the boys.

"I think the more you talk about it, it gets less." He shrugged. "It won't ever go away, but it gets less."

"I don't know if I can tell my dad . . . my mom," Ian said.

"For me, the worst part wasn't telling my dad about it. It was sitting in school and wondering what everyone was thinking."

The boys lowered their eyes to the floor, sneaking glances at one another. None of them had known how they would talk with their parents about what they were forced to do or how they would tell their parents what had been done to them. And not surprisingly, none of the boys discussed this with each other. Not even Tim and Brett.

"Do me a favor," Randy said. "I want each of you to think of the worst thing you had to do."

He paused and saw the boys thinking, disgust registering on their faces.

He leaned forward, looked at the boys and said, "It took me a long time to figure out, but what I learned was that no matter what anyone thought about me, no matter what anyone said about me, no matter what anyone called me, it was nothing like what had already happened to me." He paused and said, "Think about that."

"We survived," Tim said.

"Yeah, you survived," Randy said.

The boys reached out and either took each other's hands or put their arms around shoulders and moved together in a tight circle.

"We have each other," Tim said. "And we'll never be alone." This last, he said to Brett.

"It's scary," Randy said. "It'll take a long time, but you have to get up every morning, look in the mirror and say, 'I survived'." Then he laughed and added, "Someday, you might actually believe it."

The boys laughed with him.

"We need to visit Johnny," Brett said.

"He's still pretty sick though, and the doctors don't know if he's going to make it, but you're right," Tim said. "Let's go see Johnny."

"There are some other guys we need to thank," Brett added. "I heard one guy's still here in the hospital, and one cop got shot and another died in Kansas City. We need to thank them."

The boys nodded, filed out of the room and filled the hallway. Already gathered in the hallway were the Pruitts, the Ericksons, the Baileys, Pete, Summer, Chet, Jamie, Jack O'Brien and Jeremy. Several nurses, orderlies and doctors had stepped out of rooms and nurses' stations to see what was happening. One by one, the boys shook hands or hugged the adults standing there, saying thank you.

"Where are you guys headed," Pete asked.

"To see Johnny," Brett said.

"I don't think he's allowed visitors," Pete said.

"He'll see us," Brett said with a smile. "We need to be together."

"Ian, why don't you and Patrick lead," Tim said. "But go slow. If Mike's butt hurts as much as mine does, this could take us all day."

The boys laughed and formed up two by two.

"Randy, can you help Stephen with Mike?" Tim asked.

Randy stepped around Tim and Brett, and Mike reached out and slipped his arm around Randy's shoulder. At the end just behind Randy, Mike and Stephen were Tim and Brett, holding onto each other.

"Mom and Dad, I'll be back in a bit," Tim said.

"Us too," Stephen said.

Mike smiled and waved at his parents, who waved back. Under all the bruises and missing teeth and guarded shuffle, the adults saw a glimpse of Mike's playfulness.

Brett pulled Tim close to him leaning his head on Tim's.

"Just a minute," Brett said.

The group stopped and turned back to see what was up. Brett stepped away from Tim, came back and shook Skip's and Jamie's hand once again. He then stood in front of Pete, who reached out and held Brett in a long hug, careful of his shoulder.

"Thanks. Thanks for everything," Brett said softly.

"No problem, Kiddo. Anytime."

As the boys slowly walked down the hallway, the doctors, nurses, all of the adults and even some of the patients cheered and clapped for them. The boys hugged each other, probably none tighter than Tim and Brett.

"We survived," Tim said.

"Yeah, we survived," Brett answered.

Shattered Lives

Whoever fights monsters should see to it that in the process he does not become a monster.

Nietzsche

PART ONE
A NOT QUITE SAFE HAVEN

CHAPTER ONE

Waukesha, Wisconsin

. . . He faced the man with the gun. He couldn't quite make out his features, but he seemed to be medium height, maybe shorter than that, and well-built but not overly so. At least he didn't seem to be a bulky, weightlifter kind of man. His voice was cold and flat, which is what George would remember the most about him. That and the gun pointed at the boy next to him, a boy George did not know.

Jeremy was George's bookend on the other side of the boy. Behind the three of them was a door to a room that

George didn't know. In fact, he didn't know the room he stood in, but somehow knew the room and the house they were in. At least, the house and room seemed familiar to him. He just couldn't place it.

But more importantly, Jeremy, the boy and George stood between the man and the door, and George wasn't sure what or who was on the other side of the door, only that the three of them formed a human shield between it or them and the man with the gun.

As the man took aim, George knew with certainty that Jeremy would step in front of the boy. George couldn't let that happen, so he moved in front of Jeremy and the boy as the gun went off . . .

George slammed upright in bed, gasping for breath and pulling the sheet up to his chin, yanking it from Billy who slept soundly next to him facing the wall, mouth slightly open on his left side in a semi-fetal position. Billy didn't seem to notice or care that he was no longer covered. The night was warm and the breeze so light a sheet wasn't actually needed, even though the windows were open, and the ceiling fan was on. Jeremy Evans, the father of the twins, Randy and Billy, didn't like to run the air-conditioner at night, preferring open windows and night breezes.

The room was on the small side and made even smaller now that Billy had the idea to substitute the single bed he had slept in for the past two years for the double bed in the spare room, so that the three of them could sleep in the same room. He and George shared the double bed. George looked over at Randy three feet away on the other side of the room, who was sound asleep on his back, one knee up, arms almost spread-eagle, head off his pillow, breathing deeply and slowly just as Billy was.

He covered Billy with the sheet again and slowly, quietly, swung his feet over the side of the bed and sat with his elbows on his knees, his head in his hands trying to remember the dream. His dark, handsome, and almost noble face, along with his chest and back, the color of bronzed copper, were covered in a sheen of sweat, and his hair, the color of midnight and hanging down just passed his shoulders, hung over his face. His dark eyes were squinted shut as he tried to grasp the wisp of the dream that turned to vapor and disappeared as quickly and easily as he tried so determinedly to remember it.

George didn't know the man with the gun who had faced the three of them. He couldn't see him clearly in the dream. He didn't know who the boy was, and he wasn't certain it was the boy the man had come to kill. Perhaps it was whoever was on the other side of the door that was shut behind the three of them.

Confusing, odd, and disturbing.

George was a traditional Navajo, and he believed as some of the elders of his people believed, that dreams were messages from the spirit world. The trouble with dreams though is that they almost always needed someone to interpret them. It had always been his grandfather who had helped him understand what the spirit world was trying to tell him, but his grandfather was no longer there to help him.

His grandfather was dead.

He had been murdered- executed- along with his mother, grandmother, two brothers and sister because George had witnessed the murder of a fourteen year old boy and had come forward to report it. He was now alone with no one to return home to except for his Navajo people and a cousin. Jeremy and the twins had asked him to live with them, but he wasn't certain if he was going to accept their offer, or if he'd return to Arizona and his Navajo Nation. Waukesha, Wisconsin was a long way from Arizona and all of the trees and city life very different from the Arizona desert and rural life he had grown up in.

Quietly, slowly, so as not to wake up either of the twins, he got out of bed, smoothed the sheet over Billy and picked up his knife. It sat on the nightstand along with Billy's iPod dock that served as music for the three boys, as well as the alarm that would get up first George at 5:00 AM and then the twins at 6:00 AM. The clock face read 1:17 AM, far too early to get up, but George did so anyway.

The knife was a gift from his grandfather for his twelfth birthday two years ago in a coming of age ceremony on top of a plateau near their ranch. The razor sharp blade was eight inches long, and the handle, made of elk bone, was an additional four inches bound to the blade with leather. It fit his hand perfectly, and he had practiced each morning since receiving it under the guidance of his grandfather. To the casual observer, the movements looked oriental, such as with Tai Chi or Karate, and it was defensive in nature. George could use the knife in either hand effectively, and he had done so earlier that week.

The knife had been returned by Detective Jamie Graff just the morning before, along with a permit to carry it. It had been taken by the police because George had used it to kill a man sent to kill him, Jeremy and the twins. It was a dream and vision of his grandfather that led him to the side of the house where he found the man with the gun intent on murdering them. But the police and the district attorney had judged that George had acted in self-defense since the man had a gun and a rap sheet dating back more than twenty years.

Self-defense or not, a man was dead, and George had killed him. He had told the police, the FBI and the Evans family about the dream and the vision of his grandfather, but George was certain none of them had understood the Navajo belief about dreams and visions. He was sure it had sounded crazy to them, and he couldn't help but feel that it sounded crazy to him too.

And now a new dream- the dream he didn't understand. He was certain he wouldn't share it with anyone unless and until he needed to- if he needed to.

George tip-toed down the hall, down the stairs and out the kitchen door and sat down on the steps to the back patio that faced the yard beyond it just as he had the other night when he had spotted the man in the hedge line in the backyard and killed him. He shivered slightly at the memory and hugged himself. George turned and looked at the corner of the house, half-expecting to see someone rounding the corner with gun in hand. Of course, no one was there.

Just before he confronted the man, Jeremy had come out of the house and sat on the step next to him and had asked George to consider living permanently with him and the twins. But that was before George had killed the man.

And even though Jeremy had made that offer again afterward, and even though the twins had told him they wanted him to live with them, George wasn't sure how he had felt about it.

It had been a very difficult day.

Jeremy and Randy had traveled to a hospital in Chicago, so they could talk to the boys who had been held in captivity as part of a human trafficking ring, so George didn't have much of an opportunity to talk to either of them. He and Billy spent much of the day planting flowers for Miss Bert and Mr. Jon, the Lanes who lived next door and who seemed to be unofficial grandparents to the twins. At least, that was how they treated the twins and how the twins treated them. George liked them. While Billy acted as if nothing unusual had happened, and while the Lanes said nothing about what had happened, he knew the Lanes knew about it, and it seemed that at least they had treated him differently. Maybe it was just his imagination. Maybe not.

The kitchen door opened and was shut quietly, but instead of Jeremy, it was Billy. He was barefoot and dressed just as George was; in boxers and wrapped in a light blanket. He sat down next to George and gave half of the blanket to him, who wrapped himself in it, and the two boys huddled together.

"Sorry if I woke you up," George offered after a bit.

Billy yawned, shrugged and said, "I couldn't sleep either."

George knew he was just being polite, but he accepted his statement.

"How come you're up?" Billy asked.

George didn't say anything, and he stared out at the backyard not focusing on anything.

"When I was little and had a bad dream, my dad would sit up with me while I told him about it. It made it go away. Now, Jeremy does, but I don't have bad dreams that much anymore."

George looked at him curiously.

Billy shrugged and said, "I was adopted twice. My first dad died of a heart attack."

George nodded.

"So?" Billy said.

George shook his head.

"So, have you decided whether or not you're going to live with us?"

George shrugged noncommittally. As many reasons as he had for staying, he had an equal number of reasons for not. Well, not really as many reasons for not. Actually, not that many at all. Truth was he was scared: scared of staying, scared of leaving, just plain scared.

Billy had come to know George well enough in the last two days to understand that George was quiet and only spoke when he wanted to, so he gave up trying.

Billy and Randy were identical twins and only those who spent time around them knew how to tell the difference. Both had brown hair cut short in the same style. Both had large brown eyes, though Randy's seemed sad even when he smiled. Billy had a bit of a crooked smile and had a habit of cocking his head when he listened. He was older by eight minutes, born four minutes before midnight, while Randy was born four minutes after midnight. The twins were fourteen years old, a month or so older than George, and all three boys were headed for eighth grade in the fall, one and a half months away.

George liked them both and felt he could easily become friends with them. Randy was gentle and a listener. Billy was a joker and a talker. Even though Billy was older, it was Randy who made the decisions. Most of all, George liked watching Jeremy interact with them. He saw the love they had for each other and envied them, and it reminded him of just how lonely and alone he was.

Billy sighed and not really understanding why, said, "I think I killed my first dad."

George turned to look at Billy who quickly wiped away some tears on the blanket wrapped around them.

"Why do you think that?"

Billy looked down at his bare feet and then out at the yard.

"I was pissed at my mom for not telling me I was adopted. My parents got divorced, and I lived with my dad but spent a lot of time with Jeremy and Randy." He wiped more tears off his face with the blanket and said, "My dad missed my mom, and he was lonely. He died of a heart attack."

George nodded, letting the silence envelope them like the blanket wrapped around them.

Billy shrugged.

"Are you happy living with Mr. Jeremy and Randy?"

Without any hesitation, Billy said, "Oh yeah. I love them. Jeremy's my dad now, and Randy's my brother. They're my best friends." Then he was quiet for a moment and said, "I just miss my first dad every now and then."

George nodded.

"When my dad died, I was hoping Jeremy would let me live with him and Randy. He adopted me like he did

Randy, but I kept my dad's name . . . you know . . . out of respect, kind of." Billy shrugged and said, "It seemed like the right thing to do."

George nodded. That seemed right to him too. He thought that if Mr. Jeremy would adopt him, he'd keep his last name, Tokay, out of respect for his family, his grandfather in particular.

That thought startled him.

No one had asked him if he had wanted to be adopted. There was the offer to have him live with them, but he didn't know if he was going to accept it, and didn't know if that meant Jeremy would adopt him.

"You and I are sort of alike," Billy said, shaking him out of his thoughts.

"How?" George asked.

"I didn't have anyone after my dad died, and there was no way I was going to live with my mom. Jeremy offered to have me live with him, and now he's my dad and Randy's my brother. He's always been my brother, but you know what I mean. You don't have anyone, and dad asked you to live with us." He shrugged and said, "We're kind of alike."

Not wanting to get into it, he said, "It's late. We should probably get back to bed."

He got up, and Billy followed him back into the kitchen and up the stairs to bed.

CHAPTER TWO

Indianapolis, Indiana

His idiot partner had tipped him off accidently by calling to let him know that two Feebs showed up at the precinct carrying a warrant and telling a story about his involvement in a nationwide human trafficking ring. His partner knew it couldn't possibly be true.

It's not possible, right? Some sort of mistake, right? his partner had asked.

He had fooled his partner, just like he had fooled everyone else. He was, after all, much smarter than any of them.

He had just finished his workout at the gym but had to get back to his house, and in and out before the Feebs showed up. Get in and out undetected. Had to hurry, because he knew they'd eventually come to the house if he didn't show up at the station. He had no intention of doing that, though he had told his partner that he'd be there to straighten it all out in about an hour. He thought that might buy him some time.

He told his partner to chill. That was his partner's favorite word, and it was one of the many things he had hated about his partner. That and his picking his teeth with his long-ass fingernails after each and every meal, listening to hip-hop crap on the radio trying to fit in with the Spades and the Spics on the force, and drinking green tea like a fucking Yuppie.

He hated his stupid-ass, farm-boy partner, and if the opportunity ever presented itself, he'd take his .45 and pull the trigger sending a slug smack dab into the middle of his forehead so it would rattle around in his empty skull and blow a baseball-sized chunk out the back. Would serve him right, the stupid asshole.

He had seen the first reports of the human trafficking ring bust while working out at the gym. He had stepped off the treadmill and grabbed a towel, wiped down his face and draped it across his shoulders. He grabbed his water bottle, drank deeply and walked over and stood at the back of a crowd who had stopped their workouts and watched one of the several flat-screened TVs mounted on the wall. Three of the screens were tuned to CNN; two to ABC; two to CBS; and three to ESPN. No one paid any attention to the ones tuned to ESPN.

The group he stood behind listened to and watched a talking head while a videotape played on the half-screen showing cops wandering around the street and walking in and out of a building in Chicago. EMT trucks and cop cars had been coming and going all morning, but the cameras hadn't shown any of the passengers.

He had recognized the building in Chicago, because he had been there many times.

Every now and then, it would cut away to Kansas City or Long Beach. The stories were the same: A human trafficking ring had been busted. Prominent local, state and national political officials, sports and entertainment figures arrested. Kids - all boys who had been kidnapped and held captive, some for more than two years - had been freed and taken to local hospitals to be checked over before they were released to their parents.

Walking nonchalantly to the locker room, he had gathered his things and left without showering. He had to get home and get moving. He had things to take care of.

Driving slowly, taking care not to draw any attention, he parked a block from his house on a side street of a normal-looking tree-lined drive with white picket fences and bright, sunny flowers growing under front windows and around mailboxes, with bicycles, skateboards and scooters in driveways. He sat in his car with the window down breathing deeply of freshly mowed lawns. He got out of his car and locked it but didn't bother to wipe it down because a simple check on his tags would tell everyone who it had belonged to. By the time they got around to looking for it, he'd be long gone anyway.

Slowly, he surveyed the streets and houses for anything and anyone out of the ordinary.

Nothing.

He crossed the street to the alley and walked down it as if it were something he did every day.

At six-two, two-hundred and twenty pounds, he moved like the athlete he was. After all, he worked out at the gym three or four days a week with free weights and pounding a heavy bag every now and then. He jumped rope for twenty minutes every day and ran six to ten miles before dawn in any kind of weather. He was proud of his body and the shape he was in, viewing it as an asset, a weapon.

He knew this day would come eventually and had been planning for it for a long time. He had stashed money away and had created an account at a different bank from the one he used to pay the bills. He had created two other identities, complete with social security cards and drivers licenses using a weasel from the streets who specialized in creating identities. One of the many weasels he had cultivated from his years on the force. He had secured credit cards with large available balances under both names, along with a car titled and registered in a garage of a townhouse in a northwestern suburb of the city leased under the name of one of the identities he had created.

Knowing the day would come is different from the day actually arriving.

He had rehearsed. He had planned. He had already tied up loose ends. Like the Weasel.

The Weasel no longer existed. Body gone. Any evidence vanished in a fire described as suspicious, more than likely arson, and it was done so there was absolutely no possible blow back to him.

At the back of his house, he paused at the garbage cans lined side by side in the alley pretending to tidy up a bit but watching and listening for anything out of the ordinary.

Nothing.

He moved quickly to the backdoor, pulled the screen door back and used the key he had pulled from his pocket to unlock the deadbolt. He entered quickly and shut and locked the door behind him and pulled his gun from the pocket of his navy-blue Indianapolis Colt hoodie as he did so.

No sound.

Moving quickly, he went to the guest bedroom, knelt down and loosened the thread in the carpet just to the left of the closet and lifted it up revealing a ten by ten square piece of three-quarter inch plywood. He used the point of his key to work around an edge of it and lifted it up revealing a drop box of sorts.

He pulled out a fully loaded, unregistered Glock .9M and two magazines loaded with .9M hollow point bullets. The serial numbers had been filed off making the gun temporarily untraceable, courtesy of another one of his weasels, this one a cocaine dealer who supposedly died in a drug deal gone bad. Not coincidently, the bullets found in his skull came from a Glock .9M just like the one he shoved into his waistband. Temporarily untraceable, because the firing pin, like any other firing pin, had a serial number, few, if any gun owners, knew about.

Underneath the gun were ten banded bundles of cash, all fifties.

A half-million. Emergency money.

Underneath the money were a passport and a wallet with a driver's license and social security card of one of his identities, two credit cards in the same name and a set of keys.

He took a careful look out of the corner of the living room window, and satisfied that there wasn't anything unusual, he pulled the hood over his head and left the house as easily and as quickly as he had arrived. He carried two duffle bags, splitting the money evenly between them and threw some clothes on top to help conceal it.

Four easy blocks away was a metro bus stop that would take him downtown to the station where he'd catch another bus to the North side suburb where his townhouse was located. The trip would take him thirty-seven minutes.

He knew this because he had rehearsed.

He was ready to disappear. At least, for a while, but he would be back. He had some unfinished business to attend to.

TRUE VISIONS
PUBLICATIONS

NOW ACCEPTING
SUBMISSIONS

Become a part of the family that is home to the #1 Bestseller Dirty Laundry!!!!!

New and Aspiring Authors, do you have a vision you would like to see come to life? It is True Visions Publications mission to make that happen for you.

Submission Guidelines:

1. Email the first 3-5 chapters typed and double spaced or your full manuscript to truevisionspub@gmail.com

2. Synopsis and possible title

3. Contact info including full name, number and email address

4. Genre - Street/Urban Lit; Erotica; Mystery/Thriller; Romance; Action; Fantasy